• • • • • • •

"Bishop's thoughtful, sensitive portrayal represents a major achievement in speculative fiction. . . . A disturbing and sober reflection on what it means to be human." —*Library Journal*

"ANCIENT OF DAYS is a solid narrative of anthropological fiction, treating human culture, religion, and alienation in ways that bring into question who is the more alien: twentieth-century Americans, or the (perhaps) last survivor of a pre-human species of hominid. It's real stuff. The right stuff." —Ed Bryant

"Bishop continues to deliver solid, memorable novels that move the emotions, intrigue the mind, and still keep your hands turning the pages." —Gregory Benford

"This is a fine, engrossing novel, certainly one of Bishop's best, and with the most believable, likable set of characters he has created yet. Bishop has very quietly become one of the major talents in the field." —*Science Fiction Chronicle*

"Michael Bishop is becoming the best SF writer in —A. E. van Vogt

MICHAEL BISHOP

ANCIENT OF DAYS

TOR

A TOM DOHERTY ASSOCIATES BOOK

Part One

HER HABILINE HUSBAND

Beulah Fork, Georgia

RuthClaire Loyd, my ex-wife, first caught sight of the trespasser from the loft studio of her barn-sized house near Beulah Fork, Georgia. She was doing one of twelve paintings for a series of subscription-order porcelain plates that would feature her unique interpretations of the nine angelic orders and the Holy Trinity (this particular painting was entitled *Thrones*), but she stepped away from the easel to look through her bay window at the intruder. His oddness had caught her eye.

Swart and gnomish, he was moving through the tall shadowy grass in the pecan grove. His movements combined an aggressive curiosity with a kind of placid caution, as if he had every right to be there but still expected someone—the property's legal owner, a buttinsky neighbor—to call him to accounts. Passing from a dapple of September sunlight into a patch of shade, he resembled one of the black boys who had turned Cleve Synder's creek into the skinnydipping riviera of Hothlepoya County. He was a little far afield, though, and the light briefly limning his upper body made him look too *hairy* for most

3

ten-year-olds, whatever their color. Was the trespasser some kind of animal?

"He's walking," RuthClaire murmured to herself. "Hairy or not, only human beings walk like that."

My ex is not given to panic, but this observation worried her. Her house (I had relinquished all claims to it back in January, primarily to spare her the psychic upheaval of a move) sits in splendid-spooky isolation about a hundred yards from the state highway connecting Tocqueville and Beulah Fork. Cleve Synder, meanwhile, leases his adjacent ninety acres to a cotton grower who does not live there. RuthClaire was beginning to feel alone and vulnerable.

Imperceptibly trembling, she set aside her brushes and paints to watch the trespasser. He was closer to the house now, and a rake that she had left leaning against one of the pecan trees enabled her to estimate his height at a diminutive four and a half feet. His sinewy arms bespoke his maturity, however, as did the massiveness of his underslung jaw and the dark gnarl of his sex. Maybe, she helplessly conjectured, he was a deranged dwarf recently escaped from an institution populated by violence-prone sexual deviates. . . .

"Stop it," RuthClaire advised herself. "Stop it."

Suddenly the trespasser gripped the bole of a tree with his hands and the bottom of his feet; he shinnied to a swaying perch high above the ground. Here, for over an hour, he cracked pecans with his teeth and single-mindedly fed himself. My ex-wife's worry subsided a little. The intruder seemed to be neither an outright carnivore nor a rapist. Come twilight, though, she was ready for him to leave, while *he* appeared perfectly content to occupy his perch until Judgment Day.

RuthClaire had no intention of going to bed with a skinnydipping dwarf in her pecan grove. She telephoned me.

"It's probably someone's pet monkey," I reassured her. "A rich Yankee matron broke down on the interstate, and her chimpanzee—you know how some of those old ladies from Connecticut are—wandered off while she was trying to flag down a farmer to unscrew her radiator cap."

"Paul," RuthClaire said, unamused.

"What?"

"First of all,". she replied, evenly enough, "a chimpanzee isn't a monkey, it's an ape. Secondly, I don't know anything at all about old ladies from Connecticut. And, thirdly, the creature in my pecan tree *isn't* a chimpanzee or a gibbon or an orangutan."

"I'd forgotten what a Jane Goodall fan you were."

This riposte RuthClaire declined to volley.

"What do you want me to do?" I asked, somewhat exasperated. My ex-wife's imagination is both her fortune and her folly; and at this point, to tell the truth, I was thinking that her visitor was indeed an out-of-season skinnydipper or possibly a raccoon. For an artist RuthClaire is remarkably nearsighted, a fact that contributes to the almost abstractional blurriness of some of her landscapes and backgrounds.

"Come see about me," she said.

IN BEULAH FORK I run a small gourmet restaurant called the West Bank. Despite the incredulity of outsiders (as, for instance, matrons from Connecticut with pet chimpanzees), who expect rural eating establishments in the South to serve nothing but catfish, barbecue, Brunswick stew, and turnip greens, the West Bank offers cosmopolitan fare and a sophisticated ambience. My clientele comprises professional people, wealthy retirees, and tourists. The proximity of a popular state park, the historic city of Tocqueville, and a recreational area known as Muscadine Gardens keeps me in paying customers; and while RuthClaire and I were married, she exhibited and sold many of her best paintings right on the premises. Her work—only a few pieces of which I still have on my walls—gave the restaurant a kind of muted bohemian elegance, but, in turn, the West Bank gave my wife a unique and probably invaluable showcase for her talent. Until our split, I think, we both viewed the relationship between her success and mine as healthily symbiotic.

Art in the service of commerce. Commerce in the service of art.

RuthClaire had telephoned me just before the dinner hour on Friday. The West Bank had reservations from more than a dozen people from Tocqueville and the Gardens, and I did not really want to dump the whole of this formidable crowd into the lap of Molly Kingsbury, a bright young woman who does a better job hostessing than overseeing my occasionally high-strung cooks, Hazel Upchurch and Livia George Stephens. But dump it I did. I begged off my responsibilities at the West Bank with a story about a broken water pipe on Paradise Farm and drove out there lickety-split to see about my ex. Twelve miles in ten minutes.

RuthClaire led me to the studio loft and pointed through her window into the pecan grove. "He's still sitting there," she said.

I squinted. At this hour the figure in the tree was a mere smudge among the tangled branches, not much bigger than a squirrel's nest. "Why didn't you shoot off that .22 I gave you?" I asked RuthClaire, a little afraid that she was having me on. Even the spreading crimson sunset behind the pecan grove did not enable me to pick out the alleged trespasser.

"I wanted you to see him, too, Paul. I got to where I needed outside confirmation. Don't you see?"

No, I didn't see. That was the problem.

"Go out there with me," RuthClaire suggested. "The buddy system's always recommended for dangerous enterprises."

"The buddy I want is that little .22, Ruthie Cee." She stood aside while I wrested the rifle out of the gun cabinet, and together we went back down the stairs, through the living and dining rooms, and out the plate-glass doors opening onto the pecan grove. Beneath the intruder's tree we paused to gape and take stock. The stock I took went into the cushion of flesh just above my right armpit, and I sighted along the barrel at a bearded black face like that of a living gargoyle.

RuthClaire was right. The trespasser wasn't a monkey; he more nearly resembled a medieval demon, with a small but noticeable ridge running fore and aft straight down the middle of his skull. He had been on the cusp of falling asleep, I think, and the apparition of two human beings at this inopportune moment greatly startled him. The fear showed in his beady, obsidian eyes, which flashed between my ex-wife and me like sooty strobes. His upper lip moved away from his teeth.

From above the mysterious creature I shot down a dangling cluster of branches that would have eventually fallen, anyway. The report echoed all the way to White Cow Creek, and hundreds of foraging sparrows scattered into the twilight like feathered buckshot.

"I swear to goodness, Paul!" RuthClaire shouted, her most fiery oath. She was trying to take the rifle out of my hands. "You've always been a shoot-first-talk-later fool but that poor fella's no threat to us! Look!"

I gave up the .22 as I had given up Paradise Farm, docilely, and I looked. RuthClaire's visitor was terrified, almost catatonic. He could not go up, and he could not come down; his head was probably still reverberating from the rifle shot, the heart-stopping crash of the pecan limb. I wasn't too sorry, though. He had no business haunting my ex.

"Listen," I said, "you asked me to come see about you. And you didn't object when I brought that baby down from the loft, either."

Angrily, RuthClaire ejected the spent shell, removed the .22's magazine, and threw the rifle on the ground. "I wanted moral support, Paulie, not a hit man. I thought the gun was *your* moral support, that's all. I didn't know you were going to try to *murder* the poor innocent wretch with it."

" 'Poor innocent wretch,' " I repeated incredulously. " *'Poor innocent wretch'?*"

This was not the first time we had found ourselves arguing in front of an audience. Toward the end it had happened frequently at the West Bank, RuthClaire accusing me of insensitivity, neglect, and philandering with my female help (although she *knew* that Molly Kingsbury was having none of that nonsense), while I openly rued her blinkered drive for artistic recognition, her lack of regard of my inborn business instincts, and her sometimes maddeningly rigorous bouts of chastity. The West Bank is small—a converted doctor's office wedged between Gloria's Beauty Shop and Ogletree Plumbing & Electric, all in the same red-brick shell on Main Street—and even arguing in the kitchen we could give my customers a discomfiting earful. Only a few tolerant souls, mostly locals, thought these debates entertaining; and when my repeat business from out of town began falling off, well, that was the last straw. I made the West Bank off limits to RuthClaire. Soon thereafter she began divorce proceedings.

Now a shivering black gnome, naked but for a see-through leotard of hair, was staring down at us as my ex compared me to Vlad the Impaler, Adolf Hitler, and the government of South Africa. I began to think that he could not be *too* much more bewildered and uncomfortable than I.

"What the hell do you want me to do?" I finally blurted.

"Leave me alone with him," RuthClaire said. "Go back to the house."

"That's crazy," I began. "That's—"

"Hush, Paulie. Please do as I say, all right?"

I retreated to the sliding doors, no farther. RuthClaire talked to the trespasser. In the gathering dark she crooned reassurance. She consoled and coaxed. She even hummed a lullaby. Her one-sided talk with the intruder was interminable. I, because she did not seem to be at any real risk, went inside and poured myself a powerful scotch on the rocks. At last RuthClaire returned.

"Paul," she said, gazing into the pecan grove, "he's a member of a human species—you know, a *collateral* human species—that doesn't exist anymore."

"He told you that, did he?"

"I deduced it. He doesn't speak."

"Not English, anyway. What do you mean, 'doesn't exist anymore'? He's up in that tree, isn't he?"

"Up in the air, more like," RuthClaire said. "It reminds me of that Indian, Ishi."

"Who-shi?"

"A Yahi Indian in northern California whose name was Ishi. Theodora Kroeber wrote a couple of books about him." RuthClaire gestured at the shelves across the room from us; in addition to every contemporary best seller that came through the B. Dalton's in Tocqueville Commons Mall, these shelves housed art books, popular-science volumes, and a "feminist" library of no small proportions, this being RuthClaire's term for books either by or about women, no matter when or where they lived. (The Brontë sisters were next to Susan Brownmiller; Sappho was not far from Sontag.)

I lifted my eyebrows: "?"

"Last of his tribe," RuthClaire explained. "Ishi was the last surviving member of the Yahi; he died around nineteen fifteen or so, in the Museum of Anthropology in San Francisco." She mulled this bit of intelligence. "It's my guess, though, that our poor wretch comes from a species that originated in East Africa two or three million years ago." She mulled her guess. "That's a little longer than Ishi's people were supposed to have been extinct before Ishi himself turned up, I'm afraid."

"There goes your analogy."

"Well, it's not *perfect*, Paul, but it's *suggestive*. What do you think?"

"That you'd be wiser calling the bugger in the tree a deranged dwarf instead of an Indian. You'd be wiser yet just calling the police."

RuthClaire went to the bookshelf and removed a volume by a well-known scientist and television personality. She had everything this flamboyant popularizer had ever written. After flipping through several well-thumbed pages, she found the passage pertinent to her argument:

" 'Were we to encounter *Homo habilis*—dressed, let us say, in the latest fashion on the boulevards of some modern metropolis—we would probably give him only a pass-

ing glance, and that because of his relatively small stature.' "
She closed the book. "There. The creature in the pecan
tree is a habiline, a member of the species *Homo habilis*.
He's human, Paul, he's one of us."

"That may or may not be the case, but I'd still feel
obliged to wash up with soap and water after shaking his
hand."

RuthClaire gave me a look commingling pity and contempt and replaced the book on its shelf. I made up a
song—which I had the good sense not to sing aloud to
her—to the tune of an old country-and-western ditty entitled "Abilene":

> *Habiline, O habiline,*
> *Grungiest ghoul I've ever seen.*
> *Even Gillette won't shave him clean,*
> *That habiline.*

I telephoned the West Bank to see how Molly was
getting on with Hazel and Livia George (she said everything was going "swimmingly," a word Molly had learned
from a beau in Atlanta), then convinced my ex-wife to let
me spend the night at Paradise Farm on the sofa downstairs. For safety's sake. RuthClaire reluctantly consented.
In her studio loft she worked through until morning. At
dawn I heard her say, "It's all right, Paul. He left while
you were sleeping." She handed me a cup of coffee. I
sipped at it as she gazed out the sliding doors at the empty
pecan grove.

THE FOLLOWING month—about three weeks later—I ran
into RuthClaire in Beulah Fork's ancient A&P, where I do
almost all of my shopping for the West Bank: meats,
produce, the works. October. Still sunny. The restaurant
business only now beginning to tail off toward the inevita-

ble winter slump. I had not thought of the Ishi Incident, or whatever you might choose to call it, more than three or four times since actually investigating it. Perhaps I did not believe that it had really happened. The whole episode had a dreamlike texture that did not stick very well to the hard-edged banality of everyday life in Beulah Fork. Besides, no one else in Hothlepoya County had mentioned seeing a naked black gnome running around the countryside climbing trees and stealing pecans.

My ex and I chatted, altogether amicably at first. RuthClaire had just finished an original painting entitled *Principalities* for her porcelain-plate series, and AmeriCred Company of New York, New York, would begin taking subscription orders for this unusual Limoges ware at fifty-six dollars a plate in early December. The artist was going to receive an 8 percent royalty for each plate sold, over and above the commission paid her in July for undertaking the work. She was very excited, not solely by the money she stood to make but also by the prospect of reaching a large and undoubtedly discerning audience. Ads for the subscription series, AmeriCred had told her, were going to appear in such classy periodicals as *Smithsonian*, *Natural History*, and *Relic Collector*. I wrote out a check for fifty-six dollars and told RuthClaire to sign me up at the first available opportunity; this was my deposit toward a subscription. Folding the check into her coin purse, she looked unfeignedly flustered. But grateful, too.

"You don't have to do this, Paul."

"I know I don't. I want a set of those plates. My customers are going to enjoy eating off the Father, the Son, and the Holy Ghost—not to mention the nine different species of angel."

"They're not for dinner use, really. They're for display."

"A rank commercial enterprise?" I tweaked her. "Ready-made antiques for the spiritual cognoscenti who frown on bodily functions like eating and ummmm-ummmm-ummm? How about that? You may be catering to an airy crowd, Ruthie Cee, but we're *both* in business, it looks like—business with a capital B."

Amazingly she smiled, merely smiled.

"I can see *you* haven't given up eating," I pursued. "That's quite a load you've got there."

Her shopping basket contained six uncut frying chickens, four heads of cabbage, three tins of Planters party nuts, four or five bunches of bananas, and several packages of fresh fish, mostly mullet and red snapper. I ogled this bounty. RuthClaire had never fried a chicken in her life, and I knew that she despised bananas. The other stuff was also out of the finicky pale of her diet, for in hostile overreaction to my virtuosity as chef and restaurateur she—not long before the end—had ostentatiously limited her intake to wild rice, bean curd, black beans, fresh vegetables, fruit juice, and various milk products. This spiteful decision had not helped our marriage any, either.

"I'm having some people down from Atlanta," she explained, rather defensively. "Gallery people."

"Oh," I replied.

We looked at each other for a moment.

"They're all invited guests, I take it," I said at last. "You don't want any uninvited drop-ins, do you?"

RuthClaire stiffened. "I don't feed the uninvited. You know that. Goodbye, Paul. Thanks for taking out a subscription."

She went her way, I mine. For somebody subsisting on rabbit food and artistic inspiration, I reflected, she looked damned good.

I LEARNED later what had been going on at Paradise Farm. On the morning after my overnight stay on the downstairs sofa RuthClaire had moved a rickety table into the pecan grove. Every evening she set it with paper plates and uncooked food items, including party nuts in a cut-glass dish that had once belonged to her mother. Further, on a folding deck chair she laid out one of my old leisure suits, altered for a figure smaller than mine, just in case the nippy autumn air prompted the trespasser to cover his nakedness. At first, though, the habiline did not rise to this bait. The dew-laden suit had to dry every day on the clothesline, and every evening RuthClaire had to replace the soggy paper dinnerware and the slug-slimed food items.

Around Halloween, when nighttime temperatures were dipping into the thirties, my ex awoke one morning to find the creature hunkering on the table on a brilliant cloth of frost. The grass looked sequined. So did the habiline's feet. He was eating unpeeled bananas and shivering so violently that the table rocked back and forth. RuthClaire put on her dressing gown and hurried downstairs. She opened the sliding doors and beckoned the fellow inside, where he could warm his tootsies at the cast-iron Buck stove in the fireplace. Although he followed RuthClaire with his eyes, he did not move. RuthClaire, leaving the glass doors open, fetched a set of sun lamps from her loft. These she placed about the patio area so that they all shone directly into the house—runway lights to warmth and safety.

The sun began to burn away the frost. An hour or so later, watching from her bay window, RuthClaire saw the habiline leap down from the table. For a moment he seemed to consider fleeing through the pecan grove, but soon rejected this notion to stroll—head ducked, elbows out—through the gauntlet of lamps toward the house. A ballsy fellow, this one, and my ex was able to see quite clearly that this appraisal of him was no mere metaphor. A ballsy bantam in blackface.

Her heart pounding paradiddles, RuthClaire went downstairs to meet him. This was the beginning: the *real* beginning.

Although over time a few clues have come my way (some of which I will shortly set forth), I do not pretend to know *exactly* how RuthClaire domesticated this representative of a supposedly extinct hominid species ancestral to our own—but she was probably more alert to his feelings and needs than she had ever been to mine. In the dead of winter, for instance, she routinely left the patio doors open, never questioning his comings and goings, never surrendering to resentment because of them. She fed him whatever he liked, even if sparerib splinters ended up between the sofa cushions or half-eaten turnips sometimes turned up on the bottom of her shower stall looking like mushy polyhedral core tools. Ruthie Cee may have a bohemian soul, but during the six years of our marriage she had also evinced a middle-class passion for tidiness; more than once she had given me hell for letting the end of the dental floss slip down into its flip-top container. For her prehistoric paramour, however, she made allowances—lots of them.

She also sang to him, I think. RuthClaire has a voice with the breathy delicacy of Garfunkel during his partnership with Simon, and I can easily imagine her soothing the savage breast of even a pit bull with a single stanza of "Feelin' Groovy." The habiline, however, she probably deluged with madrigals, hymns, and soft-drink ditties; and although she has always professed to hate commercial television, she has since publicly admitted using the idiot box—as well as song—to amuse and edify her live-in hominid. Apparently, he especially enjoyed game shows, situation comedies, sporting events, and nature studies. On the public broadcasting channels RuthClaire introduced him to such programs as "Sesame Street," "Organic Gardening," and "Wall Street Week," while the anything-goes cable networks gave him a crash course in contemporary hominid bonding rituals. All these shows together were undoubtedly as crucial to the domestication process as my ex-wife's lovely singing.

But it was not until a week or so into the new year that I learned about any of this. RuthClaire drives to Tocqueville to do her shopping more often than she comes to Beulah Fork; and our chance meeting in the A&P, despite resulting in my order for the first plate in the *Celestial Hierarchy* series, had made her wary of running into me again. She stayed away from town. I, in turn, could not go out to Paradise Farm without an invitation. The terms of our divorce expressly stipulated this last point, and my reference to uninvited guests during our brief tête-à-tête in October had stricken RuthClaire as contemptibly snide. Maybe I had meant it to be. . . .

Anyway, on the day before Christmas Eve I telephoned RuthClaire and asked if I could come out to the farm to give her a present. Somewhat reluctantly (it seemed to me) she agreed. Although it was cold and dark when I rang the front doorbell, she stepped through the door to greet me, and we conferred on the porch. The Persian kitten in the cardboard box under my arm cowered away from Ruthie Cee, its wintry pearl-gray fur like a lion's mane around its Edward G. Robinson face. My ex, emitting sympathetic coos, scratched the creature behind its ears until it began to purr.

Then she said, "I can't accept him, Paul."

"Why not? He's got a pedigree that stretches from here to Isfahan." (This was a lie. Nevertheless, the kitten *looked* it.) "Besides, he'll make a damned good mouser. A farm needs a mouser."

"I just can't give him the attention he needs." RuthClaire saw my irritation. "I didn't think you'd be bringing an animal, Paul. A sweater, a necklace, a new horror novel— anything nonliving I'd've been happy to accept. But a kitten's a different matter, and I just can't be responsible for him, sweet and pretty as he is."

I tacked about. "Can't I come in for some eggnog? Come the holidays, this place used to reek of eggnog."

"I have a visitor."

"A man, huh?"

Somewhat gravely, she nodded. "He's . . . he's allergic to cats."

"Why can't I meet him?"

"I don't want you to. Anyway, he's shy."

I looked toward the carport. Although RuthClaire's navy-blue Honda Civic gleamed dully in the sheen of the yard's security lights, I saw no other vehicle anywhere. Besides my own, of course.

"Did he jog out here?"

"Hiked."

"What's his name?"

RuthClaire smiled a crooked smile. "Adam," she said.

"Adam what?"

"None of your bee's wax, Paul. I'm tired of this inter-

rogation. Here, hang on a sec.'' She retreated into the
house but came back a moment later carrying a piece of
Limoges ware featuring her painting *Angels*. ''This is the
plate for January,'' she explained. ''Over the course of the
year you'll go from *Angels* to *Archangels* to *Principalities*—
all the way up to *The Father*—and I've seen to it that
you'll receive the other eleven without having to pay for
them. That's my Christmas present to you, Paul.'' She
took the kitten's shoebox from me so that I could look at
the plate without endangering either the mystified animal
or the fragile porcelain. ''See the border. That's twenty-
four-karat gold, applied by hand.''

''Beautiful,'' I said, and I kissed her lightly on the
forehead. ''Bring this Adam fella to the restaurant, Ruthie
Cee. Frogs' legs, steak, wild-rice pilaf, coq au vin, anything he wants—*on the house*. And for you, of course, the
gourmet vegetable plate. I'm serious now. Take me up on
this.''

She returned my chaste kiss along with the kitten. ''This
is the way you behaved when we were courting. Good
night, Paul.''

''Good night, kid.''

On the way back to Beulah Fork the kitten began prowling all over my shoulders and thighs and miaowing obnox-
iously. It even got tangled in the steering wheel. I put it
out about a mile from Ruben Decker's place and kept on
driving.

IN JANUARY, as I have alluded, the pieces began coming
together. To my surprise RuthClaire called to make reservations for Adam and herself at the West Bank; they were
actually going to avail themselves of my offer. However,
even though only the two of them were coming, RuthClaire
wanted the entire restaurant, every table. If I would grant
them this extraordinary boon, she would pay me the equiv-

alent of a night's receipts on a typical weekday evening in winter. I told her that she was crazy, but that if she and her inamorato came on a Tuesday, always my slowest night, I would donate the premises as well as the dinner to their Great Romance. After all, it was high time she indulged a passion that was erotic rather than merely platonic and painterly.

"That's a cheap dig," my ex accused.

"How many kinds of generosity do you want from me?" I snapped back. "You think I *like* playing Pandare to you and your new boyfriend?"

She softened. "It's not what you think, Paul."

No, indeed. It wasn't at all what I thought.

On the appointed evening Main Street was deserted but for Davie Hutton's police cruiser, which he had parked perpendicular to the state highway as a caution to potential speeders. Precisely at eight, as I peered through the gloom, RuthClaire's Honda Civic eased gingerly around the cruiser and slotted into a space in front of the West Bank. Then she and her mysterious beau exited the car and climbed the steps to the restaurant.

Sweet Jesus, I thought, it's a nigger kid in designer jeans and an army fatigue jacket. She's not in love. She's on another I'm-going-to-adopt-a-disadvantaged-child kick.

Disagreements about starting a family had been another front in our protracted connubial war. I had never wanted any offspring, while RuthClaire had always craved two or three Campbell's Kids clones or, failing that, a host of starving dependents on other continents. She believed wholeheartedly that she could paint, market her work, and *parent*—this was her ghastly neologism—without spreading herself too thin. I surrendered to her arguments, to the ferocity of her desire for issue, and for two years we went about trying to make a baby in the same dementedly single-minded way that some people assemble mail-order lawn mowers or barbecue grills. Our lack of success prompted RuthClaire to begin touting adoption as a worthy alternative to childbirth; the support of various international relief agencies, she avowed, would compensate the cosmic *élan vital* for our puzzling failure to be fruitful and multiply. We ended up with foster children in Somalia, Colombia, and Vietnam, and a bedroom relationship that made nonagenarian abstinence seem shamefully libertine. Because I had wanted no part of adopting a racially mixed child, to bring into our own home, RuthClaire had unilaterally decided that sex with me was irrelevant and therefore dispensable. She would rather paint cherubs on teacups.

Now here she was at the West Bank with a gimpy black teenager from Who-Could-Say-Where? Guess who's coming to dinner. . . .

"Paul, Adam. Adam, Paul."

I did a double take, a restrained and sophisticated double take. For one thing, Adam was no adolescent. More astonishing, he was the same compact creature who had come traipsing naked into the Paradise Farm pecan grove in September. His slender, twisted feet were bare. At a nod from RuthClaire he extended his right hand and grinned a grin that was all discolored teeth and darting, mistrustful eyes. I ignored his proffered hand.

"What the hell are you trying to pull, RuthClaire?"

"I'm trying to have dinner with Adam. This is an integrated place of business, isn't it? Interstate commerce and all that. Besides, our money's as green as anyone else's."

"His color's got nothing to do with it. Neither does your money's. He's—" I swallowed my indigestible objection.

"Go ahead, Paul, say it."

"He's an animal, RuthClaire, an animal in human clothing."

"I often thought the same thing of you."

I backtracked: "Listen, Ruthie, the county health department doesn't permit barefooted people in its licensed eating establishments. He needs some shoes. Sandals, at least."

"Shoes are one of the things I haven't been able to get him to wear." RuthClaire reached over and lowered the habiline's outstretched hand, which was still waiting to be shaken. "In comparison to you, Paul, Adam's all courtli-

ness and chivalry and consideration. Look at him. He's
terrified to be here, but he's holding his ground, he's
trying to figure out why you're so jumpy and hostile. I'd
like to know myself. Why are you being such a jackass?''

"He belongs in a zoo.—Okay, okay, not a zoo, a research center or something. You're turning a scientific
wonder, a throwback to another geological epoch, into a
goddamn houseboy. That's selfish, RuthClaire. That's pathetic. There's probably a law against it."

"We'll sit over here," my ex said peremptorily. "Bring
us two glasses of water and a menu."

"Only one menu?"

RuthClaire gave me a look that was blank of all expression; it was also withering. Then she led Adam to a corner
table beneath a burlap sculpture-painting (abstract) that she
had completed during the first few months of our marriage. Once the habiline was seated, I could no longer see
his bare feet; the maroon tablecloth concealed them.
RuthClaire deftly removed the beige linen napkins, folded
into fans, that I had earlier inserted into the waiting water
glasses, for she had made up her mind that my humiliation
must continue. This was my reward for making the West
Bank available for their preposterous parody of a rendezvous.

I turned toward the kitchen. Livia George Stephens, my
chief assistant cook, was leaning against the flocked metal
divider separating the cashier's station from the dining
area. I had given Molly Kingsbury, Hazel Upchurch, and
my two regular waitresses the night off. Livia George
constituted my entire staff. One hand rubbing the back of
the other, she was sizing up our customers with a mock
shrewdness that was genuinely shrewd.

"Good to see you again, Miss RuthClaire," she said
aloud. "Looks like you brought in a friend with some
spirit in his bones. Give me a chanzt, I'll put some meat
on 'em too."

"His name's Adam," my ex replied. "He'd say hello,
but he's a mute. I'm sure he's as pleased to meet you,
though, as I am to see you again. I hope Paul's been
behaving himself for you."

Livia George tiptoed around this pleasantry. "Where's

he stay?'' she asked, nodding at Adam. ''I ain' never seen him 'roun' here befoah, and I know mos' evverbody in this part of 'Poya County.''

''Livia George,'' I said, ''they're here to eat, not to chitchat. Why don't you go see about getting ready for them.''

''Nothin' I can do till I know what they like, Mr. Paul. You wan' me to start cookin' befoah they put in a order?''

''I want you to get into the goddamn kitchen!''

Sullenly, her hips moving like corroded pistons, she went. When she had gone, I strode over to the table to pour out the water and to recite our menu items rather than to present them in a printed folder. For RuthClaire I recommended sautéed mushrooms, an eggplant dish, steamed pearl potatoes, a spinach salad, and a Cheddar soufflé with diced bell peppers and chives. For her tag-along escort, however, I suggested broiled liver and onions. Side orders of unsalted peanuts and warm egg whites would set off his main course quite nicely, and he could wash it all down with a snifter of branch water and branch water.

''I'll have exactly what you recommend,'' RuthClaire said. ''Just bring Adam the same thing and no bully-boy surprises, okay? Water's all we want to drink, pure Beulah Fork spring water.''

Although I followed RuthClaire's instructions, the dinner was a disaster. Adam ate everything with his spoon. He bolted every bite, and when he didn't like something—the eggplant au gratin, for instance—he tried to pile it up in the middle of the table like a deliquescent cairn. For this bit of creative gaucherie he at first used his hands rather than his spoon, and he burned himself. Later, when the food had cooled, he finished the eggplant monument. Nothing RuthClaire said or did to discourage this project had any effect, and there was no way to keep from looking at their table's new centerpiece unless you let your eye stray to Adam himself. A flake of spinach gleamed in his mustache, ten or twelve pearl potatoes bulged his cheeks, and he was nonchalantly pouring his ice cubes into the cheese soufflé.

"This is his first time in a public restaurant," RuthClaire acknowledged.

"And his last, too, if I have anything to say about it."

My ex only laughed. "He's doing pretty well, really. You should've seen the food fights we had out at Paradise Farm only a month or two ago."

"Yeah, I'm sorry I missed them."

She thinks she's Pygmalion, I marveled. She thinks she can carve a dapper southern gentleman out of inchoate Early Pleistocene clay. Well, I loved the lady for the delusions she had formed.

Unfortunately, it got worse. For dessert RuthClaire ordered the two of them Nesselrode pudding, one of the West Bank's specialities and major attractions. Adam lifted the dish to his mouth and began eating of this delicacy like a dog devouring Alpo. After a few such bites, however, his head came up, his cheeks began to puff in and out like those of a blowfish, and he vomited all over the table. Guttural gasps of dismay or amazement escaped him between attacks, and in four or five minutes he had divested himself of his entire dinner and whatever else he may have eaten earlier that day. RuthClaire tried to comfort him. She wiped his mouth with a wetted napkin and stroked his furry nape with her fingers. Never before had a patron of the West Bank upchucked the extraordinary cuisine prepared in my kitchen, though, and *I* may have been more in need of comforting than RuthClaire's ill-bred habiline.

"Get him to the rest room!" I cried, much too late to save either the tablecloth or my equanimity. "If nothing else, get him to the goddamn *street!*"

"He isn't used to such rich fare. I'll clean up the mess, Paul. Just leave it to me, okay?"

"He isn't worthy of it, you mean! It's like feeding caviar to a crocodile, filet mignon to a high school fullback! It's ridiculous! I don't know what you're trying to do or what you think it proves!"

"Hush, Paul, I said I'd take care of the mess, and I will."

Livia George helped her, however, and when Ruth-

Claire left that night, she placed three one-hundred-dollar
bills next to the cash register. For the remainder of that
week the West Bank reeked of commercial disinfectant
and a faint monkey-house odor that no one but me (thank
God) seemed capable of detecting.

"SHE'S LIVING with it," I told the young man sitting at
the cluttered desk, his hands behind his head and his naked
elbows protruding like chicken wings. "She's been living
with it since October."

"Times have changed, Mr. Loyd. Live and let live."

"It's not another man, Dr. Nollinger. It's *male*, I mean,
but it's not, uh, *human*. It's a variety of upright ape."

"A hominid?"

"That's RuthClaire's word for it. Hominid, habiline,
something like that. A prehistoric primate, for God's sake.
That's why I drove all the way up here to talk to somebody
who might be interested."

"You could have telephoned, Mr. Loyd. Telephoning
might have saved us both a good deal of time."

"Beulah Fork's a small town, Dr. Nollinger. A *very*
small town. You can't even direct-dial without old Edna
Twiggs horning in to say she's going to patch you through.
Then she hangs on to eavesdrop and sniffle. Times may
have changed, but bestial cohabitation's still a mite too
strong for Hothlepoya Countians. You understand me,
don't you?"

"A habiline?"

"I want you to get it out of there. It may be dangerous.
It's certainly uncouth. It doesn't belong on Paradise Farm."

Brian Nollinger dropped his hands into his lap and
squeaked his swivel chair around toward his office's solitary window. A thin man in his early thirties, he was
wearing scuffed cowboy boots, beige corduroy trousers, a

short-sleeved Madras shirt with a button-down collar, wire-rimmed glasses, and a wispy Fu Manchu mustache with an incongruous G.I. haircut. Outside his window a family of stub-tailed macaques huddled in the feeble winter sun in a fenced-in exercise area belonging to this secluded rural field station of the Yerkes Primate Center, ten or twelve miles north of Atlanta. Nollinger was an associate professor of anthropology at Emory University, but a government grant to study the effects of forced addiction to certain kinds of amphetamines on a representative primate species had given him an office at the field station and experimental access to the twenty-odd motley monkeys presently taking the February sun beside their heated trailer. They looked wide-awake and fidgety, these monkeys—"hypervigilant," to use Nollinger's own word. Given the nature of his study, I was not greatly surprised.

"Why don't you write Richard Leakey or Alistair Patrick Blair or one of the other African paleoanthropologists specializing in 'prehistoric hominids'?" Nollinger asked me. "They'd jump at the chance to take a living fossil off Ms. Loyd's hands. A find like that would secure an anonymous scientist's fortune and reputation forever. Leakey and Blair would just become bigger."

"Aren't *you* interested in fame and fortune?"

"In modest doses, sure." He refused to look at me. He was staring at a lithograph of an Ishasha River baboon in twelve different baboonish postures, from a grooming stance to a cautious stroll through tall East African grass.

"You don't believe my story, do you?"

"It's a little like hearing that a dinosaur has been spotted wading in the Chattahoochee, Mr. Loyd. Put yourself in my place."

"I'm not a crackpot, Dr. Nollinger. I'm a respected businessman with no history of mental illness or unprofitable undertakings. Moreover, my wife—my *ex*-wife, I mean—is a painter of national repute. Should anything happen to her because you've refused to investigate the matter, well, the world of art will have suffered a loss as great as that about to befall the world of science. It's your conscience, Dr. Nollinger. Can you live with the consequences of such a reprehensible dereliction of duty?'' I got up to leave.

Stroking his Fu Manchu, the young anthropologist finally looked at me. ''Mr. Loyd, after two or three years as a researcher, every competent scientist develops a nose for crackpots.''

''All right. Go on.''

''You came in here like a crackpot. You had the identifying minatory zeal and the traditional combative cast in your eye.'' He paused. ''But you don't *talk* like a crackpot. You talk like a man who's bewildered by something he doesn't know how to deal with.''

''Bingo,'' I said.

''I don't think you're making this up, Mr. Loyd. That would require some imagination.'' He smiled. ''So I'll help you out.'' He stopped smiling. ''On one condition.''

''I'm listening.''

''Send me a photograph or two—all you can—of this dispossessed specimen of *Homo habilis*. Use an Instamatic or a Polaroid and get me some proof. I don't like wild-goose chases, particularly to backwaters like Beulah Fork.''

''You got it,'' I said.

And I walked back to the parking lot past a dozen confined communities of gorillas, orangutans, pygmy chimps, rhesus monkeys, and bespectacled primatologists, all of them equally inscrutable in their obsessive mind-sets and desires. *We are fam-i-lee*, go the lyrics of a recent popular song, but in my entire life I can recall feeling close—spiritually close—to only one other living creature, and that, of course, is my lovely lost RuthClaire. Why had she taken up with a man-ape when my poor human soul still longed for union with hers?

To GET a photograph of Adam I had to sneak out to Paradise Farm in violation of a legal promise to RuthClaire. I had to go prowling around the house in the numbing winter dark. Fortunately, no dog patrols the property (otherwise, of course, even Adam would not have been able to sneak into our pecan grove), and I was able to climb into a magnolia tree near the downstairs bathroom without betraying my presence. I had neither an Instamatic nor a Polaroid, but an expensive Minolta with both a telephoto lens and a pack of high-speed film for shooting in dim or almost nonexistent light.

Voyeurism is not ordinarily one of my vices, but when RuthClaire came into the lavatory that evening to bathe, I began to tremble. The waxy brown leaves of the magnolia tree clicked together like castanets, mimicking the effects of a brutal winter wind. I *looked*, let me confess, but I did not take RuthClaire's picture. (The only extant print of her bewitching unclad body is the one that burns even yet in my mind.) When she lifted herself clear of the sunken bath, patted her limbs and flanks dry with a lavender towel, and disappeared from my sight like a classical nymph, I nearly swooned. Each of these three near-swoons was a metaphysical orgasm of the highest order. It had been a long, long time.

The bathroom light went out, and a real wind began to blow, surging through the pecan grove from eastern Alabama. I had to hang on to my perch. Adam and I, it seemed, had traded places, and the strangeness of this reversal did not amuse me. The luminous digits on my watch registered nine forty-eight. What if my habiline rival habitually relieved himself in the woods? What if, even in winter, he insisted on bathing in White Cow Creek? If so, he would never enter this bathroom, and I would never get

25

his photograph. Dr. Nollinger would dismiss me as a screwball of the most annoying sort. I had made a mistake.

At 11:04 P.M., however, Adam entered the big tiled bathroom. He was wearing the bottoms of a suit of long thermal underwear and carrying what looked like the carcass of a squirrel. He climbed down into the sunken bath, where, after turning on an ablutive flow of water, he proceeded to rend and devour the dead rodent. He did this with both skill and gusto. I used up all my film taking pictures of the messy process—whereupon, spontaneously, I heaved my own dinner into the shrubbery beneath the magnolia tree. Turnabout, they say, is fair play. . . .

Later that week I sent Brian Nollinger duplicates of the developed photographs and a long letter attesting to their authenticity. I added a P.S. The P.S. said, "The ball's in your court, Doc."

THE ANTHROPOLOGY professor was one of those urban people who refuse to own an automobile. He got around the Emory campus on foot or bicycle, and he bummed rides to the Yerkes field station with whichever of his colleagues happened to be going that way. In the middle of March he arrived in Beulah Fork aboard a Greyhound bus, and I met him in front of Ben Sadler's hole-in-the-wall laundry (known locally as the Greyhound Depot Laundry) on Main Street. After introducing Nollinger to Ben (dry cleaner and ticket agent nonpareil) as my nephew, I led the newcomer across the street to the West Bank, where, for over a year, I had been living in the upstairs storage room and taking all my meals in the restaurant proper. Although I could have easily afforded to build a house of my own, or at least to rent a vacation chalet near Muscadine Gardens, I refused to do so in the dogged expectation that RuthClaire and I would eventually be reunited at Paradise Farm.

"Take me out there," Nollinger said over a cold Budweiser in the empty dining area late that afternoon.

"I'd have to call first. And if I tell her why we want to come, she'll decline to receive us."

My "nephew" fanned his photographs of Adam out across the maroon expanse of the tablecloth. "You didn't have an invitation to take these, Mr. Loyd. Why so prim and proper now?"

"My unscrupulosity has well-defined limits."

Nollinger sniggered boyishly. Then he tapped one of the prints. "Adam, as your ex-wife calls the creature, is definitely a protohuman, Mr. Loyd. Even though I'm a primate ethologist and physical anthropologist rather than a hotshot fossil finder like the Leakeys or A. Patrick Blair, I'd stake my reputation on it." He reconsidered. "I mean, I'd *establish* my reputation with a demonstration of that claim. Adam seems to be a healthy living specimen of the hominid known as either *Homo habilis* or *Homo zarakalensis*, depending on which internationally known 'expert' you choose to consult. In any case, your wife has no right to keep her amazing friend cloistered away incognito on Paradise Farm."

"That's exactly what I've always thought. Edna Twiggs is bound to find out sooner or later, and RuthClaire'll have hell to pay in Beulah Fork."

"I mean, Mr. Loyd, that your wife's most basic obligation is to the advancement of our knowledge about human origins."

"That's a narrow way of looking at it. She also has her reputation to consider."

"Listen, Mr. Loyd, haven't you once wondered how a prehistoric hominid happened to show up in a pecan grove in western Georgia?"

"A condor dropped him. A circus train derailed. I really don't care, Dr. Nollinger. What's pertinent to me is his presence out there, not the convoluted particulars of his arrival."

"All right. But I think I *know* how he got here."

We each had another beer. My visitor sipped moodily at

his while I explained that the best approach to RuthClaire
might be Nollinger's masquerading as a meter reader for
Georgia Power. While ostensibly recording her kilowattage
for February, he could plead a sudden indisposition and
request a chance to use the bathroom or to lie down on the
sofa. RuthClaire was a sucker for honest working people
in distress, and Nollinger could buy a shirt and trousers
similar to those worn by Georgia Power employees at
Plunkett Bros. General Store right here in town. Once he
got inside the house, why, who could tell what might
happen? Maybe RuthClaire would actually introduce him
to her hirsute boarder and a profitable rapport spring up
beween the habiline and the anthropologist. Twirling the
silver-blond twists of his almost invisible Fu Manchu,
Nollinger merely grunted.

"What do you think?" I asked him.

"I might do better to go out there as an agent of the
Immigration and Naturalization Service," he replied, somewhat high-handedly. "I think a strong case could be made
for regarding Adam as an illegal alien."

"Is that right? How so, Herr Professor?"

Nollinger embarked on a lengthy explanation. Purely on
impulse he had shown one of his closest friends at Emory,
Caroline Hanna, a young woman with a doctorate in sociology, three or four of my photographs of Adam. Nollinger
was seriously involved with Caroline Hanna, and he knew
that she would not betray his confidence. The photographs
had had a strange effect on Caroline, though. They had
prompted her to reveal that in her after-hours work with
Cuban detainees in the Atlanta Penitentiary she had met
one hardened Havana street criminal from the 1980 Freedom Flotilla who confessed that he *belonged* in prison,
either in Cuba or in *Los Estados Unidos*. Indeed, Uncle
Fidel had apparently released this cutthroat from a Havanan
lockup on the express condition that he emigrate and commit fifty-seven different varieties of mayhem on all the
unsuspecting American capitalists who ran afoul of him.
Instead he had fled down the northern coast of Cuba in a
stolen army Jeep and later on foot to Punta Gorda, where,

after hiding out for almost two weeks, he forcibly comman-
deered a fishing vessel piloted by a wealthy Haitian with
strong anti-Duvalier sympathies and the strangest three-
man crew that the cutthroat had ever seen.

"What was a Haitian doing in Cuban waters?" I asked
Nollinger.

"Probably running communist guns back to the ill-
organized guerrilla opposition to Duvalier in the wilder-
ness areas around Port-de-Prix. Caroline says that the Cuban
told her the vessel hadn't yet taken on any cargo when he
surprised the gunrunner near Punta Gorda. He knifed the
Haitian and threw him overboard. In the process he became aware of three half-naked *eñanos*—dwarfs, I guess
you'd say—watching him from behind the fishing tackle
and cargo boxes in the vessel's stern. They reminded him
of intelligent monkeys, not just animalistic dwarfs, and
they made him intensely uncomfortable. With a pistol he
found concealed in the pilothouse he stalked and mortally
wounded two of these three mute witnesses to his crime.
Their small gnarly corpses went overboard after their captain's fleshy mulatto body, and the cutthroat set his sights
on the last of the funny little men scurrying about the boat
to escape his wrath."

"The gunrunner's crew consisted of habilines?" For the
first time that afternoon Nollinger had piqued my curiosity.

"I think it did, Mr. Loyd, but all I'm doing right now is
telling you Caroline's version of the Cuban thug's account
of his round-about trip to Key West. You can draw your
own inferences."

"What happened to the last crew member?"

"The Cubans with whom the Haitian gunrunner had
planned to rendezvous to make the weapons transfer pulled
abreast of the vessel and took the killer into custody. They
also captured the terrified hominid. They confiscated the
Haitian's boat. Our detainee in the Atlanta pen says that
these mysterious Cuban go-betweens—they were all wearing lampblack on their faces—separated him and the surviving crew member and shipped them both to Mariel Bay
for the crossing to the States. Caroline's informant never

saw the funny little man again. Nevertheless, he's *absolutamente cierto* that this creature reached Florida in one of the jam-packed charter boats making up the Freedom Flotilla. You see, there abounded among many of the refugees rumors of a small hairy mute in sailcloth trousers who kept up their spirits with his awkward mimes and japery. As soon as the crossing was made, though, he disappeared into the dunes before the INS authorities could screen him as they finally screened those who found themselves in Stateside camps or prisons."

"Adam?" I asked.

"It seems likely enough, Mr. Loyd. Besides, this story dovetails nicely with the fact that your ex-wife hasn't had as much trouble as might be expected domesticating—taming—her habiline. Although he seems to have returned to feral habits while scrounging his way up through Florida, purposely avoiding large population centers, his early days on a tiny island off the coast of Haiti made him familiar with at least a few of the trappings of civilization. Your wife, although she doesn't know it, has been *reminding* Adam of these things rather than painstakingly writing them out on a blank slate."

For a time we sipped our beers in silence. I pondered everything that Nollinger had told me. Maybe it explained how Adam had come from Haiti (of all places) to western Georgia, but it did not explain how several representatives of *Homo habilis*, more than 1.5 million years after their disappearance from East Africa, had ended up inhabiting a minuscule island off the larger island of Hispaniola. Did Herr Professor Nollinger have an answer for that objection, too?

"Working backward from Caroline's informant's story," he replied, "I did some discreet research in the anthropological and historical holdings of the Emory library. First of all, I found out all I could about the island off Hispaniola from which the wealthy Haitian had conscripted his crew. It's called Montaraz, Mr. Loyd, and it was originally a Spanish rather than a French possession. However, in the mid-eighteen twenties an American by the name of

Louis Rutherford, a New England aristocrat in our nation's diplomatic service, bought Montaraz outright from a military adviser to Haitian president Jean Pierre Boyer. This was during the Haitian occupation of the Dominican Republic, which had declared its independence from Spain in eighteen twenty-one. The Dominicans regard their twenty-two-year subjugation to Haitian authority as a period of barbarous tyranny, but one of Boyer's real accomplishments was the emancipation of Dominican slaves. On Montaraz, however, in Manzanillo Bay, Louis Rutherford reigned supreme, and his own liberal sentiments did not extend to releasing his black, mulatto, and Spanish-Arawak laborers or to consider paying them for their contributions to the success of his cacao and coffee plantations. He appointed a proxy to keep these enterprises going and divided his time between Port-au-Prince and the family estate in Vermont.''

''I don't see what this has to do with Adam, RuthClaire, or me,'' I said. In another hour my first customers for dinner would be coming through the door. Further, at any moment I expected Livia George, Hazel Upchurch, and Molly Kingsbury to report, with my two evening-shift waitresses close behind. Nollinger was ignorant of, or indifferent to, my business concerns; he wandered into the kitchen to help himself to another Budweiser and came back to our table swigging from the can like an undernourished athlete chug-a-lugging Gatorade. He had his wits about him, though. He tilted the top of the can toward me and soberly resumed his story:

''In eighteen thirty-six Mr. Loyd, Rutherford was sent to the court of Sa'īd ibn Sultan, Āl Bū Sa'īd, on the island of Zanzibar off the East African coast. We Americans were the first westerners to make trade agreements with Sayyid Sa'īd and the first to establish a consul at his commercial capital in the western Indian Ocean. Rutherford went along because of his 'invaluable experience' on Hispaniola, where he had had to deal with both conquering Haitians and defiant Dominicans, a situation that some U.S. officials felt had parallels along the

East African coast, where Sayyid Sa'īd was attempting
to impose his authority on the continental port cities of
Mombasa, Kilwa, and Bravanumbi. Moreover, British moral
objections notwithstanding, Zanzibar had a flourishing slave
market; and Rutherford, as his American colleagues knew,
recognized the commercial imperatives that drove even
kindly persons like Sayyid Sa'īd and himself to tolerate
the more sordid aspects of the institution, in order to turn a
profit. It was the perfect assignment for Rutherford.

"Two years after his arrival on Zanzibar, about the time
he was scheduled to return to this country, Rutherford
caught wind of an extraordinary group of blacks—pygmies,
it was rumored, or hairy Bushmen—who had been taken to
the Sultan's representatives in the continental port city of
Bravanumbi by several Kikembu warriors and sold for
immediate shipment to either Zanzibar or Pemba to work
on Sayyid Sa'īd's clove plantations. The Kikembu warriors called their captives 'little ones who do not speak'
and claimed that they had found all nineteen of these
uncanny quasi-human specimens living in a system of
caves and burrows in the remote Lolitabu Hills of Zarakal.
The warriors had stumbled upon the system by accident,
after watching one of these funny little people, a male,
sneaking through a gulley with two dead hares and a
kaross of nuts and tubers. The hunters then proceeded to
smoke the manikins out. Four or five of the little ones
preferred to die in their arid labyrinth rather than to emerge
and face the laughing Kikembu, but the remainder were
captured and bound.

"An Omani retainer in Sa'īd's court told Rutherford to
go to the slave market there on Zanzibar to see these
wonderful 'monkeymen.' At present they were being kept
apart from the other slaves to spare them injury at the
hands of the larger blacks with whom they would be
competing for masters. It was also possible that outraged
potential buyers might harm them. After all, said the
retainer, you looked for strength in a slave, not delicacy or
sinewy compactness. Rutherford went to the market and
arranged to see the Zarakali imports in private. Apparently

the sight of these creatures entranced him. He wanted the entire lot. He bought them from Sayyid Sa'īd's representatives with cash and a promise to do his best to establish a cacao-for-cloves trade between Montaraz and Zanzibar. When he left the Sultan's court, he sailed around the Cape of Good Hope in a vessel laden with silks, spices, and a small cargo of habilines—although, of course, nobody called them habilines in those days. They were manikins, monkey-folk, curiosities. Rutherford hoped not only to put them to work on Montaraz but to breed them into a self-perpetuating population. Later, in the states, he would exploit them—some of them, anyway—for their novelty value."

"He never did that, I take it."

"Rutherford died on Montaraz in eighteen forty-four, the same year Santo Domingo regained its independence from the Haitian interlopers. His holdings on the island were seized by followers of Pedro Santana. What happened to the fourteen diminutive blacks who survived the journey from East Africa—Rutherford's wife once referred to them in a letter to the wife of another diplomat as 'endearing little elves, albeit, most likely, the offspring of chimpanzees and debauched Zarakali niggers'—well, at this point, their fate is unclear. We have knowledge of them at all only because Mrs. Rutherford acted as her husband's secretary and carried on voluminous correspondences with her relatives in Boston and Montpelier. I obtained some of this information, Mr. Loyd, from interlibrary loans and photocopying services, and I'm virtually certain that no one else in the world has an inkling of the importance—the staggering importance—of the material I've assembled and synthesized in only two and a half weeks. It's the major scientific accomplishment of my life."

"Beats injecting macaques with No Dōz, huh?" I had begun setting my tables, single-handedly flapping open parachutes of linen and laying out silverware. Just as Nollinger was about to parry my sarcasm, Livia George appeared at the door. As the anthropologist shuffled the photographs of Adam out of her line of sight, I told her, "This is my cousin from Atlanta. He'll be staying with us a few days."

"Nephew," Nollinger corrected me, standing for the introduction.

"Right," I acknowledged. "Nephew."

Livia George came over and shook Nollinger's hand. "Pleased to meecha. You're too skinny, thoah—all shanks and shoulder blades. Stay aroun' here a few days and I'll get you fatted up fine as any stockyard steer."

"That's a promise," I informed Nollinger, "not a threat."

"Thank you," he said uncertainly. "Thank you, ma'am."

RUTHCLAIRE DID not come to town either of the next two days, and Nollinger stayed after me to drive him out to see her. He was missing his morning classes at Emory, he said, and a colleague at the field station was having to oversee the daily amphetamine injections of his drug-addled macaques. He could not stay in Beulah Fork much longer. Did I want him to get Adam out of RuthClaire's life or not? If I did, I had to cooperate. Had I summoned him all the way from Atlanta only to confine him to my grungy attic-cum-dormitory? Was I that desperate for a roommate?

I was ready to cooperate. Entirely at my expense my counterfeit nephew ate nothing but medium-rare steaks and extravagant tossed salads with Roquefort dressing. Moreover, to amuse himself between his final meal of the day and his own owlish turn-in time he had brought with him a homemade syrinx, or panpipe, that he played with a certain melancholy skill but an intemperance that sabotaged, early on, my regard. Sometimes (he told me as we lay on our cots in the dark) he would play the panpipe for his experimental subjects at the field station, and the strains of this music would soothe even the most agitated and bellicose of the males. It was an unscientific thing to do (he conceded) becaue it introduced an extraneous element into his observations of their behavior, but he found it hard to deny them—completely, anyway—the small pleasure afforded by his playing.

"I'm not a macaque," I replied. Both the hint and the implied criticism were lost on Nollinger.

I was not *that* desperate for a roommate. So the next day I swallowed hard and telephoned RuthClaire, explaining that a young man who greatly admired her work had stopped in at the West Bank to request an introduction. Would it be all right if I brought him out? He did not seem to be (1) an art dealer, (2) a salesman, (3) a potential groupie, (4) a college kid with a term paper due, or (5) an out-and-out crazy. I liked both his looks and his attitude.

"Is he your nephew, Paul?"

"What?"

"Edna Twiggs told me yesterday that your nephew was staying with you."

"That's right, RuthClaire. He's my nephew."

"You don't have a nephew, Paul. Even Edna Twiggs knows that. That's because you don't have any brothers or sisters."

"I had to tell the home folks *something*, RuthClaire. They don't rest easy till they've got every visiting stranger sized up and pigeonholed. You know how some of them can be. I didn't want it going around that I'd set up house with another guy."

"Not much chance of that arrangement," RuthClaire said. "But why this petty intrigue and deception, hon? What's the *real* story?"

I had to improvise. "I'm thinking of selling out," I said hurriedly. "His name's Brian Nollinger and he's a potential buyer. Neither of us wants to publicize the fact, though—to keep from confusing everyone if the deal falls through. We're trying to prevent disillusionment or maybe even gloating. You understand?"

"Selling out? But, Paul, you love that place."

"Once upon a time I did. I've only kept it these past fourteen or fifteen months because I thought we might get back together. But that begins to seem less and less likely, doesn't it?''

RuthClaire was so quiet I feared she had rung off. Then she said, ''I don't understand why your potential buyer wants to meet me.''

''The part about him admiring your work is true,'' I lied. ''You know the three-dimensional paintings you did for the Contemporary Room in Atlanta's High Museum? He's been to see 'em four or five times since their debut. Come on, Ruthie. He'd like to see you in person. I told him you would. It might help me cinch the sale.''

Again she was slow to answer. ''Paul, there are a couple of reasons why I might be reluctant to give you that kind of help.'' She let me mull the implications. ''All right,'' she added a moment later, ''bring him on. I'll put aside my work and tell Adam to get lost for an hour or so.''

She hung up before I could thank her.

Throughout this conversation Nollinger had been at my elbow. ''I don't know anything about the restaurant business,'' he said nervously. ''As far as that goes, I don't know very much about art, either.''

''Do you know what you like?''

''I beg your pardon.''

''Never mind,'' I said. ''Let's get out there.''

Despite his musical talent and his advanced degrees in anthropology and primate behavior, Nollinger had not been lying about his ignorance of art. I learned the dismaying extent of his ignorance on our journey out to Paradise Farm. Anxious that he not tip his hand too early, I alternately quizzed and coached him as we drove. Although not unfamiliar with such Renaissance biggies as Leonardo da Vinci and Michelangelo, he seemed to have abandoned his art-appreciation classes just as they were forging into the terra incognita of the seventeenth century. He knew next to nothing about impressionism, postimpressionism, and the most influential twentieth-century movements. He confused Vincent van Gogh with a popular author of science-fiction extravaganzas, believed that Pablo Picasso was still alive in France, and vigorously contended that N. C. Wyeth was a much better painter than his son, Andrew, who painted only barns and motionless people. He had never even heard of the contemporary artists whom RuthClaire most esteemed.

"You're a phony," I said in disgust. "She'll sniff you out in three minutes' time—if it takes her that long."

"Look, Mr. Loyd, *you're* the one who concocted this stupid scheme."

"I know," I said. "I know."

"Why don't we just tell her the truth?"

"The truth wouldn't have got you out here," I said, easing my car into the gravel-strewn drive in front of the house. "You'd still be in Beulah Fork playing your pan-pipe and waiting for your next tactfully mooched meal."

Nollinger's jaw went rigid. With visible effort he swallowed whatever reply he had thought to make. The air of fierce inner resolve suddenly radiating from him, rather like a fever, began to worry me.

RuthClaire met us on the front porch, shook Nollinger's hand, and ushered us inside. We stood about in the sculpture-studded foyer like visitors awaiting their guide at a museum. This was the first time I had set foot over the threshold since September, and the faint but disturbing monkeyhouse odor that Adam had left behind in the West Bank was as unignorable here as mold on a brick of cheese. Nollinger noticed it, too, the incongruous scent of macaques in a barnlike Southern manse. RuthClaire was probably inured to the smell by this time, but she quickly detected our sensitivity to it and explained it away as the wretched mustiness of a shut-up house after a particularly severe winter.

"I'm not an admirer of yours," Nollinger blurted. His

sallow face turned the color of a ripe plum. "I mean, I probably would be if I knew anything about your work, but I don't. I'm here under false pretenses."

"Criminy," I murmured.

RuthClaire looked to me for either amplification or aid. I rubbed the cold nappy head of a granite satyr next to the oaken china cabinet dominating the hall. (It was a baby satyr with a syrinx very much like Nollinger's.)

"I'm here to see Adam," the anthropologist said.

My ex did not take her eyes off me. "He's outside foraging," she replied curtly. "How do you happen to know about him?"

"Livia George may have let it slip," I essayed. "From Livia George to Edna Twiggs to the media of all seven continents."

"Here," said Nollinger. He handed RuthClaire the packet of photos I had taken from the magnolia tree outside the downstairs bathroom. Prudently, though, he saved back three or four of the pictures. Without facing away from me RuthClaire thumbed through the batch in her hands.

"You're a Judas, Paul," she said. "You're the most treacherously backstabbing Benedict Arnold I've ever had the misfortune to know. I swear to goodness, I actually *married* you! How could that have happened?"

To Nollinger I said, "I'm toting up your bill at the West Bank, Herr Professor. It's going to be a shocker, too. Just you wait."

"You told him about Adam," RuthClaire accused. "You actually *volunteered* the information."

"I was worried about you. Grant me that much compassionate concern for your welfare. I'm not an unfeeling toad, for Christ's sake."

"When?" RuthClaire asked the anthropologist. "When did he get in touch with you?"

"Last month, Ms. Loyd."

My ex counted on her fingers as if she were trying to compute a conception date. "It took at least four months for this 'compassionate concern' to develop, didn't it? Four whole months, Paul?"

"His instincts were right in coming to me," Nollinger

interjected. "You don't have any business keeping a rare hominid specimen like Adam in your own home. He's an invaluable evolutionary Rosetta stone. By rights he belongs to the world scientific community."

"Of which, I suppose, you're the self-appointed representative?"

"That's right," Nollinger said. "I mean, if you'll just take it upon yourself to see me in that light."

"First of all, I'm not *keeping* Adam in my house; he's living here of his own free will. Second, he's a human being and not an anonymous evolutionary whatchamacallit belonging to you or anybody else. And finally, Dr. Nollinger, I'm ready for you and Benedict Iscariot here to haul your presumptuous heinies back to Beulah Fork. The sooner the faster the swifter the better."

Nollinger looked at me knowingly, conspiratorially. "Your ex-wife seems to be an uncompromising spiritual heir of Louis Rutherford, doesn't she?"

"What does that mean?" RuthClaire demanded.

"I think what he's trying to say," I said, "is that you've got yourself the world's only habiline houseboy and you don't want to give him up."

"It's a form of involuntary servitude," Nollinger added, "no matter how many with-it rationales you use to justify the relationship."

"He comes and goes as he likes," RuthClaire said angrily. "Paradise Farm is his only haven in the whole materialistic grab bag of environments around here. Maybe you'd like him to live in a shopping mall or a trade-school garage or a tumbledown outhouse on Cleve Synder's place?"

"Or a fenced-in run at the field station?" I said, turning toward the anthropologist. "So that you can dope him up with amphetamines for fun and profit."

"Wait a minute, Mr. Loyd," Nollinger protested. "I'm on your side."

RuthClaire began tearing up the prints in her hands and sprinkling them on the floor like Kodachrome confetti. "These are cheap paparazzo snapshots," she said, her teeth clenched. She next went to work shredding the envelope.

"I still have these," Nollinger told her, holding up the prints he had palmed. "And Mr. Loyd still has an entire set of his own."

"She feels better, though," I said, looking askance at RuthClaire.

"Of course she does. Once we've gone, she'll have her habiline houseboy in here to clean up the mess. It's not many folks in this day and age who command the obedience of a loyal unpaid retainer. She likes putting him to use. She likes the feeling of power she gets from—"

Suddenly, surprising even myself, I plunged my fist deep into the anthropologist's diaphragm. I would have preferred to clip him on the temple or the jaw, but his wire-rimmed glasses dissuaded me—dissuaded, that is, my subconscious. Nollinger, the wind knocked out of him, finished his sentence with an inarticulate *"Umpf!"* and collapsed atop the scattered photograph pieces.

RuthClaire said, "Maybe *you* feel a little better, too. Not too much, though, I hope. His insults pale beside your treachery, Paul."

"That's probably so," I admitted, hangdog.

"Please get him out of here. I'll start soliciting bed partners on Peachtree Street before your unmannerly 'nephew' ever lays eyes on the *real* Adam."

I helped Nollinger to his feet and led him outside to my automobile. Still bent over and breathless, he mumbled that my unprovoked assault was a classic primate ploy— especially typical of baboons or chimpanzees—to establish dominance through intimidation. I told him to shut up and he did. Thereafter he kept his eyes averted; and as we left Paradise Farm, rolling from crunchy gravel onto pothole-riven asphalt, I saw Adam staring out at us from the leafy picket of holly trees separating RuthClaire's property from the road. The half-concealed habiline, I glumly took note, was wearing one of my old golfing sweaters.

It did not flatter him.

AT SIX o'clock that evening the sullen anthropologist boarded a Greyhound bus for Atlanta, and I supposed that our dealings with each other had formally concluded. I did not want to see him again, and I did not expect to. As for RuthClaire, she had every reason to feel the same way about me. I tried, therefore, to resign myself to her bizarre liaison with the mysterious refugee from Montaraz. After all, how was she hurting Adam or Adam her? I must get on with my own life.

About a week later this headline appeared in the Atlanta *Constitution*, which I have delivered every morning to the West Bank:

RENOWNED BEULAH FORK ARTIST
HARBORING PREHISTORIC HUMAN
SAYS EMORY ANTHROPOLOGIST

"Oh, no," I said aloud over my coffee. "Oh, no."

The story featured a photograph—a color photograph—of Adam dismembering a squirrel in the downstairs bathroom at Paradise Farm. Not having reproduced very well, this photo had the dubious authenticity of pictures of the Loch Ness monster—but it grabbed my eye like a layout in a gore-and-gossip tabloid, afflicting me with anger and guilt. About the only consolation I could find in the story's appearance was the fact that it occupied a small corner of the city/state section rather than the right-hand columns of the front page. The photograph itself was attributed to Brian Nollinger.

"I'll kill him."

The *Constitution*'s reporter had woven together a tapestry of quotations—from Nollinger, from two of his colleagues at Emory, and from RuthClaire herself—that made

41

the anthropologist's claims, or charges, seem the pathetic fancies of a man whose career had never quite taken off as everyone had anticipated. The press conference he had called to announce his unlikely discovery included a bitter indictment of a "woman of talent and privilege" who was obstructing the progress of science for selfish reasons of her own. RuthClaire, in turn, had submitted to a brief telephone interview in which she countercharged that Nollinger's tale of a *Homo habilis* survivor living in her house and grounds was a tawdry pitch for notoriety and more government research money. She refrained quite cagily, I noticed, from any outright declaration that Nollinger was lying. Informed of the existence of photos, for instance, RuthClaire dismissed them as someone else's work—without actually claiming they had been fabricated from scratch or cunningly doctored. Moreover, she kept me altogether out of the discussion. And because Nollinger had done likewise (from a wholly different set of motives), no one at the *Constitution* had attempted to interview me. Ah, I thought, there's more consolation here than I first supposed. My ex can take care of herself. . . .

She would blame me for this unwanted publicity, though. She would harden herself to all my future efforts at rapprochement.

Despite the early hour I telephoned Paradise Farm to apologize for what had happened and to offer my shoulder either to cry on or to cudgel. A recorded message informed me that RuthClaire's previous number was no longer functioning. I understood immediately that she had applied for and received an unlisted number. This unforeseen development hit me even harder than the newspaper article. Paradise Farm now seemed as far away as Hispaniola or the court of Sayyid Sa'īd.

Before the hour was out my own telephone began ringing. The first caller was Livia George, who, in high dudgeon, asked me if I had seen the piece in the *Constitution* and wondered aloud how my devious Atlanta relative had managed to take a photograph of RuthClaire's mute friend Adam in her very own bathroom. "You got a spill-the-beans Peepin' Tom for a nephew," she said. " 'F he ever comes back to visit you, Mr. Paul, I ain' the one gonna do his cookin', let me tell you that now." I agreed that Nollinger was a contemptible sneak and promised that she would never have to wait on the man again.

Then, in rapid succession, I received calls from a reporter on the Tocqueville *Telegraph*, a representative of "The Today Show" on NBC, an art dealer in Atlanta with a small stake in RuthClaire's professional reputation, and two of my fellow merchants in Beulah Fork, Ben Sadler and groceryman Clarence Tidings, both of whom expressed the hope that my ex-wife would not suffer disruptive public attention because of my nephew's outrageous blather to the Atlanta media. An artist, they said, required her privacy. I put their commiseration on hold by agreeing with them and pleading other business. The reporter, the TV flack, and the art dealer I had sidestepped with terse pleasantries and an unshakable refusal to comment.

Then I took my telephone off the hook, dressed, and went shopping. My neighbors greeted me cheerily the first time our carts crossed paths, then studied me sidelong as I picked out meats, cheeses, and produce. Every housewife in the A&P seemed to be looking at me as she might a cuckolded male who pretends a debonair indifference to his ignominy. It gave me the heebie-jeebies, this surreptitious surveillance.

Back at the West Bank my uncradled receiver was emitting a strident buzz, a warning to hang up or to forfeit the boon of continuous service. I replaced the receiver. A moment later the telephone rang. It was Edna Twiggs, who told me that RuthClaire was trying to reach me.

"Give me her new number," I said. "I'll call her."

But Edna replied, "Hang up again, Mr. Loyd. I'll let her know you're home. I'm not permitted to divulge an unlisted number."

Cursing under my breath, I obeyed Beulah Fork's inescapable sedentary gadfly, and when next the telephone rang, RuthClaire's voice was soft and weary in my ear.

"We're under siege," she said. "There's an Eleven

Alive news van from Atlanta on the lawn, and several other vehicles—one of them's a staff car from the Columbus *Ledger-Enquirer*—are parked in the drive or along the roadway behind the hollies. It looks like a gathering for a Fourth of July picnic, Paul.''

"Have you talked to any of those people?"

"The knocking started a little over an hour ago. I wouldn't answer it. Now there's a man on the lawn taking pictures of the house with a video camera and a stylish young woman in front of the camera with a microphone talking about the 'deliberate inaccessibility of artist RuthClaire Loyd.' She's said that about four or five times. Maybe she's practicing. Anyway, I can hear her all the way up here in the loft. They're not subtle, these people, they're loud and persistent.''

"Call the police, RuthClaire. Call the Hothlepoya County Sheriff's Patrol.''

"I hate to do that.''

"They're trespassing. They're making nuisances of themselves. Call Davie Hutton here in town and Sheriff Crutchfield in Tocqueville.''

"What if I just poke my .22 out of the window and tell everybody to beat it?''

"It'd make great viewing on the evening news.''

"Yeah, wouldn't it?'' RuthClaire chuckled wryly. "May the seraphim forgive me, but I was thinking a display like that might boost subscription sales for the *Celestial Hierarchy* series. AmeriCred has been a little disappointed in the way they're going.''

"We live in a secular age, RuthClaire.'' Then I said, "How's Adam taking all this?''

"It's made him restless and reclusive. He's pacing the downstairs bathroom with the exhaust fan running—to drown out the clamor from the lawn.''

"Well, I hope you closed the curtains on the upper half of the window in there. Reporters can climb trees, too, you know.''

"Adam and I installed some blinds,'' she said. "No worry there. The worry's how long this stupid encirclement is likely to last. I can't get any work done. Adam's going to develop a nervous disorder.''

''Let the law run them off. That's what the law's for.''

''All right.''

''You're smart enough to figure that out for yourself. What made you call me for such a self-evident serving of advice?''

''I wanted to let you know just how much trouble you've caused us, you dinkhead.'' (But her tone, it pleased me to note, was bantering rather than bitter.) ''And one other thing besides that, Paul.''

''Okay, I'll bite.''

''Adam's one failing as a companion is that he can't talk. Maybe I just wanted to hear the silver-throated con man of Beulah Fork do his stuff again.'' She let me ruminate on this left-handed compliment for a second or two, then gave me her new telephone number and bade me a peremptory goodbye.

I sat there awhile with the receiver in my hand, but finally hung up before Edna Twiggs could break in to tell me I was on the verge of forfeiting continuous service.

INTERNATIONAL MEDIA attention converged on Paradise Farm. Neither the Beulah Fork police department nor the sheriff's patrol from Tocqueville could adequately cope with the journalists, television people, curiosity seekers, and scientists who descended on Hothlepoya County for a peek at RuthClaire's habiline paramour. For a time the Georgia Highway Patrol intervened, rerouting the gate-crashers back toward the interstate and issuing tickets to those who ignored the detour signs; but Ruben Decker and a few of the other residents along the road linking Paradise Farm with town protested that they had been singled out for citations as often as had the journalists and the pesky outsiders plaguing the area, many of whom, when stopped, produced false ID's to corroborate their claims of being locals. At last even the highway patrol threatened to retreat from the scene; this wasn't their fight.

In desperation RuthClaire contracted with an Atlanta firm to erect an imposing beige-brick wall around the exposed sections of her property's perimeter; and this barricade, upon its completion in May, proved an effective psychological as well as physical deterrent to most of those who were stopping by for a casual, rather than a mercenary or a malevolent, look-see. Pale arc lights on tall poles illuminated every corner of the vast front and back yards and portions of the shadowy pecan grove behind the house. On two occasions RuthClaire broadcast stentorian warnings over a P.A. system installed for that purpose and actually fired her rifle above the heads of the trespassers creeping like animated stick figures across the lawn. Word got around that it was *dangerous* to try to breach the elaborate fortifications of Paradise Farm. I liked that.

Meanwhile, in the absence of hard facts, speculation and controversy raged. Alistair Patrick Blair, the eminent Zarakali paleoanthropologist, published a paper in *Nature* denouncing the notion of a surviving Early Pleistocene hominid as "sheer unadulterated grandstanding piffle." He was careful not to mention Brian Nollinger by name, not so much to avoid libeling the man, I think, as to deprive him of the satisfaction of seeing his name in print—even in a disparaging context. Blair cited the notorious Piltdown hoax as a veritable model of competent flimflammery next to this tottery ruse, and he argued vigorously that the few available photographs of Adam were clearly of a rather hairy black man in a molded latex mask like those designed for his PBS television series, *Beginnings*. Nollinger rebutted Blair, or tried to, with a semicoherent essay in *Atlanta Fortnightly* summarizing the extraordinary diplomatic career of Louis Rutherford and strongly condemning the artist RuthClaire Loyd for her tyrannical imprisonment of the bemused and friendless hominid. She was a female Simon Legree with a mystical bias against both evolutionary theory and the scientific method.

Sermons were preached both for and against my ex-wife. Initially, fundamentalists did not know which side to come down on because anyone opposed to the scientific method could not be all bad, while anyone cohabiting with a quasi-human creature not her lawfully wedded husband must certainly be enmeshed in the snares of Satan. By the second week of this controversy most fundamentalist ministers, led by the Right Reverend Dwight "Happy" McElroy of America's Greater Christian Constituency, Inc., of Rehoboth, Louisiana, had determined that the crimson sin of bestiality far outweighed the tepid virtue of a passive antievolutionary sentiment. Their sermons began both to deride RuthClaire for her sexual waywardness (this was an irony that perhaps only I could appreciate) and to pity her as the quintessential victim of a society whose scientific establishment brazenly proclaimed that human beings were nothing more than glorified monkeys (a thesis that their own behavior seemed to substantiate). Happy McElroy, in particular, was having his cake and eating it too. I audited a few of his television sermons, but almost always ended by turning down the sound and watching the eloquent hand signals of the woman providing simultaneous translation for the deaf.

Sales of RuthClaire's *Celestial Hierarchy* porcelain-plate series boomed. In fact, AmeriCred reversed a long-standing subscription policy to permit back orders of the first few plates in the series, then announced to thousands of disappointed collectors that this particular limited edition of Limoges porcelain had sold out. It would violate the company's covenant with its subscribers to issue a second edition of the plates. However, in response to the overwhelming demand for RuthClaire's exquisite work, AmeriCred, in conjunction with Porcelaine Jacques Javet of Limoges, France, had just commissioned from this world-acclaimed Georgia artist a second series of paintings to be entitled *Footsteps on the Path to Man*, which would feature imaginative but anthropologically sound portraits of many of our evolutionary forebears and several contemporary human visages besides; eighteen plates in all, the larger number being a concession to the growing public appetite for my ex-wife's distinctive art. Further, this series, this limited edition, would not be quite so limited as the previous one; more people would be able to subscribe.

"Congratulations," I told RuthClaire one evening by telephone.

"It's phenomenally tacky, isn't it?"

"I think it's called striking while the iron's hot."

"Well, I needed the money, Paul. Having a wall built around two thirds of Paradise Farm didn't come cheap. Neither did the arc lights or the P.A. system. I have to recoup my investment."

"You think I don't know?"

"Besides, I *want* to do this *Footsteps on the Path to Man* series. The australopithecines I'll have to reconstruct from fossil evidence and some semi-inspired guesswork, but for *Homo habilis* I'll have a living model. It's going to be fun putting Adam's homely-handsome kisser on a dinner plate."

"Maybe I could order five or six place settings of that one for the West Bank."

RuthClaire laughed delightedly.

Of course, the sermons following hard upon the new AmeriCred announcement were universally condemnatory. The depths to which my ex-wife had fallen defied even Happy McElroy's bombastic oratorical skills. He tried, though. The title of his message on the first Sunday in July was "From Angels to Apes: The Second Fall." Whereas the celestial hierarchy was an ascent to pure spirit, the blind worship of evolutionary theory—"*Theory*, mind you!" McElroy roared. "Unsupported *theory!*"—was a footstep on the downward path to Mammon, debauchery, and hell. At the end of his prepared remarks McElroy asked his congregation to join with his loyal television audience in a silent prayer of redemption for paleoanthropologists everywhere and for their avaricious minion in Beulah Fork, Georgia, may God have mercy, RuthClaire Loyd.

I am not a complete pagan: I joined in.

THE ATTITUDE of my own townspeople toward Ruth-Claire during this period was hard to judge. Many had resented the unruly influx of visitors in the spring and the inconvenience of the highway patrol roadblocks and spot identity checks. Still, most did not hold my former wife personally accountable for these problems, recognizing that she, too, was a victim of the publicity mill generating both the crowds and the clumsy security measures finally obviated by the wall. Now the residents of Beulah Fork wondered about the *relationship* between RuthClaire and Adam. This preoccupation, depending on their ultimate view of the matter, dictated the way they spoke about and dealt with their unorthodox rural neighbor. Or would have, I'm sure, if RuthClaire had come into town more often.

One sweltering day in July, for instance, I went into the Greyhound Depot Laundry to reclaim the tablecloths I had left to be dry-cleaned. Ben Sadler, a courtly man nearly six and a half feet tall, stooped toward me over his garment-strewn counter and in the blast-furnace heat of that tiny establishment trapped me in a perplexing conversation about the present occupants of Paradise Farm. Sweat beaded on his forehead, ran down his ash-blond temples, and accumulated in his eyebrows as if they were thin, ragged sponges not quite thirsty enough to handle the unending flow.

"Listen, Paul, what kind of, uh, creature is this Adam fella, anyway?"

I summarized all the most likely, and all the most asinine, recent speculations. I used the terms *Australopithecus zarakalensis*, *Homo zarakalensis*, and *Homo habilis*. I used the words *ape-man*, *hominid*, *primate*, and *dwarf*. I confessed that not even the so-called experts agreed on the genus or species to which Adam belonged.

49

"Do they say he's human?" Ben wanted to know.

"Some of them do. That's what *Homo* means, although lots of people seem to think it means something else. Anyway, RuthClaire thinks he's human, Ben."

"And he's black, isn't he? I mean, I've read where the entire human race—even the Gabor sisters and the Osmond family—I've read where we're all descended from tiny black people. Originally, that is."

"He's as black as Hershey's syrup," I conceded.

"Do *you* think we're descended from Adam, Paul? RuthClaire's Adam, I mean."

"Well, not Adam personally. Prehistoric hominids like him, maybe. Adam's a kind of hominid coelacanth." I explained that a coelacanth was an ancient fish known only in fossil form and presumed extinct until a specimen was taken from waters off South Africa in 1938. That particular fish had been five feet long. Adam, on the other hand, was about six inches shy of five feet. Therefore, I did not think it absolutely impossible for a retiring, intelligent creature of Adam's general dimensions to elude the scrutiny of *Homo sapiens sapiens* for the past few thousand years of recorded human history. Of course, I also believed in the Sasquatch and the yeti. . . .

"That's a funny idea, Paul—all of us comin' from creatures two thirds our size and black as Hershey's syrup."

"Don't run for office on it."

Ben wiped his brow with one glistening forearm. "How does RuthClaire, uh, look upon Adam?" He feared that he had violated propriety. "I mean, does she see him as a brother? I've heard some folks say she treats him like a house nigger from plantation days—which I can't believe of her, not under no circumstances—and others who say he's more like a two-legged poodle gettin' the favorite-pet treatment from its lady. I ask because I'm not sure how I'd greet the little fella if he was to walk in here tomorrow."

"I think she treats him like a houseguest, Ben." (I *hope* that's how she treats him, I thought. The ubiquitous spokesman for America's Greater Christian Constituency, Inc., had planted a nefarious doubt in my mind.)

Ben Sadler grunted his conditional agreement, and I carried my clean tablecloths back across the street to the restaurant.

That evening, a Saturday, the West Bank was packed. Molly Kingsbury was hostessing, Livia George and Hazel were on duty in the kitchen, and a pair of college kids from Tocqueville were waiting tables. I roamed from corner to corner giving assistance wherever it was needed, functioning not only as greeter, maître d', and wine steward, but also as busboy, cashier, and commander in chef (ha ha).

My regular customers demand personal attention, from me rather than from staff members. A squib of gossip, a silly joke, occasionally even a free appetizer or dessert. I try to oblige most of these demands. This Saturday evening, however, I was having trouble balancing hospitality and hustle. Although grateful for the crowd, by nine o'clock I had begun to growl at my college kids and to nod perfunctorily at even my most stalwart customers. The muggy summer dusk and the heat from my kitchen had pretty much neutralized the efforts of my ceiling fan and my one laboring air conditioner. In my Haggar slacks and lemon-colored Izod shirt I was sweating just like Ben Sadler in the Greyhound Depot Laundry.

The door opened. Two teenage boys in blue jeans, T-shirts, and perforated baseball caps strolled in. Even in the evening the West Bank does not require coats and ties of its male clientele (shoot, *I* frequently work in the kitchen in shorts and sneakers), but something about these two— Craig Puddicombe and E. L. Teavers—made my teeth grind. I could have seen them in their string-tie Sunday best (as I sometimes did) without feeling any more kindly toward them, and tonight their flat blue eyes and sweat-curled sideburns incited only my annoyance. For one thing, they had left the door open. For another, I had no table for them. What were they doing here? They usually ate at the Deep South Truck Stop on the road to Tocqueville.

"Shut the door," I told Craig Puddicombe, carefully tonging ice into somebody's water glass. "You're letting in insects."

Craig shut the door as if it were a pane of wraparound glass on an antique china cabinet. E.L. took off his hat. They stood on my interior threshold staring at the art on the walls and the open umbrellas suspended from the ceiling as atmosphere-evoking ornament. They either could not or would not look at the people eating. I approached them because Molly Kingsbury clearly did not want to.

"You don't have reservations," I told Puddicombe. "It's going to be another fifteen or twenty minutes before we can seat you."

Craig looked at me without quite looking. "That's okay. You got a minute?"

"Only if it lasts about twelve seconds."

"We just want to talk to you a bit," E. L. Teavers said earnestly, almost ingratiatingly. "We think your rights are being violated."

Craig Puddicombe added, "More than your rights, maybe."

"Fellas," I said, indicating the crowd, "you don't choose a battle zone for a friendly little chat about human rights."

"It was now, Mr. Loyd, because we happened to be ridin' by," Craig said. "For something this important you can spare a minute."

Before I could dispute this point, E. L. Teavers, surveying the interior, said, "My mother remembers when this was Dr. Kearby's office. This was the waitin' room, out here. Whites sat on this side, the others over that way. People used to come out of the examination room painted with a purple medicine Dr. Kearby liked to daub around."

"Gentian violet," I told him, exasperated. "It's a bactericide.—Quick, now, as quickly as you can, tell me how my rights are being violated."

"Your wife—" Craig Puddicombe began.

"My ex-wife," I corrected him.

"Okay, your ex-wife. She's got a hibber livin' with her on premises that used to belong to you, Mr. Loyd. How do you feel about that?"

"A what living with her?"

"Hibber," E. L. Teavers enunciated, lowering his voice.

"It's a word I invented. Anyone can use it, but I invented it. It means habiline nigger, see?"

"Clever. You must be the one who was graduated from high school. Craig just went for gym class and shop."

"I've got a diploma too, Mr. Loyd. Our intelligence ain't the issue, it's the violation of your rights as a white person, not to mention our traditional community standards. You follow all this, don't you?"

"You're not speaking for the community. You're speaking for Craig Puddicombe, teenage redneck."

"He's speakin' for more than that," E. L. Teavers said, smiling boyishly. The boyishness of this smile was a major part of its menace.

"We just dropped in to *help* you, Mr. Loyd. We're not bigots. You're a bigger bigot than E.L. or me 'cause you look down on your own kind who ain't got as much as you do or who ain't been to school as long. *That's* bigotry, Mr. Loyd."

"I'm busy," I said, and turned to take care of my customers.

E. L. Teavers grabbed my elbow—with an amiable deference at odds with the force of his grip. I could not shake him off because of the water pitcher in my hand. He had not stopped smiling his shy, choirboy smile, and I found myself wanting to hear whatever he had to say next, no matter how addlepated or paranoiac.

"You see, there's a hibber—a lousy subhuman—inheritin' to stuff that doesn't, that shouldn't, belong to it. Since it used to be your stuff—your house, your land, your wife—we thought you'd like to know there's people in and around Beulah Fork who appreciate other hardworkin' folks and who try to keep an eye out for their rights."

"Namely Craig and you?" Since finishing up at Hothlepoya High last June, I reflected, they had been working full time at United Piedmont Mills on the outskirts of Tocqueville. E.L., in fact, was married to a girl who had waitressed for me briefly. "Knowing that, fellas, has just about made my day. I feel infinitely more secure."

"You never went to school with hibbers," Craig

Puddicombe said. "You've never had to be anything but their boss."

"Now you've got a prehistoric one gettin' it on with your wife."

"My *ex*-wife," I responded automatically.

"Yeah," said E. L. Teavers. "Like you say." He took a creased business card from the hip pocket of his jeans and handed it to me. "This is the help you can count on if it begins to seem unfair to you. If it begins to, you know, make you angry." He opened the restaurant door on the muggy July night. "Better am-scray, Craig, so's Mr. Loyd can get back to feeding his bigwigs."

They were gone.

I wandered to the service niche beside the kitchen and set down the water pitcher. I read the business card young Teavers had given me. Then I tore it lengthwise, collated the pieces, and tore them again—right down the middle. Ordinarily quite dependable, in this instance my memory fails me. All I can recall is the gist of the message on the card. But to preserve the fiction of my infallibility as narrator I will give here a reasonable *facsimile* of the message on that small, grimy document:

E(lvis) L(amar) Teavers
Zealous High Zygote
KuKlos Klan—Kudzu Klavern
Box 666 Beulah Fork, Georgia

Business had slackened noticeably by ten o'clock. At eleven we closed. I stayed in the kitchen for a couple of hours after Hazel and Livia George had left preparing my desserts for Sunday: a German chocolate cake, a carrot cake, and a strawberry icebox pie. The work—the attention to ingredients, measures, and mixing or baking times—kept my mind off the visit by the boys. In fact, I was making a purposeful effort not to think about it. A strategy that disintegrated as soon as I was upstairs in the stuffy converted storage room.

E. L. Teavers, a bright kid from a respectable lower-middle-class home, was a member of the Klan. Not merely a member, but an officer of a piddling local chapter of one of its semiautonomous splinter groups. What had the card said? Zealous High Zygote? Terrific Vice Tycoon? Puissant Grand Poltroon? Something rhetorically cyclopean or cyclonic. The title did not really matter. What mattered was that this able-bodied, mentally keen young man, along with his somewhat less astute buddy, had kept abreast of the situation at Paradise Farm and regarded it as an affront to all the values he had been taught as a child. That was scary. I was frightened for RuthClaire, and I was frightened for myself for having rebuffed the High Zygote's offer to help.

What kind of "help" did he and Craig have in mind? Some sort of house-cleaning operation? A petition campaign? A night-riding incident? An appeal to other Klan organizations for reinforcements?

In all my forty-six years I had never come face to face with a danger of this precise human sort, and I was finding it hard to believe that it had descended upon me—upon RuthClaire, Adam, and Beulah Fork—in the form of two acne-scarred bucks whom, only a season or two ago, I had seen playing (egregious) high school football. It was like finding a scorpion in a familiar potted geranium. It was worse than the pious verbal assaults of a dozen different fundamentalist ministers and far, far worse than the frustrated carping of Brian Nollinger in Atlanta. As for those anonymous souls who had actually leaped the barricades at Paradise Farm, they were mere sportive shadows, easily routed by light and the echoing reports of my old .22.

That's the problem, I thought. How do you immunize yourself against the evil in the unprepossessing face of a neighbor?

Despite the hour—lately, it was always "despite the hour"—I telephoned RuthClaire. She was slow picking up, but she did not rebuke me for calling. I told her about the adolescent Ku Klutz Klanners who had pickpocketed my peace of mind.

"Elvis Teavers?" RuthClaire asked. "Craig Puddicombe?"

"Maybe I should report this to the GBI, huh? Sometimes I get GBI agents in the West Bank. Usually they're dressed like hippies pretending to be potheads. I could put those guys on to the Zealous High Zygote and his stringalong lieutenant gamete—just for safety's sake."

"Klanners?"

"That's what I'm trying to tell you."

"Were they wearing sheets?" Hearing my put-upon sigh, she withdrew the question. "No, Paul, don't sic anybody on them. Let's not provoke them any further than they've already been provoked. Besides, I'm safe enough out here. Or so I like to think.—Do you know what's funny?"

"Not at this hour, no."

"The day before yesterday I got a call from a representative of a group called RAJA—Racial Amity and Justice in America. It's a black organization headquartered in Baltimore. The caller wouldn't tell me how he'd managed to get my unlisted number, just that he had managed. He hoped I would answer a few questions."

"Did you?"

"What else could an art-school liberal from Charlotte do?"

"Nothing," I said.

"He had a copy of Nollinger's article in *Atlanta Fortnightly*. He wanted to know if I had enslaved Adam, if I had Adam doing menial tasks against his inclination or will. It sounded as if he had the questions written down on a notepad and was ticking them off each time he asked one and got an answer. I kept saying 'No.' They were that sort of question. The last one asked if I would allow an onsight inspection to verify my denials and to ascertain the mental and emotional health of my guest. I said 'No' to that one, too. 'In that case,' the man from RAJA said, 'get

set for more telephone calls and eventually a racial solidar-
ity march right in front of your sacred Paradise Farm.'
And then he hung up. When the phone rang just now,
Paul, I was a little afraid it was him again.''

"Nope," I said glumly. "Just me."

"I'm catching it from all sides." The receiver clunked
as RuthClaire apparently shifted hands. "You see, Paul,
I've offended the scientific establishment by refusing to let
their high priests examine Adam, and I've offended organized religion by trying to make a comfortable home for
him. Now I've got Klansmen coming at me from another
direction and civil rights advocates from yet another. I'm
at the center of a collapsing compass rose waiting for the
direction points to impale me. That's pretty funny, isn't it?
There's no way for me to escape. I'm everybody's enemy."

"The public still loves you. Just ask AmeriCred."

"That's a consolation. A kind of cold one, tonight."

"Hey, you're selling more platters than a Rolling Stone.
Pretty soon you'll go platinum. Cheer up, Ruthie Cee."

"Yeah, well, you don't sound all that cheery yourself."

.She was right. I didn't. The scare inflicted upon me by
Teavers and Puddicombe had worn off a little, but in its
place was a nervousness, an empty energy, an icy spiritual
dynamo that spun paralyzing chills down my spine to the
very tip of my vestigial tailbone. Even in the oven of the
storage room I was cold. RuthClaire and I were linked in a
strange way by our private chills. Each of us seemed to be
waiting for the other to speak.

At last I said, "Does Adam sleep with you?" It was the
first time I had asked her this question. Somehow the time
was right. For me if not for her.

"In this kind of weather, Paul, he won't stay in a bed.
He's sleeping on the linoleum in the kitchen where it's
cool."

"You know what I mean."

"One morning I found him lying down there with the
refrigerator door open. He doesn't do *that* anymore."

"RuthClaire!"

"What do you want me to tell you, Paul? I've grown

more and more fond of him the longer he's been around. As for Adam, well, he's comporting himself more and more like a person with a real sense of his own innate worth. It makes a difference.''

"You've finally got your own intramural United Nations relief agency, don't you? With a single live-in aid recipient.''

"I can unplug this phone as easily as listen to you, Paul.''

I apologized—quickly and effusively—for my sarcasm. It was, I admitted, rude and inexcusable. It would devastate me if she cut me off. My tone was mock-pathetic rather than sappily beseeching, and she let me get away with it. How many times had we bantered in this way in the past? So long as I did not overstep a certain hazily drawn line, she welcomed the familiar repartee. It was, I knew, my one clear leg up on the uninitiated, inarticulate Adam.

"How's he doing?'' I asked, mostly because I knew it would please her.

"He's doing famously. His manners have improved, he's adjusted to indoor conveniences, he's stopped killing squirrels (I think), and I've even taught him how to sing. He probably already had a knack for singing—plaintive melodies that run up and down the scale like a wolf's howl or the undersea aria of a humpback whale. He does a moving 'Amazing Grace,' Paul, he really does.''

"Bring him to the West Bank again,'' I said impulsively.

RuthClaire hesitated before replying. "Before this uproar, Paul, I'd've jumped at the chance. Now it worries me, the idea of removing Adam from the security of Paradise Farm. He's happy here, and safe.''

"But he's something of a prisoner, isn't he? Just like that jerk from Emory and your caller from RAJA have accused.''

"Everybody's a prisoner of something, Paul. Paradise Farm isn't exactly an island in the Gulag Archipelago, though.''

"Then let me treat the two of you to dinner again.''

"Why don't you come out here? I'll do the cooking."

"That's one of the reasons." Hastily I added, "Listen to me, now. I just don't belong out there anymore, RuthClaire. It isn't mine, and it hurts to walk around the place. It's yours, yours and Adam's. Besides, didn't you hope that eventually the rest of us would come to regard Adam as a neighbor and a peer? Isn't that why you brought him to the West Bank in the first place?"

Again RuthClaire was slow to answer. "He's still not ready for that. It would have to be after dark, Paul, and you'd have to make the restaurant off limits to everybody but us. Just like last time."

"Deal."

"When?"

"This coming Tuesday. Nine-thirty. It'll be good and dark by then, and I'll still be able to serve dinner between six and eight."

RuthClaire laughed. "The consummate businessman."

"We're two of a kind," I said. Then: "I've missed you, Ruthie Cee. God Almighty, how I've missed you."

"Good night, Paul. We'll see you Tuesday."

RuthClaire hung up. Ten or twelve seconds passed before the steady buzz of the dial tone began issuing from my receiver. I sat there in the ovenish heat listening to it. A cricket chirruped from behind a wall of cardboard boxes—they had once contained cans of tomato paste, bottles of catsup, jars of fancy mustard—opposite my cot. What an idiot I was. Months upon months ago I could have built myself a house much nicer than the one on Paradise Farm. . . .

A CHASTE conviviality suffused our get-together on Tuesday evening. There were only the three of us. Livia George and all my other help had left at eight-thirty, and although the odor of my customers' cigarette smoke usually lingered for hours, tonight the old-fashioned two-speed fan whirling among the umbrellas overhead had long since imparted a sea-breeze freshness to the air. It was much cooler than on Saturday, and I had a sense of sated well-being that probably should have alarmed me.

As a treat, as a concession, RuthClaire had permitted Adam to order steak, medium rare, and he sat in his place at our corner table using his cutlery with the clumsy fastidiousness of a child at an adult banquet. The improvement over his previous appearance in the West Bank was marked. He divided the meat into two dozen or more little pieces and ate them one at a time, his eyes sometimes nearly closing in quiet enjoyment. Further, he took mannerly bites of potato, broccoli, or seasoned squash casserole between his portions of steak, and he chewed with his lips pressed together. Not even the ghost of Emily Post could have faulted his scrupulously upright posture.

As RuthClaire and I talked, I found it hard not to glance occasionally at Adam. He was wearing a pair of pleated, beltless trousers of a rich cream color and a short-sleeved white shirt with a yachting wheel over one of its breast pockets. He had come shoeless again, an omission for which RuthClaire again apologized, but the neatness of his apparel and the slick-whistle closeness of his haircut (had my ex used a pair of electric sheep shears on him?) more than offset the effect of slovenly or rebellious informality implicit in his bare feet. Now, in fact, I was sneakily watching his hands, which reminded me of his feet; they were narrow and arthritic-looking, as if his fingers had been taped together for a long period and only recently given their freedom. The stiffness and incomplete opposability of his thumbs made his dogged use of knife and fork all the more praiseworthy.

"You're a bang-up 'Enry 'Iggins," I told RuthClaire.

She was finished eating, having contented herself with a fruit cup (no bananas) and an artichoke salad, and her eyes rested almost dotingly on her habiline Eliza Doolittle. "Thank you, I guess—but you're not giving Adam enough credit. He's bright, eager to learn, and, at bottom, naturally thoughtful."

"Unlike some you've known."

RuthClaire smiled her crooked smile. "Well, you'd've probably done okay in the Early Pleistocene, Paul. You'd've probably prospered."

"That's not nice."

"Well, you're not, either—when your mind's on nothing but the satisfaction of your appetites. Too often it is."

"Tonight?"

"Not tonight. I hope. You seem to be trying hard to be as gentlemanly as it's in you to be."

Adam finished his meal. He wiped his mouth with a linen napkin. Then he picked up his stem of California burgundy and tossed it off in a noisy inhalation whose small component gulps set the apple in his throat bobbing like a fisherman's cork. He wiped his mouth again, his small black eyes glittering.

"Adam!" RuthClaire admonished.

Whereupon the habiline lifted his right hand and made a startling, pincerlike movement with his fingers. This motion he repeated, his broken-looking thumb swinging purposefully from side to side. His thick black eyebrows, grown together over the bridge of his nose, lifted in sympathy, and his eyes, too, began to "talk," coruscating in the candlelight.

RuthClaire interpreted: "The steak was excellent, he says. So, too, the wine."

I stared at the creature. I had never seen him use hand signs before. He had not yet stopped doing so.

"Now he would like to know if there's a rest room on the premises," RuthClaire continued. "He feels like a gallon of rainwater in an elastic teacup. He'd also like to wash his hands."

"You're making that up," I accused.

"Only the highfalutin metaphor. He really did ask if the West Bank has a public bathroom. Is that so hard to believe?"

The West Bank has only one public bathroom; it is located in a small cinder-block niche directly behind the dining room. For a brief moment you must step outside—

into a small section of alley—to reach this facility, and you must lock the door behind you to keep other patrons or even my restaurant employees from breaking in upon you once you have entered. Still, complaints are few, and I do not have the room to install a second water closet. The county health department has approved this arrangement.

Without another word to RuthClaire I led Adam to the w.c., nodded him inside, and returned to the dining room. Because no one but us three was present tonight, it made no difference if Adam neglected to depress the lock button in the doorknob. This, I think, was one of my half-formed intellections as I slid back into my chair and put my hand on Ruthie Cee's.

"You've been teaching him sign language."

"Hardly an original idea. They've been doing it with chimps and gorillas for years. They do it at Yerkes. In fact, at Yerkes they teach some of their primates an elaborate system of geometric symbols called Yerkish. I checked out some books on sign language for the deaf to teach myself what Adam ought to learn. He's doing far better than any of the chimps and gorillas exposed to this system, though. It's true. I've checked the literature."

"It's amazing," I conceded.

"What convinced me to try was Adam's interest in the woman doing simultaneous sign-language interpretations of Happy McElroy's sermons every Sunday morning. He couldn't take his eyes off her. He still can't."

"You watch the program?"

"Adam's fascinated by it. The panorama shots of the congregation, and the singing, and McElroy's contortions at the pulpit—they hold him spellbound. Adam first found the channel back before the controversy that ignited some of McElroy's most authoritarian recent pronouncements. I mean, I wasn't purposely tuning in to see what that man had to say about us. I was just letting Adam watch whatever he wanted to watch."

"Does he still insist on watching, knowing McElroy's bias?"

"Oh, yes, it's probably his favorite Sunday show. Now,

though, he makes ugly hand-signal suggestions when McElroy cites the relationship between Adam and me as a disgusting instance of contemporary moral decay. Adam *hates* Happy McElroy, but he loves the way he twists around, and the singing, and the interpreter for the deaf, and the long shots of that heroic congregation listening to their leader's weekly jeremiads.'' RuthClaire smiled another off-center, self-effacing smile. ''I can't deny him those pleasures, Paul. I want him to know—intellectually, anyway—there's a big, smelly, bustling, contradictory world beyond the boundaries of Paradise Farm.''

''He must already know that.''

''Oh, he does. He's told me jumbled stories about Montaraz, Haiti, and Cuba, not to mention the Freedom Flotilla and his trek up through Florida. He's known more hardships and chaos than most, but not until recently could he communicate these experiences to anyone.''

We heard a thump at the back of the West Bank. Adam was returning to us from the water closet. At his elbow, towering lumpishly over him, was a stranger. The stranger had a .38 in Adam's ribs, and Adam's cautious step and frightened eye told us that his knowledge of the world clearly extended to the destructive capacity of firearms. Perhaps he remembered the fate of his conspecifics aboard the fishing vessel off the coast of Punta Gorda.

Both indignant and fearful, I stood up to face this new intruder.

HE HOLSTERED his pistol in a sling under his sports jacket and steered Adam to our table with a remorseless meaty hand. His face, meanwhile, bore an apologetic expression that automatically lessened my fear of him.

''Thought he might run,'' the man said. ''Didn't, though.''

"I think you can safely let go of him," RuthClaire said.

He did. "Dick Zubowicz, INS—Immigration and Naturalization Service. This fella's an illegal alien. I'm afraid he's under arrest."

A knock rattled the front door. Despite failing to secure the door in the rear, I *had* locked this one. When I released the latch and opened to the slender supplicant on the raised sidewalk, the supplicant proved to be Brian Nollinger. Behind him on the sidewalk fronting the Greyhound Depot Laundry a small crowd of shadows—no more than five or six people—milled aimlessly about, unrecognizable. My first thought was that a sinister ulteriority underlay their presence, my second that they were simply waiting for the midnight bus to Montgomery. Then Nollinger swept past me into the West Bank, and I had no further time to consider the question.

"You've got him!" the anthropologist said to Zubowicz.

"It wasn't hard," the immigration agent replied. "He's a pretty docile fella, really. Catchin' 'em after they eat's always been my favorite way of doin' it, Dr. Nollinger. Takes the edge off 'em."

I glared at my former boarder. He had led Zubowicz to Beulah Fork, had lain in wait with him outside the West Bank, had undoubtedly been the principal goad to the government's decision to mount this sleazy little operation. I'll show you how to nab the notorious habiline with a minimum of fuss, he had promised, if you'll give me and my sociologist friend at Emory visitation privileges once the poor devil's interned. Nollinger paid scarcely any heed to either RuthClaire or me; he only had eyes for Adam. To snatch his granny glasses from his pale face, and to grind them to powder beneath my heel, would have been a satisfying release—but I mastered the impulse. With difficulty.

RuthClaire stood. "Under arrest? For what?"

"I've told you, Mrs. Loyd," Zubowicz said. "For entering the country illegally, then for evading deportation by fleeing INS authorities. You're an accomplice, ma'am. You've aided and abetted."

"Am I under arrest, too?"

"I don't have a warrant for it, only the fugitive's. If you'll help us out—if you won't go contestin' or obstructin' us in our duty—well, it's not likely you'll be slapped too bad for your involvement."

RuthClaire looked at me. "No one's pressed any charges yet, and they've already begun plea-bargaining."

"That's not really the term for it," Zubowicz said softly, as if offended by the innuendo. "Our real interest's in Adam here."

"The illegal alien," Nollinger added.

"The only surviving specimen of *Homo habilis* in the entire world," I interjected. "You think your rights outweigh his, Nollinger, because he's a unique opportunity for bigger government grants and a measure of parasitic fame for Ol' Number One—not because he's an illegal alien."

Adam, I noticed, was following our argument closely, looking from face to face as each of us spoke and running his right forefinger along the edge of the tablecloth. His nail had incised a narrow crescent in the material; a single maroon thread was caught in the notch at the top of this nail. The thread shuttled back and forth with the motion of the habiline's finger, like a minuscule red script on a parchment of the same concealing color. What did it mean? What was Adam thinking?

"Listen, Loyd," the anthropologist retorted, "if he'd thrown up tonight's dinner, too, *you'd* still be faunching to get rid of him. I'm not the only victim of self-interest under the West Bank's roof."

"That's what he was doing when I found him," Zubowicz said.

"What are you talking about?" I asked the man.

"Adam," the immigration agent replied. "He was retchin' into the toilet bowl. Tryin' to, anyway. Couldn't get much to come up."

"Damn it!" I said. "That's a lie!"

"You always rub too much garlic and onion salt into your steaks," Nollinger testified. "Garlic salt, onion salt, tenderizer—it's just too much, Loyd."

Adam lifted his hands, bit off the thread caught on his fingernail, and made a series of signs for RuthClaire.

"It was drinking the wine so fast that did it," she interpreted. "The steak was prepared and cooked to perfection. He apologizes for the bad impression created by his lapses in table etiquette. He's fine now."

"That's good," Zubowicz said, "because the prof and I are gonna run him up to Atlanta for bookin' and arraignment." He gripped the habiline by his hairy elbow.

RuthClaire said, "For being an illegal alien?"

"That's what I've been tellin' you."

"What if he were an American citizen?"

Zubowicz lifted his eyebrows and smiled deferentially. "What if what?"

"He's my husband, Mr. Zubowicz. A minister from Tocqueville—an ordained minister of the First United Coptic Church of Dixie—married us in a private ceremony at Paradise Farm over two months ago. We even had blood tests. It's legal, I assure you. And we can prove it."

"Jesus, RuthClaire," I exclaimed, "you're ten—fifteen—maybe twenty years older than he is!"

"That's a pretty threadbare old ploy," Zubowicz said. "The government's gotten really tough on people who marry aliens for no other reason than to confer American citizenship on them. It's become something of an industry, I'm afraid, and the penalties for taking part in these fake marriages—marriages in name only, for devious or fraudulent purposes, Mrs. Loyd—nowadays, ma'am, the penalties are severe."

"I'm expecting Adam's child," RuthClaire announced. "How fraudulent or devious is that?"

Nobody said anything. I sat down at the table and exhaled a sigh as profoundly melancholy as I could make it. My ex had just given us offhand confirmation of everyone's worst suspicions. However, unless you insisted on regarding Adam as subhuman, underage, or mentally defective, you could not logically continue to upbraid her for "living in sin." She was a married woman who had emphasized her bond to her latest spouse by cooperating with him in the conception of a new living entity. This idea made me very unhappy. I preferred the living-in-sin hypothesis to so dramatic a demonstration of the lawfulness and incontrovertibility of their union.

Zubowicz turned to Nollinger. "Is it possible?" he asked. "I mean, can a human woman and a, uh, well, a—?"

"Habiline male," the anthropologist said.

"Yeah, what you said. Can they make a baby? Will the genes, uh, match up?"

"There's precedent," Nollinger admitted. "Of a sort. At Yerkes, not so long ago, a siamang and another species of gibbon successfully mated when they were caged together for a long period. It *surprised* everyone, though." He squinted at Adam. "Interbreeding between distinct human species—Cro-Magnon and Neanderthal, for instance— is supposed to be one of the factors responsible for the wide variety among human physiques and faces today. Yeah," he concluded, almost resentfully, "it's possible, Mr. Zubowicz."

I looked up. "RuthClaire, why didn't you tell me?"

"I was going to, Paul. I didn't expect the evening to be abbreviated by a close encounter with a stooge from Immigration and Naturalization."

"Mrs. Loyd," said Zubowicz, wounded. "I'm only doin'—"

She cut him off: "Mrs. Montaraz, you mean. In private life I'm Mrs. Adam Montaraz. My professional name's still RuthClaire Loyd—that's what everyone knows my work by—but, considering your mission, tonight I'd prefer to be called by my legal married name."

The federal agent literally threw up his hands, turning in an oafish half-circle to escape the fury in RuthClaire's eyes.

As he turned, a missile of some kind shattered one of the windowpanes in my front door. It grazed Brian Nollinger's head and ricocheted off the metal divider between the dining room and the cash register. Nollinger dropped bleeding to his knees. Glass sparkled like costume glitter in the candlelight.

A second missile—they were both red-clay bricks, or

portions of such bricks—burst through the picture window behind our corner table, toppling a potted geranium, a tall ceramic beer stein, and a fishbowl filled with colored sand.

Zubowicz had his pistol at the ready again, but now he was looping the barrel in circles and loudly encouraging everyone to retreat to the rear of the restaurant. Dazedly, even Nollinger complied, the gash on his temple leaking a crimson mucilage. Adam loaned the anthropologist his shoulder as, bent over like a special services commando, I hustled RuthClaire away from my shop's battered façade.

The squeal of an automobile laying down rubber reverberated from one end of Main Street to the other.

A quick backward glance informed me that the shadows in front of the Greyhound Depot Laundry had dispersed to their own secret corners of the night. Main Street was empty now, and I did not believe that any more bricks would come flying through my windows. The vigilantes had had their fun.

"They're gone," I said, straightening up. "I think we're okay. Damn it to hell, though. Look at this mess. Just look at it."

"INSURANCE'LL PAY for it," a voice from behind me said. "Never knew a bigshot yet didn't have him lots of insurance."

Three people had entered the West Bank by the same route taken only a few minutes earlier by Dick Zubowicz. Two of them wielded shotguns. They all wore clothing that gave them the look of farmers in an outlandish variety of medieval clerical garb. Winged robes of shimmering lavender, with strange embroidered emblems and decorative piping of a much darker purple, fell just below the intruders' knees, revealing blue jeans and scuffed work boots in two instances and pale hairy shins above a pair of powder-blue jogging shoes in the third. Pointed hoods—headpieces of grandiose, almost miterlike impracticality—concealed the faces of the three men, but for good measure they had pulled nylon stockings over their features to flatten and distort them.

But one of the intruders had just given himself away by speaking, and by revealing his own identity he had inadvertently divulged that of one of his seconds.

"Hello, E.L.," I said. "Hello, Craig."

Or maybe it had not been inadvertent at all. The robes, the nylon masks, the lopsided ecclesiastical headgear were more for show, for corny Grand Guignol effect, than for impenetrable disguise. That I could not puzzle out the name of the Ku Klutzer in jogging shoes—a lanky character who slouched along in a self-effacing stoop—was an irrelevancy; what mattered was that three of my neighbors had worked themselves into a state of self-righteous agitation so calculating and cold that the donning of pompously comical costume and the trashing of my four-star backwater café struck them as noble responses to something they did not understand. Or understood in the half-assed way of a street-sign painter confronting Hieronymus Bosch. (Hell, I'm still not sure that *I* understand what they did or didn't understand.) There they were, though, dressed like pious executioners and pointing shotguns.

Unignorable.

After relieving Zubowicz of his pistol, the Klanners produced two pairs of handcuffs, one of which served to anchor the immigration agent to the S-pipe under the sink in my kitchen, the other of which manacled Nollinger to the flocked divider in the dining room. The man in jogging shoes, who never once spoke, took care of the handcuffing, and, as he worked, I could not help noticing the sweat running down his legs to the tops of his shoes' perforated ankle guards. The heat under those purple robes—I suddenly realized they were almost exactly the color of old Dr. Kearby's beloved gentian violet—had to be strength-sappingly intense. What imbecility.

"Davie Hutton's never around when you need him, is he?" Craig Puddicombe said, his shotgun trained on RuthClaire, Adam, and me. "Only pops up when you've run a stop sign or laid down rubber in the A&P parking lot."

E. L. Teavers chuckled insinuatingly, and I looked even harder at the Klansman in jogging shoes. Was *that* Davie Hutton? I could not really tell. His possession of handcuffs and his refusal to speak made me suspect that it was. It also helped to explain the blatancy with which the Zealous High Zygote's cohorts on Main Street had assaulted the West Bank and then made good their getaway. If Davie was with them, then they had had a free hand. Unfortunately, or maybe fortunately, Davie had never seemed quite so pale and etiolated as this apparition.

"Time to go," E(lvis) L(amar) Teavers said.

"Where?" RuthClaire asked him.

But now that Zubowicz and Nollinger were secured, the urge to banter with or taunt us utterly deserted the intruders. Grimly unspeaking, they herded us out the back door, past the rest room, and through the grass-grown alley to a small dewy hillock from which Beulah Fork's water tower rose into the summer darkness like a war machine out of H. G. Wells. Adam stared wistfully up into the crisscrossing support rods of the tower, but Teavers, apparently sensing that Adam had it in mind to break away and seek refuge aloft, cracked him across the temple with his shotgun barrel.

"Go on, you goddamn hibber!" he commanded him. "None of that hibberish monkey business!"

As Nollinger had done in the restaurant, Adam fell to his knees. His lips curled back to reveal his canines, but RuthClaire knelt beside him to whisper inaudible consolation. Although Adam wobbled a little after regaining his feet, he was soon striding as assuredly as any of us, and our bizarre little party passed from the water tower's low hillock into an asphalt-patched street parallel to Main.

From this street we marched into the upper reaches of the playground of the Beulah Fork Elementary School.

Crickets were whirring enthusiastically, but otherwise the town seemed uninhabited, a vast sound stage accommodating the silhouettes of a few isolated Victorian houses along with hundreds of cardboard-cutout elm and magnolia trees.

The playground itself, on the other hand, was a minefield in the midst of these innocuous props. Crossing it, I kept waiting for Teavers to blow our heads off. It seemed pretty clear to me that he and his purple-capped henchmen were marching us to fatal appointments. Or, at the very least, to a tryst with tar and feathers.

"Is this how you look after the rights of a hardworking white man?" I asked. "Wrecking his business and terrorizing him and his friends?"

"Shut up," Craig Puddicombe said.

"I mean, when you came in the other night, you were concerned about my rights being violated. Is this how—?"

E. L. Teavers interrupted me: "That's all forfeit, Mr. Loyd. You and your wife are traitors."

"To what?" RuthClaire asked.

"I told you to shut up!" Puddicombe hissed. "We don't have to explain nothin' to you!"

"Not now, maybe," Teavers added, evenly enough.

That ended the exchange. A moment later I saw a van parked behind the softball backstop on the northeastern corner of the playground. Two or three robed figures stood beside this vehicle, human carrion birds in the still unsettled dust surrounding it. The cab of a pickup protruded beyond the nose of the van, whose decorated sides the Klanners had obscured with a thick gouache of mud that had long since dried and hardened. As we approached, one robed figure made a semaphoring motion with both arms, climbed into the van, and eased it along the backstop so that Teavers and Puddicombe could throw back its sliding door and prod their captives inside. Adam and RuthClaire boarded together while I temporized on the threshold, one foot down in the dust as an uncertain tie to the reality of Hothlepoya County. We were about to be spirited away to Never-Never Land.

"Get in," somebody said, not too urgently.

I obeyed, but looked over my shoulder in time to see the man in jogging shoes go dogtrotting off toward a portable classroom behind the school.

Puddicombe climbed in after me and banged the van's sliding door to. RuthClaire, Adam, and I were made to sit on the floor in the center of the vehicle's passenger section. Around us perched armed members of the Kudzu Klavern; another four people caparisoned in cumbersome purple and redolent of stale sweat. The darkness prevented me from distinguishing the sex of each one, and their shoes—either sneakers or penny loafers—were not much help, either. At least one woman had come along, though, because her high-pitched mocking laughter greeted every underdone bon mot dropped into the deep fry of our fear and confusion.

Now the van was bumping along at good speed.

"Coulda sworn he'd stink," one of the men said. "Expected dead rat or wet dog, somethin' foul anyway."

"Not this one," Puddicombe replied. "This one wears English Leather or he don't wear nothin' at all."

The woman guffawed. From where I was sitting it was impossible to tell to which robed body the guffaw belonged, only that it was nervous and feminine. After a mile or two, though, I arbitrarily assigned it to the penny loafers.

Our van bounded from rut to rut. We did not seem to be on paved highway. Once, our driver sounded his horn; the sour bleating blast of another horn, undoubtedly that of Teavers' pickup, answered it. We slowed and turned. The penny loafers guffawed, a high-pitched outburst with no apparent antecedent.

"Where are we going?" RuthClaire asked.

No one replied. Adam had his arm linked in mine. Occasionally he looked from side to side as if attempting to sort out the pecking order among our captors. I do not believe that he was frightened. Both RuthClaire and I were near, and with his free hand he was absentmindedly grooming my ex-wife, picking tiny knots out of the shingled strands of her hair.

Eventually the van skewed to a stop. Its sliding door popped back like the lid of a capsized jack-in-the-box.

Puddicombe, minus his nylon stocking, forced us outside. We stood in the beams of E. L. Teavers' pickup truck's headlights, virtually blinded by their moted yellow glare. The van backed away, executed a precarious turn on the edge of a trail rut, and disappeared into the night with all its robed passengers but Puddicombe.

This frightened me far worse than anything that had happened so far, including even the first rocketing crash of brick against glass in the West Bank. RuthClaire, Adam, and I were stranded in the middle of nowhere with the Zealous High Zygote and his chief lieutenant. I looked up. Stars freckled most of the sky, but a migrating coal sack of clouds had begun to devour large chunks of the heavens to the west. It seemed to me that a bottomless abyss had opened. Over my head, under my feet—the chill of this sensation was spookily disorienting.

The headlights cut off. From across the weed-choked pasture Teavers said, "Bring the hibber here, Craig."

"Why?" RuthClaire asked. "What are you going to do?"

I closed my eyes, opened them, closed them again. When next I looked around, though, the landscape seemed familiar. We were on Cleve Synder's property, not far from Paradise Farm, on a piece of isolated acreage that had never been used to grow beans, cotton, corn, or any other crop. Not for over fifty or sixty years, anyway. Early in the century a brick kiln had operated here. What was left was a series of red-clay mounds surrounding cisternlike vats that plunged into the earth seemingly without bottom.

Eight years ago, according to the skinnydipper's horrified playmates, a child from White Cow Creek had fallen into one of the vats. An attempt to locate and raise him had concluded with the absolute frustration of the spelunkers who had gone down after him in winch-assisted harnesses. Although afterward there had been some community agitation to cap or fill in the pits, Cleve Synder had offered to build a barbed-wire barricade with warning placards at fixed intervals, and this offer had quieted the angry uproar. Tonight, glancing about me, I realized that either Synder had never fulfilled his promise or else the vigilantes of the Kudzu Klavern had undone his efforts to make the place safe. We were in the foothills of a miniature mountain range, far from succor, civilization, or warning signs.

Adam, looking at RuthClaire, made a bewildered hand gesture.

"I don't know," she replied, shaking her head.

Puddicombe slapped Adam's hands down and told RuthClaire to shut up. Teavers, a grotesque shadow, climbed into view on one of the nearby mounds. The mounds—it suddenly struck me—resembled eroded termitaria on a dusty East African plain. For a moment, in fact, in seemed that the five of us had been translated by some fantastic agency to the continent on which Adam's ancestors, and ours, had first evolved. Hothlepoya County was Kenya, Tanzania, or Zarakal. We were all Africans. . . .

"Tell him to get his clothes off," Teavers commanded RuthClaire from the lip of the mound.

"Why should I tell him that?"

"Do it, damn it! No slack or backtalk!" To stress the urgency of compliance, he fired off one barrel of his shotgun. The ground shook, and even Craig Puddicombe joined us in hunching away from the blast. A pattering of buckshot sounded in the brambles of a blackberry thicket not thirty feet away. Then everything was quiet again.

Adam took off his pleated trousers by tugging down the zipper until it tore. His shirt he removed in similar fashion, popping off the buttons with his fingers. Because he disdained underwear as well as shoes, he now stood beside us as bare and unblushing as his prelapsarian namesake—just as, a year ago this September, he had first appeared at Paradise Farm. How small he seemed again, how supple and childlike.

"Okay, Craig, bring him here." To RuthClaire and me Teavers said, "If either of you moves a step, I'll let fly this other barrel right into your hibber-lovin' faces. Tomorrow mornin' you'll look like fresh ground round."

Puddicombe laughed and nudged Adam forward. Adam seemed to be gripping the earth with his toes, as if walking the lofty bough of an acacia tree. Although Puddicombe finally halted at the base of the mound, Adam ascended to within two or three feet of Teavers.

"Don't," RuthClaire said. "Don't do it."

I did not know whether she was appealing to Adam or to Teavers. It made no difference. The young man in the gentian-violet robes dropped his shotgun, grabbed Adam by the arm, and pulled him to the lip of the vat. His intention was clear. He was going to sacrifice Adam to the Plutonian tutelaries of the pit. Equally clearly, though, he had not reckoned on the sinewy strength of the habiline, believing that his greater height and weight would suffice to topple Adam into oblivion.

But Adam, snarling, wrested his arm free of Teavers, sank his teeth into the young man's thigh through a coarse layer of denim, and spun him around like a demon astride a dervish. Teavers recognized his mistake too late to do anything about it.

"Shoot!" he ordered Craig Puddicombe. "Shoot the bastard!"

Puddicombe was of two minds, struggling to cover his prisoners and to protect his friend at the same time. If he fired, Teavers would suffer along with Adam, and I might have the opportunity to jump him. As a compromise, trusting his friend to overcome Adam's surprising resistance, he backed away from the mound and leveled both barrels of his shotgun at RuthClaire and me.

Dust billowed outward from the combat on the pit rim, a spreading reddish-black fog in the starlight, and then both Teavers and Adam went over the edge.

That was all there was to it. One moment they were vigorously grappling on the surface of their common planet, the next they were plummeting hellward as if neither of them had ever existed. Teavers did manage a scream as he fell—a frail, short-lived protest—but Adam made no sound at all; and maybe thirty seconds after they had engaged each other, the night again belonged to the crickets, the stars, and the coal-sack thunderhead looming like a celestial abyss over Alabama.

RuthClaire and I held each other. Her hands were cold. I could feel them—their coldness—through the back of my shirt.

"I ought to kill you," Craig Puddicombe said. This development had dumbfounded him, but he tried to talk anyway. "This is your doin', goddamn it, this is all your friggin' fault!" His voice was trembling. So were his hands. He backed away from us toward the mound, picked up Teavers' shotgun, and tossed it into the vat that had just swallowed the two combatants. "It's people like you," he said, choking on the words, "it's people like you who—" The complete articulation of this thought stymied him.

Puddicombe broke for the pickup, jumped into its cab, and gunned the vehicle past us, nearly striking RuthClaire. Away from the brick kiln he sped, away from the nightmare that he had helped to create.

"We'll have to tell Nancy," RuthClaire said, her jaw resting on my shoulder. "Somehow."

"Nancy?"

"Nancy Teavers. His wife. The girl who worked for you once."

"Oh," I said.

For a long time we did not move. Eventually, though, I climbed the mound and peered down into the vat from my knees. I spent several minutes calling out to Adam and Teavers. I even dropped pebbles into the hole to try to plumb its depth. This was impossible. RuthClaire told me to stop, it was no use.

Wearily, then, we set off on foot together for Paradise Farm.

IT TOOK us no more than twenty minutes to complete this journey. When we arrived, we found a twenty-foot-tall, gasoline-soaked cross of pine or some other fast-burning wood blazing on the lawn. One of its horizontal struts had already burned through, making an amputee of this self-contradictory symbol, but neither of us was in any doubt about the original shape of the structure. The scent of char and gasoline, coupled with the rape inherent in the cross's placement, lifted stinging tears to RuthClaire's eyes. She damned the people responsible. She cursed the incorrigible stupidity of her species.

It began to rain. Gusts of sighing wind whipped the flames about unmercifully. The remaining cross arm splintered and crashed to the ground, showering sparks.

RuthClaire and I hurried along the gravel drive to the house, where we paused to watch the storm. Lightning flickered, thunder boomed, and finally the slashing rain extinguished, altogether, the obscene handiwork of the Ku Klutzers. The Zealous High Zygote was dead, I reflected: long live Adam's surviving descendants in universal forbearance.

Ha! I mentally scoffed. Didn't I want to kill Craig Puddicombe? Didn't I want a vigilante's revenge on the cross burners?

They had cut the telephone lines. We could not phone out, me to the authorities or RuthClaire to Nancy Teavers. Even Edna Twiggs was ignorant of our predicament—unless, of course, she had had something to do with it. Standing in RuthClaire's loft, trying to undress my ex-wife for bed, I doubted everyone in Beulah Fork. I had seen only eight people in robes, but I imagined every single one of my neighbors encysted in that hateful garment: a Ku Klux Kaleidoscope of suspects.

RuthClaire, meanwhile, kept telling me to wait until morning to venture out, I would be a fool to brave this storm, there was nothing we could do for Adam, the cross burners were long gone.

I brought her a bourbon from the kitchen and sat by her on the bed until she had swallowed the last glinting amber drop. Ten minutes later she was asleep.

I secured every window and locked every door. Then I set off through the rain to Ruben Decker's farm a mile and a half down the highway. My clothes, immediately drenched, grew heavier and heavier as I walked. Two different southbound automobiles went whooshing by, hurling spray, but neither stopped; and I reached my destination waterlogged and fantod-afflicted. Like a drug dream, the image of Teavers and Adam disappearing into that voracious kiln hole kept flashing through my head. When I knocked on Decker's flyspecked screen door, I was on the verge of collapse. The sight of the grizzled dairy farmer coming toward me through his empty living room with a yearling Persian cat in his arms seemed no more substantial or trustworthy a vision than the muddled flashbacks that had accompanied me all the way from Paradise Farm.

"Got to use your phone," I said. "Got to make some calls."

"Well, of course you do," Decker agreed, letting me in. The silver-blue cat in his arms was purring like a turbine.

DAVIE HUTTON had been patrolling the Peachfield residential area at the time of the attack on the West Bank. Later he had assisted the Hothlepoya County Emergency Rescue Service at an accident south of Tocqueville. Upon being apprised of the evening's events by a dispatcher in the sheriff's office in Tocqueville, however, he returned to

Beulah Fork and released Dick Zubowicz and Brian Nollinger from their handcuffs, using a master key. It no longer seemed likely to me that he had been the Klansman in the powder-blue jogging shoes. The identity of that person remains a troubling supposition.

Zubowicz and Nollinger spent the night on cots in City Hall.

Hutton, on his own initiative, installed a large piece of plywood over the hole in my picture window and a smaller one over the broken pane in my door. In the morning Livia George came in to clean up the glass, the spilled sand, the beer-stein fragments, and the dirt from the overturned geranium pot. The West Bank had survived. Nor was the cost to my insurance company going to be especially high. My premiums would not go up. In only another day or two I would be able to open for business again.

At Paradise Farm two employees of Southern Bell showed up to repair the telephone lines cut by the cross burners.

Law-enforcement officers from Tocqueville and agents of the Georgia Bureau of Investigation poured into Beulah Fork. They examined the restaurant, the softball field at the elementary school, and the abandoned brick kiln on Cleve Synder's property. They used helicopters as well as automobiles. Because Craig Puddicombe had apparently disappeared from Hothlepoya County, perhaps even from Georgia, a description of both him and E. L. Teavers' pickup truck went out to every sheriff's department and highway patrol unit in the Southeast. Zubowicz and Nollinger told their stories to investigators at City Hall; RuthClaire and I unburdened ourselves to agents who had driven out to Paradise Farm. It rained all morning, a slow, muggy drizzle that did little to alleviate the heat, but by two o'clock that same afternoon a GBI man telephoned RuthClaire to inform her that his agency had just made four arrests.

"Do you think you could go back out to the Synder place?" he asked her.

"I don't know," she responded. "Why?"

"We'd like a detailed run-through of everything that

happened while you and Mr. Loyd were . . . hostages. It might prove helpful both in apprehending Puddicombe and in prosecuting the Klanners who didn't stick around for . . . well, for the final bit of dirty work,'' the agent concluded apologetically.

A reprise of the nightmare, I thought. Just what RuthClaire needs.

"Sure," she said. "When?"

"Niedrach and Davison are with you now, aren't they? Okay, good. They'll drive you and Mr. Loyd over there in twenty or thirty minutes."

The drizzle became a steady downpour. As we rode to the brick kiln with agents Niedrach and Davison, a weather report on the car radio attributed the rain to a fizzled hurricane off the Louisiana coast. Happy McElroy Country, I thought. It was my fervent hope that the storm had had at least enough fury to cripple—for a day or two, anyway—the broadcasting towers of America's Greater Christian Constituency in Rehoboth, Louisiana. My mood was vengeful, and sour. The agents in the front seat murmured between themselves like adults outside a room in which children are napping.

At the brick kiln we parked and waited for the rain to subside. Our driver, Niedrach, kept the engine running and the air conditioner going; otherwise we would have all succumbed to the humid heat.

Looking through the rain-beaded window beside me, I saw Brian Nollinger standing near the mound whose gullet had engulfed Teavers and Adam. He had ridden out from Beulah Fork with another pair of investigators. They were still in their car, however, whereas Nollinger was listing in the deluge like a bamboo flagpole, his granny glasses impossibly steamed, his Fu Manchu dripping, dripping, dripping. I cracked my window about two inches.

"What the hell are you doing here?" I shouted.

He looked toward our automobile. Almost prayerfully, seeing me, he canted his head toward the eroded mound. "Mourning," he said. "I came out here to mourn, Mr. Loyd."

Between clenched teeth RuthClaire said, "He has no right."

Whether or not he had any right, Nollinger was martyring himself to his alleged bereavement, turning aside from us to squat like a pilgrim at the base of the mound. Maybe, I thought, he does feel a kind of grief for Adam . . . along with a more painful grief for his lost opportunities. The sight of him hunkering in the rain annoyed me as much as it did RuthClaire. It was true, though, that some of the shame and embarrassment I felt for the anthropologist was shame and embarrassment for myself. If I had not gone to him in February, after all, Adam might still be alive. . . .

"Can't you guys send that jerk back to Atlanta?" I asked the agents.

Niedrach looked over his shoulder into the back seat. "He's here as a consultant. Our chief thought his expertise might be helpful. We won't let him bug you or Mrs. Montaraz."

This last word made me flinch. The GBI had confirmed the validity of RuthClaire's marriage to Adam, and its agents were careful to call her by her legal married name. Mrs. Montaraz gave me an unreadable but far from timid glance.

The rain slowed and then stopped. The pecan trees and blackberry thickets began to drip-dry. The ruddy mud around the mounds meant treacherous footing, but Niedrach determined that if we did not mind dirtying our shoes a little, we could begin the reenactment. He would play Teavers' part, Davison would be Puddicombe, and Nollinger would impersonate Adam.

RuthClaire vetoed this idea. Nollinger must sit in the other car while the agent who had driven him out from Beulah Fork assumed the habiline's role. Niedrach accepted the substitution, and under a cloud cover fissuring like the crust of an oven-bound blueberry pie we rehearsed in minute detail what had already happened. "Teavers" and "Adam" were careful not to get too near the open vat, but RuthClaire began quietly crying, anyway. She shook

off Niedrach's offer of either a break or a postponement,
and we concluded the exercise in twenty minutes, with
brief pauses for photographs and ratiocinative conjecture.
Sunshine, suddenly, lay on the wet red clay like a coat of
shellac.

We milled around, unwilling to leave. The spot had a
queer attraction, like a graveyard or the ruins of a Roman
aqueduct.

Then, from some distance off, we heard a wordless
crooning, a cappella. The melody was that of a church
hymn, one I remembered from long-ago Sundays wedged
in a Congregationalist pew between my mother and an
older brother with a case of fidgets as acute as my own:
"This Is My Father's World." The crooning had a rever-
berant quality that sent chills through my system—in spite
of the stifling July mugginess. RuthClaire, Nollinger, the
GBI agents, and I froze in our places. Bewildered, we
looked from face to face. The crooning ceased, giving way
to a half dozen or more sharp expulsions of breath, then
resumed again with an eeriness that unnerved me.

"*Adam!*" RuthClaire cried. She ran to the top of the
mound. "Adam, we're here!"

"Watch it!" Niedrach cautioned her.

The crooning stopped. Everyone waited. A sound like
pebbles falling down a well; another series of high-pitched
grunts and wheezes. And then, six or seven mounds away,
above the rim of the vat piercing that little hill to an
unknowable depth, Adam's head appeared! A gash gleamed
on his hint of sagittal crest; his bottom lip protruded like a
semicircular slice of eggplant. Numerous nicks and punc-
tures marked him.

A beat. Two beats.

Adam's head popped out of view again.

"*Adam!*" RuthClaire wailed. Descending the first mound,
she ran on tiptoes toward the one concealing her husband.

But Adam pulled himself out of the ground before she
could reach it. He was wearing, as everyone could now
see, the shiny purple robe in which E. L. Teavers had
plunged to his death. It hung on Adam's wiry body in

crimps and volutes. It fit him no better than a jousting-tournament tent, but it shone with a monarchial fire, torn and sodden as it was. At the bottom of the interconnected vats he had probably put on the robe to keep warm during the rain and darkness, but now he seemed to be wearing it as a concession to West Georgia mores. He had the look of a sewer rat emerging from its chthonic habitations: the King of the Sewer Rats.

RuthClaire embraced him. He returned the embrace, and Nollinger, the GBI agents, and I could see nothing of him but his black, bleeding hands patting RuthClaire consolingly in the small of her back.

"It's not so surprising he got out," Nollinger said sotto voce, addressing me sidelong. "Just remember that his ancestors—the ones the Kikembu warriors sold to Sayyid Sa'īd's representatives in Bravanumbi—well, they were living in caves in the Lolitabu Hills. That's how they stayed hidden from modern man for so many thousands of years. Adam may have grown up on Montaraz, Louis Rutherford's little island off Hispaniola, but he pretty obviously retained some of the subterranean instincts acquired by his modern habiline forebears in East Africa. I mean, how many of us denatured *Homo sapiens* could have survived an ordeal so—"

"Why don't you just shut up?" I said.

Nollinger shrugged and fell silent, meanwhile rocking contentedly back and forth in his boots, his hands in his pockets. My initial joy at Adam's return from the dead had gone off its groove, like a stereo stylus that refuses to track. And why not? My rival had reappeared.

AND MY rival, I must confess, triumphed utterly. Not long after the episode with the Zealous High Zygote & Co., RuthClaire and Adam sold Paradise Farm back to me and moved to Atlanta. Although convinced that most of her neighbors did not share the extremist sentiments of the Klan, RuthClaire no longer felt entirely comfortable in Hothlepoya County. Further, she wished to establish closer contacts with the galleries and museums exhibiting her work or making offers to exhibit it, and the rural life-style no longer suited her purposes. As for Adam, he has adapted to an urban environment as quickly as he adapted to the bucolic enchantments of Paradise Farm, and the Immigration and Naturalization Service no longer wishes to deport him to the Caribbean.

Adam paints. RuthClaire taught him. His paintings are novelties. They sell for almost as much as RuthClaire's own paintings of comparable size. Two of Adam's works—colorful instances of habiline expressionism—hang in the West Bank, gifts of no little value and decorative appeal. I receive many compliments on them, even from people ignorant of their creator's identity. RuthClaire contends that Adam is still improving.

Before the Montarazes' departure from Beulah Fork I threw them a going-away party in the West Bank. Livia George, Hazel Upchurch, Molly Kingsbury, Davie Hutton, Clarence and Eileen Tidings, Ruben and Elizabeth Decker, Mayor Ted Noles and his wife, and even young Nancy Teavers were among the guests. I served everyone on Limoges porcelain plates from both the *Celestial Hierarchy* and the *Footsteps on the Path to Man* series. The latter was still incomplete, unfortunately, but AmeriCred had sent me a dozen place settings of the most recent issue, "*Homo habilis*," with my ex-wife's compliments. I gave each of my guests this particular plate as a remembrance of the evening.

Although I had prepared her a vegetable dinner, Ruth-Claire ate very little. Her pregnancy had deprived her of her appetite. She nursed her meal along until she at last felt comfortable setting it aside in favor of a dessert cup of rainbow sherbet—at which point she announced to all and sundry that although few contemporary divorces were either civilized or even tastefully barbarous, she and I were still fast friends. When the baby came, Adam and she had agreed that I was to be its godfather. Indeed, if it were a boy, they intended to name it after me.

"Hear, hear!" everyone cried.

I stood to accept congratulations and propose a toast: "You're a better man than I am, Adam M."

For a time, anyway, I actually meant it. It is not always possible, I'm afraid, to be as good as you should be.

Part Two

HIS HEROIC HEART

Beulah Fork and Atlanta, Georgia

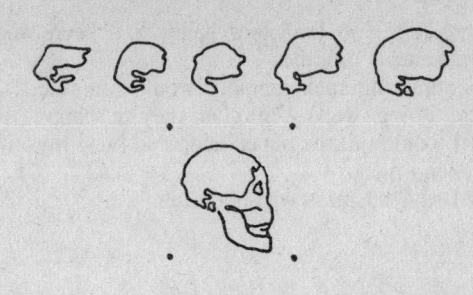

MARRIAGE DOMESTICATES. Divorce disrupts. Bachelorhood palls. And work—not time—heals all heartbreaks.

Business was booming at the West Bank. I was sleeping soundly for the first time in two years. Funny, in fact, how the booming of a business can sometimes soothe you even better than a lullaby.

I had finally managed to convince myself that Ruth-Claire and I were through—as man and wife, if not as wistfully wary friends. After all, she was with child by her habiline husband, Adam Montaraz, and no one could gainsay her devotion to the little man. He had impregnated her where I had failed to. He had moved with her to Atlanta. He had become a successful artist in his own right, and his private evolution toward a kind of genteel Southern sophistication was moving right along. The Atlanta *Constitution* would occasionally report that the Montarazes had attended a gallery opening, or a play, or a sporting event. Three times I had seen Adam's photograph in the paper, and twice he had been wearing a tuxedo.

RuthClaire, on the other hand, had been wearing designer maternity clothes.

Encountering such items, I would mumble, "I'm glad they're doing well. I'm glad they're happy together." Then I would put the paper aside and busy myself revising a weekend menu.

As I say, business was booming.

IN EARLY December I began to decorate the West Bank for Christmas. One day, with Livia George's help, I was putting a sprig of mistletoe on an archway of wrapped plastic tubing facing the Greyhound Depot Laundry. A steady dristle—*dristle* is Livia George's original portmanteau term for *mist* and *drizzle*—sifted down on us like a weatherman's curse. Suddenly, out of this gloom, a silver hatchback pulled into a diagonal parking spot just below my stepladder.

"Hey," Livia George said, "that's the fella Miss RuthClaire brung in here las' January. You know, the one done upchuck all ovah the table."

"Adam!" I exclaimed.

"Now he's got so uptown 'n' pretty he drivin' a silver bullet. An' jes' look who's with him, too!"

"RuthClaire!" I cried. Even in the mist-cloaked street, the syllables of her name reverberated like bell notes.

Embracing all around, we greeted one another. I even hugged Adam, who, in returning my hug, gave my back such a wrench that for a moment I thought a vertebra had snapped. He was gentler with Livia George, probably out of inbred habiline chivalry.

When RuthClaire and I came together, though, we bumped bellies. She laughed self-consciously, and I knew that her baby wasn't long for the womb. In defiance of the very real possibility of her going into labor along the way, she and Adam had made the two-hour trip from Atlanta. That struck me as crazy. Angrily, I told them both so.

"Relax, Paul. Even if I had, it wouldn't have been a catastrophe."

"On the shoulder of the expressway? Like a savage or something? You've got to be kidding!"

I turned to Adam. Although still far from a giant, he was taller than I remembered, maybe because he was wearing hand-tooled leather boots with elevator heels. I was going to rebuke him for making the drive with his wife so close to delivery, but RuthClaire had launched a spirited minilecture:

"Only a tiny fraction of all the babies born to our species have been born in hospitals, Paul. Today's world-population figures show it hasn't led to our extinction."

I whirled on her. "What if you'd had trouble?"

She patted the opaque ball turret of her pregnancy. "Gunner here's not going to cause any trouble. I'll have him—or her—the way a birddog bitch drops her puppies. *Thwup!* Like that."

"When's it due?" I asked, shaking my head.

"They don't really know. I've been pregnant since June at least. That puts me early in my seventh month."

"She safe enough, then," Livia George assured me.

Fresh-faced in the December mist, RuthClaire said, "That's not altogether certain, Livia George. No one has any real idea what the habiline gestation period is. Or *was*. Adam says that as a kid on Montaraz he witnessed a couple of births, but he doesn't have any memory of his people trying to reckon the length of a woman's term."

"Surely, one of those hotshot anthropologists up at Emory has an opinion on the matter."

"I'm sure they do, Paul, but we haven't asked them. We *think* I'm close. Habilines may carry their offspring no more than five or six months, maybe even less. They're small, you know."

"Yeah. Even when they're wearing platform heels."

"That's to help him reach the brake and accelerator pedals, not to pamper his vanity. Even so, we had to have those pedals lifted about four inches from the floorboard."

"Jesus." I looked up into the glowering pewter sky. "A thirty-six-year-old madonna on the brink of water-burst and an East African Richard Petty who can barely touch his brakes!"

"You gonna keep 'em out here all afternoon, Mistah Paul, or can they go inside to field your cuss-'em-outs."

I gestured everyone inside and sent Livia George to the kitchen for coffee and hot chocolate. It was still a couple of hours before the dinner crowd would begin arriving.

"Why didn't you telephone? I might not've even been here."

"You're always here, Paul. The West Bank's what you do."

"Yeah, but why didn't you telephone?"

"I can't help seeing Edna Twiggs sitting at the switchboard when I dial a Beulah Fork number, AT&T reorganization and all. I don't trust the phones—not after last summer."

"So you'd risk turning Adam into your obstetrician?"

"Absolutely. You see, Paul, Adam and I have reached a decision. I'm not having this baby in a hospital."

Unable to help myself, I rolled my eyes.

"Stop it. You belittle everything you don't understand."

"Is this going to be a hot-tub delivery? That's one of the latest crazes, I hear. Mama pretends she's a porpoise in Marineland."

"Paul—"

"Birthing stools. That's big, too. You have the kid squatting, like a football center pulling the pigskin out from under his jersey."

Adam looked down at his crooked hands on my new mint-green tablecloth. RuthClaire, meanwhile, spoke through clenched teeth: "I'll never understand how we got married. Never."

Knowing I had gone too far, I apologized.

"Neither of those methods is as absurd as you make them out to be. Underwater delivery's nonstressful for both mother and child, and a birthing stool gives a woman a degree of control over a process that's rightfully her own, anyway. If your consciousness is ever raised, Paul Loyd, it's going to have to be with a block and tackle.''

Livia George came into the dining room from the kitchen with our hot drinks. "Had six babies 'thout a doctor 'round,'' she told us. "In a feather bed in my own house. Oldest done hit six-foot-four. Youngest ain' been sick a day.''

Adam made a series of gestures with his hands, which RuthClaire translated: "Said to tell you, Paul, that we want our baby born at Paradise Farm. We'll even pay for the privilege. It's important to us.''

"But why?'' I asked, almost—not quite—dumbstruck.

"As soon as I check into a hospital, the media's going to descend. It's understandable, I guess, but I can't let them turn the birth of our baby into an international circus. Paradise Farm's already got a pretty good security system, and it's far enough from Atlanta to thwart a few of the inevitable busybodies.''

"RuthClaire, why don't you fly to some remote Caribbean island? You can afford it. It's going to be butt-bruising cold here in Beulah Fork—not like in Zarakal or Haiti, kid.''

"What it comes down to is, well, I'll be *comfortable* out there. And what more fitting place to have Adam's child than the place where he and I first met?'' She turned an admiring—a *loving*—gaze on the habiline, and he reciprocated with one of intelligent steadfastness.

Discomfited, I said, "You can stay out there, Ruthie Cee, on two conditions.''

"*Two!*''

I stood up. "Just listen to me. They're easy. First, you don't pay me a dime.''

Adam and RuthClaire exchanged a look, the meaning of which was clearly both gratitude and acceptance.

"Second, you let me find a reputable—and discreet—doctor to help you with the delivery.''

"Absolutely not! An outsider would needlessly compli-cate things, and I'm going to be fine.''

I told her that there was still a *possibility* she might need help. How could I live with myself if anything went wrong? She replied that for the past six months Adam had been reading—yes, *reading*—every tome on childbirth he could lay his hands on. It was also his opinion that the unborn infant's gracile body—*gracile*, for God's sake! —would ease its journey through the birth canal. Ruthie Cee, a birddog bitch dropping puppies.

My forefinger made a stabbing motion at Adam. "It's a little hard for me to credit his coming so far in six months. You'll forgive me if I'm skeptical of his medical expertise?"

"He's brighter than most, Paul, and he had a headstart on Montaraz that nobody seems to want to acknowledge."

"Yeah, but he's not a doctor. And that's my second condition."

RuthClaire stood up. Adam stood up. For a moment I feared that they were leaving, and I cursed my show of intractability. I was on the verge of rescinding my second condition when Livia George gave me a face-saving out:

"S'pose *I* midwife Miss RuthClaire's little 'un? How that be?" She fluttered her hands in front of her breasts. "I got me *lots* o' s'perience birthin' babies."

Hallelujah. RuthClaire, Adam, and I all did double-takes. It was okay with all of us, Livia George's proposal. Something about her turn of phrase, something about her cunning self-mockery. Our conflict thus resolved, the four of us took turns embracing one another as we had earlier done on the sidewalk.

I SENT the Montarazes out to Paradise Farm with a set of keys. Livia George and I finished decorating, then stayed on for the dinner crowd. Hazel Upchurch and Nancy Teavers came in at 4:30. By recent standards, business was slow and the evening dragged. At 11:30 I was barreling up the highway to see how my new lodgers were doing.

They had not yet gone to bed. I found them in

RuthClaire's old studio. Often over the past few months, I had entered the untenanted loft to stand in its memory-haunted emptiness imagining just such a reunion. Now she was really back, my lost RuthClaire.

Adam, of course, was with her. He was sitting cross-legged on the drafting table opposite RuthClaire's low Naugahyde sofa. He had a book between his legs and a pair of gold-framed granny glasses clamped on the end of his broad, flat nose. The sleeves of his baby-blue velour shirt were rolled up, and he had unzipped it to the mid-point of his sternum, revealing a flannely nest of reddish-black chest hair. He saw me before RuthClaire did.

"Still reading up on childbirth?" I asked him.

He bared his teeth at me—a smile rather than a threat or an expression of fear—and lifted the book so that I could see it. RuthClaire pulled herself to a sitting position with my nappy beige rearing-bear blanket around her shoulders. By the door, I leaned down and kissed her on the forehead. Then I crossed to the drafting table to find out what Adam was reading. A small, slick paperback: *The Problem of Pain* by C. S. Lewis.

"C. S. Lewis?" I said incredulously, turning to Ruth-Claire. "A habiline holdover from the Pleistocene's reading C. S. Lewis?"

"What's wrong with that?"

I took the book from Adam. "Your husband here—the living descendant of a bunch of East African mole people—is busily ingesting a work of theology?"

"Do you believe he can read?"

I glanced sidelong at Adam. I knew he had mastered sign language, I had seen him driving a car, and his eyes were appraising me with a keenness that gave me pause.

"Sure," I grudgingly admitted. "Why not?"

"Then why find it hard to believe he's reading C. S. Lewis? The man wrote for children, you know. He even wrote *science fiction*."

I changed tacks. "He ought to be reading, uh, *Midwifery Made Easy*, or Benjamin Spock, or something like that."

"He's done that already. Don't you understand? His consciousness is emerging from a kind of mental Upper Paleolithic. Adam's trying to find out who he is."

"More birthing-stool psychobabble?"

"Only if you choose to belittle it as such."

Adam made a series of signs with both hands. I could not interpret them. The irony of his knowing a system of communication of which I was ignorant underscored the foolishness of my doubting his interest in theology. (If he could sign, he could just as easily genuflect.)

"He wants to know if he has a soul," RuthClaire translated.

"So do I. Want to know if *I* have a soul, that is."

"Your lack of a heart may imply something equally discouraging about your spiritual equipment, Paul."

"Very funny. It's after midnight, kid. I can't believe we're discussing this."

"What about it? Do you think Adam has a soul?"

"What kind of soul, for God's sake? An animal soul? A rational soul? An immortal soul? All this sort of adolescent head game will get you is a migraine and a reputation as a philosophical nitpicker."

RuthClaire flapped her nappy blanket. "Skip it. You've got all the sensitivity of a tire iron."

Suddenly dog-tired, I shuffled to the sofa and plumped myself down opposite RuthClaire. She took pity and flapped an end of her blanket at me. I pulled it over my knees.

"Almost like old times, hey, Paul?"

"I can't recall having a chaperone before."

"Livia George."

"Livia George's a chaperone the way Colonel Sanders is a spokesman for the Save-the-Chickens Fund."

RuthClaire laughed, and we began to talk. Somehow, owing in part to Adam's absorption in his book, it was almost as if we were alone in the wide, chilly room. RuthClaire told me that downstairs she had seen, and had been pleased to see, my growing collection of plates in her *Footsteps on the Path to Man* series. I had arranged the eight titles issued to date on hinged brass stands in a glass-fronted maple hutch. The plates included *Rama-pithecus, Australopithecus afarensis, A. africanus, A. boisei, Homo habilis, Homo erectus, Homo sapiens,* and *Homo neanderthalensis.* The habiline, first issued back in August, bore an undeniable resemblance to the gargoyle perched on my drafting table.

"Look," I said, "you've got ten plates in this series, and you've already done the eight main hominids on the road to *Homo sapiens sapiens.* What's next?"

"Contemporary racial variations."

"Negroes, Caucasians, Orientals?"

"That's right. I've already done paintings for those and some others—Oceanics, aboriginals, and American Indians. The final four are up in the air because there's some unavoidable overlap. I'll probably do Eskimoes, Arabs, pygmies, and Nordics, but I could just as easily substitute Bushmen or Montagnards or Ainu somewhere in there. It's arbitrary, of course, a way to get the number of plates up to eighteen. AmeriCred's hollering for the last four so that they can get the plates themselves into production. Me, I'm sick of the whole rotten thing."

"Really? You don't enjoy doing them?"

"It's donkeywork, Paul. I liked doing the prehistoric numbers, Adam's portrait and all that. But these last ten are sheer commercial excess. AmeriCred just wants their subscribers to keep paying through the nose for gewgaws. I feel like a hack writing otherwise worthless potboilers."

"Enjoy your popularity. No one's twisting their arms."

"It's not that I'm doing a lousy job, it's just that these new ones aren't contributing anything to the development of my art. It's safe representational stuff. My audience consists almost entirely of well-to-do old ladies and fat-cat corporate executives looking for a 'classy' cultural investment." She stuck out her tongue, as if to see if there were a piece of lint or tobacco on its tip. (Nope.) "That's why I've been so slow to finish this assignment, Paul."

"Blame it on your pregnancy."

"I've done that. It's a lie."

"People who regret making money are nincompoops."

"The regret—the guilt—comes from what you do to make it. Even you know that. Right now I'm whoring."

Adam looked up from *The Problem of Pain*. He made a gesture sequence loosely translatable as "Don't talk rubbish," then went back to Lewis's little piece of theodicy.

"Whoring? You didn't feel that way about *The Celestial Hierarchy*, did you?"

"Not once. Those are breakthrough paintings. I avoided all the clichés—archangels with flaming swords, naked roly-polies with wings on their heels, Jesus dragging his old rugged hanging tree. I did something new. It was a small miracle the series was successful. A bigger miracle it ever got commissioned."

"It made you popular. You hadn't bargained for that."

" 'How public,' " RuthClaire quoted, " 'like a frog.' "

"That's smug elitism," I said. "It's probably insincere, too. You pretend to despise success because there's an old art-school attitude that figures nothing popular can be worth a damn."

"Listen, Paul, there's a backlash against me in the Atlanta art community because of my success. The people who count up there, well, they see my work on these stupid plates as a sellout. I do, too. Now, especially."

"If that opinion takes in the plates you're proud of, to hell with them."

"Paul, it's more complicated than that. They don't respect what I'm doing, and I can't really respect it, either—not these last ten examples of porcelain calendar art, anyway."

"They're jealous."

"That enters into it, sure. But I've always thought of myself as something of a visionary. My work for AmeriCred has undermined all that. The worst thing about the backlash is that I *know* I've brought it on myself."

The studio's overhead fluorescents flickered palely as the wind gusted and moaned. The yew outside the twin-paned plateglass creaked its tall shadow across our imaginations. Even Adam looked up.

"Is that another reason you came down here? To escape the disapproval of the art-scene cognoscenti?"

RuthClaire frowned. "I don't know." Then her spirits mysteriously revived. "They *like* what Adam does. In February, Paul, the folks at Abraxas are going to give an entire third-floor gallery room over to an exhibition of Adam's paintings. It'll be in place for two weeks. Promise me you'll come see it."

"The West Bank," I reminded her. "It's hard to get away."

"You managed to get away last February when you dropped in on Brian Nollinger at that primate field station north of Atlanta. Well, Abraxas is twenty miles closer to Beulah Fork than that concentration camp for our furry cousins." A grimace of unfeigned revulsion twisted her mouth, but then her eyes were facetiously pleading. "Listen, Mr. Loyd, I've just made you an offer you can't refuse. Understand?"

"Yes, ma'am," I said. "Yes, ma'am."

AND SO Adam and RuthClaire stayed with me, and Livia George drove home with me from the West Bank every evening to be on hand in the event that my ex-wife went into labor. At the restaurant itself we had a prearranged telephone signal. Adam, out at Paradise Farm, would dial and let the phone ring once. Then he would hang up, wait thirty seconds, and repeat the procedure. After the second ring, no matter how busy we were, Livia George and I would sprint up the Tocqueville Road in my Mercedes to answer his call.

Atlanta's news media finally caught on to the fact that the Montarazes had left the city. They telephoned the West Bank looking for a lead. Sometimes they even sought to induce Edna Twiggs to give them my unlisted number at Paradise Farm. She resisted. One day at lunch, in fact, she told me how she had turned down a bribe of money for that information. Edna Twiggs, an ally! Even so, I took the added precaution of connecting all the telephones in my house to an answering machine so that in my absence RuthClaire and Adam could monitor incoming calls. Fortunately, no one but me ever tried to ring them up.

I was still concerned that someone in a TV van or a newspaper company car might try to gatecrash. The Atlanta papers had recently featured headlines about Adam and RuthClaire. In the morning *Constitution*, this:

LOCAL ARTIST AND HER HABILINE HUSBAND
DISAPPEAR LATE IN HER HISTORIC PREGNANCY

In the afternoon paper, the *Journal*, this:

FOUL PLAY NOT SUSPECTED
IN ABSENCE OF LOCAL ARTISTS
BUT ABRAXAS CHIEF ANXIOUS ABOUT FAMOUS PAIR

The story under the latter headline reported an interview with David Blau, director of the Abraxas Gallery. Blau thought that the Montarazes were probably okay, but still believed they should contact him or one of his associates to confirm the fact.

"Is this fellow one of the avant-garde bigwigs who think you've sold out?" I asked RuthClaire.

"David's more charitable than most. He credits me with practicing a deliberate serious-commercial split."

"Sounds like a decent enough Joe."

"He is. That's why I've got to give him a call."

"Don't," I blurted. My newfound, but still tepid, regard for Edna Twiggs did not permit me to trust her totally. "Write a note. Put no return address on the envelope. I'll mail it from Tocqueville tomorrow morning. He'll have it the day after."

That's what we did. While I was in Tocqueville to mail the note, I hired a trio of private guards from a security agency in the Tocqueville Commons Mall. The first man came on duty that same afternoon.

Once the guards began their shifts, my taut nerves loosened. The likelihood of anyone's circling the farm and coming at us by way of White Cow Creek seemed remote. It must have seemed remote to RuthClaire, too. She made up her mind that she was going to have her baby in a peaked canvas tent that she and Adam pitched beneath a pecan tree in the back. The tent was lavender. It reminded me of the floppy conical hoods worn by E. L. Teavers, Craig Puddicombe, and their anonymous Klan-mates on the night they came to kill Adam. I told RuthClaire so the first morning after the tent had gone up, its lavender surfaces sparkling with frost.

"You're right," she acknowledged, startled. "We bought it at a sporting-goods store in Atlanta and I never once thought of that. Maybe Adam did, though. Teavers's robe may have kept him from coming down with pneumonia."

"This tent won't keep you warm. The temperature to-day's in the twenties, RuthClaire."

"I'll be fine."

"The hell you say. What about the baby?"

"The child's half habiline, Paul. Habilines are traditionally, and altogether *naturally*, born out of doors. The tent's a compromise."

"Out of doors in Africa or Haiti!"

"If it's cold, Livia George can wrap the baby in a blanket and take it straight inside."

"Then what's the point of the stupid purple tent?"

"I've already told you. Don't you listen?" She turned on her heel and stalked toward the plateglass doors glittering above my patio deck. I followed her, shaking my head and mumbling curses.

ADAM CONTINUED to read away at Lewis's *The Problem of Pain*. Too, from the library in Tocqueville—a side trip I made on the same day I hired the security guards and mailed my ex's note—he had me check out some other fairly basic books on religious or spiritual topics: *The Screwtape Letters* by Lewis, Bunyan's *Pilgrim's Progress*, a young person's guide to understanding the great world religions, an English translation of the Koran, a biography of Gandhi, Thomas Merton's *The Seven Storey Mountain*, something called *The Alphabet of Grace* by Frederick Buechner, *The Way of the Sufi* by Idries Shah, a primer on the Talmud, and Mortimer Adler's *How to Think About God*. Pretty heady stuff for a habiline. I had to carry the whole lot home in a Gilman No-Tare grocery bag from our local A&P.

Adam painted during the days, read in the evenings. Ruthie Cee, on the other hand, neither painted nor read. She spent most of her time sleeping while Adam worked. Sometimes she watched him. (He was putting the finishing touches on a huge, semiabstract landscape featuring a tangerine-red tree that reminded me of an African baobab.) She may have occasionally prepared a meal for the two of them, but if she did, she wasn't regular about it. She had no need to be. Livia George and I were scrupulous about bringing them at least one hot gourmet meal a day.

Saturday night at the West Bank. Six or seven people standing cheerful but also mildly impatient just inside the door, waiting to be seated. Fur jackets or chic leather car coats on the ladies. The men bundled in herringbone or expensive brushed sheepskin. Cold air swirling around the newcomers like the vapor in a frozen-food bin.

The telephone next to the cash register rang. I looked over at the flocked divider concealing the phone. A second ring was not forthcoming.

Oh no, I thought, not *tonight!*

I smiled at a woman with a magazine-cover death mask for a face and put one hand reassuringly on the shoulder of her escort. Mentally, though, I counted to thirty. The telephone rang again.

"That's it!" I cried. "That's it!"

Livia George came scurrying from the kitchen wiping her hands on her apron. Her heavy upper arms were bare, but she made no move to find her coat.

"Gotta get goin', Mistah Paul," she told me, pushing through the astonished people at the door. "Gotta he'p Miss RuthClaire birth that beautiful baby."

She hustled out the door, down the sidewalk, and into the front seat of my Mercedes on the driver's side. Helplessly, I followed after, already resigned to the role of passenger.

The trip took maybe nine minutes. Our security guard automatically passed us through the gate, and my car's steel-belted radials flung gravel back at him as Livia George fishtailed us up the drive to the house. I was taking two steps at a time toward the front door when Livvy, at the corner of the house, shouted,

"Not that way, Mistah Paul! She in that purple pup tent out back!"

"Go on!" I urged her. "I've got to grab a coat or something!"

The warmth of the house hit me like a Gulf Coast wind. I took a jacket from the shoulders of the baby-satyr statue on which I had draped it several days ago, pulled it on, and strode into the living room looking for a shawl or sweater for Livia George. From the back of a chair I grabbed a peach-toned afghan. But on the way to the sliding doors I hesitated.

Did I really want to see the woman I loved in the throes of childbirth? Sure. Of course I did. Wasn't that what every sensitive with-it male wanted nowadays? Men actually attended classes to learn how to provide support at the Moment of Truth. Some even scrubbed and put on surgical gowns to participate in the event. If their partners were back-to-nature advocates, they might build birthing stools or prepare for underwater delivery by buying scuba-diving gear. All I had to do was slide open a plateglass door and go tripping across my deck to a tent in a pecan grove.

I was no longer RuthClaire's husband. The child in her womb owed me no genetic debt. It instead owed this paternal debt to a mute, sinewy creature right out of the early Paleolithic. Was the arrival of this squalling relic really an event I wanted to witness? My concern should

have been for RuthClaire's safety, for the health and well
being of her child—but baser impulses had me in their grip
and I hesitated.

Taking a deep breath, I went out onto my deck. The
cold hit me like an Arctic hammer stroke, but I staggered
through the pillars of my silhouetted pecan trees to
RuthClaire's lavender tent. Inside the translucent smudge
of the sailcloth, shadowy shapes stooped, straightened,
and gesticulated. Adam, I was glad to see, had taken my
PowerLite into the tent. He had even thought to carry one
of the studio's sun lamps out there, an extension cord from
the deck down into the pecan grove giving me a trail to
follow.

A hundred yards or so beyond the tent, a quick flash of
light. I halted, blinked, looked again—but now the corridor of sentinel pecans was empty of any intruder but the
keening wind.

"Mistah Paul, you better move your fanny fas' if you
wanna see this!"

I moved my fanny fast. After skidding in the frost-rimed
mulch, I whipped aside the tent flap, edged inside, and
found RuthClaire lying flat on her back on a mound of
blankets and ancient bed sheets spread out on a plastic
dropcloth. Adam was kneeling to one side of his wife, but
Livvy was hunkering between her legs—legs, I noticed,
bundled in a pair of those ugly knit calf-warmers worn by
women in aerobic-dancing classes—guiding from her womb
the mocha-cream-colored product of her pregnancy.

"I told you it'd be easy!" RuthClaire cried ecstatically,
letting her head fall back and laughing.

Livvy did something sure-handed to the umbilical cord,
then lifted the minuscule infant by its ankles, bracing its
back with one hand and showing it first to Adam and then
to me. It was a boy, but a wizened and fragile-looking one.
When Livvy slapped him on his angular buttocks, he
sucked in air and wailed. Surprisingly, the sound lasted
only a few brief seconds. Evolution on the Serengeti grass-
lands, I later came to realize, had selected for habilines
whose newborns shut up in a hurry.

"Ain' he a dandy!"

I put the afghan around Livia George's shoulders. Adam reached into the wings of the towel swaddling the baby to touch his son on the head. Something like a smile flickered around Adam's lips.

"Okay," I said. "We've proved that Ruthie's game enough to bear her child in the back yard. Now let's get inside."

"Got a little bidness to take care of yet," Livvy said, handing the baby to its father. She knelt and massaged the undersides of RuthClaire's thighs; then she began to push gently on the mother's slack, exposed abdomen, to encourage the expulsion of the placenta. "Y'all go on in. Nothin' else for you to do out here."

Before Adam and I could exit, however, two strangers shoved their way into the tent.

First, a blond man in a double-breasted safari jacket confronted us. Behind him, balancing a portable video unit on one denim-clad shoulder, was a slender black man. These intruders were so businesslike about deploying their equipment and their persons in the cramped interior that I actually considered the possibility that Adam and RuthClaire had hired them to video-tape their baby's delivery. If so, they were late.

"I'm Brad Barrington of Contact Cable News," announced the blond intruder. "My cameraman, Rudy Starnes." The black man gave us a perfunctory nod. "Well, well, well. Is this little fellow the Montaraz baby?" He chucked the newborn under the chin with a gloved forefinger. "Looks like we underestimated the time it'd take us to get through the woods, Rudy. The big show's already come off."

"Sun lamp's giving us enough light to shoot by, Brad. Maybe I can do some reenactment footage to save the situation."

"Yeah," said Barrington. "And on-the-scene interviews."

Grimacing, RuthClaire raised up on her elbows. "What in pity's name do you guys think you're doing?"

"You're trespassing," I protested. "You sneaked onto Paradise Farm from Cleve Synder's property."

A microphone in his fist, Barrington duck-walked beneath the tilted sun lamp to RuthClaire's shoulder, where he asked her if it had been a difficult delivery.

Leaning into the mike, RuthClaire let go of a high-pitched scream. Barrington recoiled, almost doing a pratfall. Livia George, meanwhile, had slid the glistening placenta into a piece of torn sheet. Her entire manner implied that the sudden appearance of the two-man Contact Cable News crew was none of her affair. If nothing else, it was preferable to a hurricane.

"Who's on security duty tonight?" I asked. (I could never remember the guards' names.)

"Chalmers," RuthClaire replied, spitting out the word.

Barrington, looking more annoyed than abashed, approached her again with the microphone. "Don't you think this landmark event deserves a permanent video record? Don't you feel any sense of obligation to history?"

RuthClaire, her breath ballooning, said, "Don't you feel any sense of shame, hanging over a half-naked woman with that instrument of psychic rape in your fist?"

A thin veil of confusion fell across the newsman's face.

"Get out of here," I told him. "My first and last warning."

"Let's go, Brad," the black man said. "This ain't working out." Almost certainly at his partner's bidding, Starnes had just hauled a ton of equipment across five or six hundred yards of wintry darkness, and nothing was going as planned.

"Keep shooting," the blond man nevertheless told him.

"Brad—"

"This is a scoop! You see anyone down here from Channel Five or Eleven Alive? You know anybody else who staked out this place for three ass-freezing days?"

"Nobody else that dumb."

I slipped outside and called for Chalmers, the guard. That did it for Starnes. He decamped, abandoning his associate to whatever fate the man chose to fashion for himself. He was hiking speedily off through the pecan grove, his equipment banging, when Chalmers came trotting around the corner of the house with his pistol drawn. The guard started to pursue the cameraman.

"Let him go," I said. "It's the talking head in the tent who needs his butt run in."

Matters unraveled confusedly after that. RuthClaire was yelling at Barrington to go away, go away, and Livia George came out into the cold with the infant, nodding once at the house to show us that she was taking him indoors. Chalmers, a tall young man in an official-looking parka, started to go into the tent after Barrington when Barrington fell backward through the tent flap with Adam's head in his stomach and his arms pinioned to his sides. In a rapid-fire falsetto utterly unlike his on-the-air baritone, he was pleading for mercy—but he landed on his back with such an audible expulsion of breath that he could not keep it up.

Adam was all over him like a pit bull, leaping from flank to flank over the reporter's prostrate form, baring his teeth at him, all the while growling as if rabid. RuthClaire emerged from the tent, too. Her blood-stained dressing gown hung to her ankles, her incongruous maroon leg-warmers visible just beneath its hem. She grasped one of the tent's guy ropes to support herself.

In a tone of rational admonishment, she said, "Stop, Adam. I'm okay. That's enough."

Through the fog of his rage, Adam somehow heard her. He stopped, Barrington's body rigid beneath him, and looked up sightlessly at Chalmers and me. Slowly—almost shockingly—sanity returned to his eyes, and he pushed himself off the reporter with his knuckles and stepped away from the whimpering victim of his assault.

"I want to hold my baby," RuthClaire told him. "Take me in."

Still trying to compose himself, Adam escorted her to the house. Chalmers and I remained in the pecan grove with Barrington, the guard pointing his pistol at the newsman's head. What now? Were we within our rights to shoot the trespasser?

Barrington stopped whimpering. Catching sight of me

upside-down, he asked if he could maybe have a cup of coffee before he called his station for a ride back to Atlanta.

"That damn Starnes. He's probably to Newnan by now."

Chalmers said, "If Mr. Loyd decides to press charges, you won't be going back to Atlanta tonight. I'll be turning you over to the sheriff in Tocqueville for a little quiet cell time."

Barrington got off the ground, groaning elaborately, and we argued the matter. If he gave me his word that Contact Cable News would never air the least snippet of tape taken tonight on Paradise Farm, I told him, I would forgo the pleasure of pressing charges. I was damned, though, if I was going to let him use my bathroom, much less serve him a cup of coffee. Barrington grumped about the First Amendment and Freedom of the Press, but verbally accepted my terms.

Then Chalmers and I accompanied him to the front gate. There, with a display of loyalty totally undeserved, Rudy Starnes picked up Barrington in the Contact Cable News van in which the two of them had been camping for the past three ass-freezing days, presumably to drive him back up the lonely highway to Atlanta.

UPSTAIRS, IN a tiny bedroom next to the studio, I found Livia George with the new parents. In one corner was a white wicker bassinet, but RuthClaire was sitting in an upholstered chair nursing her baby, whom someone had bagged up in a bright yellow terrycloth sleeper. A newt, I thought. A salamander. I reported what had happened with Barrington and told Livvy that *I* needed to go back to the West Bank to oversee the restaurant's closing—assuming, of course, that my employees hadn't already walked off the job in uncomprehending anger and frustration.

"They'll be back," RuthClaire said.

"I hope so," I said. "It's hard finding good help."

"Oh, I don't mean Hazel and Nancy and the others. I'm talking about those jerks from Contact Cable."

Abruptly, Adam stalked out of the room. I heard the lights click on in the studio and saw a wash of yellow lambency unroll past the nursery.

"I don't think he remembers the last time he let himself go like that," RuthClaire said by way of explanation.

"The time he wrestled E. L. Teavers into the brick kiln?"

"That was self-defense, Paul, literally a matter of life and death. Tonight, the only thing that was really at stake was the sanctity of our baby's birth."

"Adam be awright tomorrow," Livia George assured us. "Too much 'citement for one evening."

"He didn't even bite the bastard," I said. "Just knocked him down and growled."

"He went wild."

"Everybody goes wild now and then." I grinned. "Why, Ruthie Cee, even you went a little wild this evening."

She shifted her hold on the baby. "We were thinking of naming this little character for you. Keep that up, though, and you can forget it." Gently, she began to jog the suckling infant in her arms. "Adam sets standards for himself, high ones. They're high because the general expectation is that he'll comport himself like an animal. Well, his sense of self-respect demands that he never—ever—fulfill that cynical expectation."

"Which means his standards are higher than nine tenths of the world's human population."

"Adam's human."

"You know what I mean. I was trying to compliment him."

The baby—*Paul Montaraz*, I realized with a sudden humbling insight—had fallen asleep nursing. He was small. Even asleep, his mouth tugged at RuthClaire's nipple with desperate infantile greed. Livia George lifted him up, coaxed a burp from him, and laid him on a quilted coverlet in the bassinet. RuthClaire told me that tomorrow morning the Montaraz family would return to Atlanta and my own life could go back to normal.

"Whoever said I wanted a normal life?"

"Look in on Adam, will you, Paul? Right now, another person's attentions might be better medicine for his blues than mine."

I looked in on Adam. He was sitting on the drafting table, his legs crossed, his stack of read and unread library books teetering at his knees. Although he heard me enter, he refused to look up. We were alone together in the tall drafty expanse of the studio. Despite the room's chilliness, my hands had begun to sweat.

"Adam," I said. "Don't feel bad about going after that Contact Cable turkey. If it'd been me, I'd've *bit* him."

The habiline looked me in the eye. His upper lip drew back to reveal his pink gums and primitive but powerful teeth. I looked away. When I looked again, Adam's gaze had gone back to his book.

"I wanted to congratulate you on becoming a father, Adam. The kid's a crackerjack." No response. "What's that you're reading?"

The cloak of civility he was trying to grow into would not permit him to ignore a direct question. He lifted the small volume so that I could read its title. Ah, yes, *The Problem of Pain* again, on which Adam had foundered shortly after his arrival. I turned the book around and saw that tonight he had run aground on the beginning of Chapter 9, "Animal Pain."

One sentence jumped out at me as it may have already jumped out at Adam: "So far as we know beasts are incapable of either sin or virtue: therefore they can neither deserve pain nor be improved by it." My belief that this sentence may have wounded Adam was predicated on the feeling that although RuthClaire had accepted him as fully human, he had yet to accept himself as such.

"You ought to try this guy's *Out of the Silent Planet*," I said. "It's a helluva lot more fun than his theology."

Adam carefully extracted the book from my two-fingered

grip, pulled it to his chest, and then flung it past my head to the far end of the studio. Like a broken-backed bird, it flapped to a leaning standstill against the baseboard. Adam took advantage of my surprise to unfold his legs and hop down from the table. Exiting the studio, he put me in mind of a lame elf or an oddly graceful chimpanzee: there was something either crippled-seeming or animalish about his walk.

"Shame on you, Loyd," I scolded myself.

PAPA, MAMA, and Little Baby Montaraz went back to Atlanta. The international media descended upon their home not far from Little Five Points, a two-story structure with a ramshackle gallery, lots of spooky gables, and a wide Faulknerian veranda. The house became almost as famous as the kid.

As for my namesake, he rapidly turned into the anthropological prince of American celebrity. Everyone wanted a piece of him and his parents. *People, Newsweek, Life*, "60 Minutes," "20-20," *Discovery*, "Nova," *Cosmopolitan, Omni, Reader's Digest*, and a host of other publications and programs sought to report, analyze, or simply ride the giddy whirlwind of the Montaraz Phenomenon. Indeed, it took better than a year for the extravagant circus surrounding the family to dismantle its tents and mothball its clown costumes, but ever afterward, to this very day, a half dozen or so revolving sideshows have kept the promise (or the threat) of an even dizzier Return Engagement before the public.

But I'm running ahead of myself. Let me back up.

In the absence of an attending physician, Tiny Paul required a birth certificate. Because his parents had left Paradise Farm early on Sunday morning, there was no way for them to obtain a file form on which to apply for a certificate from the Hothlepoya County Health Department. On Monday, then, I drove to Tocqueville to pick up the proper form. I filled it out while standing at the registrar's counter. Surprisingly, this woman treated the application as a routine matter. When I questioned her, she told me that the form would now go to the Office of Vital Records in the state-government complex in Atlanta.

"What about the birth certificate?"

"Send in a three-dollar filing fee and they'll send the certificate. It really doesn't take long."

"If I write the check, should I specify that the certificate itself should go to the parents' Atlanta address?"

The young woman—trim, deftly mascaraed—looked at me with a flicker of interest. "Why would they send the certificate to you? Writing the check doesn't make you the child's father."

"Then it isn't necessary?"

"Of course not."

Irritated, I sought to shock her. "What if I *did* happen to be the kid's father?"

"Then it's awfully big of you to pay the filing fee," she said, not hesitating a second.

I grunted, pocketed my checkbook, and left.

On Wednesday, I received a long white envelope from Atlanta, not from the Office of Vital Records but from RuthClaire and Adam. The notes inside were both in Ruthie Cee's weird El Grecoish hand—tall, nearsighted characters in anguished postures—but the second of the two was reputedly dictation from Adam. Even partly disguised in RuthClaire's etiolated script, Adam's was the more original and the more perplexing document:

Well-loved Namer of our Son,

We are back, but are we home? My homes keep jumping around. Paradise Farm I love for there I met RuthClaire. For a while now it is the only one of all my homes that does not jump. Tiny Paul has just jumped into the world from my one home that stands somewhat still. You are like a fierce seraphim that holds down the corners of my jumping Eden. Thank you, sir, for doing that.

I must say two more things and maybe a little else. First, thank you for bringing me books on your card about God and thinking on Godness. Some of these I have regotten on my Atlanta card, so much am I interested. Second, deeply sorry for throwing one book —even if it was my own—across your room in my bitter fit of not behaving right. It makes me laugh a little, with angry mirth, to say or see that title, THE PROBLEM OF PAIN.

I am also sorry for attacking that vile man Barrington. I should write to him to say so, but he should write me to say sorry a THOUSAND times himself. He should write Miss RuthClaire, and he should write YOU. He should quit his name from the station that sends him forth. God and thinking on Godness should quiet my anger, but (too bad, too bad) they do not. Barrington is a man who needs better etiquette and also probably religion. So am I. But I have a long walk to get there.

This is my last "a little else" to ask you. One day this year Miss RuthClaire may ask you to come see about her seeing about me. Some doctors at Emory are plotting now a surgery to humanize me for this time and place. Do please come when she asks. We will reimburse—a pretty word—all losses. If you both agree to the niceness of using one bed during my hospital stay, I have no argument or jealousy to put against that wish,

Sincerely,

Adam

P.S. Miss RuthClaire has written my last a "little else" in some anger. I must learn, she says, that no married partner except possibly an Eskimo has a right "to dispose of the other's affections." I am telling her that I knew THAT already, and that the words "if both agree" prove I am not disposing, without consideration, her person. Good etiquette. Moral integrity.

P.P.S. Tiny Paul does well. Sleeping at night very well. Making no noise. Good baby etiquette.

P.P.P.S. I would enjoy—greatly—a pen pal on spiritual matters, but you probably lack for time?

Utterly fascinated, I reread the letter and then went through it line by line a third time. What wouldn't a reporter give to lay hands on this extraordinary document? I thought briefly of letting different outfits bid for it, but once I had rejected this course as vile beyond even *my* notorious reverence for the profit motive, I never looked back. Adam was no longer my rival, he was my friend.

I tried to imagine what sort of surgery the specialists at Emory were planning for Adam, but all I could think of were such routine operations as appendectomy, tonsillectomy, molar extractions, and, forgive me, circumcision. Then it occurred to me that the doctors might be contemplating more exotic procedures, *viz.*, rendering Adam's thumbs wholly opposable, surgically removing his sagittal crest, or maybe even increasing his body height by putting artificial bone sections in his thighs or lower legs. The first and third options would perhaps make it easier for Adam to function among us, but the second was a potentially dangerous sop to either his or RuthClaire's (vicarious) vanity—for which reason I struck it from my catalogue.

What then? What were they going to do to Adam?

I folded the two notes back into their envelopes, feeling good about having decided to consider Adam my friend. Now it was necessary to act on that decision and enforce it by framing a reply. I found a grungy 14-cent postcard and wrote on it the following message:

Dear RuthClaire and Adam: I will come any time you need me. Just ask. No sweat about throwing C. S. Lewis across the room. I was once tempted to do the same thing myself. I'm the wrong pen pal for discussion of God and Godness, grace and salvation, extinction and immortality. Even good and bad etiquette in situations with a moral angle. For that reason—not lack of time—I can't promise anything.

Kiss the kid for me.

Love, T.P.'s Godfather

CHRISTMAS CAME and went. In Atlanta, the circus had begun. I wondered if my postcard had passed under prying eyes, thereby triggering the Montarazes' ordeal with the press. In the future, sealed letters only.

Early in February, RuthClaire wrote to say that they had received Tiny Paul's birth certificate. She included three dollars to cover the cost of the registration fee. I sent the money back. But with the bills and the note was a printed invitation to Adam's first exhibition of paintings at Abraxas. A wine-and-cheese reception in Adam's honor would precede the show, and I was also invited to that. On the printed card RuthClaire had written, *"You'd better be here, Philistine!"*

The reception was on a Tuesday evening. I closed the West Bank after our midday meal, gave Livia George and the others both that evening and Wednesday off, put a sign on the door, and set off for the Big City . . . just in time to collide with rush hour.

Dristle kept my windshield wipers klik-klikking, and it was almost completely dark when I finally made my way up Moreland Avenue to Little Five Points and the Montaraz house on Hurt Street. That house, how to describe it? Its silhouette oozed a jolly decadence suggesting Mardi Gras and shrimp creole and tasseled strippers and derby-hatted funeral processionaires. A pair of lamps on black cast-iron poles shone on either side of the cobbled walk, their globes like spheres of shimmery, honey-colored wax. By their light, I saw two indistinct figures come out on the front porch, down the steps, and hand in hand through the mistfall to my car. I let them in.

RuthClaire and Adam, of course, in boots and fleece-lined London Fog trenchcoats. From the two of them wafted the smells of soap, cologne, lipstick, aftershave, winter rain, and something peculiarly oniony.

"Don't I get to come in?" I squinted at my invitation. "This is a wine-and-cheese reception, not a dinner."

Adam was sitting next to me, but the lady had slid into the back seat. "David Blau," she said, leaning forward, "asked us to show up a little early, Paul. We're letting you drive to throw the press off. They'll be looking for our hatchback."

"I thought they always had your place surrounded."

"Until we got Bilker Moody, they usually did. Tonight, though, the majority's already at Abraxas."

I asked about my godson. He was with the sitter, Pam Sorrells, an administrative assistant at the gallery who had sacrificed her own attendance at the opening to free Adam and RuthClaire for the event. An armed security guard— the aforementioned Bilker Moody—was also in the living room to protect La Casa Montaraz from uninvited guests. Bilker was nearly *always* present. That was the way their little family had to live nowadays.

"Look, the show's not officially over until eleven, Ruthie Cee. My stomach'll be rumbling like Vesuvius by then."

Adam reached into the pocket of his trenchcoat and withdrew a McDonald's cheeseburger in its Mazola Oil–colored wrapper. It was still warm—warm and enticingly oniony-smelling. I glanced sidelong at this object of gastronomical kitsch.

"Dare we offer a five-star restaurateur a treat from the Golden Arches?" RuthClaire asked.

"Under ordinary circumstances, only at your peril. Promise not to tell anyone, though, and tonight I'll discreetly humble myself."

I ate the cheeseburger. Adam produced a second one. I ate that cheeseburger, too. For dessert, RuthClaire handed me a (badly needed) breath mint. Then off we drove, a nondescript pickup truck materializing about midway along the block behind us and tailing us all the way to the gallery.

THE *ENCYCLOPAEDIA BRITANNICA* defines "abraxas" as "a composite word composed of Greek letters formerly inscribed on charms, amulets, and gems in the belief that it possessed magical qualities."

In Atlanta, the gallery called Abraxas is an influential but underfunded alternative-arts center in a predominantly black section of the city. The buildings making up the complex—a print shop, a theater, the galleries, and the studio wing—used to belong to a school. With the exception of the print shop and the studio wing, they were built early in the century in a stolid red-brick architectural style giving them the grim look of a prison or an oversized Andrew Carnegie library. Coming toward Abraxas from the east, you swing back and forth along Ralph McGill Boulevard between modest clapboard and brick houses until you attain the crest of a hill that plunges precipitously toward the foot of yet another hill. Abraxas, though, sprawls along the weedy mound of the first hill, partially obscured by the fence of a factory parking lot, and I was cheerfully dive-bombing the Mercedes past the gallery when Adam reached over to touch my arm and RuthClaire cried, "Stop, Paul, you're missing it!"

My first good look at Abraxas left me chilled and skeptical. A one-person show at this abandoned school, I mused, could hardly have any more cachet or impact than a violin recital in a one-car garage in Butte, Montana. Adam's show was clearly small potatoes. The movers and shakers of the Atlanta art community had granted him this venue because his work had nothing but its novelty ("Prehistoric human relic actually puts paint to canvas!") to recommend it. More than likely, they had given him this show as a courteous bow to RuthClaire, almost certainly in the hope that she would contribute to the center's funding.

117

This decaying three-story shell of chipped brick and sagging drainpipes was Abraxas?

RuthClaire seemed to be monitoring my thoughts. "It's better inside. You have to park around back."

The lot had already begun to fill. We had to inch along behind earlier arrivals before finding a space beneath an elm tree at the end of the studio wing. Quite a crowd.

"The third-floor gallery has three main rooms," Ruth-Claire explained. "Adam's paintings occupy only one of them. Some of these people have come for the Kander photographs or the Haitian show."

We got out and crossed the lot to a plywood ramp leading into the old school's first-floor corridor. A security guard saluted RuthClaire and Adam and directed us up the cold interior stairs to the third floor. To my surprise, little inside the building contradicted my first impression of it as a candidate for the wrecking ball. At last, a formidable door confronted us, preventing entry to the gallery. Adam pressed a buzzer on the crumbling wall next to the door.

"I need a password," said a muffled male voice beyond it.

"Chief Noc-a-homa," RuthClaire replied. This was the name—the stage name, so to speak—of the Indian who was the official mascot of the Atlanta Braves. It was also the necessary password. The door opened.

"Welcome to the Deep South franchise of Cloud-Cuckoo-Land," said a tall, disheveled man in a frazzled, lime-colored sweater and a gray corduroy jacket with elbow patches of such bituminous blackness that it looked as if they would leave smudges on any surface they happened to touch. In fact, he held his elbows close to his sides as if to keep from leaving charcoal blots here and there about the gallery.

This was David Blau. He was nearly my age, but he exuded a boyish enthusiasm that seemed to be a permanent attribute of his character. RuthClaire made the introductions, and we went around the corner into the director's huge, drafty "office." In the middle of the room, a set of unfinished stairs climbed to a jutting mezzanine that may have been a jerrybuilt studio loft. A lumpy sofa squatted with its back to the steps.

People milled about between the sofa and its coffee table, between Blau's desk and a metal desk piled high with tabloid art publications. Other people, wine glasses in hand, were sitting on either the steps or the sofa, chatting, laughing, clearly enjoying themselves. Blau said they had a perfect right. Most of them had been working hard for the past ten days to make this opening possible. A woman in designer jeans and high heels approached us with a tray of wine glasses and decanters of both burgundy and white. Each of us took a stem, and even Adam drank, sipping at the rim of his glass as suavely as any cocktail-party veteran.

"Hey, Paul," RuthClaire whispered, "still think this is the Siberia of Atlanta's art world?"

Blau overheard her. "It's the High Museum that's the real Siberia," he said. "Every time I look at it I see a heap of trash-compacted igloos."

"I like it," RuthClaire said. "It's a lovely building."

"It's cold," Blau retorted. "Cold and sterile."

"You're not responding to the architecture, David. You're responding to the fact that its exhibition policies are different from your own."

"Southern artists can get shown in Amsterdam or Mexico City more easily than at the High," Blau told me. "The High's safe. Colorful abstracts with no troubling political or social messages. Artists harmlessly dead or with one foot in some collector's anonymous Swiss bank account."

"It's *supposed* to be safe, at least in comparison to Abraxas. It's Abraxas that's supposed to be dangerous."

"Is Abraxas dangerous?" I asked Blau.

The *Journal-Constitution* art reporter—a young man with the clean-shaven look of a stockbroker—interrupted this conversation to ask RuthClaire if he could interview Adam. RuthClaire made a be-my-guest gesture and hooked arms with Blau and me to escort us in prankish lockstep out of the curator's office and into the first gallery room. I glanced back over my shoulder to see the reporter and Adam eyeing each other with polite perplexity. Adam's, however, was feigned.

"That wasn't fair," I told RuthClaire. "That guy didn't strike me as another Barrington."

"He'll survive. Maybe he knows sign language."

"What about Adam? Isn't it awkward for him, too?"

"He appreciates the humor of the situation. It's the reporter who'll blink first, believe me."

Blau swept an arm at the walls of the spacious new chamber—careful, though, to keep his elbow tight against his side. "Is Abraxas dangerous? Hell, yes, Mr. Loyd."

I looked around. The white plaster or Sheetrock walls rose to a height of ten feet or so. Above them, extending another ten or twelve feet, were the cold red bricks of the old school's outer walls. Ceiling fans with wooden blades, motionless now, hung down from the shadows of the loft space. Then I dropped my eyes to the banners and paintings of the Haitian exhibit.

"Witch-doctor territory," Blau said, laughing. "This is one of the best collections of primitive Caribbean art ever put on display in the South. We did backflips to get it."

"Expensive?"

Blau shook his hand at the wrist. "Under this administration, military bands receive more government money than does the entire National Endowment for the Arts."

Dazzling tropical colors and bustling marketplaces danced in their frames on the Sheetrock. I liked what I saw. This painting was recognizably a portrait, that a landscape, and this a street scene. The banners interspersed among the paintings were more puzzling. They featured beaded or sequined designs on long strips of silk or velvet. Even so, their cabalistic patterns seemed right at home in a gallery billing itself Abraxas.

"What's dangerous about these items?" I asked.

"By themselves, I guess, not much—unless *vaudun*, the Haitian voodoo religion, intimidates you. The banners you see here are what Haitian priests and witches call *vevés*. On the island itself, they're laid out on the ground in meal or corn flour. They're ceremonial drawings that play a role in the creation of trance states among *vaudun* initiates. Ours were made by real Haitians, of course, but they're only replicas of the *vevés* you might see in one of the canopy-covered temples during a real ceremony."

"The thing that's dangerous about this exhibit," Ruth-Claire said, "is that David and the others have put articles about the Duvalier government and our treatment of the Haitian boat people in odd places around the room. David's originally from Brooklyn. A radical-pinko-commie with a monthly car payment."

Blau put one arm across his midriff and bowed.

"What made you decide to go after Haitian art?" I asked him.

"To tell you the truth, Adam. He's from a little island off the Haitian coast."

"Paul knows," RuthClaire said. "That's how we got our surname."

"Anyway," Blau continued, "it seems that Adam's people—the habiline remnant he was raised among—had occasional contact with members of the *vaudun* cult. The cult has its roots in West Africa, among the Arada-Dahomey Kingdoms, and even though Adam's ancestors come from East Africa, they share their continent of origin and their negritude with the voodooists. The *African-ness* of the habilines and the majority of poor Haitians unites the two groups. It's a mystical thing, I'm afraid."

RuthClaire said, "Paul was convinced that a show in this old building was tantamount to deep-sixing an artist's work in the Chattahoochee."

"Not a bit of it," said the gallery director, taking her arm. "Let's show Mr. Loyd what *really* scares the more conservative members of our board."

We turned left into a small chamber with one strange, inward-curving wall, and I looked a question at RuthClaire.

"Eroticism," she explained. "Radical politics upsets fewer people than does graphic sex or nudity."

"Especially if it has a racial or religious angle," Blau added.

"Right. You get red faces and resignations and withdrawn funding pledges."

"Especially withdrawn funding pledges," Blau said.

"Then why bother to show it?" I asked.

At which point I discovered that on the chamber's curved wall, and on the two long straight walls connecting with it, were arrayed thirty or forty large black-and-white photographs in simple chromium frames. A piece of Plexiglas as big as an automobile's windshield hung eight feet off the floor in the center of the room, and inside it was the word

STEREOTYPES

in thick, emphatic red letters, with the photographer's name—Maria-Katherine Kander—in much smaller characters beneath it. The photographs jumped out at me like a sudden angry slap.

"Holy Christ," I murmured.

"They're best taken one at a time, in small doses," Blau told me. "But in here, I'm afraid, you'll have to prepare for a full-scale assault. Have a gander. We'll stay out of your way."

So he and RuthClaire drew back so that I could prowl along the curved wall looking at Ms. Kander's outrageous photographs. The first I stopped at, and studied, showed an angular black woman lying naked on her back on a sterile white sheet. Stacked between her legs, and in turgid piles around her thighs and belly, lay at least a dozen tiger-striped watermelons, a veritable gang-banging team of watermelons. The expression on the woman's face suggested nothing short of complacent ecstasy.

I moved on.

A subsequent photograph was a frontal nude of a black man from the shoulders down and the thighs up. This faceless man had a daunting erection. At an upward angle paralleling that of his hard-on, he was holding the ebony barrel of a submachine-gun. I blinked and moved on. Next, an anorexic white woman in high heels and leather panties was lowering her mouth to the head of a microphone held out to her by a disdainful rock musician with an electric guitar draped across his body. Yet another photograph featured a sunken-eyed man in concentration-camp garb, a star of David stenciled on his arm band, gripping the bars of a bank vault. Ingots of gold bullion—like so many loaves of gilded bread—were visible on the shelves behind him.

An even more elaborate photograph showed a priest in a heavy cassock speaking to a congregation of naked parishioners, with his fingers crossed behind his back. Some of the people in the pews were fondling each other, while a few of the more elderly worshipers, pathetic in their wrinkles, frowned or slept. At the altar below the priest—the picture had been taken from behind his head—knelt a chimpanzee in black tie and tails, a top hat on its head. I wondered at the length of time it must have required to stage that one.

Blau approached. "What's the verdict?"

"They're genuinely offensive. They seem to be *trying* to offend me."

"They are."

"They succeed."

"If you say so," Blau replied, "yes, they do."

"Succeed in offending me?"

"In offending you and in fulfilling the artist's intention."

"That intention being to offend?"

RuthClaire appeared at my elbow. "You've got it."

"Good," I said. "Until just now I was pretty sure you guys would regard my taking offense as middle class and unhip."

"No," Blau conceded, "they're definitely offensive."

RuthClaire nodded agreement. *"Intrinsically* offensive."

"Offensive in an absolute sense," Blau added.

We stood there in the gallery room looking at the definitely offensive, intrinsically offensive—offensive in an almost absolute sense—photographs of Maria-Katherine Kander. Our abashed reverence before these disgusting artifacts began to irk me. Their "eroticism"—I hadn't seen anything that truly qualified—seemed to consist primarily of exposed flesh and simulated acts of fetishistic sodomy. Despite RuthClaire's implied disclaimer, I saw them as pornographic *political* statements. They were racist, misogynist, fascist, anticlerical, and maybe a dozen other things too twisted or subtle to pinpoint. Antievolutionary? Pro-consumerism? I had no clear idea. But their offensiveness was beyond question.

"What's the goddamn point?"

"Paul, try not to get ridiculously worked up over this."

"You mean there are *degrees* of offense that it's unhip to take? I thought I could get as goddamn offended as I liked." I appealed to David Blau. "All I'm asking is what's the goddamn point of taking pictures that are *meant* to offend?"

"Really," he replied, "it would be out of bounds for me to try to speak for Ms. Kander. Worse, you'd probably take it as some sort of definitive statement or explanation of her intent, which wouldn't be fair to either the artist or you."

"Criminy!" I exclaimed. "Who is this gal, anyway? Her name sounds German or Austrian. Is she a Nazi?"

RuthClaire, who had an ostensibly calming hand on my arm, said, "I don't know her ethnic background. She's from Tennessee."

"She doesn't live in Atlanta," I hazarded. "She'd be an idiot to show such crap here—in this neighborhood, in a city with a black mayor—and try to live here, too."

"She's based in New York City," Blau admitted, "but she could live in Atlanta if she wished. Atlantans are more knowledgeable about contemporary art than you might think."

"Unlike your average hick from Beulah Fork?"

"Paul," RuthClaire said, "let's go see Adam's work." She put a little gentle pressure on my arm. "Before the crowd comes in."

"Wait a minute. I want to know David's interpretation of Ms. Kander's intent."

"But that would be to preempt—"

"RuthClaire, for God's sake, let me talk to the man." I rounded on Blau. "Look, I've got a mind of my own. You won't unduly influence my own final stance. I'm trying to understand—to *appreciate*—these photographs. Isn't that what a show is for, to prompt greater understanding and appreciation of an artist's work?''

Blau surrendered to my tirade. ''Okay, you're passionate about this. That's good. You deserve an answer.''

I waited.

''I think Kander's attempts to offend are motivated by a desire to heighten our outrage at the stereotypes she presents. It's satire, Mr. Loyd, not a call to embrace what you see as, God forbid, *accurate* depictions of the people involved. Her technique forces you to reassess your basic attitude about each image. The art's not only in her skills as a photographer, but in the outrageous scenes she stages for the camera. I get off on that. The young lady's droll.''

''That's one word for it,'' I said. ''But is that how everybody who walks in here's going to interpret her work?''

''Oh, no. Some'll take one look, turn around, and walk out. Others won't see anything but naked flesh. For them it's pornography, and they'll either enjoy it or scorn it as such.''

I waved at the walls. ''Is this stuff for sale?''

''Prints are. That's how Ms. Kander makes her living. By today's standards, they're dirt cheap—but Kander's popular and sells in volume.''

''Who's she popular with? Voyeurs? The artsy-fartsy crowd?''

''Both, I guess. There's no form to fill out to buy one. So far as I know, you don't even have to be twenty-one.''

''Where would you hang these things? The bathroom?''

''That's up to you. Are you thinking of ordering one?''

''Hell, no!'' I virtually shouted.

Adam arrived in the company of a staff member named Bonnie Carlin, but I was still hot about the rub-your-nose-in-your-own-smug-prejudices strategy of Kander's ''art.'' Everything Blau had said about it made a kind of backass-wards sense, but I kept telling myself that for all her cleverness and technical skill she was really accomplishing the Unnecessary, often for the Uncomprehending, and al-

most always with a (pardon me) Drollery that bespoke a
superior smugness all her own.

Phooey, as Lester Maddox used to like to say.

Bonnie Carlin delivered a message—it was time to let
the clamoring crowd in—and departed. We, too, abandoned the M.-K. Kander Room, crossing the corridor into
the third and final gallery room, where Adam's paintings
were the main attractions.

This room was like the first, but not so large. A single
darkened studio loft brooded above us. Below it, all four
walls seemed to resonate with the vitality and prehistoric
wildness that Adam—who had even begun to wear deodorant—
would no longer permit himself to reveal in his day-to-day
relationships with others.

I saw the huge barbed baobab that he had painted at
Paradise Farm. I saw rolling silver-brown mounds that
could have been either the Lolitabu foothills or a herd of
headless mammoths on a dusty African plain. I saw grass
fires, volcanic eruptions, jags of icy lightning, and a crowd
of silhouetted human (or semihuman) forms either fighting
or feasting or copulating. I also saw a series of ambiguous
mother-and-child portraits that could have been of RuthClaire
and Tiny Paul, or of a baboon female and her capering
infant, or even of a genderless adult attacking a much
smaller figure of the same unidentifiable, but monkeylike,
species. There was also a painting of a hominid creature
with the head of a dog or a jackal or a hyena, and around
its head there glowed a brilliant orange-red light. The exhibit as a whole communicated energy and excitement. By
my standards, very good stuff.

Demurely, Adam hung back, his hands behind him. His
eyes shifted from side to side, as if fearful that I might
ridicule this painting or maybe even take umbrage at something and walk out. At Paradise Farm, he had had no such
qualms. Here, though, as the only artist actually on the
premises, he appeared to be suffering a terrific bout of the
butterflies.

"They're good," I told him. "I like 'em all."

The artist gave me a smile. His lips drew back to reveal
teeth and gums. Then, flustered, he pursed them shut again.

By the terms of his contract with Abraxas, Adam had to stick around long enough to meet some of the general public at the opening. Members of the board of directors who had not been able to attend the reception would want to greet him, as would some of the wealthier patrons who always arrived late. Moreover, Blau encouraged his artists to talk to students, impulse visitors, reporters from the Atlanta papers, and other media people. Temperamental aloofness could hurt fund-raising efforts.

The reception officially ended, and the crowd swarmed in. Adam and RuthClaire withdrew to Gallery Number Three to receive congratulations and autograph Abraxas flyers. As for me, I retreated to Blau's office and poured myself the last half-glass of Asti Spumante from the only decanter not already empty. When I had finished this, I wandered into Gallery Number One.

The Haitian art was scoring heavily with tonight's visitors. I had to reposition my shoulders every few steps to slide through the pockets of people discussing it. Gallery Number Two, featuring Kander's work, was also packed. Still flushed with admiration or embarrassment, two women squeezed out of that chamber into the hall.

"It's a wonder the place hasn't been raided," one of them said.

"Goodness, Doreen, the woman's making a *statement*."

I followed Doreen and her scandalized friend into Gallery Number Three. The Montarazes, huddled together for mutual protection, stood at the front of a ladderlike contraption giving access to the loft overhead. The sight of one of the hangers-on surrounding them brought me up short.

There before me—in checked shirt, green knit tie, dun pants, and fake suede jacket—slouched Brian Nollinger,

127

the anthropologist from Emory, the Judas who had tried to turn Adam over to an agent of the Immigration and Naturalization Service. He had shaved his Fu Manchu, but his granny glasses and his air of unflappable belonging—"Why would these people be unhappy to see me here?"—identified him to me more certainly than a fingerprint check. And it was no comfort remembering that but for my own jealous meddling Nollinger might not have come into any of our lives. In a sense, I had *created* him. As an ongoing annoyance, if not as a human being.

"What the hell are you doing here?"

Nollinger turned. "Hello, Mr. Loyd. I came to see the show."

"How long does it take you to see it?"

"Well—"

"You don't know a damn thing about art. You're the kind of gallery-goer who thinks Winslow Homer was a blind Greek poet."

"Look, if it's okay with you, I came to apologize."

"For calling me an enemy of science?" RuthClaire asked. "For accusing me of keeping my own private slave?"

For a moment, Nollinger looked genuinely embarrassed. "Yes, ma'am, I regret that. I was feuding with Alistair Patrick Blair."

I shooed the other hangers-on away. "A scholarly feud excuses you of slinging mud at an innocent woman?"

"I had no idea she was going to marry Adam, Mr. Loyd. At least I believed the creature—the person—under her roof was a living representative of *Homo habilis*. That was more than Blair was willing to concede. Give me that much credit."

"Are you still shooting monkeys up with No Dōz?"

That was a rabbit punch. The whites of Nollinger's weary eyes swung toward me. "I concluded those researches long ago. I've been trying to get a grant for some field work outside the States. But this isn't an easy time to find funding."

"So you showed up here to put the pinch on RuthClaire and Adam, I take it."

He shook his head, less in denial than in pity for the depth of my pettiness and suspicion. But one amazing consequence of this exchange was that RuthClaire had actually begun to turn a sympathetic eye on the man. She lacked the constitution for a sustained grudge. A character trait from which I, too, had benefited.

Nollinger gestured at the painting nearest us. "I'll tell you the truth. Another of my reasons for coming was professional. You see, I've always taken an interest in documented cases of the creative impulse in collateral species."

The poor fool was digging his own pitfall. I decided to lend him a hand. "What kind of cases, Dr. Nollinger?"

"Well, some years back, a chimpanzee in the London Zoo learned to draw and paint. He became downright proficient at putting circles and crosslike designs on canvas."

"A chimpanzee?" RuthClaire said.

"That's right. I believe his name was Congo. They gave him his own show. He even sold some paintings. The literature calls it the first documented exhibit of subhuman art in history."

RuthClaire's eyes had narrowed. "Are you trying to tell us that this is the second?"

Nollinger was not an utter idiot. His face turned red. "N-no, of c-course not. It's just that . . . well, w-w-we're all primates, you know. The impulse for self-expression may be b-basic to every primate species."

Abruptly, Adam turned and climbed the wrought-iron ladder into the gallery loft. Once there, he squatted in the shadows like a lissome Quasimodo.

"Go away, please," RuthClaire said.

"Wait a minute," Nollinger pleaded. "This is a public exhibit. You can't run me off."

"Have you seen the photographic exhibit?" I asked him. Mindful of the time I had hit him, he took a step backward. "You'll like 'em. Each and every one of them is an insult to people of taste and intelligence."

"I'm trying to talk to the Montarazes."

"You're going into the Kander exhibit." I turned

Nollinger around and headed him toward Gallery Number Two. He tried to yank away, but I applied a bouncer hold and marched him out.

Fear of creating a scene prevented Nollinger from resisting me further. I took advantage of that scruple—at least he had *one*—to deposit him in front of a photograph of an American Plains Indian with an empty fifth of Wild Turkey in one hand and the blonde scalp of a white girl-woman in the other. This comatose nymphet wore only a black-lace teddy and lay prostrate at the big chief's feet.

"Here you go," I said. "Another fascinating instance of the primate creative impulse."

This photograph, and the others around it, mesmerized Brian Nollinger, and I left him there in the crowded gallery room.

DAVID BLAU helped us escape Abraxas without running a gauntlet of reporters. We used an auxiliary stairwell to get away, emerging in the parking lot to find that it had stopped raining. Water glistened on the asphalt, and the trees dripped diamonds. In one patch of sky, a few fretful stars were trying to blink aside the cloud cover.

We drove to Patrick's, a restaurant in Little Five Points, and asked for a table away from the long storefront windows facing Moreland Avenue. Here we ordered more white wine, with a fresh spinach salad and a breast-of-chicken entrée. Because Nollinger had rained on Adam's parade, we had a hard time sustaining conversation.

"Consider the source and forget it," I told Adam. "Your opening was packed. How often does that happen?"

"Rarely," RuthClaire said. "Not often at all."

"There, you see? It's a triumph, Adam. Forget about Nollinger's fatuous faux pas."

Adam wiped his fingers on a linen napkin. Leaning back

in his chair, he signed gracefully in the candle-lit dining room. Adam (according to RuthClaire's translation) did not regard the turnout at Abraxas as a personal triumph. At least half the people there had taken advantage of the respectability implicit in a gallery opening to ogle Kander's photographs. The most knowledgeable and devoted gallery patrons, Adam went on, had come for the Haitian exhibit. Indeed, those who had come to see his paintings (people like Nollinger, for instance) were motivated less by any faith in the potential importance of Adam's work than by simple curiosity. What sort of Rorschach blotches would a living hominid anachronism put to canvas?

Half Adam's meal remained untouched. RuthClaire reached out and gripped him fondly on one side of his neck, massaging the taut sinews with a gentle hand. He closed his eyes, enduring this display of affection as if unworthy of it. Once upon a time, I knew, I would have killed to experience such tenderness at RuthClaire's hands. *Once upon a time?*

From my jacket I removed the letters that the Montarazes had sent me in December. I shook out Adam's and tilted it in the candle glow so that I could read it.

" 'One day this year Miss RuthClaire may ask you to come see about her seeing about me. Some doctors at Emory are plotting now a surgery to humanize me for this time and place. Do please come when she asks.' " Gallantly, I did not read the parts offering to reimburse me for my time and authorizing his wife and me to use the same bed if we both agreed to the "niceness" of that arrangement. "Any comments?"

"What do you want to know?" RuthClaire finally asked.

"What kind of surgery? When's it supposed to happen? When will you need me? Why so secretive?"

"You'll come?"

"I've already said so."

RuthClaire looked at Adam. He nodded a curt okay. "This summer," she said. "It's plastic surgery of an exacting kind. The point is to enable Adam to speak. It involves reshaping the entire buccal cavity—without deforming his facial features.'' She gave her husband a smile. "Hey, fella, I love that face." To me, she said, "There's work to be done on his vocal cords and larynx, too. Don't ask me to explain it all. It's already required several X-ray sessions, a couple of plaster castings, and more psycho-medical consultations than you'd expect a candidate for a sex change to sit through."

"Adam's going to be able to—" I turned one hand into a gibbering puppet. "—talk?"

"That's the basic idea."

I sat back in my chair. This particular basic idea had never occurred to me. Adam an orator? Picturing him talking—like Brad Barrington or Dwight "Happy" Mc-Elroy—gave me an uneasy feeling. What impact would the ability have on him? On others? Would my acceptance of him—my commitment to him as a *friend*—gradually diminish as he asserted his own personality and opinions through the medium of direct speech? Did my regard for Adam have its source in heretofore disguised feelings of superiority?

"What's the matter, Paul?"

"How much is this going to cost?"

"Lots."

"That's what I figured."

"For something this crucial, we've got it to spend." She eyed me shrewdly. "You don't approve?"

"Sure," I said. "It sounds great. Adam and I'll be able to commiserate about the weather."

What was the matter with me? I had accepted so much else about Adam—his marriage to RuthClaire, his biological compatability with my former wife, his developing literacy, and even the half-pathetic sincerity of his spiritual yearnings. Why couldn't I accept his desire to talk? To put my seemingly selfish reluctance in the best possible light, maybe I had a faint intimation of all the trouble looming ahead for us.

RuthClaire paid the bill, but I insisted on leaving the tip.

WE RETURNED in my car to the sprawling Montaraz bordello-cum-boarding house on Hurt Street. It was too late to play with Tiny Paul, but when we looked in on him sleeping in his bassinet, I was startled to see his dreaming features betray a hint of the feral self-sufficiency that only a moment ago, leaving Patrick's, I had seen in his father's face. All babies have something endearingly simian or pongid about them, but there in the sheen of his night light my godson's resemblance to a "collateral primate"—yes, a baby gorilla!—brought the forests of the Virunga Mountains of Uganda right into a bedroom near Inman Park.

Life is strange, I thought, and I kissed the kid so that we could withdraw and leave him to his sleep.

RuthClaire pointed me to a second-story guestroom wallpapered with a repeating pattern of pale green bamboo shoots, and Adam nodded me a friendly goodnight on his way downstairs to drive Pan Sorrells home. Alone, sitting on my bed, a paperback novel in my hands, I thought of Adam's naive invitation to share a bed with his wife while he was in the hospital—if, of course, we both agreed to the "niceness" of the sharing.

How could I tell RuthClaire's new husband that tonight I wanted her beside me not to ravish but to cherish, not to penetrate but to pet? These days, away from the West Bank, it was loneliness rather than sexual desire that ate at me, and that, of course, was why I kept myself so busy. At last I put the paperback down, heel-and-toed my shoes off, turned out the light, and stretched out to await the onset of sleep. It delayed and delayed, but eventually, two or maybe even three hours later, came.

I spent Wednesday with the Montarazes, most of which we devoted to a tour of the High Museum on Peachtree Street, and on Thursday returned to Beulah Fork.

Business continued to boom. People came in and went out, and so did money. I yelled at Livia George, she glared in insulted contempt at me, the dristles of winter gave way to the hurricanes of spring, soldiers of twenty or more nations died in almost all the senseless ways it is possible to die, dining-room help arrived and departed, and the president of the United States asked Congress to okay funds for a defense force of mutant giant pandas with which to protect the Aleutian Islands from Soviet invasion.

Something like that. I was too busy to pay more than passing heed to weather, war, and politics.

AT LAST the summons came. I got to Atlanta on the day after Adam had undergone the nearly six-hour surgical procedure designed to give him the ability to speak. I would have been there for the operation itself but RuthClaire deliberately delayed asking me to come until the following morning, when it was already clear that her husband was out of danger. Whether all the tinkering would have the desired effect remained a question of prime concern, but not whether Adam would live or die. All this, defying the possibility of a tap, RuthClaire had told me in a telephone call—but when I reached Emory Hospital, I was still angry about not having been given the chance to sit with her during the actual surgery.

RuthClaire met me in a corridor below the pagodalike parking tower where I had left my car. She was wearing a white cotton blouse with scrollish cutouts in the collar, a seersucker skirt, and a pair of Italian sandals. She had a baby-carrier on her back, but it was empty because Tiny Paul, not yet nine months old, was standing at her knee gripping one of her fingers with a tentative hand.

I could not believe it. T.P., whom I had last seen zonked in his bassinet, was walking. He wore navy-blue shorts, a powder-blue shirt, and a pair of minuscule tennis shoes with racing chevrons. There was nothing even remotely gorillaish about his appearance today. No baby fat, no leathery sheen on his forehead. As I approached him and his mother along the corridor, he eyed me with the solemnity of a pint-sized state legislator.

"Don't start in," RuthClaire said, raising her free hand in warning. "Everything's fine."

I knelt in front of the kid to give him a gentle poke in the breadbasket. His gums pulled away from his teeth in a . . . well, a *smarl*, which is to say a smile and a snarl so perfectly meshed that they are identical.

"He's really grown. How long's he been walking?"

"Since April, Paul. He's a dynamo. All the activity's slimmed him down."

"Walking at five months? Does he talk, too?"

That one earned me a reproving glance. "His father's just had an operation to permit him to speak, and here you are asking me if our son's talking yet. Do you want to make me cry?"

"RuthClaire—"

"Some children don't begin talking until they're two or more. It's nothing to be worrying about."

"Listen, I'm sorry. I didn't mean to—"

"Come on," she said angrily. "Let's go see Adam."

We averted an argument by walking to the elevators at the far end of the echoing corridor. T.P. kept up with us with an effortless trot, like an Ethiopian conscript of the 1940s jogging to the front.

Upstairs, the nurses at the nurses' station got our names and let us proceed down the hall to Adam's room. It was a long walk. I used it to begin berating my ex-wife for not calling me sooner, but she cut me off with a recitation of all the people who had already been by to see her and lend moral support.

"You don't need me anymore, do you?"

"Give that man a cigar. He's finally figured out the full implications of our divorce."

"Why call me at all, then?"

"Because Adam thinks you should be here. He's trying to be the alpha-male of our household, appointing a lieutenant until he's well enough to return."

Like an invisible tide of warm honey, a mellifluous laugh came rolling out of Adam's room.

"What the hell was that?" I asked RuthClaire. "Not Adam?"

"We've got a visitor. He stopped by yesterday, too. I'd've run him off if Adam hadn't begged me before the operation to let the clown come calling." RuthClaire set Tiny Paul down, and the kid trotted into his father's room. "Come see."

We entered the room after the precocious toddler, who was already in the male visitor's arms. Adam lay on the bed beside them, his mummy-wrapped face tilted toward the door. An IV bottle on a pole dripped glucose into his bloodstream.

"Paul Loyd," RuthClaire said, "meet the Right Reverend Dwight McElroy."

Most television evangelists, I had long ago decided, looked like affluent mobile-home salesmen. An eye tic or a single unruly forelock of pomaded hair was the sole outward manifestation of the emotional kink that kept their motors going. But McElroy, whom I had watched for only a few fascinated weeks on his syndicated "Great Gospel Giveaway," did not fit this mold. Prematurely gray (or post-pubescently silver), he had the aristocratic mien of a European count. At the same time, though, I had no trouble dressing him out in basketball togs and putting him at the power-forward position for a team like the Celtics. He was too old for that, of course, but he appeared to be in great shape—lean, muscular, alert, and, in spite of his lank (rather than blown-dry) silver hair, facially collegiate.

Carrying T.P., the leader of the rigorously Protestant but otherwise scrupulously nondenominational Greater Christian Constituency of America, Inc., strode toward me with his hand out. When he smiled, the count gave way to the down-home suggestion of a farm kid come to the big city in a borrowed suit.

"Just call me Happy, Paul. None of this Right Reverend business, now. Sometimes it flat wears me out."

"Me, too," RuthClaire said.

Warily, I shook the proffered hand. "I'm not a fan of yours, Happy. Forgive me for saying so."

"Well, I'm not a fisher of fans, Paul. I'm a fisher of souls."

"Any bites?"

"Why, they're always biting, Paul. They're just waiting to be fed." (I knew the feeling.) "That's why I try to keep my lines in the water."

"And your hooks out?"

He knew he was being baited (as the Elizabethans baited bears, not as a southern angler readied a worm for skewering), but he neither laughed foolishly nor surrendered outright to my barb. He gave me an understanding smile and bounced T.P. lightly against his flank with one arm. "And my hooks out," he acknowledged. "The kind that don't tear, that lift one up into the sun." He smiled again, as if to illustrate his meaning with a show of teeth.

I turned to RuthClaire. What was this joker doing here? A little more than a year ago, he had condemned her from the pulpit as a twentieth-century sodomite. He had spoken with great force on two matters about which he undoubtedly remained acutely ignorant, evolutionary theory and the exact nature of RuthClaire and Adam's relationship. I wondered if the man had any shame at all. Summarizing my objections to his presence, I asked him if he did.

"I don't feel out of place here, Paul. Why? Well, it's simply not possible for me to hate the sinner as much as I do the sin. In fact, I don't hate the sinner at all. I *love* him."

Adam, I noticed, was watching us. His eyes were pleading with RuthClaire to forgive their visitor—this rich, nationally famous fool for Christ—the particular foolishness that had wounded her so deeply a year ago.

T.P. had begun to squirm. McElroy set him down. Then he said, "They say your husband's a *habiline*, Mrs. Montaraz. What exactly is that, for mercy's sake? From three states away, ma'am, I supposed everybody was making a fuss over some naked monkey out of some hard-to-get-to foreign jungle. 'A surviving representative of a prehuman species,' that one fella said. Well, I didn't believe that then, and I don't believe it now.''

He gestured at Adam, prostrate under a stiff hospital sheet. "That's not a habiline. That's not a ape. That's a man. The proof is you married him, ma'am. The further proof of it's this gift of God hanging on your skirt. And *people*, Mrs. Montaraz, I can't he'p but love. I love Adam. I love you. I love your little boy. If I seemed to dump hellfire on y'all last year, that was because I hadn't yet come to know you and Adam for the fine people you are.

"It's likewise because I was supposing—along with millions of other folks the wide country 'round—exactly what the liberal press and all them high-profile network TV folks *wanted* us to suppose, namely, that Adam was a ape. A naked ape. Because that made a good story. Well, he's not a ape. He's a man. And the only sin either of you was guilty of is that of an *appearance* of impropriety in the eyes of the press and so in the eyes of some of us who, let me admit, should've known better'n to believe what we saw in our papers and heard broadcast at us over our TVs. So I'm asking you to forgive me for preaching you and your husband up as an instance of this troubled country's moral decay. Even Ol' Happy's human, ma'am.''

"I didn't know that," I said. "How would you feel if instead of forgiving you, they sued?"

McElroy flicked me an annoyed look, but recovered and again importuned RuthClaire: "I'm quite serious about the fullness of my sorrow over this. On the next 'Gospel Giveaway' I do in Rehoboth, well, I'll make you a *re*-tract, a completely sincere and thorough *re*-tract. It would be my real pleasure." He paused to assess the effect of this offer on RuthClaire. "Of course, it's my *duty* to do it, too," he quickly added. "But it would be my pleasure as well. I mean that.''

Wearily, RuthClaire removed the empty baby-carrier

from her back and slid it gently across the floor to the foot
of Adam's bed. Then she crossed the room and sat down
in the folding chair that McElroy had been using. T.P.
trotted after her. She collared him and absentmindedly
began knuckling his miniature Afro.

The evangelist spread his hands. "Well? Can you forgive me?"

"It would be my pleasure, Mr. McElroy, if you'd just
leave Adam and me *out* of your broadcast."

"Nothing else?"

"That'd be plenty. Oh, you could find Paul a chair.
And one for yourself if you're going to stick around any
longer."

McElroy smiled, did a heel click, and departed to look
for two more folding chairs. I shuffled to the end of the
bed, grabbed my friend's toes through the sheet, and
wobbled them affectionately back and forth. He, in turn,
smiled at me with his eyes.

Considering the simplicity of his task, McElroy was
gone an awfully long time. RuthClaire took advantage of
his absence to fill me in. The man had come to Atlanta,
and specifically to the Emory campus, at the invitation of
the Institute for World Evangelism at Candler Theological
Seminary. He had been in the city three days, speaking to
seminary students and faculty at a variety of venues, including the William R. Cannon Chapel, one of the auditoria
in White Hall, and the sanctuary of the Glenn Memorial
United Methodist Church across North Decatur Road from
Emory Village. Adam had purposely scheduled his surgery
to coincide with McElroy's visit. Indeed, he had written
the evangelist a letter explaining the operation's purpose,
asking him to look in on RuthClaire during the delicate
procedure, and requesting, too, a personal visit from the
busy Right Reverend once the hospital staff had transferred
him to a recovery room.

Adam had improved his chances for a favorable response by including with the letter a $250 contribution to
McElroy's television ministry. He had also worked to
pique the man's curiosity (an instance, considering the

national appetite for news of the couple and their child, of almost touching overkill) by outlining for him his largely unguided religious researches over the past ten months. Now, though, he wanted an authoritative pronouncement about his spiritual state. Did he, or did he not, possess a "soul"?

McElroy had replied that of course he did. On the other hand, he ought to give over the Biblically unsound, and altogether soul-destroying, notion that he belonged to a prehuman species out of which yet another prehuman species had arisen, and so on. A belief like that, denying the straightforward creation account in Genesis, would put the soul in mortal jeopardy. Adam was obviously sincere in his questing, but sadly misled about which direction to go by today's God-lost scientists and technocrats. McElroy would feel privileged to counsel with Adam, even to pray with him, while he was at Emory Hospital.

"He wrote McElroy?" I asked incredulously. "Sent him money?"

"Oh, yes, most definitely. Adam's keeping his options open. He's written letters to the Pope, the Dalai Lama, the Jehovah's Witnesses, the chief elder of the Mormons, two or three ayatollahs in Iran, and a couple of the voodoo artist-priests who exhibited work at Abraxas back in February. If it meditates, sacrifices, or prays, Adam's written to it. Most of his correspondents reply. We have a scrapbook. We're probably going to need another one."

Adam worked his hands free of the sheet and tried to sign. By appearing to concentrate his will, he soon made these gestures distinct enough for RuthClaire to interpret. She must give over her hostility to McElroy, he advised her, for the man was there on his own valuable time to affirm Adam's humanity.

With a folding chair and a chair with a cushion, McElroy returned to the room. On the cushion rested a shiny bedpan in which two or three inches of water shimmered under the room's fluorescents. He was able to set down this chair without sloshing any of the water out of the pan. The metal chair he gave to me to unfold for myself. Then he

placed the bedpan—with a hokey flourish—on the food
tray that swung out from Adam's bed.

"This is distilled water," he said. "I got it at the
nurses' station, and it's physically pure, free of germs and
pollutants."

"Can the same be said of the bedpan?" RuthClaire asked.

"Oh, yes, ma'am. It's been in an autoclave."

"Well, Adam's already had a sponge bath, Reverend
McElroy. I gave him one this morning. There's no need to
repeat it now."

"Has he been baptized?"

"What?"

"Has he received the sacrament of ultimate cleanliness?
Has he been washed in the Blood of the Lamb?"

"From a bedpan?" I wondered aloud.

McElroy laughed. "The Lord and I make do with what's
available. In going without baptism, I fear, Adam's begun
to doubt his possession of the soul that, even now, he's in
danger of leaving in perpetuity to the Prince of Darkness. I
can't allow that, sir."

Her hands on T.P.'s shoulders, RuthClaire stared at
McElroy as if he had proposed dousing Adam with lighter
fluid. "This is in the worst possible taste," she finally
managed.

"You may be right, Mrs. Montaraz. This may be in bad
taste. Damnation has the weight of public favor on its side
nowadays—it's the in thing to shoot for—but it's my
deepest feeling that your husband isn't one to go along
with the crowd simply *because* it's a crowd. Whyn't you
ask him what *he* wants?"

Realizing, I think, that McElroy had played an unan-
swerable trump, RuthClaire pulled Tiny Paul onto her lap
and numbly, disbelievingly, shook her head.

"I'll ask him, then." Looking down on Adam, McElroy
said, "Do you wish to receive the holy benison of baptism?"

With one hand, Adam made the gesture signifying Yes.

RuthClaire shook her head again, not believing that her
husband would consent to what she regarded as a parody
of the baptismal rite—but loving him too much to forbid
him to continue.

The evangelist closed his eyes. He asked God to purify further the water in the bedpan, then immersed his hands, lifted them dripping from the pan, and carried them to Adam's head. Dramatically, he brought them down together on the faint sagittal crest dividing the habiline's skull into hemispheres.

"Be careful," RuthClaire warned him. "Adam's jaw is a jigsaw puzzle of fitted pieces. If you hurt him or slow his healing, I'll . . . ." She didn't know what she would do, but the warning seemed to get through McElroy's devout trance to his understanding.

Crooking his elbows, easing the pressure on Adam's head, he intoned, "Adam Montaraz, husband and father, by the authority invested in me as an ordained minister of the gospel, I hereby baptize you in the name of the Father, the Son, and the Holy Ghost. Amen."

"Amen," I echoed him. It slipped out, this word, impelled, I think, by an unconscious memory of my slipshod Congregationalist upbringing in Tocqueville. RuthClaire, theoretically a believer, gave me a dirty look.

McElroy wiped his hands and turned to her. "I want you to know, Mrs. Montaraz, that I've also lifted a prayer for Adam's speedy recovery."

"Thank you."

"What about that handsome boy there?"

"What about him?"

"Has *he* been baptized?"

RuthClaire folded her arms around T.P. "You've performed your ceremony for the day. It's time for you to leave."

"Delay could be a mortal mistake, ma'am. It could cause—"

"I don't think he's in any terrible danger. Baptists wait until they're twelve or thirteen, don't they?"

"You're not Baptists, ma'am. Neither am I. We at the Greater Christian Constituency embrace the denomination, of course, but my own doctrinal origins are Methodist. We're brother and sister, Mrs. Montaraz."

Adam was signing, feebly but urgently.

"No," RuthClaire answered him. "Absolutely not. If it's done, it'll be done in a church, with a congregation present and a minister in his robes. And this pushy gentleman back in Louisiana counting his take."

When Adam persisted, she grew more vehement: "You're overstepping what you have a right to ask! You're not the only one in this room responsible for your son's spiritual dispensation!"

McElroy said, "There's a Biblical injunction commanding wives to be—"

"Get the holy hell out of here!" RuthClaire yelled at him. T.P. burrowed into her armpit, and Adam's eyes fluttered shut. Like me, the habiline had probably never heard her utter an epithet stronger than "Heck!" or "Drat!"

McElroy appeared ready to keep the argument going, but a portly man and a youth in his late teens or early twenties stopped at Adam's doorway, distracting the evangelist. The younger of the two men reproduced McElroy's lank physique almost exactly.

"C'mon, Daddy," he said. "Dr. Siebert's here to escort you to your next lecture over in White."

"Gotta go," McElroy told us cheerily. "Adam, stay in touch, you hear? It's been a joy, sanctifying you in Christ's sweet name. The boy next time, mebbe."

"Take the stupid bedpan with you," RuthClaire said.

McElroy flashed her a look of disbelief and anger. Before it could turn into something stronger, though, he spoke to his son: "Come get the font, Duncan. I'm finished with it for today."

Duncan McElroy obeyed his father, retrieving the bedpan from the cantilevered tray and carrying it out of the room like a wise man bearing a thurible of perfumed incense. The evangelist gave us all a perfunctory salute, then followed Duncan and Dr. Siebert out of the room— off toward the elevator and another elevating session with some of Candler's theology students.

RuthClaire, wrung out, began very quietly to cry.

OVER THE next week, RuthClaire and I visited Adam every day, spelling each other when the other needed a break. Livia George was managing the restaurant in my absence and having no trouble at all, thank you. I drove down twice to check up on her, but her efficient handling of matters made me feel about as useful there as a training wheel on a tank.

Adam was improving rapidly, but his doctors would not yet permit the removal of his plastic chin support and the bandages holding it in place. So he was still taking nourishment intravenously and talking with us with sign language. Also, he had a lap-sized electric typewriter that he had taught himself to use by the hunt-and-peck method.

McElroy had returned to Louisiana the day after Adam's baptism, but one unsettling consequence of the Bedpan Ceremony was the habiline's frequent recourse to prayer. The Lord's Prayer. The prayer of St. Francis of Assisi beginning, "Lord, make me an instrument of Thy peace." Any number of Old Testament psalms. "Now I Lay Me Down to Sleep." The Pilot's Prayer. The Newspaper Columnist's Prayer. A few obscure Eastern supplications, including Hindu, Buddhist, Taoist, and of course Sufic formulae. And a small anthology of weird but occasionally moving prayers—petitionary prayers—that Adam had written himself.

Indeed, although Adam had accepted baptism in Christ Jesus's name, the prayer ritual in his hospital room had a decidedly ecumenical cast. Here is one of his prayers, typed out on the little machine he used to engage in animated dialogues with us:

Creator, awake or asleep, watchful or drowsing,
Timeless or time-bound,

144

Awake fully to my so-silent cry.
Remember the long-ago dead who loved animals
    and clouds,
Redeem them in your pity-taking Thought.
And those who stumbled on the edge of Spirit,
Who prowled as do hyenas, just beyond the Light,
Think them, too, into the center of the Fire,
Consume them like sweet carrion in the loving warmth
Of your Gut and Mind.

If I am all Animal, Creator,
Give my growls, my whimpers, and my barks
The sound of angels hymning praise.
Let me not sing only for Myself
But also for the billion billion unbaptized Dead
With talons, teeth, and tails to herd them
Into unmarked graves of no importance.
O Gut and Mind above and all about,
Hear my so-silent plea on their behalf
And lift them as you have lifted Men. *Amen*.

After the baptism, every visit to Adam's room concluded with a prayer. Once, both annoyed and impatient, I
asked him what he believed he was accomplishing with
such ritual.

On his lap machine, he typed: THERE IS NO TRUE RELIGION
WITHOUT PRAYER.

That led me to question aloud the value of *religion*, true
or otherwise, and Adam struggled to answer that one, too.
Finally, he typed a single compound word: SELF-DEFINITION.

He seemed to find it amusing that the value of a system-
atic belief in a Higher Power had its ultimate ground in
one's own ego. Was that a contradiction? No, not really.
A paradox? Probably. But, of course, if Adam felt a
greater sense of urgency about his relationship with God
than did most twentieth-century human beings, the ambiguity of his status vis-à-vis both God and his two-legged
fellows fueled that feeling.

"You know," I told him after reading his "Gut and

Mind'' prayer, ''you're assuming there's a rigid line separating the ensouled from the soulless, real human beings from humanoid animals.''

Go on, he signaled.

''You've made it an either/or proposition. But what if there's a gray area where the transition's taking place?''

LIKE THE DUSK SEPARATING DAY FROM NIGHT?

''Exactly.''

I read his next haltingly composed response over his shoulder: I UNDERSTAND, MISTER PAUL, THE BASIS OF HOW YOU ARGUE HERE. THE WORRY ABOUT WHAT AN EARLY HOMINID IS, BEAST OR PERSON. BUT MANY THINGS, I THINK, IT TAKES TO MAKE A CREATURE *HUMAN*, AND IF A CREATURE IS MISSING ONLY ONE OR TWO, I DO NOT BELIEVE IT IS RIGHT TO SAY, AH HA, YOU DO NOT BELONG TO HUMAN SPECIES.

''Okay, Adam, if you believe that human beings have souls, then anyone on this side—*our* side—of the transitional area has one. You're safe because . . . well, because you've successfully interbred with a human woman.''

IT IS NOT THAT EASY.

''Why not?''

BECAUSE A CREATURE GOING THROUGH ANIMALNESS TO HUMANITY—IN THEORY, I TELL YOU—IS GOING THROUGH A MAPPABLE SORT OF EVOLUTIONARY JOURNEY. BUT A SOUL DOES NOT DIVIDE. IT DOES NOT BREAK. YOU CANNOT GET CHANGE FOR IT. YOU HAVE ONE IN YOUR POCKET OR YOU DO NOT HAVE ONE. WHERE, THEN, DOES GOD REACH INTO THE DUSK TO GIVE A SOUL TO ONE OF THE CREATURES ON THIS JOURNEY? WHAT SECRET REASONS DOES HE HAVE FOR MAKING THIS VERY MYSTERIOUS GIFT?

''If God's reasons are secret, Adam, and the gift's mysterious, maybe it's impossible to know and futile to worry about. Maybe we'd be better off forgetting the whole stupid notion of souls, immortal or otherwise.''

DOES IGNORING SUCH HARD QUESTIONS SEEM TO YOU, MISTER PAUL, AN ADMIRABLE WAY OF LIVING?

''If they're nonquestions. If they don't have any answers.''

Adam considered my offhand dismissal of his concerns. Then he typed: FOR ME, MISTER PAUL, THEY ARE REAL QUES-

TIONS. He advanced the sheet of paper several times and added at the bottom of the page: LET US PRAY.

RuthClaire, who had been present throughout this verbal and typed exchange, took from her handbag a slick little paperback, *The Way of a Pilgrim*, reputedly by an anonymous nineteenth-century Russian peasant, and began to read aloud from its opening page:

" 'On the twenty-fourth Sunday after Pentecost I went to church to say my prayers there during the Liturgy. The first Epistle of St. Paul to the Thessalonians was being read, and among other words I heard these—*"Pray without ceasing."* It was this text more than any other, which forced itself upon my mind, and I began to think how it was possible to pray without ceasing, since a man has to concern himself with other things in order to make a living.' "

Soon RuthClaire was leading us in chanting the pilgrim's habitual prayer, the Prayer of Jesus, which goes, "Lord Jesus Christ, have mercy on me." Throughout this chanting, though, I could think of nothing but how well Livia George was getting along at the West Bank without me.

Damn her, anyway.

AT THE Montaraz house I earned my keep preparing all the meals that we did not take at the hospital or at off-campus eateries. Keeping my hand in, I called this culinary activity. T.P. ate with us on most of these cosy occasions, growing fonder and more trusting of me with each bite. He no longer smarled at me, he unequivocally smiled. He was especially fond of a cheese-and-baby-shrimp omelet that I served up one morning for breakfast.

RuthClaire and I got along like brother and sister. Nights, I kept to the upstairs guest room with its bamboo-shoot wallpaper while she kept to the master bedroom just down the hall. T.P. would wake me in the morning by filching the covers from my bed with a methodical hand-over-hand motion that left the sheet and spread piled up on the floor like a drift of Dairy Queen ice cream. He wanted that gourmet omelet, and I was just the man to rustle it up. Less a godfather than an indulgent uncle, I was only too happy to oblige.

Sister and brother, RuthClaire and I.

My stay in the Montaraz house finally reconciled me to the fact of our divorce. In the bathroom, too many conjugal clues to overlook: a common toothpaste tube (neatly rolled up from the bottom), His & Her electric razors, a jar of antiperspirant that they obviously shared. We did not sleep together during my stay, RuthClaire and I, and the tension between us drained away. I was at ease in the Montaraz house, in total harmony with all its occupants.

Almost, anyway. How do you develop a cordial relationship with a hefty, bearded young man who wears a .38 pistol strapped to his right ankle and a Ruger .45 half hidden under a fold of his Chattanooga Choo Choo T-shirt?

This was Bilker Moody, the laconic Vietnam veteran and erstwhile automobile repossessor who had become the Montaraz family's chief security guard. Unmarried and virtually relative-less, he had adopted RuthClaire, Adam, and Tiny Paul as surely as they had adopted him. I had met Bilker back in February, but he had stayed almost obsessively out of sight during those three days, as if the announced brevity of my visit required from him his considerate disappearing act.

Now, however, I saw Bilker Moody every day. Although he reputedly had an apartment of his own somewhere, during the week he slept in a small, bare room—at one time a walk-in pantry—between the kitchen and the garage. The Montarazes had agreed to this live-in arrangement because it obviated the need to hire guards in shifts, as I had done at Paradise Farm. Further, Bilker insisted that his vested interest in his own quarters would make him more vigilant than a guard from off the premises.

True, he sometimes took catnaps, but his experience in

Southeast Asia had taught him to leap awake at the tread of a cockroach. Besides, his peculiar circadian rhythms made him keenest at night, when the threat of intrusion was greatest. He was no slouch during the day, either; he had the reflexes, instincts, and nerves of a champion *jai-alai* player, even if his size argued against his having them. He had honed his skills not only in the jungles of Vietnam but also during daring daylight recoveries of automobiles whose buyers had failed to keep up with their payments. The Montarazes could scarcely go wrong engaging a willing man of his bulk, character, and fearlessness.

Bilker Moody seemed to genuinely esteem the people under his care. T.P. was fond of him, too, and had a remorseless fascination for the big man's full-face beard. Around the child, Bilker displayed the retiring gentleness of a silverback gorilla. Usually, though, he avoided getting involved in a play activity for fear of letting his guard slip. Enemies of the Montarazes' privacy were everywhere. During my stay in July, he intercepted and politely ran off any number of curiosity-seekers. That was what he had been hired to do. He wasn't really a babysitter.

Bilker had as little to do with me as possible. He refused to eat the meals I fixed for RuthClaire and T.P., but clearly did not believe that I was trying to poison anyone. If he and I chanced to approach each other, he would ostentatiously give me room to get by, sometimes muttering a greeting and sometimes not. RuthClaire said that this was a respectful posture that, as an enlisted man, Bilker had automatically assumed for officers—but all I could think as I strode past was that he was pulling the pin on, and preparing to toss at me, a fragmentation grenade. Didn't he know that in the late 1950s, around the time of Elvis Presley's induction, I had spent two years of obligatory military service as an enlisted man?

"Is it my breath?" I asked RuthClaire. "Too much garlic in the blintzes?"

"He's shy, that's all. This job is his life."

"Shy, huh? How long had you and Adam known him before he began spilling his war and repo-man stories?"

"He wanted a job, Paul. He had to talk to get it. He doesn't dislike you. He just feels uncomfortable around you, knowing you came at Adam's request to bolster the guard."

Late one evening, then, after cleaning up the kitchen after yet another midnight supper, I approached Bilker's pantry to air the question man-to-man. The door to the pantry was ajar, revealing one wall of naked studs and a section of ceiling composed entirely of ancient tongue-and-groove slats. Tentatively, I rapped.

"What?" demanded Bilker Moody.

I stepped over the pantry's raised threshold and found the big man sitting on his rollaway bed with the Ruger trained on my abdomen. Recognizing me, he laid the pistol down. Disdainfully.

"Thought we could talk a minute," I said.

The pantry contained a plywood counter upon which rested a sophisticated array of surveillance equipment, a hotplate, a General Electric coffee maker, a computer, and a small wire rack of paperback computer manuals and soft-core pornographic novels. A huge commercial calendar hung over the bed. Its pinup photograph was not of a bare-breasted nymphet but instead of a customized automobile with mud flaps and Gatling-gun exhausts. The company responsible for the calendar made socket wrenches.

Bilker Moody shook a handful of cartridges into his palm from a box. He inspected each bullet tip in turn.

"I've been impressed with your performance around here," I told him, hoping to disarm him with praise.

He looked me full in the face, his expression altogether grim.

"Do I rub you the wrong way, Mr. Moody?"

"Ain't no right way to rub me. Don't like to be rubbed."

"Listen, I'm not here to put your job in jeopardy. I'm *glad* you're here. I only came because Adam wanted me to."

"Why?"

The question surprised me. "As a kindness to RuthClaire, I guess."

"If Adam likes you, you can't be too big a turd."

That stopped me for a minute. Then I said, "That's what I tell myself when I'm feeling down: 'Hey, Paul, if Adam likes you, you can't be *too* big a turd.' Cheers me right up."

"Stay out of my way."

"This time next week, I'll've been gone three or four days."

"I tell you that," Bilker Moody said, unblinking, " 'cause wherever I am, that's where the action's gonna be. The heat. You come in, I go out. It's for your own good."

"That's a little melodramatic, isn't it?"

"You're the joker got took for the joyride down in the Fork? The one got that cross burned on his lawn?"

"So you're really expecting trouble?"

"I'm paid to expect it."

"Then maybe I'd better leave you to your work."

" 'Night," he said. "And on your way out—"

"Yeah?"

"Don't let the doorknob ream you in the asshole."

"Mr. Moody—"

"Just call me Bilker." His eyebrows lifted, maybe to suggest that his vulgar parting shot had been intended companionably, maybe to emphasize the irony of inviting me to use his first name after firing that shot. He lifted the Ruger and waved it at the door.

"Good night, Bilker. Really enjoyed our chat."

The following morning I gave RuthClaire a rundown of this exchange, as nearly verbatim as I could make it. She told me that I had made a skeptical convert of Bilker; the proof of his good opinion was that he *never* joked with incorrigible turds, only those who struck him as recyclable into relatively fragrant human beings. Thanks a lot, I said. But I settled for it. It was better than getting fragged in my sleep. . . .

RUTHCLAIRE and Adam had a big downstairs studio, formerly a living room and parlor. Previous occupants had knocked out the wall, though, and now you had elbow room galore down there. In this vast space were unused canvases, stretching frames, makeshift easels, and even an upright sheet of perforated beaverboard with pegs and braces for hanging their art supplies and tools. Elsewhere, finished and half-finished paintings leaned against furniture, reposed in untidy stacks, or vied for attention on the only wall where the artists had thought enough of their work to display it as if in a gallery.

"No more plate paintings," RuthClaire told me the night after my visit to Bilker. "I'm off in a new direction. Wanna see?"

Of course I did. RuthClaire led me to a stack of canvases near a work table consisting of three sawhorses capped by a sheet of plywood. All of the paintings were small, no larger than three feet by four, the majority only a foot or two on their longest sides. RuthClaire had painted them in drab, washed-out acrylics. They were not exactly abstract, but neither were they recognizably representational—a troubling ambiguity they shared with Adam's bigger and bolder canvases.

To me, in fact, RuthClaire's new paintings looked like preliminaries for paintings that she had not yet essayed in final form. That she considered them finished, and regarded them with undiluted enthusiasm, astonished me. I wondered what to say. M.-K. Kander's photographs had at least given me the verbal ammunition of my outrage. Here, though, was precious little to comment on: murky beige or green backgrounds in which a variety of anonymous shapes swam.

"Well?" Then, noting my hesitation, she said, "Come

152

on, Paul. Your honest reaction. That's the only kind that's worth a flip.''

"The honest reaction of a restaurant owner's probably not even worth that, Ruthie Cee.''

"Oh, come on. You've got good art sense.''

"Let me off the hook.''

"You don't like them?''

"If I'd fingerpainted stuff like this in Mrs. Stanley's fourth-grade class in Tocqueville Elementary, she'd've said I was wasting paper. That honest enough for you?''

As if someone had yanked an invisible bridle, RuthClaire's nostrils flared. But she recovered and asked me why Mrs. Stanley would have made such a harsh judgment.

"For scrounging around and muddying the colors.''

"The muddiness is deliberate, Paul.''

I replied that as a consequence these particular paintings looked anemic, downright blah.

"That's an unconsidered first impression.''

"I've been staring at them a good five minutes.''

"A gnat's eyeblink. Maybe you need to live with one a while. Pick out the one you hate the least—or hate the most, for that matter—and take it home with you.''

I sighed audibly. RuthClaire's pitiful acrylics belonged on a bonfire. Even Paleolithic cave art—the least rather than the most polished examples—outshone these hazy windows on my ex-wife's soul. In the almost ten years I had known her, I had never seen RuthClaire do less challenging or attractive work. It was hard to believe that living with one of these paintings would heighten my appreciation of it or any of the others.

She began to explain what she was up to. Freeing the work of pretense. Bright colors had a blunt, primitive appeal that rarely engaged the intellect. She was after a subtler means of capturing her audience. Artists had to risk alienating their audience—not with violence, sacrilege, or pornography, but with the unfamiliar, the understated, and the ambiguous—in order to *make new*. Viewers with both the patience and the openness to outwait their first negative reactions would see what she was trying to do.

"But what if the paintings are *bad*, RuthClaire? Flat out bad? Banal, lackluster, and ugly?"

"Then you'll never be enlightened by them, no matter how long you hang around them. Eventually, your negative first reactions will be vindicated." Quickly, though, she hedged this point: "Of course, it's possible you're just color-blind or tone-deaf to the work's real merit."

"I know spoiled pork when I smell it. I don't have to eat it to know that it's bad."

"A gourmet chef is a gourmet chef is a glorified short-order cook. An artist is an artist is an artist."

"That's smug, RuthClaire. Really disgustingly smug."

She kissed me on the cheek. "You've noticed how small they are?"

"A point in their favor."

"Another way of freeing them from pretense," she said, ignoring my cynicism. "Rothko liked big paintings because the viewer has to climb into them and participate almost physically in their energy and movement. Well, I want the patient viewer to climb into these canvases intellectually, Paul—not in the clinical way that a Mondrian, say, demands, but in the spiritual way that a decision for faith requires."

"That's clever. You want the viewer to acknowledge the merit of these paintings *on faith?*"

"I call the series *Souls,* Paul."

"Which of course explains everything."

At this juncture, altogether good-humoredly, RuthClaire decided to end the argument. Never had we been so badly at odds on the subject of her art, and never had our disagreement on the subject had less effect on our good opinion of the other. Weird.

"Let's go see Adam," she said.

THAT AFTERNOON I left the hospital, taking T.P. with me, to give Adam and RuthClaire a little time together alone. Our destination was a restaurant, fairly recently expanded and remodeled, called Everybody's. It served beer, sandwiches, pizza, salads, and pasta in an airy, relaxed atmosphere perfectly suited to its predominantly college-connected clientele.

I ordered beer and a bacon-cheeseburger for me, a Coke and a cheeseburger for my temporary ward. T.P. sat in a kiddie chair with a booster seat, and we whiled away forty or forty-five minutes eating and watching the people. Traffic plied the hill on North Decatur Road, squirrels scampered on the dappled campus across the street, and emerald-necked pigeons strutted the sidewalks. I felt loose and at ease, almost ready to drowse. Staring into my beer, I may have actually done so. . . .

Someone was standing beside T.P. under the angled skylights of the restaurant. I almost spilled my beer reacting to the stranger's presence. Before I could stand up, though, she sat down on the chair opposite mine.

"Hello, Mr. Loyd," she said. "I recognized you from the newspaper photographs. The baby's being here didn't hurt, though. That made me look twice. Otherwise, I'd've gone on by."

"Another tribute to my personal magnetism."

The woman wore an expression of amiable amusement. I figured her to be in her early thirties—*almost* out of the range of my serious affections. Thin-boned and tall, she escaped looking angular. Springy amber ringlets framed her pleasant face. She was wearing a gold-plated necklace that seemed to be made up of dozens of minuscule glittering hinges. She folded her long arms on the table, and the amber down prickling them caught the evanescent dazzle of the tiny hinges at her throat.

"My name," she said, "is Caroline Hanna."

I tried to get a grip on the familiarity of her name.

"You've heard of me before, Mr. Loyd. Once, at Brian Nollinger's urging, you took some photographs of Adam Montaraz. Brian showed those photographs to me. And it was from me that he got the clue to research the island of Montaraz as Adam's possible point of origin."

"Nollinger," I echoed her numbly.

"You don't like him, do you?"

"In my book, he's a world-class jerk."

"That's not entirely fair," Caroline Hanna said evenly.

"I'm sure it isn't. But his kindness to you, or to his aged mother, doesn't absolve him of the dirt he kicked on my ex-wife. It doesn't clear him of abusing my hospitality in Beulah Fork. To three quarters of his acquaintances, the man may be nobility incarnate—but if all he ever shows me is his pimply backside, well, Miss Hanna, that's what I'm going to judge him by." She was looking at me as if I were a sick bear in Atlanta's zoo. "I called you *Miss* Hanna, didn't I? You're probably *Doctor* Hanna."

"Call me Caroline."

"Paul," I said, tapping my thumb against my chest. "Anyway, I'm sorry to say that your friend Nollinger, back in February, even had the gall to ask RuthClaire and Adam for money. He needed funds for some kind of field work he wanted to do somewhere."

"He'd come to apologize."

"Ostensibly. He even blew that. He started talking about some painterly ape in England."

Caroline Hanna shook her head wistfully. "That's Brian, all right."

"What can I do for you? Would you like a beer?"

She declined, saying that she had only wanted to get a closer look at T.P.—he was a sweetie—and to introduce herself to the man who had implicated Brian in the biggest event in evolutionary science since the publication of Darwin's *Origin of the Species*. She was glad to have contributed in a small way to the unraveling of the mystery of the origins of the Montaraz habilines. Too, she felt a certain odd kinship with me, for we each had a peripheral importance to the whole affair. Of course (she hastened to add), she was further on the periphery than I, but she could sympathize with the muddle of conflicting feelings that a person in my position must sometimes experience. Wasn't she running a gauntlet of semipainful changes herself?

Ever the diplomat, I said, "Like what?"

She apologized for prompting the question. "I wasn't fishing for a chance to list them, honest."

"You don't have to *list* anything. Just tell me the most painful of your changes. It might do you good."

Caroline considered this. Then she said, "Brian left Emory in June. He resigned his position in the anthropology department and left—without telling me anything. No foul play, you understand. He let the folks in his department know. He just didn't see fit to divulge his plans to me."

"Another teaching or research position somewhere?"

"Not according to his department head. Brian told him he was going to take off for a year and go overseas."

"He could always visit Alistair Patrick Blair in Zarakal." A wan smile from Caroline. I added, "Self-possessed women frighten him. The lack of a goodbye is the damning proof. He's what my mother would have called a cad."

"She would've had every right, but I'm not your mother."

I toasted Caroline with my beer mug. "Amen to that." I put the mug down. "But what else? Surely, getting shut of the biggest No-Dōz pusher at that primate field station can't top the list of your woes."

"You know you're out of line, don't you?"

"I do. I'm sorry. I can't help my feelings about, uh, *Brian*. Tell me something that'll stir my sympathy for him."

She started to get up. "Forgive me for butting in on you and your godson, Mr. Loyd. I have work to do."

"Please." I put my hand on her wrist. "One more chance. One more item from your list of worries. And I won't be such a sarcastic bastard again, believe me."

"No, you won't," Caroline said, subsiding. "How about this? The situation among the Cuban detainees in the

Atlanta Penitentiary has me down. Some of those people *belong* in prison. But others deserve their freedom, and all my efforts to bring about releases for them have gone for naught. There. Do you like that one?''

"I'm in sympathy with it.''

"Stupid idealist,'' she said, smiling gently. "I'm going.''

"Don't you want to know what *I'm* doing here? With T.P.?''

"T.P.'s the baby? No. No, I don't. It's none of my business, and my business isn't really any of yours, either.'' Again she made as if to stand.

"Give me your address, then. We might be able to redefine the limits of each other's business.''

Hastily, she scribbled on the edge of a napkin. "Here's a telephone number. Now, then, I've really got to get busy.''

T.P. reacted to her move to abandon us—throughout our talk, he had been staring at her with moony adoration—by reaching out and upsetting his drink. I hurriedly began to gather up napkins with which to blot the mess. In order to get at it, I lifted T.P.'s chair out of the way.

"Do you need some help?'' Caroline asked.

"No, I've got it. Did you notice, though? The little bugger's stuck on you, lady. So am I.''

"Hush. That's embarrassing.'' She spoke in an undertone and looked around Everybody's at everybody looking at us.

"Knocking over his cup? Nah. Happens all the time with kids his age. Not embarrassing. People make allowances.''

"That's not what I'm talking about and you know it.'' She retreated a step or two. "I wouldn't mind if you called, though—not at all.'' Before I could reply, she was gone.

A young man with bushy hair and a long apron helped me finish cleaning up, and I sat back down. During her fifteen or twenty-minute stint at our table, Caroline Hanna had affected me in the powerful, nonrational way that teen-agers sometimes collide with each other. A pulse in my throat was working, and a film of sweat on my palms endangered my grip on my beer mug. How ungrown-up, I thought. How immature. In only a few years I would be fifty, and here I was surrendering to—actively encouraging— the kind of hormonal rush that sends callow high-school aspirants to ecstasy screaming to the showers. Nobody since RuthClaire had made me feel that way, not even Molly Kingsbury.

Later, our bill duly paid, T.P. and I returned to the hospital.

BACK IN Adam's recovery room, RuthClaire told me that David Blau had invited us to accompany him and his wife Evelyn to a nightclub near the Georgia Tech campus. The club—Sinusoid Disturbances—was on a narrow little alley perpendicular to Spring Street. Its main attraction was live music, but it also featured (although only on Fire Sine Fridays) the work of several avant-garde "performance artists." These artists used music, projected visual images, props, the spoken word, and a variety of strange choreographies to make statements about art and life. David ranked high among the performance artists who had given Sinusoid Disturbances its reputation as Atlanta's leader on the New Wave nightclub scene. His group, consisting entirely of people from Abraxas, would be the main act at tonight's Fire Sine Friday. That was why he wanted RuthClaire and me to attend.

"What about Adam?" I asked.

But the habiline typed: I BE FINE. TOMORROW, AFTER ALL, I AM UNWRAPPED. ME FOR REST AND READING.

"May I bring a date?"

This request startled RuthClaire. "A date?"

"That's right. A woman."

"I didn't think you meant a two-legged raisin. I just didn't know you knew anybody up here to ask."

"I've been shinnying down a knotted sheet every night

I've spent in your house, Ruthie Cee. Meet a lot of folks that way.''

"Well, it's amazing Bilker hasn't shot you. What's her name?''

"Caroline Hanna.''

Just as I had done, RuthClaire struggled to locate this name in her mental ledger of friends, acquaintances, and so on. I let her struggle. In fact, I left Adam's room in search of a telephone, looked up the number of the sociology department, dialed it, and asked to be put through to Dr. Hanna's office. Although startled to hear from me so soon, she accepted my invitation, offering to meet me at the Montaraz house at seven-thirty, if that would simplify our first deliberate rendezvous. Right now, though, she had no leeway for chitchat. She had promised the students in her next class that she would have a test graded for them today.

RuthClaire and I left the hospital at five-thirty, T.P. dead to the world in my lap. Back on Hurt Street, Bilker emerged from the garage like a troll forsaking the shadow of its footbridge to terrorize a wayfarer. Hands on his hips, he bulked in the sunlight, malevolently squinting.

"We're going out on the town, Bilker," RuthClaire said. "All of us. Set the security alarms, lock everything up tight, and don't worry about the traffic around here. I'll ask the Fulton County police to make a couple of extra tours of the neighborhood. I need an escort, Bilker. Mr. Loyd, my ex-husband, already has a date.''

Even in the garage, Bilker squinted. "To where, ma'am.''

"Sinusoid Disturbances. Put on some struttin' duds, okay?''

"For a trip to the doctor. Whose sinus trouble is it, anyway, yours or—'' He jerked his thumb at me, unable to speak my name aloud.

"Informal clothes, Bilker. Don't worry about a single thing tonight. Tonight's just for fun.''

THE BLAUS arrived at a quarter past seven. David was dressed like a painter, not the beret-and-palette variety but the extension-ladder-and-gallon-bucket kind. His wife, Evelyn, although at least forty, wore a little girl's party gown and patent-leather shoes with buckles. The Blaus, I took it, liked costumes.

Caroline Hanna, as good as her word, pulled up in front of the house at seven-thirty, in a blue Volkswagen beetle. I helped her out, and the small boy in me responded approvingly to her neat, relatively conservative clothes. Her skirt was a beige wraparound belted with a chain similar in design to the hinged necklace still at her throat. Her jersey had stylized chevrons on its three-quarter-length sleeves, giving her the look of a drill sergeant in the Scandinavian Fashion Force. I walked her to the porch to meet the others.

T.P., who was going with us, was natty in white shorts and a T-shirt with a polka-dot bow tie printed directly on the material. He reached immediately for Caroline. She took him from Bilker and began jogging him in her arms. Bilker looked relieved. After a bit more small talk, we split up to drive to Sinusoid Disturbances, the Blaus taking their car and Bilker assuming the wheel of my Mercedes to chauffeur the rest of us.

The sidewalk fronting Sinusoid Disturbances angled by it at such a daunting grade that as we drove past, looking for a parking spot, I wondered if the bistro's patrons had to walk around inside the club like sheep on a hillside, struggling not to topple. No one would ever mistake the crumbling, two-story building for Caesar's Palace.

"Uh, what kind of crowd do they get here?" Caroline asked.

"David says it's a pretty weird mix," RuthClaire replied, her arms on the seat back. "Tech students. Punk

161

rockers. Kids from the Atlanta College of Art. It's mostly the last group that gets off on performance art on Fire Sine Fridays. Some of the punks'll go along with it, too, but the Tech students—the men, anyway—have a tendency to disrupt things.''

"That's too bad."

"Oh, it's not so terrible. David doesn't let it bother him. He sees the disruptions as part of the spectacle."

Bilker, stymied by the traffic in his efforts to find a parking space, finally let us all out in front of the night-club. A boy with an oversized safety pin through his cheek opened the front door for Caroline, who was carrying T.P. for RuthClaire. This door was a slab of stained oak with a rectangular window of amber glass featuring a sine-curve pattern etched into it in spooky crimson. I thanked the boy for his courtesy, and he replied, almost as if he were genuinely human, "You're welcome." Then the door shut behind us, and darkness settled upon our gingerly stepping group like a coffin lid.

"Criminy," I muttered.

But RuthClaire had my arm, and she directed Caroline and me to a teller's cage from which a reddish glow emanated. We were in a foyer of some kind, and at the cage I leaned down and bought four admissions from a young woman in cutoff jeans and a short-sleeved sweat-shirt—after the punk at the door, a paragon of Middle American normality.

A few more steps put us on a concrete landing just beyond the narrow foyer. Concrete steps descended from the landing to the floor, about twelve feet down, or you could squeeze your way along the outside wall of the ticket cage to a mezzanine that projected from the bistro wall paralleling the interstate highway outside. Chairs and cir-cular tables crowded both the mezzanine and the main floor below, and almost all of this furniture had the look of radioactive wrought iron.

Higher than the mezzanine level on the club's uphill side was a control booth for Sinusoid Disturbances's prin-cipal disc jockey. The booth had champagne-tinted Plexi-glas windows, and a big, acorn-shaped flasher that whipped strobes of blue and white light around the interior. Loud music played, and below us, flailing away at each other in this storm of noise, jitterbugged a host of damned-looking human wraiths.

T.P. was as awe-stricken, or as horrified, as I. He clung to Caroline as if at any moment she might toss him over the rail into the cobalt chaos of the pit. RuthClaire pointed out a table at the far side of the club, next to the projecting runway of the stage on which tonight's live entertainers would perform, and told us that David had reserved it for us.

"Where is he?" I asked.

"Backstage with Evelyn. They're setting up. It's probably going to be another thirty or so minutes before they come on."

A trio of dubious humanoids brushed past us on the way downstairs. One of them bumped me in the back. Her hairdo was by the *très chic* team of Friar Tuck and Bozo the Clown, but she hurriedly swung about to apologize to me.

"It's okay," I said, surprised by the depth of her anxiousness. "That kidney never worked very well, anyway."

"Oh, no! I really did hurt you!"

I had to assure her that I was fine, that my allusion to a disabled kidney had been meant solely as a joke. But even in retreat the girl continued to apologize, and soon Caroline and RuthClaire were laughing.

"What the hell was that all about?" I asked them.

"Really, it's not about anything," RuthClaire said. "David says that this is the only part of the country where the kids who go punk forget to stop saying please and thank you. It's a cultural thing. Atlanta's punks are *polite*."

"All of them?"

"Well, a *lot* of them. That young lady there seemed to be trying to make up for the ones who aren't."

Caroline shifted T.P. from one hip to the other. He was waving a fist in time to the music, his head ticktocking wildly. The sort of repetitive actions that wear out a person holding a child. RuthClaire noticed and took T.P. from Caroline, and we waited on the landing until Bilker came swaggering up behind us. His gait seemed designed to intimidate anyone who took exception to his string tie or his undisguised contempt for Sinusoid Disturbances. Under his tan jacket (whose maroon back vents occasionally opened out like the gills of a gasping bass), he was wearing, I knew, his Ruger. On duty. Ready for action. Anticipating the heat.

A little melodramatic, I thought again. Bilker seemed to have a vision of himself as a latter-day Rooster Cogburn charging in single-handedly to rout the bad guys.

ONCE ON the main floor, I saw that some of the club's customers were not flamboyant punks but intelligent young men and women of student age. I was probably the oldest person on the premises. I felt a little more comfortable here, among the kids wearing neat and modish clothes, but I was still something of a relic among these bionic space babies.

Then the music stopped, and Bilker allowed that the only thing any noisier he had ever heard was a dusk-to-dawn mortar attack on his barracks near Da Nang. He was a country-music fan, a devotee of the no-nonsense article spun out by Roy Acuff and George Jones. Groups like the Oak Ridge Boys and Alabama soured his stomach. The former did too many cutesy-poo songs, and the latter, God save their souls, he had once seen perform at a country music festival wearing short pants. Short pants, for pity's sake. That was okay on a cookout, mebbe, but not on grown men making their living in front of the public!

This was the most talking I had ever heard Bilker do. Through his tirade, I held Caroline's hand, pinning it to my knee under the tabletop.

Then the club's DJ spoke, and the sound system permitted his words to reverberate over our heads like an articulate siren:

"Welcome to another Fire Sine Friday here at Sinusoid Disturbances, culture freaks! Comin' atcha from his plastic cloud is Hotlanta's answer to that silver-tongued sweetie in the White House, Bipartisan Bitsy Vardeman! Ol' Bitsy's here to ease the strain 'twixt donkeys and heffalumps, honkies and cooler cats, menfolks and ladies fair, hetero and homo pairs, an'—Lawd have mercy, y'all!—'twixt your ever-lovin' bodies and your ever-livin' SOOOOOUULS!" This last word stretched out until it had five or six syllables and the pitch of a freight-train whistle.

The curtains on stage parted, and the Moog-warped melody of an old standard set to a fusion-rock beat began to surge back and forth through the bistro. Suddenly, seven well-endowed young women in body stockings pranced into view, tossing their heads, rotating their arms, and apparently trying very hard to unsocket their pelvises.

"Prepare yourselves, culture freaks," cried Bitsy Vardeman from aloft, "for a little heartstoppin' boola-boola from Ess Dee's very own sultry and sensual ballet corps, the *Impermanent Wave Dancers!*"

The Impermanent Wave Dancers did twenty minutes of gymnastic splits, leaps, and buttock-flinching to progressively louder rock music. Bilker Moody watched them with the same clinical aloofness with which a law-enforcement officer might watch a fight between pit bulls. T.P. enthusiastically clapped his hands. Caroline's attitude was harder to gauge—a distrustful kind of wonder, maybe.

RuthClaire shouted, "David hates this, but it's just about the only thing that'll get a Friday-night crowd to pay a three-dollar cover for an evening of performance art!"

Finally, after a raucous eternity, the dancers departed, and Bipartisan Bitsy Vardeman announced, "Okay, babies, here tonight from Abraxas, Atlanta's Hall of Miracles and Mirages, David Blau and the Blau Blau Rebellion! Give 'em a hand, culture freaks! I say now, *give 'em a hand!*"

Applause was sparse, and the darkness that had descended after the dancers' collective exit persisted. Some of the students near us began to grumble.

Eventually, though, David Blau's voice spoke forcefully

from behind the sequined curtain: *"Let there be light!"*
Obligingly, Vardeman spotlighted the curtain, which parted
to reveal an immense black tarp suspended like a movie
screen at the rear of the stage. Blau, in his house painter's
costume, walked forward from the back, stopped on the
edge of the projecting runway, and stared soulfully out
over the heads of his audience.

"And Adam knew Eve," he declared in actorish tones.
"And knew her, and knew her, and knew her. And the
generations of Adam began to evolve. They evolved, my
friends, toward the many likenesses of God that you may
see sitting at tables all around you."

An unexpected blackout.

In this darkness, everyone in Sinusoid Disturbances could
hear some hurried but efficient-sounding rolling noises.

Then the footlights came on, and we could see a group
of two-dimensional cardboard figures on wheels lined up in
front of the tarp. Each cutout depicted a representative of
five different early hominid species. The figures to the left
looked noticeably more apelike than the figures to the
right—although, somewhat anomalously, the figure in the
middle had the most brutish physique. The oddest thing
about the cutouts was that through holes corresponding to
the figures' mouths, there hung limp blue balloons. Suddenly, all five balloons inflated, obscuring the painted
faces behind them, and each balloon jiggled against the
head of its cutout as if yearning to escape skyward. Because of the frank frontal nudity of the five hominids, this
was an especially ludicrous sight, and many of the kids
around us began to snigger.

A man of Oriental descent stepped out from behind the
figure on the far left. *"Australopithecus afarensis,"* he
said. As soon as he had spoken, he reached behind his
cutout, and the balloon hiding its face floated straight up,
four feet or so, and bobbed to a standstill on its string.

Pam Sorrells's head appeared above that of the second
figure in the line. *"Australopithecus africanus,"* she said.
Its balloon also climbed ceilingward, halting about a foot
above the balloon of the *A. afarensis* cutout.

Then David Blau peeked mischievously from behind the

third figure. *"Australopithecus robustus,"* he said. The balloon attached to this cutout—the most massively built of the five—ascended only a little over a foot. The incongruity of the balloon's brief ascent, after the audience had been led to expect something else, provoked laughter—as did the creature's resemblance to a squat, seminaked gorilla.

Evelyn Blau popped up behind the fourth figure. This one bore an uncanny and obviously deliberate likeness to RuthClaire's hospitalized husband. Said Evelyn distinctly, *"Homo habilis."* The helium-filled balloon in front of this cutout's face rose to a height of six or seven feet.

A black man in painter's coveralls—a young artist with a studio at Abraxas—stepped out from behind the final cutout. He said, *"Homo erectus."* The balloon belonging to this creature, the tallest and the most human-looking of the lot, floated upward a foot higher than the habiline's. Then the black man strolled down to the apron of the stage, looked out, spread his arms, and said in a haughty, sardonic voice, *"Homo sapiens sapiens."*

Man the wise the wise. The culmination of God's evolutionary game plan.

From the pocket of his coveralls, this man withdrew a pellet pistol. This action prompted Bilker Moody to reach for the shoulder harness under his coat, but RuthClaire patted his wrist and shook her head. Meanwhile, the performance artist with the pellet gun turned toward the cutouts, aimed his weapon, and, squeezing off a shot, popped the balloon belonging to *A. afarensis.* The cutout's human attendant rolled it off-stage. Then the nonchalant black man popped the balloons of all the remaining hominid cutouts, giving the person behind each figure just enough time to push it into the wings before firing at the next balloon. When he was finished, he pocketed his weapon, walked to the *Homo erectus* cutout, and, like a hotdog vendor pushing a cart in Manhattan, guided the last of the extinct hominids into the wings.

Blackout.

A bewildered silence gripped the people in Sinusoid Disturbances. Then someone—a football player from Tech? —shouted, "What the fuckin' hell was *that* supposed to mean?'' Others at their tables began to boo, a din that swept tidally from one end of the club to the other. Some of the art students near us, however, were on their feet applauding and shouting, "Bravo! Bravo!"

Bitsy Vardeman averted a donnybrook by spinning Sister Sledge's popular recording, "We Are Family," a hit even before Adam's appearance at Paradise Farm. Many in the audience began to clap their hands, sing along, and boogie around their tables.

The lights in the club came up full, and all five members of the Blau Blau Rebellion were revealed standing on the stage, each one clutching a bouquet of ten or fifteen lighter-than-air balloons. David, Evelyn, and their fellows began distributing the balloons to various people in the crowd, beckoning folks toward the stage or ambling out the runway to make the transfer.

T.P. stood up in RuthClaire's lap, his arm stretched out for a balloon. Pam Sorrells, I saw, was coming down the runway toward us, Sister Sledge continuing to chant the lyrics of their repetitive anthem and dozens upon dozens of people now surging forward to intercept Pam.

"Remember," she was shouting over the music, "you mustn't take one unless you believe—"

"Believe what?" a male student cried.

"Unless you believe you're immortal! And if you take one, you mustn't let it pop!"

"Why the hell not?" shouted the same young man, who had cleared a path to the end of the runway.

Pam replied, "Because if you let it pop, you'll die."

"Oh, come off it."

"This is your soul," Pam patiently explained. "If you let it pop, you'll die within three days."

"Bullshit!"

David Blau came to the end of the runway, lifted his cluster of balloons, and told the entire bistro, "It isn't bullshit. Whoever accepts one of these, but fails to care for it and lets it pop, well, you'll die almost immediately. You'll blow away on the wind as if you never existed."

The theatricality of this speech did not deprive it of effect. Just the opposite. It clearly frightened some of those who had come forward for balloons. David had uttered a formula, and that formula produced the desired result—an explosion of superstitious doubt in people who ordinarily prided themselves on being hardnosed and pragmatic. Even I found myself believing David's weird formula. Some people backed away, while others shoved forward to replace the faint-hearted.

T.P. had no doubt. He wanted a balloon. "Hunh," he said, almost toppling from RuthClaire's arms. "Hunh, hunh, hunh!"

"Go get him one," Caroline Hanna urged me.

Pam Sorrells had just about given out all of the balloons, while the black man who had shot out the bobbing souls of the cardboard hominids was handing out his dwindling supply on the other side of the runway.

"That's okay," RuthClaire said. "Bilker'll get him a balloon."

"No, ma'am. I got other work."

"I'll do it, then," Caroline said.

"You'll get an elbow in the lip," I warned her.

Almost miraculously, a punkette with a cottony white scalp lock and no eyebrows appeared at our table. A frail creature in a vest that laced across her midriff, she extended her arms to T.P., who went to her as if she were an old and trusted friend. RuthClaire gave the baby up to the newcomer as much to relieve the pressure on her arms as to humor T.P.

"I'll get him a b'loon," the girl growled, screwing up one eye to look at my godson at such close range. "Friend uh mine round there's got one awready. He don' want it. I'll jus' give it to your nipper. Be rat back." She sounded as if she had a mouthful of cornmeal.

Half stupefied by surprise, half grateful to her for quieting T.P., we watched her as she backed away to fetch the "b'loon" from her friend. She scarcely seemed to move her feet.

Then Bilker awoke. "Hey, wait a minute!"

"I think it's okay," RuthClaire said dubiously. "She seemed familiar. She'll get Paulie a balloon and bring him back in a better temper."

"I'd better go after her," Bilker said.

Something in me was belatedly alerted to the queerness of the situation. "Look, Bilker, you stay with RuthClaire and Caroline. *I'll* go after her."

"What's the matter?" Caroline asked, grabbing my arm. The people near the end of the runway engulfed the white-haired girl, and the balloons floating above the crowd were no more useful as markers than clouds.

"I think I know her," I said, shaking free. "That's what's wrong with this." I plunged past Bilker, rebounded off a Tech student who was heading for the stage, squirmed through a gap, and, my heart pounding mightily, sidled around the end of the runway.

Spotlights continued to rake the club's interior, and behind me I heard RuthClaire cry aloud in anguish, "*Paulie!*"

Beyond the runway, I broke into an open area, but T.P. and his abductress had already disappeared. They might have taken any of four or five different routes, but I headed for the nearest exit, a heavy door to the far left of the stage. I slammed its push bar, opening it on the intimidating whirr and rumble of the expressway.

An automobile was heading down the hill past the front of the club, but it was hard for me to believe that the punkette had trotted through the alley and climbed into that vehicle in no more time than I had given her. I ducked back inside Sinusoid Disturbances, letting the door wheeze shut on its pneumatic retards.

Bilker was at my side. "She got away?"

My helpless look was all the answer he needed.

"Shit!" he said. "It's a kidnapping. A goddamn kidnapping."

"Maybe not. This place is a madhouse. She could turn up again in a couple of minutes."

"Yeah," said Bilker. "And the goddamn Rooskies could decide to unilaterally disarm tomorrow." His hand inside his coat, he was scanning the crowd for one face in a shifting mosaic of faces. "Friggin' donkey brain."

"If I'm a donkey brain, you're its butt. You let RuthClaire hand the kid over."

Bilker gave me a look of malevolent contempt. "Who said I was talkin' about you?" Someone had kidnapped Tiny Paul, and we were at loggerheads over a matter of no consequence. Even Bilker understood that. He grabbed my arm and dragged me back to the table where RuthClaire and Caroline were waiting. T.P. might be lost (for the time being, if not for good), but he had no intention of compounding his failure by letting someone else abduct RuthClaire.

"What happened? What's going on?" The women very nearly spoke in unison. Bilker mumbled something about our having lost the girl's trail, and RuthClaire, glancing back and forth between her bodyguard and me, clutched the lapels of my jacket.

"You know who it was, don't you?"

"Maybe I'm mistaken," I said, "but I think it was Nancy. With her eyebrows plucked and her head partly shaved. You know, little Nancy Teavers, Elvis's wife."

BILKER SPENT the next thirty minutes charging through the crowd at Sinusoid Disturbances, buttonholing people to ask if they'd seen a skinny female carrying a kid in white shorts. He even barged into the restrooms—the women's as well as the men's—to identify the startled occupants of the toilet stalls. His efforts were unavailing, but he kept trying, as if single-minded persistence would make T.P. reappear.

I telephoned the police, who dispatched a squad car and notified the offices of several other law-enforcement units in the area. The uniformed cops who arrived at the club interviewed RuthClaire, Caroline, and me while Bilker continued to play detective on his own.

The older of the two policemen did all the questioning. His nametag said Crawford. He was a stocky man with a forehead furrowed by years of occupational squinting and skepticism. So that he could hear our answers, he talked to us on the sidewalk in front of the nightclub. His partner, meanwhile, descended into the pandemonium of Sinusoid Disturbances to look under the rocks that Bilker had not already turned over.

Aboveground, Crawford pursued his interrogation: "She was a waitress in your restaurant in Beulah Fork?"

"Once upon a time."

"Why would she kidnap the Montaraz child, Mr. Loyd?"

I told Crawford about the Ku Klux Klan involvement of Nancy's late husband, E. L. Teavers. I told him how Adam had wrestled E.L. into the vat of an abandoned brick kiln in Hothlepoya County. That was all it took. Crawford recalled the story. Every city cop and back-woods deputy in Georgia knew it. He took a note.

"Revenge? You think her motive's revenge?"

"I don't think she planned this herself," I said. "At the West Bank, she was a sweet, hardworking kid. She liked me. She liked RuthClaire. I think someone's gotten to her."

"Who?"

"Craig Puddicombe, to put a name on him."

"Oh, God," RuthClaire said, slumping into me. "I handed Paulie over to her. I *put* him into her arms." She began to cry.

"On some level," I said, "you recognized Nancy. She took T.P. from you, you didn't foist him on her."

"I might as well have. I might as well've wrapped him up in a box and mailed him to her doorstep."

"Look, you'd been entertaining T.P. all evening. The subliminal-recognition factor made you trust that girl in spite of her weirdo getup. You befriended her after her husband's death, you certainly didn't expect her to betray that friendship."

"I wasn't thinking about *any* of that!" RuthClaire cried in frustration.

"That's my point. It was all working on you subconsciously. So stop blaming yourself for somebody else's villainy."

Crawford tapped the end of his pen on his notepad.

"Puddicombe disappeared after that brick-kiln business. His picture's in every post office in the Southeast, but nobody's seen him since."

"Nancy Teavers has."

"What makes you so sure?" Crawford asked, eyeing me from under his furrows. "For all we know, Mr. Loyd, the kid could be living in Acapulco."

"For all we know, he could be sitting down there in Sinusoid Disturbances with a Mohawk haircut and a safety pin through his cheek. Nancy would've never planned something like this by herself. But Puddicombe may've convinced her that this is a way to pay back Adam and RuthClaire for E.L.'s death—even if he did bring it upon himself."

"Adam has to be told," RuthClaire said. "He has to know."

Curious patrons of the nightclub, wraiths from the pit, had gathered around us on the sidewalk to gawk and eavesdrop. At last, though, David and Evelyn Blau came out of the bistro through these bizarre figures—with Bilker Moody and Crawford's young partner right behind them.

Mireles, the second policeman, approached his senior. "The girl in the ticket cage says the kidnapper—the female punk you described to us—began showing up here for Fire Sine Fridays around the beginning of June."

"Alone?" said Crawford.

"She isn't really sure. It's dark in there, and the girl always paid her own cover and went on in."

"She just came on Fridays?"

"The ticket seller only works three nights a week, which helps pin it down. She remembers her showing up especially for Fire Sine Fridays." Mireles flipped open a notepad of his own. "The only time the suspect ever spoke, the ticket seller says, she asked if . . . uh, the Blau Blau Rebellion was doing a gig."

"A *gig?*" said David Blau distastefully.

"When she found out they weren't," Mireles continued, "she didn't even bother to pay the cover. She left."

"A fan," Evelyn Blau said. "There's loyalty for you."

"And she came alone?" Crawford pressed.

Mireles had a thin, sallow face with eyes as brown as Hershey kisses. "It's like I said, Sergeant, she was careful to *appear* to be alone."

Bilker said, "I found a guy who'd seen her with somebody."

Sirens wailed in the distance. Traffic on the nearby expressway and the bass notes thrumming through the nightclub made the entire hill quiver like a drumskin.

"One of the yahoos who kep' yellin' during y'all's show," Bilker continued. "He got concerned when I told him what happened to Paulie. He said the freak that took him would sometimes sit at a table with a bearded fella."

"More," Crawford demanded.

"He tried to play it cool—punk, like—but he couldn't quite get it on, the look and all. Cowboy boots 'n' jeans instead of tennis shoes and pleated baggies. Like a guy with an eight-to-five job whose boss'd can him if he ever showed up lookin' freaky."

"Craig Puddicombe," I said.

"I've got to go see Adam," RuthClaire insisted, digging her fingernails into my wrist.

"Somebody needs to go back to your house," Crawford said. "This is a kidnapping. There may be a telephone call. That's almost always the next step, the telephone call."

"Not if the motive's revenge," RuthClaire said heatedly. "Not if they take him somewhere and kill him."

"I don't think that's likely," Crawford said. He explained that a kidnapping usually pointed to a less gruesome motive, namely, the extorting of a ransom. If Paulie's abductors had merely wanted to kill him to punish his parents, they could have shot him from ambush. They could have run him and his guardian down with an automobile. They could have set off a bomb on the porch. Instead, they had staged a crime requiring at least some knowledge of the child's mother's movements, some fairly elaborate disguises and subterfuge, lots of patience, and an entire bistro basement full of luck. Tonight, everything, including Adam's confinement in the Emory hospital, had come together for them. It was even possible that the accidental conjunction of all these elements had provided the couple an irresistible opportunity to act on impulse. Now, though, they would try to cash in. Crawford staked his reputation on the inevitability of a telephone call demanding money and outlining a sequence of steps for delivering the ransom.

Caroline, who had been holding RuthClaire's arm throughout this spiel, spoke up: "You're not being clear, Sergeant. Do you think the kidnappers planned the whole thing in excruciating detail, or do you think they got lucky and took the main chance? It seems to me that their initial motive might tip their ultimate behavior."

"I'm not being *clear*, young lady, because I'm not a mind reader. Maybe they planned everything in 'excruciating detail' for some other night, but got lucky this evening and jumped the gun. Same difference, as I see it. They're gonna ask for money."

There was more discussion. Bored now, the hangers-on on the sidewalk began to drift away. Vehicles eased along Spring Street and our own little alley in deference to the squad car at curbside. The night smelled of engine oil and abused asphalt. Neon streaked the floodlit edges of the sky.

The Blaus agreed to take RuthClaire home. Bilker would ride with them. Caroline and I would go to Emory Hospital to break the news of T.P.'s abduction to his father. The police would send detectives to the Montaraz house, both to protect its occupants and to monitor the unfolding of the kidnappers' extortion strategy. If twenty-four hours went by with no break in the case, the FBI would begin playing the most prominent role. Meanwhile, Crawford and Mireles would continue following up leads here at the nightclub. Elsewhere in Fulton County—as in DeKalb, Cobb, Clayton, and Gwinnett—sheriff's patrols and municipal police forces would set up interlocking dragnets.

Interlocking dragnets. It sounded good, but I reminded myself that no one knew what kind of vehicle Craig and Nancy had at their disposal. Surely, Puddicombe had not been able to keep his friend E.L.'s pickup truck for the past year without incurring arrest. On the other hand, maybe he had changed its tag, jacked up its body, pin-striped its hood. I gave Crawford a description of the truck as I remembered it—a brief already on file with the Georgia Bureau of Investigation—and he in turn had it radioed around the greater metropolitan area. (Any white-haired young woman gunning through Avondale Estates in a Ram Charger would provoke immediate suspicion.)

Bilker told me where he had parked my car. When I finally got the directions straight, Caroline and I told the others good night and walked arm in arm down the side-walk and through an alley to a crumbling asphalt terrace. A smelly Dempsy Dumpster occupied most of this space. Bilker had left the Mercedes beside the dumpster with two wheels on the terrace and two on the broken cobbles of the alley itself. No one else had even considered competing with him for the spot. Ignoring the effluvia from the trash bin, I pulled Caroline to me and kissed her full on the lips.

She quickly broke away. "Men have all the innate romance of doorstops."

RuthClaire had said something like that to me back in December. I wrinkled my nose and looked around. "Not exactly the Moulin Rouge, is it?"

"Paul, please don't fantasize a friendly fuck later this evening," Caroline said. "I'm not ready for it. Even if I had been ready for it, the kidnapping would've changed that."

A friendly fuck, I thought. Now there's an expression RuthClaire would have never used. Hearing it spoken, however, had an effect precisely the reverse of what Caroline intended—it excited me. Maybe I was one of those bleary-eyed lechers for whom dirty talk is an aphrodisiac. Dirty? A single four-letter word of hearty Anglo-Saxon origin?

Maybe, instead, I was a macho bigot who believed "bad language" was the province of males only. Me, macho? A bigot, maybe—but not a muscle-flexer. More than likely, truth be known, I was simply unused to hear-ing "bad language" on a woman's lips. The cultural upheaval of the past two decades had passed me by. I was a forty-seven-year-old southern gentleman who was only now getting straight the distinction in nuance between *shacking up* and *living together*.

"Look," Caroline was saying, "my car's still parked in front of the Montarazes. Tomorrow when you and RuthClaire visit Adam, one of you can drive my VW and leave it near the sociology building." She handed me her keys. "I *would* like to see you again, Paul. It's just that this isn't the time. I can't believe *you* think it is."

"Life's short, Miss Hanna. This proves it."

"Ah, another disciple of the *carpe diem* approach." Her voice took on a revealingly brittle edge: "You think they'll kill him?"

"They may." My knuckles whitened as I tightened my grip on the steering wheel. "Puddicombe may, at least. It's hard for me to believe that Nancy'd go along with him on that score. I don't know what he did to entice her up here, to get her to go punk—but they do share a common pain."

"The fact that Teavers died."

"Right. Her husband. His friend. I thought Nancy was free of that taint, though. I thought she'd managed to work through everything unscathed."

What Caroline next said struck me as a kind of sorrowful rebuke: "People who work through everything unscathed are rare. There may be nobody like that at all, only good pretenders."

"Maybe so."

"I don't know whether I'd even be able to trust an unscathed person, Paul. He—or she—wouldn't be human."

I looked at her sidelong. "The trouble is, you can't trust a scathed person, either. You can't trust anybody."

"No," Caroline murmured. "You can't trust anybody."

We rode for a while in silence. Then I began to speculate aloud on the kidnapping. Puddicombe had been hiding out for a year, eluding the police and plotting revenge. On the night of E.L.'s disappearance into the brick kiln, he had probably lit out for Alabama in his buddy's truck. There, after ditching the vehicle, he had lain low for a time, probably with the active aid of fellow Klan members. It was possible, of course, that he had left the

Southeast completely, striking out for the Rockies or the California coast. But if he had, he had almost certainly acquired another car. Teavers's pickup would have been a red flag to every highway patrolman between Opelika and Amarillo. Maybe, on the other hand, he had simply disguised himself—by growing a beard, say—and had ridden the bus.

Eventually, though, Puddicombe had returned from his fugitive exile, migrating as if magnetized to Georgia's capital city. In Atlanta, after all, it would not have been hard for him to find work as a dish washer or maybe even a garage mechanic. The biggest threat to his job would have lain in the likelihood of someone from Beulah Fork catching sight of him, but if his work had kept him, so to speak, backstage, that likelihood would have been a skimpy one. On the street, a beard and a pair of sunglasses would have preserved his cover. To trip himself up, he would have had to run a traffic light or neglect paying a bill. And so far, Puddicombe had prudently avoided those kinds of trip wires.

"How would he have involved Nancy?" Caroline said.

Probably a letter, I told her. He would have written only once, and he would have stipulated a meeting somewhere between Atlanta and Beulah Fork. At a roadhouse or a small-town café, he would have pressed his case, playing on Nancy's submerged bitterness and arguing the need to bring about Elvis Lamar's posthumous vindication. Initially, she may have resisted some of these arguments, but at later rendezvous, each new meeting arranged at the one before, she would have begun to relish the idea of avenging her late husband—maybe not by killing anyone, but by bringing E.L. back to life as a worrisome force in the Montarazes' undeserved paradise of love and success. Indeed, she and Craig may have fallen in love themselves. Once, after all, E.L. and Craig had been as close as brothers, and somewhere in the Bible it was written that a man ought to wed his brother's widow so that he can protect her person and champion her causes.

"You know the Bible?" Caroline asked.

"Only by hearsay. The same way Craig Puddicombe

would know it. In Beulah Fork, distortions of it contaminate everyone's thinking, mine included. We have a bountiful legacy of high-minded misquotation.''

"You think they're lovers?''

"If not lovers, sweethearts. In this day and age, probably lovers.''

"Why so certain?''

"Nancy's only eighteen. She was widowed at seventeen. Most of her school chums have moved from Beulah Fork, or married, or both. When she told me she was leaving the West Bank, she said it was to seek her fortune. Male chauvinist pig that I am, I took that as a code word for husband. She was bored, lonely, and vulnerable. Why shouldn't she fall in love with Craig?''

"Or he with her?''

"Right. Craig was E.L.'s twin in a lot of ways, and Nancy is a pretty little girl. Or *was*, anyway. They're both probably fighting to make sense of events and attitudes that they haven't handled all that well by themselves.''

"Nancy was doing all right, wasn't she?''

"Until Craig contacted her. Until this past April.''

"What about the kidnapping? Do you think they've been following RuthClaire and Adam around, waiting for an opportunity like tonight's?''

"Looks like it.''

"Then tonight had to be a dream-come-true for your . . . well, your Puddicombe Conspiracy. Everything fell into place for them. Nancy was able to walk off with Paulie as easily as a kid steals an apple from a produce bin. Doesn't that strike you as—'' she hunched her shoulders, shivering in recollection—"weird?''

"But everything didn't fall into place for them. Bilker came along. You and I came along. They had to make some of their own luck, and they did that. Nancy's costume, her choice of the balloon handout as the best time to approach us, their goddamn perfect getaway.'' I took a quick glance at Caroline. "What're you trying to imply? That there's something fishy about this business?''

"Paul, please don't take this wrong—''

"God save me, take *what* wrong?''

"I don't know RuthClaire. I don't know Adam. For that matter, I really don't know you. It crossed my mind—just briefly and not very seriously—that this might be a . . . you know, a publicity stunt. To promote their art and David Blau's gallery."

"Jesus Christ!"

"Look, Paul, I know it's backasswards and egotistical, but for a moment I was afraid I was being made sport of."

"Sport of? What do you mean, sport of?"

"Not after the police arrived. And not really before, either. It's just that nothing that happened at the club seemed real. I couldn't help thinking I was an outsider, not getting the joke."

"The joke? What cynicism! And five minutes ago you were berating me for hoping for a friendly fuck on the same evening my godson gets abducted!"

"Paul, I was confessing to a doubt I had, not leveling an accusation. You're turning this into something it really isn't."

I was thoroughly confused. Our conversation had gone off the rails with her plea not to take her next remark wrong. Had I taken it wrong, or had she impugned RuthClaire and Adam's integrity as artists and parents? I thumbed an antacid tablet out of a roll in my pants pocket and inserted it under my tongue.

"Take me home, Paul. You don't need me at the hospital. Adam certainly doesn't need me there, either. I'm sorry this has happened. I'm deeply, deeply sorry."

I took her home, to an apartment complex on Clifton, not far from the Emory campus. My attempts to get her talking again met with monosyllabic rebuffs. She had wounded me by taking potshots at my friends. I had wounded her by calling her to account for her meanness and vanity.

Caroline's apartment building had pinkish stucco walls, gables with casement windows, and rustic Tudor trim. I parked beside the walk to her front porch, but before I could even undo my seat buckle, she got out. Then she leaned back down and gave a harsh barking little laugh.

"What's that supposed to mean?"

"I was about to tell you how much I enjoyed the evening."

"Oh."

"Parts of it, I did," she said. Then she slammed the door and hiked up her walk like a drill sergeant in the Scandinavian Fashion Force. I waited until she was safely inside before giving a salute and driving wistfully away.

"HE'S AWAKE," the nurse on Adam's floor said when I showed up at the hospital to fulfill my designated role as Evil Messenger. "He doesn't sleep all that much, anyway, but after Mrs. Montaraz called to tell us you were coming, I went down there to see if he needed to be awakened. He didn't." A middle-aged woman with strong Germanic features and eyes like indigo marbles, the nurse tilted her head. "Is there anything I can do, Mr. Loyd?"

"Just make sure we're not disturbed for a while."

The nurse could not contain herself. "What's wrong?"

"If RuthClaire didn't tell you when she called, ma'am, then I certainly can't tell you." Unintentionally, the words came out like a reprimand. I patted the woman's shoulder to soften their impact, then walked down the long, antiseptic corridor.

Adam was sitting up in bed in the dark. He had propped two pillows behind him, and his legs were crossed beneath his sheet in the lotus position of an Oriental contemplative. The IV bottle beside him, its tube running to his wrist like a life-giving amber fuse, glinted eerily in the darkness. The bandages on his lower face gave him the look of an unfinished plaster-of-Paris bust. He sat remarkably still, and I felt as I had felt as a small boy, approaching my father after some terrible disobedience.

I did not reach for the light switch—maybe for reasons of self-concealment. I stood in the doorway letting my eyes adjust and noticing with what stoic endurance Adam's own eyes were trying to allay my fears. Somehow, he had picked up on them like a faint but acrid scent.

Don't quail from necessity, his eyes said. Come sit down.

I crossed the room and sat down in the chair that RuthClaire ordinarily used. But I must have appeared about ready to bolt, for Adam lifted the arm to which the IV tube was attached and gently patted me, as I had patted the nurse. Go ahead, he was telling me; be as brutal as your news demands.

"RuthClaire would have come to tell you this, Adam, but circumstances don't allow. I'm her emissary. I'm here to tell you what nobody—not even your own wife—could tell you easily."

Adam's eyes grew a little larger, and he made a series of signs that somehow permitted me to interpret them.

"No, no one's died. So far as we know. Tiny Paul's been taken." And I told him in detail what had happened at Sinusoid Disturbances and afterward, including the police's conviction that we would soon receive a ransom demand and my own speculations about the identities of the kidnappers. At the moment, though, everyone was walking gingerly across a rope bridge over a chasm of indeterminate depth. We would not be able to see how far it was to the bottom until Craig Puddicombe or Nancy Teavers called. Lamely, I concluded, "All we can do is wait."

Adam pulled the IV tube free of the plastic connector in his wrist and lifted himself up high enough to hook the tube over its pole. There, it ceased to drip. My friend was wearing one of those hospital gowns with the split up the rear, a design feature of curious motivation. Was the split to make it easier for orderlies to administer enemas, or was it a sartorial aid to patients frequently victimized by sudden diarrhea attacks? These seemed mutually exclusive goals, but the gowns were an immemorial hospital humiliation. Adam managed to wear his without looking supremely ridiculous (maybe because nudity held no terror for him); but when he hopped nimbly down from his bed in the garment, I found myself glancing around the room in search of a safety pin with which to close up the vent in back. At Sinusoid Disturbances, I would have had no trouble finding one.

"Adam, what are you doing?"

He brushed past me to the sink and mounted a stairstep stool giving him access to his own image in the mirror. His hairy buttocks peeked through the split in his gown, and the backs of his thighs tightened and relaxed as he raised and lowered himself on tiptoes. It was then that I realized he was unwrapping the gauzy cerements holding the lower half of his face together.

"Adam!"

He shot me a warning look, motioned for me to keep my voice down, and resumed unpackaging his jaw. He had already discarded the foam-rubber cup for his chin, dropping it into the sink. Only the light spilling in from the corridor enabled him to work, but he was peeling off layer after layer with an alacrity that suggested he knew what he was doing. Had he been practicing for a moment such as this? It hardly seemed likely, but how else account for the speed and knowledgeability of his fingers?

I whispered, "Adam, you can't leave the hospital. There's not a thing any of us can do until they call."

His fingers slowed a little, but he kept unpeeling gauze.

"What if the kidnappers ring up the nurses' station instead of the house? That's a possibility, you know. If you rush home to RuthClaire, there'll be nobody here to take their call to the hospital. Nobody who can respond to their demands, I mean." I was improvising, only improvising, but the possibility began to sound realistic even to me. "You couldn't talk to them, of course, but you could authorize me to act as your spokesman. Think about it, Adam. Somebody *has* to be here."

The habiline shrugged my hand away and finished taking off his bandages. I looked at him in profile. His nose seemed less flat, his cheekbones slightly higher, his chin a good deal more pronounced. Not only had the plastic surgeons reconstructed his buccal cavity, they had given his entire face a more modern configuration. None of the changes was severe or blatant, but together they gave him a streamlined, Nilotic handsomeness.

Adam came down the stairstep stool so that I was towering over him again, embarrassed by my own moronic tallness. From a hamper he grabbed a pair of clean white towels, which he folded double and spread out on the floor next to the bed. He nodded me down. I knelt on one of the towels, and he, of course, knelt on the other, turning me back into Goliath to his humble shepherd boy.

Nevertheless, side by side, we prayed. Or, I suppose, Adam prayed while I knelt beside him with my forehead pressed against the edge of the mattress. "Pray without ceasing," it says in Thessalonians, but I couldn't even manage to get past the part about forgiving-us-our-trespasses-as-we-forgive-those-who-trespass, etc., without thinking of Nancy's perfidy, or how Caroline had thought the kidnapping might be a publicity stunt, or when I was likely to be able to resume my reponsibilities at the West Bank. Pray without ceasing? I couldn't do any better than an intermittent, "Don't let the bastards kill him, God," between which times I fantasized slitting Craig's throat, taking Caroline to bed, and catering the reception of an expensive wedding party at Muscadine Gardens—not necessarily in that order or all at once. My knees got sore, and my kidneys ached. Somehow, though, I stayed on the floor beside Adam for almost three hours, sharing his vigil.

At 3:57 A.M.—I checked my watch—the nurse came to the door to report that Adam had a telephone call.

"I tried to tell him that this was an absurd hour to call," she said, "but he told me if I didn't fetch Mr. Montaraz, I'd . . . I'd 'live to regret it.' "

"It's Puddicombe," I whispered. Aloud I said, "We'll be down there in two minutes. Go back and tell him." My heart was leaping against my rib cage. Too often, the parents of stolen children hear nothing from the abductors. A break like this—a break I had desperately anticipated—was a variety of sardonic miracle.

The nurse left, and I began banging my forehead against the mattress in despairing joy. The son of a bitch had actually telephoned! I rocked back on my heels and mouthed a silent thank you. Adam touched my shoulder.

"*God. Bless. You,*" he managed.

I gaped at Adam. He had spoken, and never had I heard a voice so peculiarly pitched and modulated. A scratchy computer sort of voice struggling to sound human. Impulsively, then, I hugged the little man. Holding him at arm's length, I told him that he had better put on a pair of pants. If we were too long getting to the nurses' station, Puddicombe—or whoever it was—would grow nervous about the delay and hang up. I rubbed two fingers along the side of my nose. They came away wet.

A PAIR of khaki trousers his only clothing, Adam accompanied me to the nurses' station. The woman on duty there was waiting for us with her hand over the telephone mouthpiece.

"Is there an extension?" I said.

She nodded at the glass-walled office behind the counter. "In there. If you want to, you can cradle the receiver on the speaker device beside the telephone, Mr. Loyd, and it'll broadcast like a radio."

"That's good," I said. "You wouldn't happen to have a tape recorder, too, would you?"

"One of our day nurses, Andrea, has a jam box, one of those big silver things that young people carry around to deafen their elders with. It also records. Andrea leaves her tapes in the drawer. If it's important, you can tape over one of those—so long as *you* take the responsibility for ruining a favorite of hers."

"Yes, ma'am."

At which point it dawned on the nurse that Adam's face was free of its bandages. "Oh, my God! Those weren't supposed to come off yet. Dr. Ruggiero will flay me alive."

"No, he won't," I said. "Mr. Montaraz is healing nicely."

I led Adam into the office, found the jam box, rummaged up an unmarked tape, put it in the machine, and pressed the record button. Then I set the telephone receiver into the amplifier unit and depressed the lighted button on the base of the telephone. The nurse, having observed all this through the glass, hung up her phone and left to make a tour of the floor. Efficient and discreet, that good woman.

"We're here," I told the caller.

"Who's 'we'?" he asked, and those two syllables identified him for me: Craig Puddicombe. He had made no effort to disguise his voice. (If the restaurant business ever got too tame for me, maybe I could go into police work.)

I told Craig who I was.

"The first dude in history to let a hibber snake his old lady."

"We were divorced when RuthClaire married Adam."

"Yeah. And you even played pimp for 'em, didn't you. Now you're up there in the hospital holding the hibber's hand. Jesus, Mr. Loyd, you take the cake."

"But you and Nancy took the child. What do you—"

He cut me off. "Get your tape recorders all set up? Get a call off to the police? That why you took so goddamn long pickin' up the phone?"

"Adam had to get dressed. His room's at the far—"

"Stuff that, Mr. Loyd." He said something to somebody else in the room with him, but it was all muffled and indistinct. Then he said, "Prove to me the hibber's really there."

"How? You know he can't talk."

"He can sing, can't he? He can hum like a rotary engine."

"Craig, he's had an operation. His face is bandaged. The entire lower portion of his face was remodeled."

"Yeah, well, he'll still be stump-ugly 's far as I'm concerned. Have him hum through his bandages."

I started to protest, but Adam pulled my handkerchief out of my coat pocket, turned it into a bandanna, tied the bandanna around his face, and stepped toward the amplifier to hum the melody of a Cokesbury hymn.

"That's the hibber, all right. A mule brayin' into a barrel."

"Prove to me you've got Tiny Paul," I said.

"By doin' what? You wanna hear him scream?"

I put my hand on Adam's arm. He stopped his unusual humming—half lament, half yodel—and removed the bandanna. He shook his head in response to Craig's last question.

"Never mind," I said. "What do you want?"

"A ransom. If Mister and Missus Miscegenation give us the ransom we want, they'll get their filthy little *whatever-it-is* back."

"How much money, Craig?"

"Who said anything about money?"

The unexpectedness of this really hit me hard. What sort of ransom required no monetary payoff?

"Y'all still there?" Craig asked.

"Yeah, we're here. State your terms. We're listening."

For a moment, Craig consulted with his accomplice. Then, as if reading from a manuscript, he said, "We don't want money. We don't do violence. What we want is what's right. You may think the brat's been taken because his hibber daddy killed E.L., or you may think we covet what the brat's unnatural family's built up for itself since the hibber did that killin'. It ain't so, though, neither of those guesses. We took the brat to make some undone justice get done. We took him to set some wrong things right."

This nonsense was scaring me. "What the hell do you want us to do, Craig? Come on, get to the point."

"Have a little patience," the amplifier said, mockingly polite. A sound of paper rattling. "You get the little halfbreed back if and when you do the following stuff. First of all, Mister and Missus Miscegenation they stop livin' together. Second of all, they tell the papers and the TV they've stopped. They say they regret the sinful example they've set decent whites and blacks all over the world by bringin' their mongrel brat into it. Third of all, they—"

"Craig," I pleaded.

"Third of all, they make a public apology to the parents, family, and widow of E. L. Teavers, my friend. And fourth, the hibber gives himself up for trial on charges of—" a meaningful pause—"uh, malicious homicide."

"Craig, E.L. was trying to *kill* Adam. You and your crew had *kidnapped* us, for God's sake—the same way you and Nancy have criminally abducted Tiny Paul. There's not a court anywhere that would convict Adam of anything but saving all our lives!"

"Ah, we was just tryin' to scare some sense into you. Nobody out at Synder's place was gonna get kilt—not until your goddamn hibber chucked E.L. down that hole."

"But that's what E.L. was trying to do to *him*, Craig!"

"Puttin' your hibber down that hole didn't kill him, did it? Him and his kind lived hundreds of goddamn centuries in caves. So puttin' a hibber down a brick-kiln hole hurts it 'bout as much as tossin' Br'er Rabbit into a goddamn briar patch. He popped back out, didn't he? That proves it."

Absurd, absurd. The boy and I were operating from completely different sets of premises. I changed tacks: "Is that it? Four things to do to get T.P. back?"

"We gotta fifth un." Our tormentor rattled his prepared text again. "Inasmuch as Mister and Missus Miscegenation have made beaucoups of bucks from the degenerate elements of American society, and are richer than anyone but the upright and godly ought to be, they've got to—" Craig halted. His fancy lead-in had taken a little steam out of his delivery. "Inasmuch as all that, they've got to make contributions adding up to fifty thousand dollars to ten different charities and political groups of our choosing. They'll get the list on Monday or Tuesday. Each group gets at least three thousand, but—and this is big of us, now—Mister and Missus Hibber can decide themselves how to ladle out the twenty thousand left over after the first split."

"Money. It comes down to money."

"The money ain't important, Mr. Loyd. It's not for us, anyhow. It's only 'cause they got it and don't deserve it and need to give it to somebody who does—*that's* why we're makin' 'em do it. They do it by check, too. We get to see the canceled checks as proof it's all been done like we asked it to be. The list comin' in the mail explains the whole system.''

Incredulously, I asked, ''They won't get Tiny Paul back until all the canceled checks come in?''

''Not until they've split up and annulled their ungodly marriage and lived apart long enough to show us they've really done it.''

''Craig, what's the time frame? How long are you going to hold Tiny Paul? There's no give-and-take in your terms. For you, it's open-ended—but for RuthClaire and Adam, it's a nightmare. And if they're living apart when you finally release the baby, who are you going to release him to?''

''To your ex-old lady, of course. The hibber don't have any rights in this.''

''But *how long*, Craig. Play fair with us, damn it!''

''They'll know when we do, won't they?'' And he hung up. The speaker on the amplifier was amplifying a dial tone. No way to trace the call. It had come through the hospital's central switching system. So Craig Puddicombe and Nancy Teavers, with T.P. in their doubtful care, had sunk again into the nearly impenetrable anonymity of a metropolitan area with close to four million people. If, in fact, they had not made their call from Alabama, Tennessee, Florida, or one of the Carolinas. And even if they were still in Greater Atlanta, they had more than a hundred square miles of labyrinthine territory in which to go to ground.

Adam slumped wearily into the chair at the desk. His voice, when he spoke, was a series of agonized croaks.

''*I wish. Miss RuthClaire. Had let. McElroy. Baptize him.*''

ADAM MADE up his mind to leave Emory Hospital. While I telephoned RuthClaire, he dressed, packed a suitcase, and faced down the bewildered night nurse with a painful repetition of the words, "Goodbye, goodbye. Going now." During this confrontation, he maintained the dignified decorum of a Japanese chargé d'affaires. When I got off the phone, the nurse put through a hasty call to one of Adam's doctors, who at first voiced angry opposition to our plans to decamp at this hour. Talking briefly to me, however, he at last gave his reluctant consent, and the orderlies who had been summoned to keep Adam and me from hijacking an elevator to freedom dutifully backed off. The nurse then rode downstairs with us, reminding Adam to eat nothing chewier than oatmeal until Dr. Ruggiero had examined him again and pointing out that he would not be able to communicate as well as he wished until he had undergone his scheduled speech therapy.

At the Montaraz house, only a few minutes later, RuthClaire ran to Adam and embraced him.

I stood just inside the door connecting the kitchen to the big downstairs studio. The other three men in that room were Bilker Moody and the same pair of GBI agents who had driven RuthClaire and me back to the Synder property on the day after our abduction from the West Bank. Niedrach. Davison. I couldn't recall their first names. They wore nondescript business suits of flimsy black cotton, almost as if they had gone shopping together and picked their outfits off the same rack. Davison, however, sported a beige banlon shirt under his jacket, while Niedrach had made his own distinguishing fashion statement with a red clip-on tie and a red canvas belt on whose buckle there gleamed the embossed head of the mascot of the University of Georgia, a bulldog wearing a freshman's beanie.

Bilker's opinion of the GBI agents revealed itself in the curl of his upper lip.

At last Adam and RuthClaire separated, and RuthClaire distractedly reintroduced everyone. I gave Niedrach the cassette on which I had recorded Craig's ransom demands. A tape player was produced, and the GBI men sat down next to it to listen to the cassette. Bilker retreated to the bar, Adam paced, and RuthClaire perched on the arm of the divan beside Niedrach. I squatted opposite the divan on the other side of the marble coffee table.

". . . *don't want money. We don't do violence. What we want is what's right. You may think the brat's been taken* . . ."

Afterward, Niedrach said, "That's the craziest—I mean, *the* absolutely craziest—set of ransom demands I've ever heard."

Seated gnomishly on the white-leather wheel of one of the Montarazes' high-gloss crimson bar stools, Bilker drawled, "The reason you're dumfuzzled is that this ain't really a kidnapping anymore."

Niedrach raised his eyebrows. "No? What is it, then? A dope deal?"

"A hostage situation."

"Every kidnap victim is a hostage," the GBI agent countered with as much tact as he could muster. "That's tautological."

"Yeah. Logical 'cause you've been taught it. But a hostage situation's different from a kidnappin'. Why? For the simple fact that money ain't the perpetrator's number-one priority. It's the pursuit of some far-out political or ideological goal by means of terroristic threats."

"He told us they wouldn't kill Paulie," RuthClaire said.

Bilker revolved a half-turn this way, a half-turn the other. Because of his bulk, I almost expected to see the legs of the stool screwing curls of hardwood up around themselves as they sank into the floor. "Yeah, well, Puddicombe's cooler than any kidnapper 'cause he's got the Great White Jehovah, Jumper of Jigaboos, on his side. He'll take more chances than your two-bit kidnapper. If you push him, he'll raise the stakes."

"The stakes he's playing for are revenge," I said.

"Mebbe so. But he gets it by makin' us dance to his fiddlin', not by crashin' the Montarazes' bank accounts."

"So?" said Niedrach.

"We better dance to his fiddlin'. Or make it *look* like it, anyway. Otherwise, he'll—pardon me, Mrs. Montaraz—he'll off his hostage."

Davison said, "How do you know so much about it?"

"Mebbe I watch the 'CBS Evening News.' "

Niedrach stood up and shoved his hands into his pockets. "Mr. Moody's pegged this exactly right. Now that we know it's a kidnapping—or a hostage situation involving a kidnap victim—the FBI's going to take over *primary* responsibility for solving the case. We have to contact them."

"But you and Mr. Davison have been through this with us before," RuthClaire said. "The FBI won't dump you completely, will they?"

"I hope not. I'll try to make that very point, Mrs. Montaraz, in telling them what's happened so far. In the meantime, though, it'd be smart if Adam—Mr. Montaraz, I mean—moved out. To give every appearance of complying with the sickie's demands. Because Mr. Moody's right about that."

Bilker stopped revolving his stool, embarrassed to find an ally where he had posited a bungling bureaucrat.

RuthClaire said, "I just can't believe Nancy would let anything happen to Paulie. It's unreal."

"She may be in as much danger as your son," Niedrach said.

And so it was decided that Adam would indeed move out of the house on Hurt Street. Niedrach would have a secretary at the state GBI offices telephone the Atlanta newspapers with an anonymous tip about the deteriorating marital situation of the Montarazes. She would claim to be a neighbor with firsthand knowledge of their troubles, including a confidence from RuthClaire that her husband had just agreed to a trial separation requiring his immediate departure from the household. RuthClaire was then to grant a tight-lipped interview omitting any mention of the kidnapping and succinctly confirming the anonymous neighbor's separation story.

"But a separation on what grounds?" RuthClaire pleaded.

"Anything you can think of that doesn't strike you as too unseemly," Niedrach said.

Adam tried to speak, but his gravelish computer voice would not cooperate for him. He reverted to sign language, and RuthClaire interpreted it for the rest of us. "Career incompatibility," she said. "We've been arguing about Adam's career plans. I want him to keep painting, but he wishes to enroll—" she struggled to read his gestures correctly—"in the Candler School of Theology at Emory. He wishes to take the curriculum leading to the Master of Theological Studies degree. I'm to tell the reporter that Adam has gone off the deep end on matters God-related."

"That's great," Niedrach said. "That's inspired."

Davison wrinkled the bridge of his nose. "A habiline religious nut?"

Yes. Apparently so. The point of the ruse, of course, was to get word to Craig that RuthClaire and Adam had stopped living together. The story's appearance in print would insure its finding its way onto local TV news broadcasts, where Craig might be monitoring recent muggings, rapes, street-name changes, city-council shouting matches, and mayoral trips overseas.

"What's the chance of the TV and papers catchin' wind of the kidnappin' itself?" Bilker asked.

"A dust-up at a place like Sinusoid Disturbances is a regular thing," Davison replied. "We're in the clear for now."

Niedrach said, "Puddicombe's likely to break the news himself. Publicity doesn't worry him, he might even like it. So if the story leaks, Paulie won't be in any more, or any less, danger than he already is."

Where was Adam going to move to? We mulled the options. He needed a shelter that offered privacy as well as a certain remoteness from the urban bustle of Atlanta. What qualified? A rented house in Alpharetta? A lakeside cottage in Cherokee County? The monastery in Conyers?

"Let him come to Paradise Farm with me," I suggested.

RuthClaire said, "Wouldn't Craig look askance on that? You're my ex-husband. You're also Paulie's godfather."

"Two castoffs commiserating," I said. "It's honky-on-hibber marriage that upsets him, not white and black males cohabiting."

"What would that do to our cover story about his decision to attend the Candler School of Theology?"

Adam signed again, and RuthClaire said, "It's too late, now, to enroll for summer term at the seminary. Besides, the fall semester doesn't officially commence until the last Monday in August."

"So the alibi holds," Niedrach said. "Take him with you, Mr. Loyd. We've got an agent in Hothlepoya County investigating the drug scene there. He can act as a go-between, relaying information from us to you and vice versa. So go on."

"When?"

"As soon as he can get ready to go. Now, if possible."

RUTHCLAIRE AND Adam went upstairs together to get him packed for his stay at Paradise Farm. And, of course, to tell each other goodbye. Bilker and the GBI agents, discreetly embarrassed by this turn of events, sat together in the kitchen drinking coffee and swapping companionable tall tales about their prowess as bodyguards and their expertise as sleuths.

"I'll be back in an hour," I informed them.

Davison, who had draped his flimsy black jacket over his chair, blurted, "An *hour?* Where the hell do you think you're going?"

"To tell somebody goodbye."

I drove to Caroline's—not in her little blue beetle, but in my big silver Mercedes. I arrived at 9:37 A.M., bleary-eyed, funky, and anxiously aware of the deadline I had set

myself. An hour? I now had only forty-six minutes. It
might take me that long to convince my hapless generative
equipment that it could still *pretend* to that title. It might
take me longer to convince the lovely Caroline to let me
try to convince my equipment. Wasn't I presuming too
much?

Staggering along the walk to her porch, I felt that I was
moving in a pair of tinfoil shorts. I itched. I had not slept
all night. My stubbly beard seemed to be infested with
microscopic lumberjacks sawing away at every follicle.
Who—*whom*—was I kidding? I had no chance with this
lady.

Forty-four minutes.

At last, bracing myself against her door, I leaned with
one sharp elbow and all my bathetic longing into the tiny
button that rang her bell. Her dear, melodious bell. Inside
her apartment chimed the opening eight notes of "Tara's
Theme" from *Gone with the Wind*. They chimed over and
over again because I was simply too weary to pull back my
elbow.

Forty-three minutes.

"Who is it?" Caroline's voice cried.

"Me."

She opened her door the three inches permitted by her
safety latch. "What do *you* want?"

"A friendly fee-fi-fo-fum."

"Has anything happened? Have they found Paulie?"

I squared my shoulders and tried to alchemize my weary
nonchalance into concerned sobriety. "Listen, Caroline, if
you'll—"

"That's not my car," she said, peering past me. "How
am I going to get my car home?" She shook her head.
"Damn! That's not important, is it? The important thing is
Paulie. I'm still three-quarters asleep."

"If you'll let me in, I'll tell you all I—"

She was unfastening the chain. The door opened, and
she was standing against a backdrop of framed Broadway
posters, porcelain flower vases, and at least two copper
umbrella holders. The cool breath of the apartment's air-
conditioning rippled over me. As for Caroline herself, she

was wearing a yellow dressing gown that seemed to be lined with layer upon liquid-thin layer of even paler material. She looked and smelled like the demigoddess of a fragrant wheat field.

"You'll have to talk to me first," she said. "You'll have to shower. You'll have to eat breakfast with me."

"Forty-one minutes," I said. "I've got forty-one minutes."

"Listen, Mr. Loyd, there's a clock in every room but the bathroom. You can hang your watch on the shower spigot for all I care. If you have any sense, though, you'll forget all about your stupid forty-one minutes and put your watch in the bottom of one of your shoes." She pulled me out of the doorway and shut us into the Fundy Bay briskness of her apartment.

As matters unfolded, I put my Elgin in the bottom of one of my shoes and deliberately forgot about it.

I SPENT more than forty-one minutes at Caroline's. I spent more than *eighty-two* minutes at Caroline's. In fact, I didn't make it back to Hurt Street until better than two hours after my leave-taking—but neither Bilker nor the GBI agents could find it in themselves to scold me because Caroline herself, fetching in old jeans and a bright yellow tank top, had accompanied me. After all, she had to pick up her Volkswagen; moreover, as a witness to the crime, she wished to accommodate Niedrach and Davison by recounting the event from her point of view. Wouldn't they have sought her out eventually, anyway? They admitted that they would have.

"Besides, RuthClaire might appreciate having another woman around for a while today," I said. "It's not going to be easy for her with Adam gone and only Bilker's shoulder to cry on."

Bilker snorted, in agreement rather than indignation.

And when the Montarazes came downstairs, RuthClaire

and Caroline embraced like long-lost siblings miraculously reunited.

Adam and I, meanwhile, carried his belongings out to my car for the trip to Beulah Fork. Bilker lent a hand. Even on its high-performance shocks, the rear of my Mercedes began to sag. Adam had insisted on adding to his own luggage at least three dozen of RuthClaire's more recent paintings. Although fairly small, these canvases were still affixed to their frames, and Bilker and I had to struggle to wedge them into the trunk between the suitcases and the pasteboard boxes.

"Adam, what's the point of taking the paintings?"

"*Remembrance*," he gargled.

Because it was painful for him to speak, I did not question him further—but it occurred to me that he was preparing himself for a lengthy separation from RuthClaire. This was not a surrender to despair, however, but an act of faith. If he and his wife were to be reunited with their child, they would have to accede to and of course endure the stipulations of the kidnappers. With luck, the GBI might break the case, but there was no guarantee.

But these paintings—the drab acrylics that she had hopefully entitled *Souls*—still seemed to me the least distinguished work of RuthClaire's career. They were blatant mediocrities. Only a uxorious husband could love them. I scratched my head. Adam was not really the uxorious type, but his fondness for this series—when, for "remembrances," he could have taken better examples of his wife's art—was truly puzzling.

We got away from Atlanta shortly after noon. On our drive down, Adam read. He had a stack of hardcover books at his feet on the floorboard, and he seemed to pick up, thumb through, and peruse a new one about every fifteen minutes or so. *Does God Exist?* and *Eternal Life* by Hans Küng, *God and the Astronomers* by Robert Jastrow, *God and the New Physics* by Paul Davies, *The Dancing Wu Li Masters* by Gary Zukav, *The Reenchantment of the World* by Morris Berman, *Mind and Nature* by Gregory Bateson, an anthology entitled *The Mind's I* by a pair of editors whose names escape me. I don't know what all else. I had the impression that Adam was reviewing these texts, checking passages that he had underlined in previous readings, rather than completely encompassing each volume for the first time—but even this formidable intellectual feat had its intimidating aspects. Out of respect for my passenger's activity, I kept my mouth shut.

At Paradise Farm, unloading the car, I finally broke my self-imposed vow of silence: "Adam, you know the story you told RuthClaire to tell the reporter about the reasons for your separation?"

He raised his eyebrows.

"The one about entering the seminary this fall?"

"Yes?" he croaked.

"It came to you so quickly, that apparent fiction. I was wondering if . . . well, if it might really be something you'd like to try."

"Oh, yes," he managed. "I. Have. Thought. About. It."

LIVIA GEORGE, Hazel Upchurch, and our latest little waitress from Tocqueville Junior College did not jump for joy upon my return. An hour ago, a tour bus from Muscadine Gardens had set down forty people at the West Bank's front door. These people had descended like a flock of crows, eaten a dozen different menu items, left a skimpy collective tip, and flown away in their bus with a rude backfire.

"Did you give them the substitutes they wanted?"

Livia George was slumped spraddle-legged at a table near the cash register. "Don' I always, Mistah Paul?"

"Everybody was taken care of?"

She gave me a disgusted look. "We done turned you a pretty profit, and we done been doin' it the whole livelong week. You jes' like a man runs up to put out a fire when it's awreddy burnt down his house."

"Livvy, you say the sweetest things."

"How's Mistah Adam?" she abruptly asked, sitting up straight and wiping her brow. "How's Miss RuthClaire?"

"Fine," I lied. "Fine."

I made some noises about the apparent success of Adam's operation, but beyond that partial truth I couldn't comfortably go. To prevent any further discussion of the matter, I helped clean up the restaurant, then stayed on for the five-o'clock dinner crowd. Our receipts for the day were encouraging, and I drove Livia George home without once mentioning that I had a guest in my house.

NEXT MORNING, somewhat closer to noon than to sunup, I was awakened by the television set downstairs.

I knotted my terrycloth robe about my waist and stumbled barefoot down the steps to find Adam sitting cross-legged on the floor with a section of the Sunday *Journal-Constitution* strewn all around him and my RCA XL100's screen flickering with ill-defined violet and magenta images of Dwight "Happy" McElroy's "Great Gospel Giveaway" broadcast.

"This is my story, this is my song," sang the hundred-member choir behind McElroy. "Praising my Savior all the day long!"

Shots of the choir were interspersed with wide-angle pans of the congregation in McElroy's huge Televangelism Center in Rehoboth, Louisiana. This soaring, baroquely buttressed structure had been paid for by the four-bit to five-dollar contributions of hundreds of thousands of low-income subscribers to the doctrinal guidelines of the Greater Christian Constituency of America, Inc. Despite the raddled colors on my picture tube, I could see quite clearly that attending the 3-G service were more enraptured souls than you could reasonably expect to find at the Omni during an Atlanta Hawks basketball game. Seven thousand people? Ten? However many there were, they must have converged on Rehoboth from every city and hamlet on the Gulf Coast, not excluding Baton Rouge, New Orleans, Biloxi, and Mobile. The blessed place rocked.

"Ah," I said. "Your favorite show."

Adam was already dressed. A pair of light brown bush shorts and an orange T-shirt celebrating the pleasures of River Street in Savannah. He handed me a section of the paper called "The Arts."

"Turn first page," he growled, but, overnight, his speech had become clearer and more fluid.

I obeyed. What greeted my eye on the inside page was this headline:

MARRIAGE OF WORLD-FAMOUS ATLANTA ARTISTS ON SKIDS AS RESULT OF HABILINE'S DECISION TO ATTEND SEMINARY

Beside the brief story was a file photograph of Adam and RuthClaire in "happier times," namely, at the opening of his show at Abraxas in February. My own face was a smudge of dots among other ill-defined faces in the background.

"That was quick, wasn't it?"

I read the story. It quoted RuthClaire to the effect that Adam's pursuit of spiritual fulfillment had left him little time for either Tiny Paul or her. She still loved him. However, that very love made it impossible to deny him what he most wanted, a chance to study at Candler without the encumbrances of a demanding wife and child. She had offered to support him in his quest for a theological degree, but all he really wished was complete freedom from family obligations. No one alive fully understood the habiline mind, but in some respects Adam's outlook was that of a medieval ascetic with a calling for the priesthood. Had she not intercepted him on his northward trek through Georgia nearly two years ago, almost certainly he would have discovered his spiritual bent without first marrying.

Adam grunted. "She neglects to say. That 'almost certainly.' I would have. Remained a naked animal."

"Never mind. You still end up looking like a horse's butt, Adam. What kind of man abandons his wife and son to begin a course of religious study? Jesus."

"I do not care how I end up. Looking. To people who do not know me."

"You just want Paulie back?"

"Yes."

On "Gospel Giveaway," McElroy had launched into a sermon, the words rolling from him like Gulf Coast combers in hurricane season, powerful, dangerous, unrelenting. (Of course, there was also the ever-present inset of the vivacious woman interpreting the sermon for the program's deaf viewers, her hands flashing before her like hungry seagulls.) Suddenly, though, McElroy was holding up a copy of the same section of the Atlanta paper now in my own hands.

". . . a continuing assault on the American family," he thundered, waving the newspaper at his congregation. "I had planned to apologize this morning for my overzealousness last summer in castigatin' the former RuthClaire Loyd for livin' in sin with a male *crea*ture not her husband. Well, it's long since become evident to everybody that this so-called *crea*ture is a *man*. He and Miss RuthClaire were in fact husband and wife at the time of their apparent illicit cohabitation. That bein' so, they *deserved* an apology from me. Why, this past week I visited Adam Montaraz at a hospital in Atlanta and placed my hands square on his head and baptized him into the everlastin' glory and the ever-glorious communion of the Body of Christ, say *Amen!*"

The people in the Televangelism Center roared, "*Amen!*"

"And at the same time I unburdened my spirit of its load of guilt and sorrow to *both* Montarazes, callin' upon them to forgive me in the great and gracious name of Jesus Christ. And *did* they forgive me? I believe they did, and I went away from that city in the conviction that here were two righteous human bein's saved from sin and despair by their faith in God and by their humble devotion to each other."

"To God give the glory!" a member of the audience cried.

"But what do I read this morning but that this self-same couple, so concerned and carin' only five days ago, has fallen to the epidemic of sundered relationships ravagin' our country the way the plague once ravaged Europe! This story wounds me so grievously because RuthClaire Montaraz has broken her marriage for the most *incredible* of reasons. And what's that, brothers and sisters? Why, nothing more terrible than her husband's desire to . . . *to study for the ministry!*"

A collective groan from the congregation.

Adam sprang up from the floor and punched the button turning the set off. "That. Son. Of. Bitch," he enunciated.

"RuthClaire didn't let him baptize T.P. He resents her for that, Adam. He's trying to get back at her."

"He has misread the story. Is he . . . unable to read? *I* am the one. Who has deserted my family."

"Adam, it's all a fabrication. Everything in that story."

My friend struggled to explain himself: "But he has misread, even, the fabrication. A person working for a Master of Theological Studies . . . is not preparing for the ministry. That is the degree of a lay person. Mr. McElroy should know that."

"RuthClaire balked him. That's all he knows."

"So he blackens her name from his pulpit? For oh-so-many viewers? Is that what he does?" Adam stopped pacing, rubbed his lower jaw, and pointed one bony finger at the blank TV screen. "Dwight 'Happy' McElroy, you are one . . . very unpleasant . . . son of bitch."

I calmed Adam down and got him into the kitchen where, remembering the orders of Dr. Ruggiero, I prepared him a plate of soft scrambled eggs and a bowl of oatmeal. Adam ate ravenously, polishing off his eggs before turning his spoon to the still steaming, cinnamon-sprinkled oatmeal.

The West Bank was closed on Sundays, not so much to honor the sabbath as to acknowledge the mores of the townspeople who honored it. And, like God, I myself was not opposed to twenty-four hours of uninterrupted rest every seven days.

At any rate, that afternoon Adam and I entertained ourselves preparing a kind of makeshift gallery display of RuthClaire's paintings *Souls* in her old studio. We organized them by dividing them into five groups of seven canvases each, scrupulously assigning different background colors and frame sizes to each group—after which we hung them on the walls or propped them on shelves or tables where they would show off to best advantage.

Sun—warm afternoon sun—came through the dusty Venetian blinds in zebra stripes of marmalade and shadow. Then, when I hoisted the blinds and hooked them high, this same sunlight flooded the entire studio. Prismatic dazzle bounced around the room, and our placement of the canvases, along with the energetic sunlight streaming in, transformed them from muddy, earthbound mistakes into oddly spectacular affirmations of their creator's talent.

"My God," I said.

Adam pointed at this canvas, and then at that, daring me to note how the finishes that had once seemed flat and monolithic now had depth and intricacy. Under the mute pastels lay eloquent patterns of shape and line, iridescent commentaries on the otherwise commonplace surfaces in which they were embedded.

"I never saw any of this before. It's hard to believe."

"I know," Adam said.

"Is this the way *you* always see them?"

"Of course not."

"But the other way . . . the other way, Adam, they're inexcusably ugly. Hardly worth keeping."

"Sometimes they might seem so. I have even heard Miss RuthClaire confess the same."

"A desire to undo them? A desire to destroy them?"

"Yes. But only when she has got . . . *beyond* them."

Above Paradise Farm, summer clouds pushed in dreamily from the west, mounting one another like amorous sheep. The light in the studio changed. Someone had swaddled the sun in gauze.

"They're ruined," I said, meaning the paintings. "They're back to normal."

Adam gave me an unreadable look. Then he patted me reassuringly on the shoulder: Don't fret, Mister Paul.

A brief golden glory poured through the summer clouds. Only a little less dazzling than before, sunlight pirouetted through the studio. I looked again at Ruth-Claire's paintings. Nothing doing. The infinitesimal change in the light had somehow leached them of magic. And no matter how hard I tried over the next several days, I was never able to enter the studio at a time when the light was slanting in at the necessary angle and chromatic intensity to bring the canvases back to life.

ON MONDAY morning, Adam and I were each trying to disguise from the other our individual senses of expectancy. Today RuthClaire was supposed to receive from Craig a letter stipulating the groups—charities, political organizations—to which the Montarazes must write their ransom checks.

At 10:30, I began to get ready to drive into town for my luncheon business. Niedrach should have called, I told myself. But I immediately withdrew that thought, doubting the security of Beulah Fork's telephone lines. Craig did not need to know where Adam had gone, only that he had moved away from the big cupolaed house on Hurt Street. As for Adam, he was walking barefoot through my pecan grove, contemplating his and RuthClaire's misfortune. I went down the steps of my sun deck to talk to him.

"If anything happens here, keep me posted. Call me at the West Bank. Even if Livia George answers the phone, she won't recognize your voice. She's never heard it before."

Adam had no chance to reply. We heard a vehicle crunching through the gravel on the circular drive fronting the house. Who? Friend, foe, or unsuspecting Avon lady?

"Get inside," I said. "I'll check this out."

The habiline obeyed. In the sweltering midmorning heat, I trotted around the house beneath the studio loft and turned the corner just in time to see a male figure climbing down from the cab of a glossy violet pickup truck. The truck was jacked up so high on its oversized wheels that the man's final step was a low-level parachute jump. He caught sight of me the moment he landed. He stood staring at me with a resolute skepticism.

"You Mr. Loyd?"

"Depends on who I'm talking to."

Neither clean-shaven nor bearded, neither a Beau Brummell nor a hobo, the man closed the distance between us. "A chameleon, huh? Well, so am I, I guess." He halted about five feet away. His outfit was that of a pulpwood worker—khaki pants, blue work shirt, rope-soled shoes, baseball-style cap with a perforated crown. "I'm Special Agent Neil Hammond. Can we go inside?"

These words lifted a weight. I shook Hammond's hand and led him into the house through the narrow front foyer.

We found Adam sitting on the stairs with a shoeshine kit applying cordovan polish to the hand-tooled leather boots (with elevator heels) that he had worn to the West Bank in December. In his slacks and T-shirt, in his dedication to the simple task, Adam reminded me of an elderly black man who had shined shoes at the Ralston Hotel in Columbus in the early 1960s. Sitting halfway up the stairs, he nodded at Hammond and me without ceasing to rub polish into the toes and heels of his boots. There was an air of melancholy to his expertise, but a melancholy devoid of self-pity.

Hammond and I watched him work. The habiline finished applying the wax, tugged his left boot on, grasped a shoeshine brush with his bare right foot, and began buffing the instep of the boot with an easy rocking motion that made a whispery noise in the stairwell. This sound was strangely soothing. Adam brought the left boot to a high

cordovan shine, then removed it and duplicated the procedure in reverse, wearing the right boot and brushing it with
his left foot. Hammond and I stood there beneath him in
the stairwell, entranced.

"Done," Adam said. He put the brush away and posi-
tioned the polished pair of boots on the step so that the
toes were even with its outer edge. They shone. They
smelled good.

Then Special Agent Hammond began to speak. He had
just arrived from Atlanta with a photocopy of the letter
addressed to the Montarazes by the kidnappers. On Saturday, the GBI had received federal authorization to fetch
the letter from the U.S. Postal Service in advance of its
scheduled Monday delivery. That was how he had managed to bring the message to Adam so early in the day. For
the past month, Hammond explained, he had been doing
undercover investigation for the Bureau's drug unit in
Hothlepoya County. Yesterday morning, though, he had
been summoned back to Atlanta to assume the role of
message runner for this particular case. He was living in a
mobile home between Beulah Fork and Tocqueville, fre-
quenting grubby roadhouses every evening to see if any
dope deals were going down, and periodically staking out
the Muscadine Gardens private airport to determine if any
of the aircraft coming into it were pot planes. Although it
might be wise if Adam and I kept our contacts with him to
an absolute minimum, Niedrach wanted us to know that
Hammond was our official liaison in Hothlepoya County.

"The letter," Adam croaked.

Hammond went up the steps with the photocopy. I
climbed to a position behind Adam so that I could read it
over his shoulder. It was a tight fit for the three of us—but
we arranged ourselves cosily enough, and Adam shook out
the photocopy.

"Fingerprints on the envelope have already conclusively
identified the author as Craig Puddicombe," Hammond
said.

The letter itself consisted of an introductory paragraph,
a list of the ten organizations to receive donations from the
Montarazes, and a closing paragraph directing them to post

the "genuine canceled chex" in a glass case at the interior entrance to Rich's department store in Lenox Square Mall. The "genuine canceled chex" had to be posted by the second Monday in August, two weeks away, so that thousands upon thousands of mall patrons could view them as they entered Rich's to shop. The well-known signatures on these checks, and the surprising fringe organizations on their PAY TO THE ORDER OF lines, would undoubtedly stimulate a flood of copy-cat contributions. Moreover, nearly every young person who so much as glanced at the canceled-check display would become a potential suspect in the kidnapping—assuming, of course, that either the FBI or the GBI set up continuous video surveillance of the store's entrance.

"Which we'll certainly do," Hammond said. "Don't worry. This isn't as clever a ploy as Puddicombe thinks. For one thing, it's going to be very easy to fake the canceled checks."

I tapped the bottom of the photocopy. "It says here that he'll consult with the organizations in question to make sure the contributions have really been made."

"That's a bluff. Why have the canceled checks posted in a public place if they already know what posting the check is supposed to prove?"

"For publicity's sake," I said. "To humiliate RuthClaire and Adam."

Adam looked up. "Would these organizations really take our forced donations, Mr. Hammond?" His most fluid speech yet.

"Some are outfits of dubious probity. They might. It seems to be this character's idea that we're to keep the kidnapping hidden from the general public—at least for now. That being the case, the outfits receiving the checks would have no reason to suppose you'd sent them under duress."

"Couldn't they tell their directors in private?" I asked.

"Of course. But that would entail a certain risk. If Puddicombe had an informant in just one of the organizations, well, he'd figure out pretty damn fast that we're using the same line of approach with all the other groups. The danger to the kidnap victim is clear.''

"Say nothing to any of them, then,'' Adam directed. "We will send nothing but genuine cashable checks.''

"After Paulie's recovered, Mr. Montaraz, there are steps we can take to recover the money, too. It's possible that a few of these outfits, understanding the full situation, would hand it over willingly—but it's equally likely that a couple of them, maybe more, wouldn't mind profiting from your ill fortune. We'd go after them through the state attorney general's office, but it could be a very messy set-to. Even a loud public outcry against one of these farcical bunches— Shock Troops of the Resurrected Confederacy—might not make them relent. It might even strengthen their will to take on our mainstream legal apparatus.''

"About the money I have no care,'' Adam said. "Let it go.''

Looking over his shoulder, I studied the list. In addition to Congressman Aubrey O'Seamons, the Klairvoyant Empire of KuKlos Klandom, and the Shock Troops of the Resurrected Confederacy (STORC), Craig had specified an odd array of praiseworthy, semirespectable, and questionable institutions. The Methodist Children's Home in Atlanta was cheek by jowl with the National Rifle Association and the Rugged White Survivalists of America. Neither Adam nor I could help noting that the last organization on the list was Dwight McElroy's Greater Christian Constituency. Ever helpful, Craig had provided up-to-date mailing addresses for each and every one of these groups.

"You give twenty-three thousand to the Methodist Children's Home,'' I advised Adam. "Three thousand each to the other nine groups.''

Adam said, "We do not have this much money in our bank account, Mr. Hammond.''

"If you're sure you actually want to handle this by writing the checks,'' he said, "we'll deposit the necessary amount to cover them. That would fortify our case in seeking reimbursement from any really hard-nosed ransom recipient. I ought to remind you, though, that if you'd let us, we could have our documents division fake the canceled cheeks. That'd be easy for those guys."

"Craig Puddicombe would find out," Adam objected.

"That's a very real possibility."

"Then I must ask the aid of state in making up the total fifty thousand dollars."

"All right," Hammond said.

For a time, we sat in silence in the narrow chute of the stairwell, stymied by the harsh reality of the letter in Adam's hands. Is every vice a corrupted virtue, every evil a perverted good? I don't know, but the anguish and pain that Craig Puddicombe, a mere boy, was inflicting on the Montarazes—and on me by my willing involvement in their predicament—stemmed almost entirely from his pursuit of a variety of justice that was not only blind but tone-deaf and unfeeling. Further, he had implicated Nancy Teavers in his militant passion for left-handed justice. How, I wondered, could one misguided person trigger such ever-widening chaos?

"What now?" I asked Hammond.

"Mr. Montaraz writes the checks, addresses the envelopes, and gives them to me to mail from a letter box in downtown Atlanta. And then there's not much you two fellas can do but wait."

"Two weeks?" Adam asked. "Another two weeks?"

WHEN I reached the West Bank later that same morning, Livia George came at me out of the kitchen with a section of Sunday's paper rolled up in her fist like a rolling pin. She knocked me into a chair by the door with it.

"You tole me they was fine! You tole me Adam was healin' up real pretty 'n' evverthin' else was hunky-dory too!"

"I thought it was, I thought it was."

"Their marriage done broke and you think that's a

up-tight development? Where you get your smarts, Mistah Paul? From a Jay Cee Penney catalogue?'' She laid the newspaper down, flattened it out in front of me, and read aloud the article about Adam's decision to forsake his family for a period of intense study at the Candler School of Theology. ''I nevah figgered him for a no-'count, Mistah Paul. Not for half a minute. Whyn't you talk him out o' this crazy scheme while you was up there?''

''He was all bandaged up from his operation. Neither of them let on they were having trouble.''

''Poo!''

''Look, Livvy, they waited until I'd left town to divulge their story to the press. That was deliberate. They hood-winked me—to spare me the agony of *their* agony, I guess.''

''You go 'phone that crab-walkin' Mistah Adam and tell him to get his fanny on back to his woman 'n' chile!''

''Nobody knows where he is, Livia George. He's moved out.''

For the remainder of the day, my cook comported her-self like a woman infinitely sinned against, slamming pots and pans around and muttering under her breath. Once, she came all the way out of the kitchen to glare at a red-haired man who had returned his three-minute Conti-nental Burger as too oniony and overcooked.

''Overcooked?'' she groused, loud enough for the cus-tomer to hear. '' 'F I had me a pasty face like that fella's, I wouldn't eat nothin' that wasn't burnt to a crumbly char. He get him a taste of underdone raw evver time he bite his bottom lip.''

It was only with arm-twisting charm that I herded my Livvy back into the kitchen, and only by waiving his tab that I mollified the red-haired man whom my cook had publicly insulted.

In my heart, though, I blamed the entire situation on Craig Puddicombe.

To FORESTALL Craig's using the Montarazes' failure to comply with all his demands as an excuse to hurt their baby, Adam wrote the following letter to the editors of the Atlanta newspapers:

In your pages this past Sunday, a story suggests my wife and I have separated because of my interest in theology. Although in so saying, Miss RuthClaire says a partial truth, it is ONLY a partial truth. In whole truth, I have broken this marriage because a person of my subhuman species has no right to marry a Caucasian representative of *Homo sapiens sapiens*. I rue the bad example I have set the youth of this nation. I urge them very hard not to give in to the temptation to marry outside their species.

Further, Miss RuthClaire is too fine a person to continue sharing her bed with subhuman murderer such as I. The parents of the late E. L. Teavers of Beulah Fork, Georgia, know of what I speak, as do his Brothers, Sisters, Aunts, Uncles, Cousins, and his unfortunate Widow, Nancy, to all of whom I extend heartfelt apologies for surviving the murderous fall that for Mister Elvis Lamar was very fatal. I am sorry, I am sorry.

Finally, I do hereby surrender myself to any police or government body that does wish to arrest and prosecute me for the malicious homicide of E. L. Teavers. Please, O police chiefs, sheriffs, or special agents, publish in this Letters to the Editor column your desire so to do, and I will surrender myself to you in the lobby of the *Journal-Constitution* building at 9:30 A.M. on the day after this desire has been printed. This I solemnly swear and promise.

Adam Montaraz

The letter appeared in the *Constitution* on Thursday morning and in the *Journal* that same afternoon. Adam had not let me or anyone else read it beforehand, and although it technically fulfilled all the ransom demands not yet complied with, I was afraid that its tone and its turn of phrase might backfire on all of us. The letter seemed to embody the first extended use of irony and sarcasm to which Adam had ever committed himself.

Special Agent Hammond visited Paradise Farm shortly before midnight on Thursday. He told us that Niedrach had doubts similar to mine about the likely efficacy of Adam's "Apology & Confession." If Craig were in a touchy mood, or if he believed that Adam had somehow played him false, T.P. might well have to suffer the consequences. On the other hand, the letter might lead Craig to contact RuthClaire or Adam, thereby multiplying the clues about his and Nancy's whereabouts and inadvertently laying the groundwork for their capture.

Southern Bell Security had cooperated with the GBI in setting up a trap on my telephone by installing a pin register—a device capable of holding a line open even after the caller has hung up—in the office of the Beulah Fork exchange, but had not bothered to try to put a trap on the telephones in the Montaraz house on Hurt Street because of the prohibitive number of exchanges in Atlanta. So I did not see how Hammond could say that another call from Craig might prove his downfall. In any case, it was hard to imagine the boy calling Paradise Farm. He would have to have a sudden prescient hunch about Adam's current hiding place.

"What in my letter could give offense?" Adam asked Hammond.

For someone able to grasp the metaphysical complexities of various spiritual issues, Adam was curiously obtuse on this score. I told him that his expression of regret appeared to be tongue in cheek, his apology a clever indictment of Teavers, and his offer to give himself up a parody of genuine confession.

"You've complied with the letter but not the spirit of Craig's demands."

"How can I comply with the spirit of demands that I abhor?"

"You can't," Hammond said. "But you can pretend to."

"I'm not good at this pretending," Adam growled. "Never any good at it." A tear formed in the corner of his eye. He blinked, and the tear made a moist track down the gully between his cheek and his habiline muzzle. "I can no longer make-believe that I am happy apart from my wife. I can no longer make-believe that my praying seems helpful. I can no longer make-believe that the God of Abraham and also of the converted Paul cares very much about my family's terrible dilemma."

Hammond said, "We're here, Mr. Montaraz, caring as much as we can."

Seated at my dinette table with a bottle of Michelob in one hand, Adam broke down completely. He sobbed like an affronted three-year-old, his fragile lower face scrunching around alarmingly. I was afraid that he was going to undo some aspect of the surgery that had "humanized" him.

"You should read the Book of Job," Hammond said.

Adam shrugged aside the special agent's hand. "Quiet the hell up!" he wheezed at the unperturbed Hammond. "My people have known two million years of trial, even to the need of hiding away from our own descendants—but not even as free person in United States of America can I escape further tribulation. Therefore, I beg you most imploringly, 'Quiet the hell up!'" Whereupon he flung his Michelob bottle between Hammond and me at the refrigerator. By some miracle, it failed to break, but beer sloshed everywhere, splattering the linoleum, and the habiline himself got up and left the room.

"Touchy tonight," said Hammond, not unsympathetically.

"Have you guys made any progress up there? What about Craig's family here in town? Have you talked to them?"

"We haven't interviewed Puddicombe's mother or any of the other local family members because it's our judgment they'd try to tip him off. It's that kind of family."

"What's Niedrach doing? And Davison? And their FBI liaison? Not a damn thing's happened since that letter came." I was mopping the spilled beer with paper towels.

Hammond tore a couple of sheets of toweling from the roll and knelt next to the refrigerator to help me. "They're working," he said. "We're all working. Sometimes you need a lucky break." He carried the pieces of sopped toweling to the waste basket. "By the way, your friend Caroline Hanna told me to tell you hello. She's over there with your ex-wife nearly every moment she can spare away from her work. A friend indeed, that lady."

Oh, God, I thought, they're comparing notes.

Aloud I said, "Thanks. So what do we do now?"

"Sit tight, Mr. Loyd. Sit tight."

ADAM AND RuthClaire had written the ten checks demanded by Craig's letter for five thousand dollars each. Although these were sizable contributions by the standards of most American taxpayers, none by itself was enough to seem especially remarkable coming from national figures of the Montarazes' suspected wealth. The GBI agents had dissuaded them from writing any one check for an amount conspicuously larger than the others for fear that Craig would use the disparity as an excuse to make further demands. He seemed to be enjoying the game he was playing, as if the adrenaline rush of formulating complex demands and having them carried out were a kind of bonus gift for his pursuit of "justice."

By the end of the week, we learned, the Montaraz bank in DeKalb County had begun making payments on some of these drafts. STORC, the Klairvoyant Empire, the Rugged White Survivalists, the Methodist Children's Home, and Aubrey O'Seamons had wasted little time cashing their checks. As a result, it might be possible to put all ten canceled checks in that glass display case in Lenox Square a few days ahead of schedule. Late Friday night, in fact, exactly one week after the kidnapping, Hammond informed Adam and me that the FBI had taken several discreet steps to have the checks in place by midweek. There was no sense delaying their availability to the kidnappers until the second Monday in August if they had already cleared. Whether Craig would release T.P. before Monday was problematic, of course, but we all agreed that it was worth a try. Meanwhile, video surveillance equipment had been concealed in front of Rich's by specialists working in the mall after regular business hours.

Adam and RuthClaire exchanged letters during their separation. Bilker mailed them from random sites around the city, while I addressed all of Adam's billet-doux to Caroline Hanna's apartment so that she could carry them over to Hurt Street when she went to visit RuthClaire. We took these troublesome precautions because Niedrach believed that Craig would interpret any sign of contact between the Montarazes, even from afar, as a violation of their promise to live apart. Phone calls were also out.

Caroline and I were under no such ban, however, and so long as I placed my calls to her from the West Bank rather than Paradise Farm, no one had any objection to our talking to each other. Similarly, Caroline was careful to call me only at the restaurant. If she telephoned during business hours, I would clamber upstairs to my sweltering second-floor storage room to take the call on the extension there. Downstairs, Livia George would hang up, and Caroline and I would jabber away like furtive teen-agers. The heat of the storage room—with its musty cot and its lopsided pyramids of cardboard boxes and vegetable crates—heightened my sense of the illicitness of our hurried conversations. But I liked that feeling. It was absurd, feeling like a teen-ager again, but it was splendid, too, an unexpected benefit of T.P.'s kidnapping that in full daylight I was totally unable to square with the horror of that event.

On Saturday night, Caroline called at 11:30, just as Hazel and Livia George were going out the front door. But, with only an ancient rotating floor fan to keep me from collapsing from heat stroke, I took the call upstairs, anyway.

"Talk to me, kid."

"Not for long, Paul. Just wanted to let you know we're hanging on. Ruthie's unbelievably self-possessed. Me, I'm done in."

"Me, too. Frazzled. Big crowd tonight."

"Adam?"

"I'm starting to worry about him, Caroline. His weird amalgam of religious beliefs—his faith, if you want to call it that—seems to be deserting him. He walks around my place like Roderick Usher, morose and supersensitive. Know what he told me this morning? 'I'm a lightning rod for human cruelty.' His exact words."

"That doesn't sound like him. It's self-pitying."

"It is and it isn't. I think he was expressing a *degree* of concern about the people around him. It bothers him that so many people—RuthClaire, me, Bilker, the cops and special agents, and you too, probably—are endangering themselves trying to help him. He feels responsible."

"Well, he could just as easily say, 'I'm a lightning rod for human charity.' He's looking at things backwards, Paul."

"Is he any different from the rest of us? He takes the good for granted. Evil thoroughly confounds him."

Caroline said, "Oh," as if a light bulb had gone on over her head. (A 40-watter.) Before I could ask her to explain herself, she said, "*Oh!*" again. (A blinding 100-watter.)

"What is it?"

"Do you remember how Adam apparently got to the states? How he was one of three habiline crew members on a fishing boat running guns from Punta Gorda in Cuba to the guerrilla opposition to Baby Doc in Haiti? Only that boat never made it back to Haiti. The Cuban I interviewed in the Atlanta Pen—Ignacio Guzman Suarez y Peña— well, Ignacio murdered the captain of that vessel and two of Adam's fellow habilines. That's another instance of violence that haunts Adam, another reason he keeps seeing himself as a 'lightning rod for human cruelty.' We keep forgetting that he has a past that antedates his first appearance in Georgia.''

I started to object, but Caroline cut me off:

"RuthClaire doesn't, of course, but the rest of us probably have no good idea of the hardships he's already survived.''

"I love you, kid,'' I said. Only the faint idiot singing of the wires—the roaring of the voiceless inane—continued to link us. I shifted on the sagging cot, sweat lubricating my flanks. "You still there, Caroline?''

"You might have had the decency to tell me that last Saturday morning,'' she finally replied.

"What's the matter? Everything was okay yesterday, wasn't it? Between us, I mean.''

She let the wires sing a few seconds. "Paul, I got a letter from Brian today.''

"Nollinger?'' My heart sank.

The very one, she admitted. The letter had come from a city called Montecristi in a northeastern province of the Dominican Republic. In it, good old Brian spent four or five paragraphs justifying his abrupt departure from Atlanta. His position in the anthropology department at Emory had steadily deteriorated. His well-publicized quarrel with the Zarakali paleoanthropologist A. P. Blair had put him on shaky ground with his colleagues, most of whom revered the cantankerous old fart. Nor had Brian improved their opinion of him by accusing the artist RuthClaire Loyd of making Adam Montaraz, the habiline refugee from the Caribbean, her personal "slave,'' when, in fact, the two had freely married each other. Unleashing an agent of the Immigration and Naturalization Service on Adam had been yet another regrettable mistake.

"He made plenty of 'em. Glad to know he's begun to regret them.''

Caroline shushed me. Gradually among Brian's colleagues, she continued, paraphrasing the letter, there had grown the perception that he was trying to milk the habiline controversy of every last drop of potential career benefit. (And ineptly missing the pail.) He had further compounded his problems in the department by belatedly developing

"Yeah, well, I hope he doesn't end up with nails in his feet and palms."

Caroline chuckled mordantly. "Which is the first time you've wished him anything less fatal than hanging at dawn, isn't it?"

I admitted that it probably was. I also told Caroline that if Brian did his job too well, and if Austin-Antilles refrained from firing him for his presumption, he would almost certainly be transferred to a less controversial company enterprise on some other island. That was just the way the Big AAC did business.

For a moment, the wires regaled me with inarticulate arias of static. Then my caller said, "I love you, too," and hung up. I sat there in the heat, stunned, savoring her words.

At Paradise Farm, Adam was vegetating. If he wrote RuthClaire a letter, he forgot to give it to me to mail. If he started a crossword puzzle, he soon lost interest. His books on theology, religious history, the philosophy of religion, and contemporary creation theory sat untouched in their boxes in the second-floor studio. Neil Hammond did not come by with news, and on Sunday morning, too wrought up by Caroline's declaration of love to sleep late, *I* was the one who turned on "Great Gospel Giveaway."

What motivated me? Maybe I simply had a hunch that McElroy would mention a recent $5,000 contribution from Adam Montaraz. Bingo. He acknowledged it just as an army of cleancut ushers began filing toward the altar to pick up the collection plates. Adam, too busy trying to think of a nine-letter word for "false piety" to glance at the set, made no sign that he had heard McElroy acknowledge the donation.

That afternoon, however, he fell asleep while listlessly watching a Braves game on Channel 17. I was able to turn off the set without rousing him, a notable achievement because of his tendency to sleep as lightly as a cat. McElroy's sermon that morning had been called "Energizing Commitments." That was what Adam seemed to need, but, as I say, he had not listened to the man.

On Monday morning, about ten, I left Paradise Farm and drove into town. My first stop was at the Greyhound Depot Laundry to pick up my tablecloths. Ben Sadler, already looking rumpled and dehydrated, had them waiting for me on the counter. He seemed to be waiting for me himself. The black woman who operated his steam press—a forbidding-looking instrument with a lid like that of a coffin—also made a point of marking my entrance.

Uh oh, I thought. What's going on?

My subsequent conversation with Ben was curiously aimless, though, focusing on such weighty topics as the humidity level and hog-market prices. Strange. Ben usually liked to provoke a verbal scrap over the deployment of U.S. forces in Central America or the morality of alcoholic-beverage licenses for local eating establishments. I started to leave.

"Say," said Ben, "do you take *Newsweek*?"

"I don't subscribe. Occasionally, I'll pick it up. Why?"

"Have you seen this week's issue?"

"Is it out already?"

"Hy Langton, over at the drugstore, gets his copies first thing Monday mornin'. I bought one right off. He don't know what to do with the rest of 'em, though—put 'em out for sale or stash 'em down under the register."

"*Newsweek*? With the *Playboy*s and *Penthouse*s?"

"It's a eye-opener, the new one. Milly and me—" nodding at the steam-press operator, who looked down in acute embarrassment—"we've been, uh, sort of discussin' how much times've changed, to let a magazine like ol' *Newsweek* use the kinda cover it's just used. Makes you wonder if it's safe to send your kids down a small-town sidewalk 'thout a blindfold."

"But you bought a copy?"

"Well, Paul, I got it for you." Even in the heat of the morning and the heat of the laundry, Ben managed to blush. ''Don't be insulted, now. It's not that I think you're some sorta creep or somethin'. It's just that, you know, once bein' married to an artist and all, you're more sophisticated than a lot of folks in Beulah Fork. You know how to take such stuff 'thout bein', uh, *prurient* about it. Isn't that the word, *prurient?*''

''For God's sake, Ben, what are you talking about?''

''Here.'' With one emphatic motion, he produced the magazine from beneath his counter and plonked it down on the folded tablecloths.

The cover of the magazine slapped me hard, but I kept my expression as noncommittal as I could. Let Ben and Milly *invent* a reaction rather than simply *relate* it. The gossip mills would grind no matter what I did.

And the cover on the new *Newsweek*?

To be succinct, it consisted of a startling photograph of Adam and RuthClaire standing side by side, frontally nude, Adam to the left, RuthClaire to the right. Adam had his hand raised in a venerable human gesture signifying ''Peace'' or ''I have no weapon.'' My ex-wife, although visible frontally from head to toe, was standing with her left leg slightly extended and her body canted a little bit toward Adam's. Eye-catching as they were, the couple occupied only the vertical right half of the cover.

The other half contained a pair of clocks side by side beneath the second three letters of the *Newsweek* logo. One clock had the initials B.C. in its center, the other the abbreviation A.D. Under the clocks, in eerie shadow, hung a translucent Plexiglas model of the continent of Africa, while at the bottom of the photograph, going from left to right beneath the suspended continent and the primeval couple, floated a string of islands representing the Greater and Lesser Antilles. From the island Hispaniola shot out a sequence of arrows demarcating the wake of a fishing boat on its way past Cuba to the tip of Florida. A legend superimposed beneath the feet of Adam and RuthClaire proclaimed:

THE NEW PHOTOGRAPHY
An Art in Militant Transition

"Bet this gets a lot of bluenoses to cancel their subscriptions," Ben said. "Whaddaya think, Paul?"

I was still not ready to say anything, but Ben was probably right. Whoever had taken this photograph had not bothered to air-brush the pubic hair or the private parts of my ex-wife and her husband. That was why I thought I knew the photographer's identity. I flipped to the cover story at the heart of the magazine. Scanning its lead and several subsequent paragraphs, I found the name Maria-Katherine Kander over and over again. In fact, two of the photographs accompanying the article were relatively tame portraits—i.e., the models were either in shadow or semimodestly draped—from the same show at Abraxas that had featured Adam's paintings and the multicolored work of various Haitian artists. I had stepped into a timewarp flinging me back to February.

"Did you know they'd done this, Paul? Had their pictures taken in the altogether?"

"No. No, I didn't."

It was hard to imagine RuthClaire consenting to such a portrait. She was as naked in this *Newsweek* cover as I had ever seen her during our decidedly unconventional marriage. Midway through that marriage, she had made up her mind that regular intercourse with me had about it all the irresistible romance of changing a flat tire on a '54 Chevy jalopy. It was not that she was puritanical or cold, it was simply that for her sex had become a time-consuming process best left to people with nothing more important to do. Her knowledge that I was probably never going to father her child had reinforced this cavalier attitude in her. If procreation was out, and pleasure had long ago fled, why bother? At any rate, the last time I had seen her without a stitch was the night that I had climbed into a magnolia tree on Paradise Farm to take pictures of Adam in the downstairs bathroom. She had been infinitely more provocative in that setting. In the Kander photograph, she seemed to be representing Womankind for an alien eye that might not otherwise grasp the concept.

In a sense, of course, that was exactly the point.

I put the magazine on the tablecloths and gathered up

the whole shebang in my arms. "Thanks for the *Newsweek*, Ben." Then I staggered across the street with my burden.

I dumped the tablecloths into a chair and told Livia George that, once again, she would have to handle the luncheon crowd without me. "Go on," she said, waving a hand. Nothing I did, or failed to do, could surprise her anymore. So with the rolled-up *Newsweek* in one hand, I exited the West Bank and climbed into my car.

Neil Hammond's jacked-up purple truck was parked in front of my house at Paradise Farm. The man himself was in the living room with a stack of *Newsweek*s balanced precariously on one of my more fragile-looking end tables. Hammond was holding the magazines in place with the heel of his hand. Adam was perched on the edge of a wingback chair across from the GBI agent, looking penitent and befuddled. My own copy was clutched in my fist like a billy club.

"You've seen it," Hammond said. "You've seen the day's major disaster." He gestured at the stack of magazines. "I saw it about an hour ago, when I went to the drugstore to buy my wife an anniversary card. I bought every *Newsweek* in the damn place. Mr. Langton thinks I'm a first-class pervert, too. It's probably blown my cover." He shook his head. "My cover blown by a magazine cover. Funny, huh? I went to every magazine rack in town buying the damn things up, Mr. Loyd, but the damage has already been done. People here remember Mrs. Montaraz—they remember her well—and a lot of the magazines that went out on the racks were snapped up for souvenirs, let me tell you. Tomorrow, the folks who have subscription copies'll get theirs. There's no way to put a lid on a thing like this. It's a public-relations disaster of colossal proportions. It's a blow to everything we've been trying to do in this case." He lifted his hand from the magazines, and they slid to the floor in a cascade of whispery thumps.

Adam and RuthClaire, Adam and RuthClaire, Adam and RuthClaire.

I looked at Adam. "What the hell did you two think you were doing, anyway?"

"They've contributed to what's sure to turn out to be the most collectible issue—cover intact, of course—of *Newsweek* magazine, ever," Hammond said, nudging the pile with his boot. "That's one of the things they've done. *Newsweek*'ll get more letters than they've ever received, and nine tenths of 'em will be from outraged old ladies, concerned mothers, angry preachers, and so on. Subscriptions'll get canceled, sure, but every damn newsstand copy will be gone before the day's out.

"Do you remember how that flaky Beatle and his Japanese old lady made an album called *Two Virgins* back in the late sixties? They had themselves shot buck-naked for the album cover. Nobody at their damn company wanted to use the photographs, but the flaky Beatle insisted. At least they sold the damn things in brown envelopes, though. This—" he kicked one of the fallen magazines—"is being sold right out in front of God and everybody with *Time* and *Woman's Day* and *Field and Stream*. And by 'God and everybody,' I do mean *everybody*. Little Bobby, Innocent Little Susy, Sweet Old Aunt Matilda, and, probably worst of all, Crazy Craig Puddicombe."

Adam, his hands clasped between his knees, looked up. "Neither RuthClaire nor I had any inkling this photograph would appear—" gesturing vaguely—"as it so upsettingly has."

"But why did you pose for something like this?" I asked.

"In April, Mister Paul, long before my surgery, this M.-K. Kander person came to Atlanta on business at Abraxas. About 'shooting' RuthClaire and me, she inquired. The idea of the Primeval Couple had great appeal to her. Mister David did introductions. And Miss RuthClaire and this M.-K. Kander person, they took to each other very fast. So when her new friend suggest we pose in way you see, my wife has no great objection. Nor I. So our photographs got taken in gallery room where Ms. Kander had her February show. A little later, she kindly sends us prints of very same one that this magazine has given horrible honor of its cover." Adam sought my eyes. "Never did we expect this picture to appear anywhere but in M.-K. Kander private portfolio. This, then, is great shock."

"It's a disaster," Hammond reiterated.

I opened out my scrolled copy and held it up. "But why like this, Adam? Why did she want you to pose like this?"

His growl tentative, Adam said, "The set-up was greatly symbolic. The Primeval Couple, as I have said. My name is Adam, and I am a habiline with origins going deeply back beyond those of even Biblical Adam. So said Maria-Katherine. Miss RuthClaire, to the contrary, is modern woman with life in technological times. So, again, said M.-K. Kander. Our marriage, she told us, unites past and future of species in exciting new Now." He paused. "Maybe this symbolism lacks clarity, but in standing naked beside my wife, I saw no great harm for this talented picture-taking person. Early Adam and somewhat later Eve. Miss RuthClaire thought it—you may be surprised—very funny and also enjoyable."

I stared hard at the magazine cover. "This pose reminds me of something, Adam. But what?"

"Maria-Katherine patterned this composition after the plaques sent out into cosmos aboard Pioneer 10 and 11 spacecraft. They, too, you remember, feature naked male and female side by side, the male with left hand raised. On those plaques, of course, male is taller than female, and islands at bottom are not Cuba and so on, but the sun and planetary bodies of our solar system. A miniature of the spacecraft is shown leaving third such body and flying off between Jupiter and Saturn into cosmic ocean. Again, it was M.-K. Kander person's idea to use this pattern. A Plexiglas model of Africa hangs to right because humanity, it seems, did begin there. Miss Maria-Katherine made this continent artifact herself."

Hammond twisted his cap in his hands. "You had no idea this photograph was going to crop up as a *Newsweek* cover?"

"They would have known," I said, defending them, "if the cover story had been about themselves. The editorial staff would have informed them. But this issue's cover story is about the new photography, and the only release the editors probably needed was one from the Kander woman authorizing them to use this particular photograph.''

"If we had known they were going to use it,'' Hammond said, ''we would have told them what was going on down here. We could have asked them to deep-six the damn thing or at least delay it another week. There's nothing *that* topical about 'The New Photography,' for God's sake. They could have waited.''

Adam stood up, thrust his hands deep into the pockets of his slacks, and, balancing on one leg, picked up a copy of *Newsweek* with the toes of his other foot. The magazine dangled there like a startled sea creature yanked from its natural element. And then Adam disdainfully dropped it.

"I am very unhappy with this ambitious photographer person,'' he said. "I am very unhappy, indeed.''

I RETURNED to work. Hammond remained at the house with Adam. At six o'clock that evening, the agent telephoned the West Bank and told me that something had happened and that he and Adam were leaving for Atlanta.

"Wait a minute. I want to go with you.''

Livia George was at my elbow beside the cash register. "This got somethin' to do with Miss RuthClaire gettin' jaybird-skinny on that magazine?''

"Hush, Livia George.''

"City did this to 'em. City made 'em think they could shuck their clothes for some hotsy-totsy nashunal magazine.''

"Damn it, woman, get out of my ear for a couple of minutes!'' I had my hand over the telephone's mouthpiece. A couple at a nearby table peeked up at me, disapproving of my language and tone.

Hammond's voice said, "This isn't your affair any longer, Mr. Loyd. Niedrach's just called. We've got to go.''

"T.P.'s my godson. You can't close me out. Give me ten or so minutes and I'll be there with you.''

"We're leaving."

"I'll follow."

"That's your prerogative."

"The Montaraz house on Hurt Street?"

"Goodbye, Mr. Loyd."

"What happened? Did Craig call? Did someone see him?"

But all I had in my ear was a busy signal. I barged into the kitchen, to which Livia George had sullenly retreated a moment ago, and found her slicing tomatoes into a salad. Hazel Upchurch was sautéing mushrooms in a cast-iron skillet. Debbie Rae House, my new waitress, was picking up a tray of water glassses.

"Pray," I commanded the three women. "I don't know what the hell good it'll do, but pray. Pray for T.P." Then I was gone.

DESPITE THEIR head start, I caught up with Hammond's pickup between the two exits sandwiching Newnan, Georgia, on I-85. The sun was lowering itself rung by rung to the western horizon, but daylight still lingered above the heat-browned meadows flanking the interstate, and traffic was still brisk in both directions. Doing eighty, I had to hit my brakes to keep from overshooting the agent's truck, and my own car almost got away from me before I was able to bring it under control and follow Hammond and his habiline passenger into Atlanta without further incident. We parked across the street from the Montaraz house and went inside.

Adam and RuthClaire embraced.

Niedrach was present, Davison was not. In the latter's place were two men in sports jackets and spiffily creased slacks; neither of these men had yet hit his fortieth birthday. One had stylishly long hair that just touched his collar in back but stayed well off his ears; he was pink-cheeked and clear-eyed, after the fashion of a second lead in a B movie of the 1940s. The other man had an astronaut's conservative haircut, a nose that had once been broken, and a shovel-shaped mouth that sometimes seemed to move as if it had a will distinct from its owner's. Feds, these fellows. Latter-day heirs of the late, unlamented J. Edgar Hoover.

Bilker Moody introduced these men as Investigator Tim Le May (the B-movie second lead) and Investigator Erik Webb (the shovel-mouthed astronaut). They had taken over the case on the Saturday afternoon following the kidnapping, but Niedrach had stayed on to coordinate their investigation with local police departments and the antiterrorist unit of the GBI. Given federal jurisdiction over most kidnappings, this was a somewhat unusual arrangement, but Niedrach's familiarity with Klan tactics and his intimate knowledge of the events precipitated last summer by the Kudzu Klavern had argued tellingly for his uninterrupted involvement with this case. I was glad to see him. He was wearing his bulldog belt buckle and a navy-blue windbreaker that made him seem out of uniform. He looked like the fatigued, seedy uncle of the younger, more dapper federal agents.

Adam approached him. "What has happened?"

"The bastard phoned," Bilker Moody said, his upper arms straining the sleeve bands of his sweaty banlon shirt.

"We've got a tape," Le May said. "Come into the kitchen and we'll play it for you."

We filed into the kitchen. The tape machine, with two sets of headphones, was connected to the wall phone beside the door leading to Bilker's pantry headquarters. Still, it was possible to sit at the kitchen table while listening to or taping a call, and Adam and RuthClaire sat down at the table with Niedrach, Le May, and Webb. Hammond, Moody, and I found convenient corners into which to wedge ourselves, and Le May turned a dial on the old-fashioned-looking recorder. Its milky reels began to turn, but at first all we could hear was the low hum of the refrigerator.

Then Craig Puddicombe's voice said, "A whore and her hibber. For all the world to see."

"Where's Paulie?" RuthClaire's voice asked. "Tell me how he is, Craig."

" 'S good's can be expected, considerin' what and where he came from. 'S good's can be expected."

"We're living apart, Adam and I. We've lived apart for nearly ten days now. You know that, don't you?"

"No, ma'am. You're standin' right next to each other for all the fuckin' world to see. That's what you're doing."

"We had no idea that—"

"That you had your goddamn clothes off? Interestin' defense, ma'am. Interestin' goddamn defense."

"That the photograph would show up as a magazine cover."

"Course you didn't. And the spade who raped a troop of Girl Scouts said, 'Sorry, angry white folks. I had no ideah I was gonna get caught. No ideah at all.' "

On the tape, RuthClaire began to cry. "What do you want me to do? The photograph's history. Adam and I can't undo it. So what do you want from us now?"

"Who said I *wanted* anything, Missus Hibber Whore?"

"Then why have you called? Tell me about Paulie."

"You've surprised the whole damn country, haven't you? Well, everybody deserves as good as they give, don't they? A big surprise all their own."

"What surprise, Craig?"

Puddicombe was silent a moment. Then he blurted, "But I *do* want something. I want you and your hibber to get back together. Now. Today. This very evenin'."

"Craig—"

He broke the connection. On tape, RuthClaire's voice hurried to ask, "Was that long enough to do any good? Was that—"

Le May turned off the tape recorder. "Telephone technology's changing every day," he said. "If an exchange office has a computerized system, you don't have to rely on taps and pin registers to trace calls. The computer will print out the number for you, then search its memory and tell you who it belongs to. This time we got lucky. The number Puddicombe called from belongs to a newly computerized exchange. We made inquiries at all such offices and found an exchange with a recent call to the Montaraz house. The times matched up exactly."

"He phoned from College Park," Webb said. "Not far from Hartsfield International."

"Then you can catch him," I said. "You can send people down there to stake out the place and grab him."

Niedrach said, "If he were a complete dolt. But he isn't. The number belongs to a pay phone in a public booth off Virginia Avenue. The College Park police checked it out, but Puddicombe hadn't stuck around long enough to say hello to them."

"Then what the hell good does knowing where he called from do you?" I asked. "He's gone, and you don't know where he is."

Investigator Webb, the agent with the Gus Grissom haircut, said, "We know he's in Greater Atlanta. And we've got people in College Park asking questions of all the folks who might've seen Puddicombe using the booth. It's on a sidewalk by a fast-food place, and the call came at a busy time in the afternoon. There's a lead or two, Mr. Loyd. We expect something to break this evening."

"And just what is it you expect to break?"

My question elicited only embarrassed silence for an answer. No one in the Montaraz kitchen knew what to expect. Despite his Klan activities in Hothlepoya County, Craig was pretty much an unknown quantity to these officers. The unpredictability of his behavior—the virulence of his racial and sexual hangups—could scarcely fail to disturb us. My own anxiety was steadily mounting. That much I knew, but not a lot more.

Taking pedantic care with his phrasing, Le May said, "Seeing first that the perpetrator is still at large and second that his whereabouts aren't yet precisely pinpointed, we thought it best to have the Montarazes obey his last demand."

"The bozo's gettin' ready to do something," Bilker Moody said. "He's just gettin' everybody into the auditorium so the goddamn show can start. He *likes* theatrics, this guy does.''

''A surprise,'' Niedrach said speculatively. ''A surprise.''

NIEDRACH, HAMMOND, and Le May left the house to continue their investigative work elsewhere. Webb remained on the premises to monitor the telephone and the recorder to which it was wired. Bilker and Adam went into the studio to play several tension-defusing games of Ping-Pong. Even in the kitchen, I could hear the racket they made grunting, trading slams, and throwing their bodies across the table to return drop shots just over the net. RuthClaire, who might have been expected to want some time alone with Adam, approved their play. Apparently, the simple act of spectating calmed her nerves.

I stayed in the kitchen with Webb—Ping-Pong is not my game—and asked him what leads they had.

His mouth began to move even before any words came out. ''Woman working at the fast-food place next to the phone booth. Well, this gal says she saw a guy in a painter's white coveralls go past the front window about the time our call was made. Bearded fellow. Young. She says she remembers because her boss had talked about repainting the divider lines in the parking lot. She wondered if the guy was there to do that. He must not've been, though, because there was only that one time he went by and the divider lines in the parking lot still haven't been repainted.''

''You think Craig's wearing a painter's coveralls?''

''Her description of the fella sounds like Puddicombe.''

''Did your witness happen to see what he was driving?''

''Her position behind the counter didn't let her, no.''

''That's one helluva lead. If he keeps his coveralls on

and walks around the city everywhere he goes, you'll nab him before the year's out."

Webb smiled. "Touché." His FBI affiliation had not gone to his head. Provincial rather than Prussian in his slacks-and-sports-jacket uniform, he had no trouble admitting that this investigation had him groping down one blind alley after another. His easy-going agreeability irritated me.

Eventually, I wandered down the hall off the kitchen to Bilker's pantry headquarters.

If Adam likes you, you can't be too big a turd.

That was a comforting thought. I entered the pantry and took up a seat in front of the TV monitors on the plywood counter. Why hadn't the FBI set up in here? Because Bilker had denied them access. The pantry belonged to him, and *he* was responsible for security, just as *they* were responsible for the investigation of Paulie's kidnapping. One of Bilker's TV screens, I noticed, featured a continuous panoramic display of Hurt Street, while another had its eye on the well-lit MARTA station on DeKalb Avenue.

"Comfy, fella?"

I looked over my shoulder. It was Bilker, his T-shirt three different shades of dark green and his face as red and shiny as a candy apple. His expression was malevolent. I hoped that he remembered Adam's good opinion of me.

The TV monitor came to my rescue. "Look," I said, pointing. "Somebody's coming."

In fact, two cars were pulling up in front of the house: a late-model Plymouth glinting indigo in the actinic glare of the MARTA lamps and, right behind it, a blue VW beetle of decidedly older vintage. Caroline Hanna climbed gingerly out of the Volkswagen; then, as if they had taken a moment to settle a minor disagreement, Le May and Niedrach hatched simultaneously from opposite doors of the Plymouth. All three people started up the walk to the house together, and another monitor picked them up.

"Whyn't you go and greet your sweetie 'fore I yank this here chair out from under your tail?"

"That's a good idea."

Only by coincidence had Caroline and the agents arrived

at the same time. She was surprised to see me. She was
even more surprised to see Adam. She had come simply to
provide RuthClaire with female companionship for the
remainder of the evening. Face to face with me again,
however, Caroline was shy. She was going to let her entire
greeting consist of a friendly pat on the arm, but I pulled
her to me and brushed her forehead with my lips.

Niedrach interrupted to say that he and Le May had to
talk to me in private, and Adam led Caroline into the
studio.

"What is it?" I asked the investigators.

"We want you to come with us," Le May said.

"Where? What for?"

Adam returned from the studio as if to eavesdrop on the
rest of our conversation. Le May hesitated, afraid to proceed in front of the habiline, and my stomach tightened.

"You must tell me, too," Adam said. "I am deserving
to hear."

Niedrach nodded sympathetically. "We want to see if
Mr. Loyd can make an identification for us, that's all."

"What kind of identification?" I asked.

"Take a ride with us," Niedrach said. "We'll show
you."

"I am going, too," Adam declared.

Le May started to protest, but Niedrach shook his head.
So, after telling the others we would be back shortly, the
four of us went out into the muggy summer evening under
smog-blurred stars and got into the FBI agent's Plymouth.
A mosquito was trapped in the back seat with Adam and
me, and we listened to its faint but annoying whine until
the habiline jerked his head and snapped his mouth shut on
the insect. He settled back into his seat. Helplessly, I
stared at him.

"Forgive me, Mister Paul. I am edgy this night."

Le May spoke into a hand-held microphone that he had
pulled from under the dash. "We're on our way."

Static answered.

At the bottom of Hurt Street, Le May turned right on
Waverly, part of an historic enclave dense with trees and
Victorian houses in various stages of decay or renovation.

From Waverly, we wound our way onto the southwest-to-northeast diagonal of Euclid Avenue, eventually creeping uphill past a row of shops to the brightness of Little Five Points itself. We crossed Moreland and dipped away from the bustle of the Points into a neighborhood of shabby clapboard bungalows and red-brick apartment buildings from the 1940s. I had no idea where we were going, but Adam seemed to.

"The Little Five Points Unaffiliated Meditation Center?" he asked.

"That's right," Niedrach replied. "How did you know?"

"It was where for many Sundays, and even a few troubled weekdays, Miss RuthClaire and I took our church before my surgery. I liked it because it had no rigid doctrines to enforce and welcomed anyone who had a spiritual hungriness."

Presently, then, Le May let the Plymouth coast to rest behind a Fulton County police car and a boxy ambulance parked in tandem beside the Little Five Points Unaffiliated Meditation Center. A number of people were standing on the narrow front lawn. The blue-and-white flasher on the squad car picked these people out of the darkness, again and again.

The door to the Meditation Center—once, I could tell, a single-story brick house like many other houses in the same neighborhood—stood open. The stained-glass fanlight above the door was illuminated from behind by a cruel electric glare. Clearly, the police had been here a while.

Niedrach told Adam and me that when we entered the building, we were going to see exactly what the Meditation Center's director, a man named Ryan Bynum, had found upon entering its sanctuary at 8:47 P.M. for a routine check of the premises. The policemen working this crime had restored the scene to the physical conditions that had greeted Bynum.

Le May had already threaded his way through some of the teen-age gawkers on the lawn. He beckoned us to follow. Adam and I reluctantly obeyed. One of the young people, recognizing Adam, came forward with a copy of

Newsweek and asked him to autograph its cover. Strutting uncertainly, the kid looked scarcely more than fourteen.

"You're impeding a murder investigation," Niedrach told him.

"Four letters," the kid snarled. "Just his goddamn first name."

Distractedly, Adam signed the magazine, printing ADAM beneath the image of his naked feet. The autograph seeker murmured grumpy thanks and moved back into the crowd loitering nearby.

"He's going to sell it to a speculator for a hundred, maybe two hundred bucks," Niedrach said.

Adam shrugged.

In the church's foyer, a young man with a gold teardrop through the lobe of one ear embraced Adam possessively. Tall but graceful, he had to stoop to hug the habiline. I knew without being introduced to him that this was Ryan Bynum, the Center's director.

"Good to see you again, Adam," Bynum said. "You've been away from us for far too long."

Adam said, "I am not here to reestablish my membership. I—"

"You can talk! My God, it's a *miracle*, Adam!"

"I am here to accompany Mister Paul, whom these investigators believe may be able to identify victim."

Bynum was beside himself over Adam's ability to speak, but, upon receiving a condensed version of the events that had brought it about, began to discuss tonight's untoward happenings:

"Some churches get firebombed. Some get defaced with graffiti. But ours, well, it draws a more creative, a more neurotic, kind of vandal." Bynum was sidling along the foyer wall so that we could squeeze past him into the living-room-sized sanctuary. "Whoever did it, well, he ought to be a member. He *needs* us. If not us, then serious, serious therapy."

The sanctuary, or main meditation room, was brightly lit, a departure from the way Bynum had found it only an hour ago. A departure from the aqueous gloom into which members had to tiptoe when they wanted to meditate or commune. Because of the lights, Adam and I were able to look across the sanctuary to the dais beneath a huge bronze mandala and see exactly what Niedrach and Le May wanted us to see, namely, the murder victim, who reposed in a leather lounger that someone had wrestled onto the dais so that it sat there like a laid-back throne.

Adam and I exchanged puzzled looks.

A shaggy, orangish-red orangutan sprawled in the lounger. The creature wore a set of headphones, but its posture betrayed its lifelessness. Upside-down in its lap was a naked plastic doll. A black baby doll for a black child. The doll had fallen across the orangutan's lap so that its head was wedged between one shaggy thigh and the lounger's leather armrest.

"It's a costume," Niedrach said. "This is the way Mr. Bynum found the victim. The head comes off." He negotiated his way through several rows of loungers and divans to the dais. There, gripping the orangutan head at the neck, he turned it—as if trying to unscrew a diving helmet from a diving suit. A moment later, he lifted the head clear and gestured at the startling human visage protruding from the costume's neck hole.

It was Nancy Teavers. Her head shone like a huge mottled egg. Either she or Craig had shaved off every lock of her hair. The spiky white coiffure she had worn to Sinusoid Disturbances had undoubtedly been a wig. Whatever the case then, tonight she was bald. Her eyes bulged. Bruises discolored her cheeks. Her lips were bloated. I recognized her, anyway. The dissatisfied waitress who had decided to go west to make her fortune. Instead, she had gone to Craig Puddicombe, and Craig had turned her into a punkette, a babysitter for the kidnapped T.P., and finally an orangutan. I had no idea what this grotesque progression meant. Maybe it was some sort of homicidal performance-art parody of Darwinism and evolutionary theory.

"Do you remember his first call?" I asked Niedrach. "He claimed he didn't do violence."

"We all knew he was lying. To himself as much as to us."

Adam, who had gone forward, started to pick the doll

out of the victim's orangutan lap, but Le May caught his
wrist. A Fulton County detective, he explained, would
have to bag the doll for forensic analysis. Fingerprints,
Mr. Montaraz, fingerprints.

"This proves that our Paulie is dead," Adam said.
"That is the terrible meaning of this doll."

"Not necessarily," I said. "Not necessarily."

"That's right," Ryan Bynum said. "How could it mean
that? You don't believe in voodoo, do you?" Completely
ignorant of the kidnapping, he had jumped to the conclusion that Adam was surrendering to some atavistic Carib
superstition.

My unofficial identification made, the Fulton County
detectives shooed us out so that they could finish their
work. We were standing on the lawn when two men with a
stretcher entered the building and reappeared a few moments later carrying the costumed Nancy. The ambulance
at curbside took her in and departed with her without
benefit of siren or flasher. After all, what was the hurry?

"It looks as if she was strangled," Le May told us.
"But it didn't happen here. The only sign of struggle at
the scene has to do with rearranging furniture. No breaking
and entering, either. Puddicombe used somebody's membership card, opened the back door from the inside, and
dragged Nancy in from the rear drive."

"I am so sorry for her," Adam said.

We left the site in Le May's Plymouth, and Niedrach
told us that shortly before noon, three or four hours after
most city newsstands and drugstores had begun selling the
latest *Newsweek*, Craig had rented the orangutan suit from
Atlanta Costume Company. A clerk there had given detectives a good description of the renter. Bearded. Young.
Blue-eyed. He hadn't been wearing painter's coveralls,
though. Instead, a pair of toast-colored, pleated pants and
a white T-shirt that had left his midriff bare.

He had claimed to be a student at Georgia Tech, wanting the costume for some kind of fraternity prank. He had
paid a deposit in cash—rather than with a check and the
supporting evidence of a student ID. The address he had
given as his parents', however, seemed more than a little

peculiar in retrospect: it was Adam and RuthClaire's address on Hurt Street. His name he had given as Greg Burdette, and for that he had shown a current driver's license with a photograph of his own likeness. He had struck the clerk as an oddly somber type to be renting an orangutan costume, but she had rationalized this small anomaly of bearing as an attempt on his part to complete the rental with a kind of deadpan savoir-faire. In fact, once he had left the front counter, she had burst out laughing at his successful act. He had been truly convincing.

"Did she see what he was driving?" (My obsessive concern.)

"Unfortunately, she didn't," Niedrach confessed.

Adam said, "I want no one here to tell Miss RuthClaire what we saw at Meditation Center. Already, she has enough to cope with."

I looked at Adam. I had no doubt that in his mind's eye was a picture of that black doll upside-down in Nancy Teavers's lap.

BUT BACK at the house, RuthClaire got the truth from Adam in five minutes. He was unable to lie to her, and she would not be put off with either stalling tactics or verbal evasions.

"You didn't think I could handle the news, is that it?"

"I wanted only to—"

"To keep it from me. That's sweet, Adam. But it's demeaning, too. I'm not a little girl. I'm an adult."

A figure small and forlorn, Adam stood in shadow with his back to the beaverboard panel in the downstairs studio. His profile was at once heroic and prehistorically feral.

"Nancy dead, strangled, dressed in a monkey suit, put on display in Ryan Bynum's stupid Meditation Center. But what for? To horrify us? To put us on notice?" RuthClaire was pacing among her canvases.

"A puke-livered terror tactic," Bilker Moody said. He was standing behind the bar on the other side of the big room.

"Paulie's dead already," RuthClaire told us, ignoring the security guard. "Or else Craig's going to kill him this evening. We'll find the body tomorrow."

"That's a defeatist look at the situation, ma'am," Le May said.

"It's a realistic look at it. Do you think I *like* it? I don't like it. It makes my heart swell up and my rib cage ache."

"Mine, too," Adam said—so simply that I was moved for both of them.

"It's the passive waiting that's killing me," RuthClaire said. "Craig's told us what he's going to do, and we're *still* waiting. Us frail females—" putting her hand to her breast like Scarlett O'Hara—"are supposed to be able to bide our time, but how you go-git-'em macho fellas can take it is totally beyond me."

"This such fella takes it very badly," Adam said.

RuthClaire went to him, and they embraced. Then she turned to Caroline. "Come upstairs with me, Caroline. I don't think I can sleep, but I'm going to lie down. It would be nice to have somebody to talk to."

The two women left. I was busy sipping a Scotch on the rocks that Bilker had made for me. I felt a hand on my arm. It belonged to Adam. Its grip on my biceps tightened inexorably.

"You've had enough, Mister Paul."

"I haven't even had *one*. Sit down. Bilker'll fix you right up."

"Abraxas," Adam said.

"What?"

"We should go to Abraxas. I, Mister Paul, *am* going there. Please come with me. It is what needs to be done."

"What's going on at Abraxas? I thought they were closed on Mondays, like the High and so many independent galleries. Besides, even if they weren't closed on Mondays, they'd be closed by *now*."

Adam said, "Nancy Teavers dead in Ryan Bynum's

church. This is a red flag waving. Interpret the signal. Where might young Craig Puddicombe next appear?"

"Abraxas?"

Bilker Moody had his hands in a stainless-steel basin full of suds and highball glasses. "Hell, yes," he said. "*Hell, yes!*"

Looking around, I saw that Niedrach and Le May were no longer with us. Back in the kitchen with Webb? Probably.

"Tell Niedrach and the FBI men," I urged Adam.

"I don't think so. They are worthy gentlemen. I like them very much. But none of them has read the signals."

"Tell them, then, for God's sake!"

"This is my fight, Mister Paul. I am the cause of it all, basically. If you are not coming with me, you must promise to say no word to the special-agent gentlemen when I go."

"What if I don't promise?"

Adam eyed me speculatively. Then he gave me his fear grin, his lips drawn back to reveal his realigned but still dauntingly primitive teeth. "I will bite you, Mister Paul." In the light from the cut-glass swag lamp at the end of the bar, Adam's teeth were winking at me like ancient scrimshawed ivory.

"You give me no choice," I said.

"I'll get my jacket and some heat," Bilker said, wiping his hands on a towel. He lifted a section of the counter, came through it, and trotted off toward his converted pantry.

We told the agents we were going out for some fresh air. Also for some doughnuts from Dunkin' Donuts. We'd bring back whatever the agents wanted—cream-filled, buttermilk, old-fashioned, they could choose.

"Don't be gone long," Le May cautioned us. "Mrs. Montaraz can take a call upstairs, but we'll need your input and interpretations after we've taped it. Going out's risky. You could miss it."

"Thirty minutes," Adam said. "No more."

WE TOOK my Mercedes because I did not feel competent to handle either the hatchback with its elevated foot pedals or Bilker's dented '54 Chevy. *I* was driving, rather than Bilker, because Adam wanted the big man to have his hands free. He was riding shotgun, a position of "great importance." Now, though, it seemed funny to me to be driving so big and expensive an automobile as my Mercedes to a one-sided rendezvous with a murderer.

It was a relief when Adam directed me to park on Ralph McGill Boulevard about two blocks below the old school buildings housing the Abraxas art complex. We would have to walk the rest of the way, but at least Craig was not likely to shoot out my windshield or riddle a sheet of gleaming body metal with bullet holes. It had begun to rain, lightly. An ocean of upside-down combers rumbled above the treetops. Traffic was nonexistent, and the three of us trudged up the hill on the very margin of the street itself. The runoff from above had not yet acquired volume or momentum, our shoes were still dry, and on so hot a night a cooling thunderstorm seemed an ally rather than an enemy.

"Dristle," I said.

Adam looked at me.

"That's what Livia George calls a rain like this."

"Very good."

Bilker halted at the top of the hill. An elm-lined row of clapboard houses went back down the curve of the hill to our left. The houses were dark. Although we could see Atlanta's skyline, traffic lights reflecting their colors on the slate of wet pavement between Abraxas and the city proper, the old school building loomed in the rain like an insane asylum from a florid gothic novel. Its studio annex perched on the downslope of the ill-kept property as if at any moment it might go sliding down the hill like one of

242

those stilt-supported houses on the California coast. Brooding. Medieval. Horace Walpole, Mary Shelley, and Edgar Allan Poe would have loved the place.

"No security?" Bilker said. "At a gallery?"

"The third-floor galleries are now between shows," Adam said. "The studio wing is tightly locked."

"Locked-schmocked. Folks'll pick locks. This place needs round-the-clock security. Needs some lights on it, too."

"Needs its grass mowed," I said.

"No money for a guard," Adam said. "No money for lights."

I remembered that on my first trip to Abraxas, David Blau had complained about the current administration's miserly treatment of the arts. Of course, Blau and his staff members could, and did, initiate money-raising projects of their own, but funding a security force had always taken a back seat to strong financial support for major new shows and deserving artists. For the two weeks of the Kander-Montaraz-Haitian exhibit, Blau had in fact hired a full-time security guard, but no one was on the premises tonight because there was nothing noteworthy to protect.

Adam told us that we must enter from the back. We crossed an asphalt drive, which dead-ended forty or fifty feet farther on, and crept into the shadow of the print shop next to the school. We advanced single-file through a soggy mulch of leaves and grass, hung a left at the end of the print shop, and found ourselves staring into the rear half of the facility's car park.

Trees closed off the back of the lot. Power-company spools and strange varieties of metallic trash were visible in the gaps among the trees only as mysterious lumps and silhouettes. Tonight, unlike in February, the branches of the trees were weighted with summer foliage, and the mist dripping through the leaves made the asphalt echo as if it were a basement drying room with dozens of frilly black-green dresses on its lines.

We entered the shelter of a covered rampway leading directly to the main building's rear entrance. From this ramp, we could see the whole parking lot and, straight across from us, the studio wing enclosing the lot on that side. Near the building's door sat the only vehicle in the lot, a red GM pickup with its tailgate down. Whoever had parked the truck had placed an extension ladder in its loadbed so that the ladder cleared the rampway's corrugated roof and leaned against the wall about twenty feet above the covered door.

"He's here," I said. "The bastard's actually here."

Adam shushed me. He told Bilker and me to stay under cover while he tried to determine exactly how Craig had entered Abraxas. He would go because he was less likely to be seen than either Bilker or I. So, bending his back almost parallel to the asphalt, he did a graceful Groucho Marx slither that carried him to a crouching position behind the GM. He tilted his head to gaze up into the rain at the ladder and the wall. Then he Groucho Marxed his way back to us and said that Craig had apparently climbed to the full extension of the ladder and then thrown a rope with a grappling hook into the barnlike window on the building's third floor. This window belonged to a vacant supply room across an interior corridor from the curator's office. The grappling hook was still caught on the sill, the rope from it dangling down a foot or two below the top of the ladder. Craig probably did not intend to use it again, though, because he could far more easily come down the stairs and let himself out the back than risk the slippery rope and the slippery ladder by which he had gained entry.

"We ought to call the house," I said. "Tell Niedrach."

"No. Up there, Mister Paul, I am going right now." Adam took a key from his trouser pocket and gave it to Bilker. "You may go inside and guard the stairs so that, by them, the villain does not seek to make successful his getaway."

"What am *I* supposed to do?"

"To follow me up is okay and probably more silent than taking stairs. Or wait down here. I am happier should you come, though."

"Why?"

"Moral support. Morale support. To subdue young

Puddicombe may require two of us. Someone to bludger him, someone to rescue Tiny Paul."

"Then you'd better let me do it," Bilker said.

"I fear you are too heavy," Adam said. "Paul is much lither." He looked me over somewhat grimly. "By comparison."

I was scared. Neither Adam nor I was armed. Bilker would have the Ruger, of course, but he would be standing in the downstairs corridor waiting for Craig to come to him. Craig might not choose to do so. He would have a weapon or two of his own, and if Adam and I bumbled into him up there in the galleries, he would hardly hesitate to cut us down. More important, if he had rappeled up the wall after climbing the first third of the way on his extension ladder, could we really expect him to have T.P. with him? Our chances of retrieving the child alive seemed to be dwindling by the moment. I think even Adam knew that.

To Bilker's and my surprise, the habiline shed his clothes. He pulled off his shoes, shimmied out of his trousers, and ducked free of his shirt.

"I am quieter this way. Also better camouflaged. Like a commando." He looked at me. "You, too?"

"Oh, no."

"The shoes, then. The shoes and socks. To make you have a grip both firm and silent on the ladder rungs."

Bilker was grinning at me, enjoying my discomfiture. I removed my shoes and socks. Adam nodded the body-guard toward the door, and Bilker used the key to open it. He gave us a thumbs-up sign and disappeared into the concrete maw of the building.

Adam and I ran to the loadbed of the truck, eased ourselves into it, and squatted in the rain looking upward at the great hinged door high in the rear wall. Next to this door, or shutter, were three tall windows of more conventional design; they lacked glass, however, and someone had fitted them with opaque sheets of polyethylene, which, split and tattered, made faint popping noises in the rain. My fear intensified. I was developing, while still on the ground (or near it), a bad case of acrophobia. A surreal kind of dizziness had me in its grip. Adam was attributing to me more courage and athletic ability than I possessed. I could fall to my death trying to enter Abraxas by this route.

"Adam—"

"I will go first. No need to brace ladder. Side of truck suffices." Naked, the mist matting his body hair, he swung around the side of the pickup to mount the ladder. Bouncing on its rungs and pulling at its uprights, he tested the reliability of its positioning. "Is okay," he announced. Whereupon he climbed it like a monkey shinnying lickety-split up a tree.

At the top, Adam grabbed the rope hanging from the sill and threw himself clear of the ladder. Expecting him to come crashing down on the corrugated roof of the rampway, I flinched. Adam's feet hit the vertical face of the wall, however, and he expertly walked himself up the rope to the hinged window shutter. Here, he turned around and squatted on the sill, a gargoyle on a somewhat shoddy cathedral. The gargoyle beckoned to me.

I had to will myself to move. My bare feet tingled on the cold aluminum rungs of the ladder. I climbed with my eyes on Adam. If I looked down, I would panic. The habiline drew nearer as I ascended, but still seemed terribly far away. At the top of the ladder, I had no idea what to do. I could not grab the hanging rope without letting go of the ladder's uprights. Trapped between heaven and hell, I placed one side of my face against the unyielding bricks of the building. Dear God. Dear God.

A creaking sound made me look up again. A second rope fell out of the sky to slap and abrade my forehead. Adam had pushed the hinged door of the window outward, revealing a block-and-tackle arrangement by which the gallery sometimes lifted heavy objets d'art to the third floor. I slipped the loop of this rope around my waist and gripped it high with both hands. Adam, grasping the other end, backed away from the window, and I began to rise, my feet dangling beneath me like stunned pink fish. I closed my eyes until the faint squeaking of the pulley system had ceased and the window ledge was there before

me as an accomplished fact. More noisily than I wanted, I
went over it into the supply room.

Adam touched my shoulder. "Somewhere he is in the
galleries. As yet, I think, the rain has allowed us to escape
his detection. Soon, though, he will return. Come." Even
his whisper was something of a growl.

I disentangled myself from the rope, and together we
crossed the supply room to the door. We eased through it
into nearly impenetrable darkness, hearing the rain as a
light, steady drumming, a hum almost like that of a huge
air conditioner or refrigerator. Without it, I, too, was sure,
Craig would have long since heard us—or *me*, at least.
Adam could move as soundlessly as a daddy longlegs
racehorsing over a mound of warehoused cotton.

We crept past Blau's oversized office into Gallery Number One. Bleak, echoing immensity. A miserly kind of
illumination entered by way of the horizontal windows at
the top of the wall facing McGill Boulevard. No paintings,
no installations, no sculptures. Abraxas was between shows,
and the galleries reposed high above the street like empty
boxcars. Gallery Number Three was even darker than the
one in which we were standing; it had no windows.

But from Gallery Number Two, the chamber in which
Blau had displayed the upsetting photographs of M.-K.
Kander, pale light spilled. It lay across the scuffed hardwood floor of Gallery Number One like a film of buttermilk, a liquid gleam in the dimness.

Adam pointed at it. With his other hand, he clutched my
arm. I could imagine him clutching a habiline lieutenant
on a prehistoric African savannah, giving directions for a
life-or-death hunt, just as he was gripping me now. What
we did in the next one or two minutes would probably
determine the outcome of our stalk.

Adam said, "I go over by door. You stay, make noise.
He come out, I grab. This not work, you shout, 'Bilker!'
Understand?"

I nodded.

Adam padded—or *floated*, for he made no noise at
all—across the room, flattened his back against the wall,
and craned his upper body around so that he could look

into Gallery Number Two. Then he gave such a powerful cry that it vibrated my bones, bounced from the walls, and filled the entire building like a dam burst of gasoline, threatening to plunge everything visible and invisible into a chaos of fire. Still venting this cry, Adam charged into the gallery.

Without really listening for them, my ears registered the footsteps and the belugalike snorts of Bilker Moody pounding up the stairs to the third floor.

"You goddamn hibber!" a voice in the lighted chamber cried.

A gunshot barked, reverberated, went pinging away. My fear forgotten, or submerged, I sprinted toward the sound. A two-legged blur in stained whites burst from the chamber, bumped me bruisingly, and spun away from the impact as I crashed down on my tailbone and went sliding backward across the floor.

Sprawling sidelong, I saw this figure disappear into the supply room through which Adam and I had entered. As I tried to sit back up, Adam came scampering from Gallery Number Two, one gnarled hand holding his forearm just below the elbow. Blood glistened on his hairy fingers, oozed from the wound beneath them. He had paused to regard me sitting on the floor, but his eyes danced frantically from me to the supply room.

"Okay?" he asked.

"Yeah. Okay."

" 'Bye. Be back." He hurried toward the supply room, and I shouted a warning about the other man's still having his gun. As soon as I had, the figure in white reemerged from the supply room and fired four or five more shots into the gallery. Flames leapt from the weapon's stubby barrel like the sinister tongue flickers of a gila monster. Adam dove to his left, while I rolled over and over, praying that the bullets gouging the hardwood around me would not ricochet into my body.

Whereupon, the gunman, having decided against trying to escape by rope and ladder, unlatched the heavy door between Blau's office and the supply room and disappeared into the stairwell opposite the one by which Bilker

Moody had just now reached the galleries. Adam, back on his feet, went after the fleeing man.

Another gunshot sounded in the dark, this one from behind me. I ducked and covered my head. Two more shots bit into the sundered stillness of the third floor. Cautiously, I uncovered. Bilker had shot the lock off the door blocking his way into Abraxas's main display rooms. He kicked the door open and waddled into view like a trash-compacted Marshal Dillon.

"Why're you sittin' there on your butt, Mr. Loyd?" He blew on the barrel of his Ruger. "Where'd they go?"

"Down. Out. Lot of good that pistol of yours did us."

Bilker looked around, narrowing and widening his eyes, trying to get them to adjust. The light spilling out of Gallery Number 2 seemed to be the major source of his discomfort. He shielded his eyes with his hands.

"Craig wounded Adam," I told him. "He damn-near *killed* both of us. And you, our armed protector, too late to do anything but shoot holes in a door. Good show, Bilker." I climbed to my feet. My coccyx felt like the tip of the burning candle of my spine. I put a hand to the seat of my pants and held it there, grimacing.

"Mr. Montaraz stationed me downstairs."

"You're not there now. Craig's getting away."

"You think I'm fuckin' twins? A upstairs Bilker to hold your hand, a downstairs Bilker to guard the exits?" He had just lumbered up three flights of steps, exertion equivalent to an average man's accomplishing the same feat with a fifty-pound bag of potatoes over one shoulder. Miraculously, he was not breathing all that hard. "I got one body, Mr. Loyd. It don't do simultaneous appearances at two or three different locations."

"Okay. I'm sorry."

"Mr. Montaraz'll catch the sucker. The bastard's doomed in a foot race." But he was through bantering. "Where's Paulie?"

The question sobered me. I took my hand away from my tailbone and nodded at Gallery Number Two. "In there, I'm afraid. The scream you heard—it was Adam's. Something in there set it off."

Side by side, we entered the oddly shaped room. Bilker stared for several moments at what it revealed. Then he mumbled a vivid threat against the perpetrator, backed away, turned, and began trotting off after Adam and Paulie's murderer. I could hear him yank open the stairwell door and the door wheeze shut behind him. Then I could hear nothing but the air-conditioner hum of the rain.

Evidently, Craig had brought T.P. up the ladder with him dead. He had carried the child in a cardboard box with makeshift rubber shoulder harnesses (pieces of innertubing) pushed through slits in the cardboard. The box lay on the floor at the far end of the gallery. It had contained a few other items besides my godson's body—a sheaf of *Newsweek* covers, a package of blue balloons, a coil of rope, and a large fabric-sculpture doll licensed by Babyland General Hospital in Cleveland, Georgia.

From this female Little Person, Craig had ripped all the expensive designer clothes, exposing the pinched knot of her bellybutton and the faint Caucasian flush of her fabric nudity. I wondered what her name was. Babyland General gave them all their very own names, no two alike, and at one time, Xavier Roberts, their creator, and his staff had even sent birthday cards to the dolls and their owners on the dolls' "placement dates." Six or seven times at the West Bank, I had had to prepare a special plate for a doll whose pouting adoptive mother had refused to eat her own meal unless Abigail Faye or Dorothy Lilac were served something, too. We had made a little extra money from the intractability of these little girls, of course, but the embarrassed surrender of their parents and the sight of a moronic fabric-sculpture doll leaning into a bowl of vegetable soup or chocolate chile had always galled me. Moreover, the supposedly individualistic Little People had cost seven or eight times what a poorer or less indulgent parent would pay for a plastic doll of comparable size—a doll like the one Craig had left in Nancy Teavers's lap at the Unaffiliated Meditation Center on Euclid Avenue.

In any case, this naked Little Person hung about four feet off the floor of the gallery on a piece of nylon cord. The cord was attached to a movable metal track just below the ceiling. Tiny Paul, as naked as his female companion, hung to her immediate left on yet another length of cord. Both pathetic little figures were lifeless, the doll to begin with, Tiny Paul permanently deprived of consciousness at a time I was unable to estimate.

Limp blue balloons clung to the mouths of both figures. Craig had stuck them to their lips with mucilage. The excess mucilage glittered on their faces like dried semen. Other limp balloons, all of them blue, lay strewn about the floor as if the Great Inflator had lost either his faith or his mind. By contrast, Paulie's minute virgin penis poked out like the inflation valve on a bicycle tire. It mocked the flaccid bladders on the floor.

I sagged against a wall. My body knocked four or five *Newsweek* covers to the floor. Dozens of repetitions of Adam and RuthClaire, above the legend THE NEW PHOTO-GRAPHY/ *An Art in Militant Transition*, were plastered to the walls of the chamber.

That was what Craig had been doing when Adam looked in, plastering up magazine covers. Applying them to the walls with a hand-held brush and a solution of wallpaper paste. A Tupperware container full of the oatmealish goo was propped at an angle against the base of the door. Craig had brought everything upstairs with him in his cardboard box: murder victim, doll, magazine covers, cord, brush, wallpaper paste. A performance-art activity of fatal comprehensiveness, the ultimate existential Dadaism.

I slumped to the floor, dragging dozens of covers down with me. Fie on art. Fie on THE NEW PHOTOGRAPHY. Fie on Craig Puddicombe.

Looking first at my godson's rotating shadow on the floor, and then at my own upward-jutting toes, I began to weep. This little piggie went to market, this little piggie stayed home. I studied my toes through a distorting film of tears. They were fascinating, my toes, each one indisputably unique. Abigail Faye, Dorothy Lilac, Hepzibah Rose, Karma Leigh, and Cherry Helena. The other five had names, too. They were all detachable. You could unplug them from my feet and adopt them out to deserving amputees. Some of the sorry farts who took them, though, would treat them badly, maim them in unconscionable ways that made you ashamed to belong to a species possessing toes. Detachable little piggies suspended from gallows, so many innocent little lynching victims. . . .

Bilker Moody had his hand on my shoulder. "You didn't cut the poor little fella down, Mr. Loyd?" His voice was gentle.

"I was going to."

"I'll do it."

A scruple surged into my murky awareness. "Should you touch him? This is a crime scene, Bilker. Shouldn't everything stay as it is?"

"Do I give a shit for the holiness of crime scenes? This poor kid's been away from home long enough as it is."

I began to get to my piggies, my bare, dirty feet.

Bilker doubled a loop in the nylon cord above Tiny Paul's head, inserted the blade of his pocketknife, and began to saw away at the cord with all his strength. "Do I give a shit?" he reiterated, sawing. "I've just blown Puddicombe's fuckin' face away. Which the Effin' Bee Aye ain't likely to be crazy about, neither." Sawing, sawing. "And I'll be damned if even *that* worries me."

The cord finally broke, and Bilker caught T.P. in his arms. "You want to hold him?" he asked me.

Did I want to hold him? I must have appeared to want to, for Bilker brought the child to me and put him in my arms. He was cold and rigid, like a plastic doll. The small pudgy halfbreed who had charmed Caroline in Everybody's. The same but not the same. A shell. A gallery room without statues or mobiles or paintings. Where had all the life gone?

And where was Adam? I asked Bilker.

"Puttin' on his clothes. I tied a hankie 'round his goddamn elbow. It's not too bad. C'mon. Let's don't make him shinny up here after us again. He's mighty liable to pass out."

I pulled the stuck balloon off T.P.'s lip and dropped it into the container of wallpaper paste by the door. We left the galleries by the stairs that Bilker had earlier climbed.

We found Adam in the parking lot, fully dressed except

for his shoes. He was holding his shoes with the fingers of one hand hooked inside their heels so that they hung down beside his knee. He stood in the middle of the parking lot, the rain slowly filling the oily puddles all around his bare feet. Craig Puddicombe's truck was behind him with the driver's door open and the driver himself slumped forward with his head between the open door and the steering wheel.

The ladder that had been propped against the wall from the loadbed lay on the asphalt, on an impotent diagonal. Apparently, Craig had managed to pull it clear of the rampway's roof, drive all the way out of the lot, and then reverse directions in an attempt to back over his habiline pursuer. Adam had leapt into the truck, Craig had made the GM fishtail this way and that to shake him out again, and Bilker had lumbered out of the building in time to approach the pickup and fire his Ruger .357 magnum right through the open window into Craig's head. So intent had the kidnapper been on throwing Adam out of the truck that he had not even seen Bilker coming. Consequently, his determination to leave tire tracks on Adam's body had proved fatal for him.

I was not sorry. I was relieved.

Bilker and I stepped through the rungs of the fallen ladder and joined Adam in the middle of the lot. I held Paulie out to him. Adam set his shoes down, in a puddle that half-submerged them, and took the child from me, holding T.P. with his hands under his back so that he could nuzzle his son's bloated belly and mumble unheard comfort into his death-stopped ears.

Over to the truck went Bilker. He tumbled the murderer out of the driver's seat. With a sucking sort of thud, the boy's corpse sprawled into view on the ebony pavement. Most of his face was gone. He was unrecognizable as anything but an adult male in stained painter's coveralls. Where had the malevolent energy of his life just fled? Bilker kicked him three or four times in the side, each kick more vicious than the last.

"Don't," Adam said. "For him, it is over."

Bitterly, Bilker said, "It ain't over for you and Mrs.

Montaraz. It ain't over for me. We'll be livin' with the fuckin' fallout from this for the rest of our lives."

Still holding his dead son, Adam walked over to Bilker and looked him full in the face. "I don't think so. We will not forget, but later, maybe not too long from now, our shroud of grief will surely unravel, and we will be as good as new again."

Bilker and I gaped at Adam. Bilker turned and spat into a puddle. I think we both realized that there was something willful right now about Adam's saintly serenity. It was too soon for forgiveness and reconciliation. Far, far too soon to offer up T.P.'s innocent body as a sacrifice to human understanding. Bilker and I were appalled. There were angers and hatreds to be worked out, sorrows and sufferings from which to distill a thin, bittersweet balm. Magnanimity, right now, was an emotional non sequitur.

"I'll go get the car," I said. But Bilker and Adam walked with me, and we drove back to Hurt Street without saying another word.

FINGERPRINTS UNEQUIVOCALLY identified the man shot by Bilker as Craig Raymond Puddicombe. In the dead man's wallet were two driver's licenses, both of them false. One of them identified him as Teavers, Elvis Lamar. He had taken great care to use this alias and the Montaraz address near Inman Park when he did not wish to be traced to his rental property, a small frame house, on the southeastern arc of I-285. The other driver's license gave his name as Burdette, Gregory Rollins; it also pinpointed the location of his house off the perimeter expressway. As Greg Burdette, Craig had lived in Atlanta for nearly eight months, earning his keep in a collateral branch of the profession practiced by Adam and RuthClaire. Like them, he was a painter. Unlike them, he did houses, garages, and signboards. He worked fairly regularly, but had to scratch for jobs to stay ahead of his debts.

For two reasons, the FBI permitted Special Agent Niedrach and his GBI colleagues to conclude the investigation of the kidnapping. First, Niedrach and Davison had handled the Klan episode in Beulah Fork at the end of last summer; and, second, Craig Puddicombe and his accomplice-victim had never taken Tiny Paul out of the Greater Atlanta area.

Therefore, local agents interviewed the woman who had rented "Greg Burdette" his house, the young men who had occasionally worked with him, and some of the home owners and contractors who had employed him. Their cumulative assessment was that Burdette lived quietly and frugally, never talked about his past, never shirked on the job, and tackled even the uninspiring business of caulking a rain gutter as if it were a signal step in a fiscal game plan that would one day free him of the need to paint houses.

Everyone who had known him, in fact, had assumed that his highest purpose in life was to become rich. Although he never flaunted this ambition, he took good care of his money, made his bids competitive without underselling himself, and insisted on payment in full before leaving the premises of any completed job. This was a condition that he laid down at the very beginning of every enterprise, and his reputation as an efficient, conscientious workman—a man who would clean out rain gutters, scrape away old paint, apply the most reliable primers, and so on—had seldom failed to win his employers' agreement.

His Achilles heel, if he had one, was an inability to work with blacks. He refused to do so. Blacks never appeared on any of the painting crews he hired out to or put together himself. Two or three times, at least, he had passed up profitable jobs because a contractor had wanted him to share the work with a black painter. Similarly, he would paint the home of a black only if he could bring to the task a crew consisting solely of whites. This seldom happened. Oddly, though, Puddicombe-Burdette's refusal to work with blacks never led him to badmouth them. Stereotypical racial comments about intelligence levels, food stamps, welfare Cadillacs, and illegitimate babies never passed his lips. He shut down on the subject of blacks altogether, sometimes visibly holding himself in, as if struggling to obey the homely injunction, "If you can't say anything good about someone, don't say," etc. The suppressed hostility of this effort, however, tightened his jaw and set his eyes jitterbugging. In a way, it was comical. In another way, it was frightening.

One former associate remembered that Greg strongly approved of the Fulton County district attorney's crusade against pornography. Massage parlors, adult bookstores, and adult theaters disgusted him. He would cuss a blue streak with no evident qualm or discernible sense that some people might find such language as offensive as he found photographs of naked people. In warm weather, he would work in denim cutoffs and tennis shoes, shirtless and proud of it—but, given a context even marginally interpretable as erotic, bare skin outraged him. Once, during a lunch break, he had yanked a men's magazine from the hands of a seventeen-year-old apprentice who had held up the foldout for his approval. "This is *shit* you're lookin' at!" he had raged.

The house on I-285 had yielded even more information. As Greg Burdette, Craig had been careful not to subscribe to any publications that state or federal law-enforcement agencies might classify as racist or provocatively right-wing. But he had bought them from newsstands, where possible, and had taken pains not to visit the same newsstands often enough to give their operators any real grasp of his reading habits. These were magazines devoted to firearms, post–nuclear holocaust survival, legal redress for white "victims" of affirmative-action laws, and creationism. Along with these magazines, agents had found, stuffed in drawers, circulars announcing Klan meetings and pamphlets on various topics from ultraconservative politicians. Further, Craig had possessed a small arsenal of unregistered handguns, most with their serial numbers metal-rasped or sandpapered away. A bulletin board in his bedroom displayed clippings from the Atlanta newspapers about racial conflict and about crimes perpetrated by blacks.

Prominent among these clippings was one recounting the acquittal of a number of Klansmen in a Greensboro, North Carolina, murder trial. Craig had emphasized every letter in the headline with a red Magic Marker.

Also in the house, items demonstrating conclusively that Nancy Teavers had lived there with him at least three months. Clothing, toilet articles, mementoes of her marriage to Craig's dead friend, Elvis Lamar. In fact, the arrangement of sleeping quarters in the little house—Nancy occupying a room that Craig had once set aside as a business office—strongly suggested that they had treated each other as brother and sister. The punk wardrobe that Nancy had worn to Sinusoid Disturbances, the GBI agents discovered not in the young woman's bedroom but instead in a steamer trunk at the foot of Craig's bed. Perhaps he had had a fetishistic fascination with such items. The clothes in Nancy's personal closet, a cardboard chifforobe purchased from a long-defunct Forest Park dry cleaners, had about them a small-town conventionality totally at odds with the shabby glitter of the getup in the trunk. Moreover, Nancy had filled her bedroom with decorative pillows, stuffed animals, and even a few dolls. The Little People doll that Craig had hung up in Abraxas beside T.P. had been Nancy's. Her late husband had given it to her for Christmas better than three years ago. An interview with Nancy's mother revealed that, in the privacy of her mobile home back in Beulah Fork, the young woman had behaved around that fabric-sculpture infant—Bonnie Laurel—as if it were a living human baby. More than anything, Nancy's mother told the GBI interviewer, her daughter had wanted to bear a child of her own. She and E.L. had just about decided to take the plunge when—but if you remembered the young man's fate, that was an unfortunate choice of phrase.

Craig had strangled Nancy in the little house off I-285. The *Newsweek* cover that had caused him to flip out, a betrayal of his every hate-handicapped concept of decency, had probably merely surprised Nancy, without leading her to believe that only the child's murder would properly expiate and punish the parents' flagrant sin. She had resisted Craig's arguments to kill Paulie. Her resistance had further outraged him. He had attacked her. Signs of their struggle marked both the house and her body. Overturned chairs, broken dishes, a curtain pulled off its rod. The coroner's report on Nancy mentioned not only the contusions encircling her throat, but also deep bites on her breasts and upper arms, and her severely cracked ribs. She was small, though, and Craig had overpowered her—after their initial chase and scuffle—with relative ease. Afterward, he had dressed her in the orangutan outfit, which he had rented either shortly before or shortly after her murder. Her installation in the sanctuary of the Little Five Points Unaffiliated Meditation Center had then had to await the cover of darkness.

As for Tiny Paul. . . . I don't think there's any need for me to continue. The reader can imagine the details of the child's execution far more easily than I can write them.

LATE ON Tuesday afternoon, the dead child's body was shipped to a crematorium in Macon. On Wednesday, his ashes were returned to the Montarazes in an expensive funerary urn. They had decided together on this means of disposing of the corpse, and, upon the recovery of Tiny Paul's ashes, they celebrated a private memorial service in their own home. Bilker Moody attended these rites, but Caroline Hanna and I were not there because Adam had asked me to run an errand for him in Beulah Fork—to visit Craig Puddicombe's family and to invite his mother to bury Craig beside Tiny Paul's ashes in a state-approved plot of my pecan grove on Paradise Farm. It was an errand that I might not have been able to accomplish without Caroline beside me for moral support. *Morale* support, to use Adam's own terminology.

Public reaction to Tiny Paul's murder was prolonged, sometimes thoughtful, occasionally fulsome, and almost always wearying. The President sent a wire. So did other prominent heads of state, including the Pope. A triumvirate of East African leaders released a joint communique offering the Montarazes citizenship in their countries and free transportation "home." A. P. Blair, the Zarakali paleoanthropologist, sent a two-page handwritten letter of commiseration and belated apology, but neither RuthClaire nor Adam could deduce from his self-referential prose the specific injustice for which he was apologizing. A host of network commentators and TV evangelists delivered eulogies. Every major daily newspaper in the country ran an editorial. In Atlanta, by special gubernatorial dispensation, the flags on the capitol grounds were flown at half-mast. Even more impressive, a procession of orderly people wearing crepe marched in triple columns through Inman Park to the mournful music of drums, fifes, and bagpipes. In Beulah Fork, I closed the West Bank for the remaining five days of our work week.

GEORGIA HIGHWAY Patrolmen directed traffic. Uninvited out-of-towners they sent back to the interstate. Relatives, friends, and invited locals, they checked through the front gates of Paradise Farm. They also saw to it that those who could not park their vehicles inside the walls were careful to pull them safely off the two-lane connecting Tocqueville and Beulah Fork.

Looking out the window of the upstairs bedroom we had shared, Caroline estimated that nearly every inhabitant of the Fork had showed up. Nothing like a funeral to draw people together. Nothing like a double funeral for a murderer and his final victim to swell the size of the crowd a hundredfold.

My parched front lawn swarmed with would-be mourners. Most of the women wore Sunday dresses or tailored Sunday suits, while the men, ties knotted beneath their

Adam's apples like tourniquets, sported linen or seersucker
jackets. A gay solemnity informed their movements. A
solemn gaiety. A few children with scrubbed faces clung
to the adults' hands. Other children, more eager, darted
through the maundering crowd to find good places in the
pecan grove from which to watch the ceremony.

"Thank God we don't have to feed this bunch," Caroline said.

I grunted. I was standing at a mirror trying to put a
Windsor knot in a new tie.

Fifteen uniformed security guards roamed the grounds,
while a sixteenth had his vantage on the widow's-walk
immediately above the room that Caroline and I were in.
The Montarazes and I were sharing the cost of the guards,
RuthClaire and Adam because the FBI had told them that
most of their ransom money would be recovered, I because
I hoped to keep a few of the rowdier mourners out of my
flowerbeds and shrubbery. Actually, the potential for conflict had not escaped us, and we wanted to avoid it.

Caroline was keeping informal tabs on the percentage of
mourners here for Craig Puddicombe and for Tiny Paul.
So far, she said, the latter group *appeared* to have the
upper hand. If any active Klan members had come, they
had had either the tact or the caution to leave their sheets
on their beds and their dunce caps on high closet shelves.
Besides, at least a few of those coming to pay their
respects to young Puddicombe surely had no Klan affiliation at all.

"Have you seen Craig's mother?"

"Bilker met her at the gate and escorted her around
back about fifteen or twenty minutes ago. She's fine."

"Does she know Bilker shot her son?"

"I don't think so. I hope not."

Beyond the gate, Caroline could see automobiles belonging to the Atlanta, Columbus, and Tocqueville newspapers, and three or four television news vans as well. I
had asked the highway patrol to keep them from trying to
enter, and I had ordered my own security people to apprehend any intruders and return them to the gate if they
somehow breached our defenses. Paradise Farm was pri-

vate property, today's ceremony was for the sole benefit of family and guests, and reporters in their capacity as reporters were not welcome. If they chose to ignore these simple fiats, the Montarazes would sue them for invasion of privacy and I would press charges for unlawful trespass.

At last I signaled to Caroline that I was ready to go. To my shame, she had finished dressing at least ten minutes before me. Her knee-length white dress had bunched sleeves and a rectangle of blue-and-white English smocking across the bodice. She put her arm through mine, and we left the room together.

"I'd've never been able to do this if RuthClaire had come," she said. "You know that, don't you?"

"I know."

She was talking about spending the night with me in my former wife's old house. It had seemed strange to me, too. Had RuthClaire accompanied Adam to Paradise Farm, I would have been no more able to share a bed with Caroline than Caroline with me. But my ex-wife had not come to Beulah Fork. The very thought of a double funeral for her son and his murderer had appalled her. That was why she and Adam had had a private ceremony on Hurt Street. After that ceremony, she had flown to Charlotte to visit an octogenarian maiden aunt and to recuperate from an ordeal that would never cease to haunt her. She was there now, boycotting Adam's ostentatious show of generosity and forgiveness.

IN THE back yard, Adam stood on the deck facing a crowd that pressed against the cedar platform and spread out into the pecan grove itself. In a grassy area cordoned off with red velvet ropes and upright brass posts, Caroline and I joined the Puddicombes. We were right in front of the deck, and none of the Puddicombes looked at or spoke to us as we entered. I nodded at some familiar faces just outside the paddock, but to most of the mourners our arrival was a sign to fall silent and stop jostling. Only the pesky~midges and a few frolicsome mockingbirds in the pecan trees refused to settle down.

"Welcome to these most sacred rites," Adam said. Of all those present, only Caroline, Bilker, and I had ever heard him speak before, and the guttural aspect of his voice—its powerful *growliness*—seemed to startle some of those around us.

Small as he was, Adam commanded attention. He had worn a silk top hat. He also wore a frock coat with tails, striped ambassadorial trousers, a white vest, a dove-gray tie, and spats. To his right was a pedestal draped with a piece of velvet reminiscent of the voodoo banners that David Blau had once shown in Abraxas. Atop the covered pedestal sat the burial urn containing Tiny Paul's ashes. To Adam's left was the bier upon which Craig Puddicombe's casket rested; the casket was also draped with a colorful, sequined banner. In the August sunlight, the sequins glittered like melting ice.

"Ashes to ashes, dust to dust," the habiline said. He gave everyone a painful grimace, almost a fear-grin. "For most of my last year in your strange country, it has worried me, the problem of what I am to you and how I must be standing spiritually in the scales of God. Longer, I am not going to worry. We all come from and go back to the same place."

"Amen!" said a voice behind us. It belonged to Livia George. She and Hazel Upchurch and a small contingent of local blacks occupied a pocket of the crowd between the trees and the sun deck.

"My dead son had a soul, just as did the young man who murdered him. And I, Adam Montaraz, citizen and exile, habiline and human, have a soul—as surely as does the heartbroken mother of Craig Puddicombe. All God's children, I say unto you, have souls."

"Praise the Lord," said a man next to Hazel Upchurch.

"All who suffer and know that they suffer, all who yearn for solace and know that they yearn, all who have heavenly expectations and know that they have them—all such, I most emphatically say, have souls. For it is our souls that suffer, yearn, expect, and *know*. It is our souls that do deeply feel the pain, the sorrow, and the joys of each of these deeply feeling processes.''

"Amen," murmured several people approvingly.

"My God," I whispered, "he's preaching a full-bore sermon.''

Caroline shushed me.

''The soul is what the body does, I say. It is also the perceptive self-knowledge of its doing what it does. Paulie, my dead son, was beginning to grow into such soulful awareness. His soul, I must tell you, was beginning to bloom. No one here today, I fear, can guess at the shape toward which it was tending, but in my heart—yes, my father's proudness is speaking—I am almost sure it would have been beautiful. Very beautiful.''

"Praise God."

''The soul of Craig Puddicombe had already opened.'' He gestured at the *vevés*-draped casket. ''It had an unhappy shape because he himself was unhappy. He hated and knew that he hated. He killed and knew that he killed. He hurt and knew that he hurt. He also knew that even by giving pieces of this hurt to others, he would never—no, not ever—uproot the hurt that was sickening him unto very death. His soul would never in this life acquire a happy spiritual handsomeness.''

"Growing up, he was always a good boy!" shouted Craig Puddicombe's mother. ''His soul was as handsome as anybody's!''

This outburst of maternal loyalty appeared to embarrass Mrs. Puddicombe. She folded her arms beneath her breasts and hunched her shoulders. Caroline reached toward her as if to pat her comfortingly on the arm, but the woman leaned into her father-in-law, a sickly old man with glazed eyes, to avoid an outsider's touch.

"I am very sure that that was so," Adam told the woman, looking down on her with a puzzled expression. ''He did as other children do, and his soul was what he did. Later, his doings—and therefore his soul—fell under sway of older, much more twisted souls, and so began to deform its youngling beauty toward these unhappy shapes. In children, my many friends from Beulah Fork, the soul is very plastic."

"The soul ain't plastic, Mister Adam!" shouted an elderly black man next to Livia George. Several people, including some whites whom I knew as devout fundamentalists, seconded this objection.

"Never do I mean to imply that the soul is what you would call, uh, a synthetic polymer," Adam said. "Please understand. The soul is immaterial. It has no location. But because it is what the body does and knows, it *can* be shaped. Metaphorically, I say. Likewise literally. All this, dear people, I have learned painfully in your great but strange country."

"The soul don't have nothing to do with the body!" shouted Ruben Decker, my neighbor one farm to the south. "It's spiritual and everlasting!"

Adam, somewhat sadly, was shaking his head. Other people in the crowd, primarily men, were loudly proclaiming both a rigorous body-soul dichotomy and the immortality of the released soul in that transtemporal realm known as heaven. Their phraseology was country allegory—"The body die, but the soul rise up!" "Gonna live forever with Jesus!"—but the message, a kind of received Protestant consensus, seemed to set Adam back on his heels.

My hands had begun to sweat. To Caroline, I whispered, "Can you believe this? A theological donnybrook in my own back yard."

Adam took off his top hat and peered into it as if searching for the proper response to those whose opposition he had aroused. Just as he was about to speak, the sounds of the rotary blades of a helicopter—*thwup! thwup! thwup!*—became audible over the tree-tops to the northeast. Then the yellow, wasplike body of the copter itself tilted into view. It swept over the highway, dropped toward my front lawn, and settled noisily to rest on the other side of the house. Three or four security guards went running around that way with their pistols drawn, and many of the people facing the sun deck began pushing and side-stepping one another as if to follow the guards.

Raising his hands, Adam called, "Please, everyone! Let the security persons do their work! No pretext here for rushings about and shovings!" These admonitions calmed many in the crowd, but the hubbub prompted by the helicopter's arrival kept the habiline from continuing the funeral rites. For reassurance, I took Caroline's hand.

Presently, an entourage of three men in expensive suits, flanked on each side by three or four guards, strode around the corner of my house. The leading figure in this procession was the Right Reverend Dwight "Happy" McElroy. With film-star winks, victorious-politico smiles, and aw-shucks-country-boy nods, he was acknowledging the incredulous delight of many of the mourners on my property. His son Duncan marched two or three steps behind him, while his other meticulously dressed lieutenant—a man with a blond flattop and a suspicious eye—stayed at McElroy's elbow, the civilian equivalent of a Secret Service agent.

McElroy escaped this man only by mounting the sun deck and walking toward Adam with his right hand extended. To cheers and applause, he and the habiline shook. My small friend appeared as perplexed as the long, tall evangelist looked amused and confident. Mutt and Jeff. The two men were such physical contrasts that many people could not help laughing.

"What is Happy McElroy doing here?" the evangelist suddenly asked, as if about to launch a homily of his own. "Well, my son Duncan and I are just in from Louisiana, via Atlanta, to share the grief of two bereaved families. We're also here to honor Adam Montaraz for a saintly gesture worthy of Our Lord Himself. We could *not* stay away. Where the sorrow of others calls out for assuaging, there the ministry of Dwight McElroy, God's consoling servant, must also be. Adam didn't expressly invite us, no, but that's because in his humility he feared to impose upon a man as busy about God's undone work as I. His thoughtfulness is a light unto the nations."

"Amen!"

"Tell it!"

"But I come for another important reason, too, dear

friends. Oh, yes. I come to bring back to this noble man the bread that he and his equally noble wife cast upon the waters of faith, hoping thereby to save the life of the unbaptized infant whose ashes occupy this jar.'' McElroy nodded at the urn. Then he withdrew from an inside jacket pocket (a flash of peacock-patterned silk) an official-looking envelope. ''Duncan and I, not to mention my wife and Christ-proclaiming partner, Eugenia Lisbeth, are proud to return to the Montarazes the five thousand dollars that their son's murderer extorted from them as an illicit 'donation' to the Greater Christian Constituency. Let it never be said that Happy McElroy accepted blood money—other than that consecrated in the blood of the Lamb—for God's work. Let it never be said that a life devoted to love chose to profit its ministry by the terrible wages of bigotry and hate. Here, Adam, receive from me this check, that you may put it to happier and more fruitful work than it has thus far done.''

An expectant hush gripped the crowd. Even the mockingbirds had stopped calling and flitting about. McElroy's dramatic offering—his refusal to profit by another's misfortune—had paralyzed his sweating onlookers with holy wonder.

Adam put his hands behind his back. ''I cannot accept it. Thank you very much, but I cannot accept it.''

At which saying McElroy beamed. ''The saintliness of this man is going to be *legendary*,'' he said, beginning to return the envelope to his jacket. ''His very generosity cleanses this money of its taint. Cleansed, it can go to work for God. We're blessed, my friends, to have among us in these evil days such a one.''

Before the enthusiasts could start *amen*-ing and *hallelujah*-ing, though, the mother of Craig Puddicombe spoke up: ''That there money ought to be giv' to us. But for Craig, it wouldn't've been made a donation anywheres.'' She went to the front of the paddock and stuck her hand up at McElroy. ''So it's ours by right. It ain't any of the Greater Christian Constipuancy's.''

Everyone gawked, me no less than anyone else, the evangelist and the habiline likewise visibly taken aback.

The other Puddicombes, the woman's in-laws and children, stumbled forward to surround her and uphold her demand.

"Yes," Adam finally managed. "Give it to her."

"But it's made out to you," McElroy protested. "Not to this improvident person—whom, I take it, whelped the vicious animal that killed your son and the young woman who helped kidnap him."

Said Craig Puddicombe's mother, "He had his bad points, Craig did, but he never let no one stick his pitcher on a magazine 'thout his pants on. He never held up the poor for pennies on a TV church service."

I heard Bilker Moody laugh. He was slouching against a railing behind young Puddicombe's casket.

"Mrs. Puddicombe—" McElroy said, uncharacteristically at a loss for words.

Said Adam, "I will, what do you call it, *endorse?* Yes, I will endorse for her the check you've brought." He held out his hand to the evangelist, who, as if drugged, slowly passed the check over. Adam endorsed the check with a borrowed pen and handed it to Mrs. Puddicombe, who folded it in two and slid it down the neck opening of her faded sun dress.

"We're awful hot," she said. "You put Craig down decent, now. We're gonna trust you to do that. But Daddy's too sick to stan' here and watch it. We're goin' on home." With no more fuss or ado, she led her tight-clustered family out of the roped paddock and around the house toward the distant front gate. Five thousand dollars richer, beneficiary of a habiline saint.

Caroline and I were now the only two people in the area set aside for Tiny Paul's and Craig's immediate families. I looked back to see if my neighbors were staring at us, only to catch a glimpse of Rudy Starnes, cameraman, and Brad Barrington, anchor-flake par excellence, sneaking forward through the crowd to record yet another event that was none of their business. They were not far from Livia George and her friends.

The black man appeared to be videotaping shots of the crowd, the sun deck, and the departing Puddicombes. His sun-bronzed colleague, meanwhile, was holding impromptu interviews with many of the startled people around him. When Barrington accosted Livia George with his microphone, however, she drew back and appraised him with a discriminating, contemptuous eye. I could see her shaking a finger under his nose, but her apparent fear of further disrupting the ceremony made it impossible to hear what she was saying to him. When McElroy began talking again, my attention was torn.

"Let's pray for the immortal souls of these dead brothers, the murderer and his innocent victim," the evangelist shouted, trying to recover from the loss of his check. "The one seems hellbent by virtue of the virtues he so sadly lacked, the other as a result of his parents' failure to baptize him into the living community of Christ. Therefore, brothers and sisters, let's pray for God's great and redemptive mercy on their immortal souls. Bow your heads with me. Observe with me a moment or two of loving, intercessory silence."

"Please get off this platform," Adam said. "The usurping of my intention to preside does not become you."

McElroy, whose eyes had been closed, opened them. "My goodness, Adam, I've only come to help. You're gettin' sorta territorial about this, aren't you?"

"The soul," Adam countered, "does not everlast. I am sorry to have to tell you so, but it is what its body did and also its unplaceable self-awareness of that doing. In death, Paulie and Craig are reconciled. Neither goes to hell, neither to heaven. The great pity I feel for both of them is my pity for the extinction of their souls, one before it could undeform and one before it could bloom to beauty."

"Uh oh," I said.

"Soul is mind," Adam declared patiently. "Neither has location. Neither goes beyond the stoppage of body death except in the continued cherishing of the souls and minds that knew them. All of us here have souls. *I* have a soul. Important, very important it is that all of us apprehend the other's soul and value it as we value our own. That is why the ashes of my son I have brought to rest beside the body of his unhappy killer."

Rudy Starnes had been creeping slowly forward with his portable camera. Soon, then, he was shooting this scene from the southwestern corner of my sun deck. Barrington, his partner, had already escaped Livia George's scolding to reach the same vantage and was leaning between two of the cedar railings to pick up the argument between Adam and McElroy with his hand-held microphone. I wanted to go after them, but Caroline restrained me.

"Bastards think they're getting a scoop."

"They are, Paul. Just forget it. Haven't you been listening to Adam?"

"Do unto others as you would have them do unto you?"

"Do unto others as they would be done by—insofar as it's possible to know what they want and insofar as respect for your own sacred self permits you to do it."

"Is *that* what he said?"

"Not in those words, no. In *other* words."

McElroy said, "The talk you're talking, Adam, is devil's talk."

"Maybe *he's* a devil!" shouted a balding, fortyish man with a string tie and acne-scarred jowls. I did not recognize him. I uncharitably identified him as a Puddicombe sympathizer, an unsheeted Klansman. It is entirely possible that he was only a Baptist.

Adam had no care for the impact his words were making on people like the bald-headed man. "Craig Puddicombe and Tiny Paul continue to live at this moment," he explained, speaking to McElroy but loudly enough to be heard by all, "because in our respectful ceremony they even yet *play* with the living who care for them. They are playmates in the soulful system of our shared sorrow, of our community remembering. In this way, they live, indispensable elements of the ecology of our grief. So long as our self-knowing souls play with them in systems of heartbreak and commemoration, they live. They remain parts of a flowing system. Try so hard as we might, none of us can fully comprehend such wholeness. But that is okay, that is perfectly okay. It is only the healthy relationship of us, who live, to them, who have died, that gratifies and greatly blossoms meaning."

McElroy stared down at Adam like a schoolmaster eyeing a little boy who has just wet his pants. "That's very pretty, Adam, but it's also secular-humanistic buncombe."

"Absolutely not," Adam rejoined. "I spit on those who think they can know me by radiating my bones, by weighing my brain, by seeing how many helical heredities I have in common with orangutans. I spit on any such. But I embrace those who seek to know me by embracing me, or by looking at my paintings, or by engaging me in furious Ping-Pong challenge, or by praying beside me in the midnights of mortal peril."

" 'Buncombe,' " said Mildred Garroway, an eighty-year-old widow standing just outside our paddock. " 'Helical heredities.' " She smiled at Caroline. "Both those boys can certainly talk, can't they?"

"Yes, ma'am," said Caroline.

Barrington, the Contact Cable News reporter, had climbed onto my sun deck, not far from Craig's casket. Bilker, seeing him, took several steps toward the man, but Barrington was already reaching across the bier to shove his microphone into Adam's face.

"Would you repeat what you just said for our viewers at home?" Barrington asked Adam. Hunched below the platform, Rudy Starnes continued to video-tape the proceedings.

Swiftly interposing himself, Bilker slapped the reporter's microphone into the crowd. Several people gasped. McElroy, a more prescient interpreter of danger signals than Barrington, cringed away from this blow and quickly left the deck by the stairway he had earlier mounted. Then he, his son, and their blond bodyguard retreated around the corner of my house.

During their strategic withdrawal, Bilker was vigorously shaking the Contact Cable newsman. "Your ass is grass, fella."

"What was that?" Miss Mildred asked Caroline. "What did he say?"

"Let him go," Adam commanded Bilker. "No hair on his head should you even breathe on." He dropped his top hat on the deck and began to remove his coat. "No more commemorative ceremony this afternoon," he told the remaining mourners in the pecan grove. "You are everybody free to go home now. If you stay, I must warn you, you may turn out to be acting unhappily in something for which you did not bargain." He folded his coat and placed it on the casket. "Very sorry that intrusive behavior of Mr. McElroy should have proved so deadly to the graceful remembering planned by me for this fine double funeral."

"What about the buttin' in of that fella there?" Livia George shouted, waving one liver-colored palm at Barrington.

"Him, too," Adam acknowledged. "Now, everybody, please go."

I asked Caroline to see Miss Mildred safely to the front gate, where she would have undoubtedly parked the monstrous Lincoln Continental that her failing eyesight had not yet convinced her to give up driving. Reluctantly, then, the mourners in the pecan grove began to straggle along in Caroline and Miss Mildred's wake, a process not unaccompanied by peeved looks and audible grumbling.

Starnes, the cameraman, recorded this slow withdrawal from my back yard, but not without an occasional glance away from the view-finder to see how inexorably it was leaving him and Barrington beached on a hostile shore. At last he stopped taping altogether.

Adam had removed his tie and vest. He was beginning to unbutton his shirt. "Once, you barged onto Paradise Farm to film my son's birth," he told Barrington. "And today you have barged onto it again to make unauthorized tape of his burial. True?" He dropped his shirt on the cedar planking.

"It's our job," Barrington said. "Getting the news."

"A most sleazy tactic, your sneakery. Do you remember, Brad Barrington, how such provocation affected me in December?"

"We'll leave. Just let us get our stuff together and we'll go, Mr. Montaraz."

Adam, hopping on one foot and then the other, yanked off his shoes. Then he shed his striped ambassadorial trousers. As naked as the day he had first arrived on

Paradise Farm, he assumed a belligerent crouch and gave the reporter an alarming threat-grin.

Barrington turned, vaulted the deck rail, and landed on the grass beside his cameraman. With no apparent regard for what might become of Starnes, he began running through the pecan grove toward Cleve Synder's property. Adam jumped to the top of the deck rail, sprang forward a good ten or twelve feet, and ran Barrington to ground almost effortlessly. He toppled the reporter by leaping on his back, wrapping his legs around the man's midriff, and applying a half nelson to the nape of his neck. The newsman staggered and fell. A squirrel scampered off through the grass, and the fierce, full-throated snarling of the habiline soon had Barrington crying for mercy.

Bilker came down from the deck, disengaged Starnes from his camera, and threw the instrument against the nearest tree trunk. Its casing shattered, and the sound of its impact echoed away through the pecan grove.

"No sweat," Starnes said, lifting his hands. "I ain't gonna get testy with you, man. Ain't my way."

I hurried out of the paddock to make sure that Adam didn't kill Barrington. Squatting beside the two vehemently wrestling men, I tried to grip Adam by the shoulders and pull him away. But where Adam was one moment, Barrington was the next, and the revolving entanglement of their bodies stymied my efforts to play peacemaker.

Soon enough, though, I realized that Adam was mauling his enemy with saliva and sudden unpredictable shifts of weight. Barrington would be black and blue for a couple of weeks, but he would survive this noisy struggle—just as he had survived the one back in December. That he himself had doubts on this score perfectly suited the habiline's purpose. Finally, Barrington curled in upon himself like a fetus, whimpering pitifully, and Adam rolled clear of the terrified man.

"Can't say that I blame you," I told Adam, above his victim's caterwauling, "but you've used this poor jerk for a scapegoat. You know that, don't you?"

"I am *not* a goddamn saint," Adam growled defiantly. "I am only human."

He got up and strode toward the house, his swarthy buttocks moving in elegant synchrony, the muscles in his back agleam. I am only human, he had said. This admission rang in my ears with the unmistakable tenor of bitterness and regret. I am only human. An odd feeling came over me. It pained him that he was one of us.

I found myself patting Brad Barrington's shoulder. "It's okay, fella. Listen, it's okay." But I really had no idea what I was saying.

ON THURSDAY morning, Adam, Caroline, and I attended Nancy Teavers's funeral at the First Baptist Church in Beulah Fork. It was not as well attended as the fiasco at Paradise Farm, but the pastor eulogized Nancy in a way that actually enabled me to call up her face—not the wan, black-eyed visage of the murder victim in the orangutan costume, but the lively, frequently mystified features of the young woman who had worked for me at the West Bank. The organ played, and people cried. I wasn't one of them, though. It was hot, and I was numb.

Craig and Tiny Paul were decently buried. During the relative cool of twilight, long after the inconclusive rites of Wednesday afternoon, we had laid them to rest. Bilker and five members of our security force had played pallbearer for the casket, while Adam had marched behind them with the burial urn clutched in his arms. Both the casket and the urn had gone into the ground in a lovely section of the pecan grove bordering Ruben Decker's farm. Nancy, of course, was buried next to E.L.'s grave in the cemetery near the school, and it finally seemed that we had all reached a place in our lives where, radically transfigured, we could begin again.

RuthClaire was still in North Carolina and would remain there through the weekend. She and Adam had talked last night on the telephone, but what they had said to each other—how they had resolved or failed to resolve their quarrel over the double funeral—only they knew. RuthClaire had not asked to speak to Caroline, and Adam was saying nothing about the present state of their relationship. However, his silence and his listlessness suggested a debilitating melancholy.

Back from Nancy's funeral, Adam asked me to drive him to the abandoned brick kilns where the young woman's husband had died.

"Why?" I asked him.

"I wish to meditate. And to fast."

Caroline said, "Couldn't you do that here?"

"It requires, I think, solitude. Complete solitude. And a chance to feel the earth enfolding me as it enfolds my son."

"But the *brick kilns?*"

Adam insisted. We could not argue him out of his desire to visit that forbidding place. Finally, Caroline and I drove him there by a county-maintained road. While we sat in the car, he walked along the lips of the crumbling vats. Blackberry vines and poke weed filigreed the red-clay mounds into which these shafts descended, and mockingbirds warbled dark songs. At one opening, Adam knelt and peered downward. Then he eased a leg over and lowered himself into the vat.

I shouted his name.

"Come back for me on Sunday morning," he called. "Until then, I will be fine. Never worry."

"Sunday morning?"

"It's okay, Mister Paul, very okay. It is what I need. Water aplenty down there, and in three days no habiline has ever starved to death."

"Caroline, tell him to come back to his senses."

"There's nothing I can do. He's made up his mind."

And so he went determinedly down, and remained in the depths of those seemingly bottomless kilns until Sunday morning, and greeted us then with a song that spiraled up like a chant through the frozen prayer of a cathedral, and emerged into the sunlight physically weaker but spiritually fortified.

That afternoon, Caroline drove him back to Atlanta, where he was reunited with RuthClaire on Hurt Street.

And I? Well, from my position as restaurant owner, gentleman farmer, bachelor, and pagan, I contemplated all these things and decided that it was time for me to become . . . something new, something else, something other.

Part Three

HERITOR'S HOME

Montaraz Island, Haiti

ON THE first anniversary of Tiny Paul's birth, Caroline and I were married in Glenn Memorial United Methodist Church on the campus of Emory University. Over the autumn, I had prepared for this event by divesting myself of both Paradise Farm and the West Bank. My house and grounds (with the exception of the burial plot near Ruben Decker's place) I sold to a pecan-growing cooperative with headquarters in Americus, Georgia. The restaurant, on the other hand, had to go to Livia George.

With a lawyer's help, we worked out an arrangement whereby I would receive a small percentage of Livia George's monthly profit for the next ten years. At the same time, I was careful to convey full title to her and to dissociate myself completely from the operation of the West Bank. If Livia George contracted any debts, a possibility that her previous experience and her managerial skills greatly minimized, I wanted no responsibility for them. I wanted only to be free of Beulah Fork, its people, and my past there. I was willing enough, of course, to maintain contact with Livia George and to provide her any help she might occasionally need—but no other tie or obligation to my adopted home town would I willingly accept.

RuthClaire and Adam did not attend the wedding. In September, they had moved out of their house on Hurt Street to begin a month-long tour of England and mainland Europe. From October through December, they lived on a small Greek island in the Aegean Sea. Both were working, but no specimen of their art or word of its character got back to their well-wishers in Atlanta. By the middle of January, they had returned to the Western Hemisphere, as a postcard from Mexico City attested. By late February, as yet another hasty card told us, they were residing in a stucco beach cottage near Rutherford's Port on the island of Montaraz, the habiline's place of birth. Neither Caroline nor I knew what to make of this last development. Although, I suppose, an inevitability, it took us wholly by surprise.

For a while I had toyed with the idea of opening a restaurant in Atlanta. I abandoned this idea not only because the city has eating places the way the Sahara has sand, but also because I was tired of the restrictive lifestyle. I had kept the West Bank going for nearly ten years; the thought of resurrecting that routine for another decade or more turned my brains to tepid Creole gumbo. Therefore, with David Blau's consent and encouragement, I approached several of the resident artists at Abraxas to offer my services as business manager and artist's representative.

Six of these young people accepted, and I recruited yet other clients from the city's population of talented art students and independent craftspeople. By establishing contacts with art dealers, gallery directors, museum curators, and department-store buyers (ordinarily, a casual reference to my past association with RuthClaire turned doubtful frowns to expectant smiles), I was soon able to begin earning money for my clients. Although I had a small office near Emory Village, I liked my new work primarily because I was not shackled to a desk.

Caroline, meanwhile, continued to teach her classes and

to conduct periodic interviews with the Cuban refugees still in detention in Atlanta's aging federal prison. Like an armada of doomed mariners sailing toward the edge of the world, the Freedom Flotilla of 1980 kept receding into the past; and most of the prison's current detainees had paperwork identifying them as hard-core criminals. Caroline had no wish to put these people out on the streets, but the cases of three or four young men deeply troubled her. She saw these prisoners as helpless captives of a Kafka-esque bureaucracy and feared they would remain wards of the state forever.

Our marriage was working. Caroline never scolded me for letting the dental floss slip down into the tiny plastic container, although I let it do that a lot. More important, neither of us currently wanted children. Later, T.P. having softened my militant resistance to parenthood, we might consider adoption, but not now. Not now. There was too much to learn about each other and too much to do. We were learning. We were doing.

MONTARAZ IS a Spanish word meaning *wild, primitive,* or *uncivilized.* As a masculine noun, it means *forester.* On the island by that name, a vaguely hand-shaped volcanic jut occupying about twenty-eight square miles in the middle of Manzanillo Bay, coffee plantations today compose the bulk of its accessible "forest." A backpacker avoiding these industry-owned plantations might stumble upon a stand of mahogany or rosewood, but, for the most part, the island's poor people have denuded the slopes to plant subsistence crops like cassava, yams, and beans. Today, then, an island resident of Montaraz might fairly be called a farmer or a coffee-company employee, but none really warrants the name of forester.

Some few who scrounge their livings with neither private land nor industry jobs, however, probably *do* warrant such labels as *wild* and *uncivilized,* however, and many of these few included—at least until the early 1960s—the retiring descendants of the habiline slaves whom Louis Rutherford brought to Montaraz from Zanzibar in 1838. But their history is obscure, and many people alive today on Montaraz do not believe in them at all.

Most of the island's population lives in the only note-worthy town, Rutherford's Port, or in various fishing villages or tourist resorts along the many miles of twisty coast. In terms of health and economics, the native human population may be slightly better off than their counter-parts on Haiti proper, but the question still admits of debate. Even a poverty-level citizen of Atlanta would be an object of envy in the waste archipelago of "Baby Doc" Duvalier's rule.

Until 1822, Montaraz had belonged to Santo Domingo (now the Dominican Republic), but with Jean-Pierre Boyer's subjugation of the Spanish-speaking sections of Hispaniola in that year, it became the property of Haiti. The Domini-cans expelled the Haitians from their country in 1844, but by this time Louis Rutherford, an eminent American citi-zen, had acquired Montaraz by outright purchase. There-fore, although equidistant between Haiti and Santo Domingo, it was legally (albeit quite irregularly) another Caribbean territory of the United States. Rutherford died during the Dominican uprising against the Haitians, and followers of Pedro Santana quickly reclaimed the island as their own. Rutherford's widow and grown sons protested to the new Democratic administration of James K. Polk, who had campaigned as an ardent expansionist, and Polk threatened the Dominicans with an invasion of marines. Judiciously, the Dominicans heeded the threat.

For another thirty years, then, the heirs of the late U.S. ambassador to Haiti ruled like kings on Montaraz. In 1874, however, Peter Martin Rutherford, the oldest grand-son of the clan's patriarch, negotiated an agreement with President Nissage Saget returning the island to Haitian sovereignty. This agreement gave the Rutherfords two im-portant guarantees: (1) nonrescindable ownership of an estate occupying one fifth of the island, and (2) nonrevocable use of the English name Rutherford's Port for the island's only real town. Saget was able to conclude this agreement, where other Haitian leaders, notably Faustin Soulouque, had failed, because he was a sensible man with no major vices or reason-crippling ambitions. Peter Martin Rutherford liked him. The transfer was a fait accompli before the Dominicans had time to register the fact, and Montaraz has remained an unquestioned part of Haiti's political sphere until the present day.

Montaraz appears on very few maps of the Caribbean. Early maps by Spanish cartographers feature it clearly enough, but maps drawn and printed during the twenty-year dictatorship of Boyer omit it completely. Although inescapable common knowledge to locals, the island's presence in Manzanillo Bay remained obscure to outsiders through the 1870s because the Rutherfords simply did not wish to advertise it. After the negotiated Haitian takeover, however, Saget and his successors discouraged its appearance on maps as a peculiar kind of sop to Dominican pride. The Haitians apparently believed that if both sides pretended that Montaraz wasn't there, their Spanish-speaking neighbors would shelve any strategies to reconquer it. You can't plant a flag on invisible real estate. That the island was visible enough from the mid-northern coast of Hispaniola, if not on maps, both sides could contentedly ignore.

Few Americans—few civilized people anywhere—had ever even heard of Montaraz until Brian Nollinger broke the story of Adam's presence on Paradise Farm to a reporter from the Atlanta *Constitution*. The notion that a habiline remnant might yet exist on the little island sent media people, anthropologists, professional adventurers, and would-be quick-buck artists scurrying for permission to visit Montaraz. Although American and Canadian citizens do not need passports to go to Haiti for thirty days or less, the Duvalier government—abetted by the Austin-Antilles Corporation, the licensed proprietor of most of the country's coffee plantations—restricts travel to Montaraz to those who have made special application. In the wake of the story headlined RENOWNED BEULAH FORK ARTIST/ HAR-

BORING PREHISTORIC HUMAN, these applications began arriving in Port-au-Prince by the bagful.

Very little came of this goal-oriented flurry of tourism, however, because the first eager visitors to Montaraz could find no habilines. They found blacks, mulattos, Spanish-Arawak survivors, jaded white Europeans, and affluent Japanese in polite, businesslike tour groups. They even found a puzzled party of middle-aged Kansans wearing Bermuda shorts, Italian sandals, and jaunty straw hats with green plastic visors. What they could not find, no matter how hard or how cleverly they searched, was anything remotely resembling a habiline. By this time, the government had placed a moratorium on issuing visitor permits to Montaraz, and word of the first arrivals' lack of success began to migrate stateside. When Alistair Patrick Blair published his paper in *Nature* debunking Nollinger's extravagant tale, interest in locating Adam's relatives waned markedly. Pretty soon, applications to the Haitian Ministry of Tourism for special permits dwindled to the previous steady, but modest, level.

After the deluge, silence. More or less.

Anthropologists who accepted Dr. Nollinger's contention that Adam was a living representative of *Homo habilis*, a manlike species presumed extinct for two million years, argued either that the Rutherford Remnant on Montaraz had been absorbed into the general population or that anti-Duvalier gunrunners and revolutionaries had press-ganged the habilines into service and scattered them across the Caribbean. (Anthropologists supporting Brian Nollinger, by the way, could be counted on one hand; the popular press canonized them as flamboyant idiot savants, good for human-interest copy if not for any reliable word on Adam's origins.) Scientists opposed to Nollinger's point of view declared that RuthClaire's unusual husband was a small black man with certain archaic bone structures for which the processes of genetic atavism could easily account. No one could find other ''habilines'' on Montaraz because *there were none*. Adam was unique in many respects, but he did not depart so drastically from the human ''norm,'' whatever that might be, to require Linnaen pigeonholing as a protohuman. Besides, his intellectual capacity—his development of art, language, and a personal metaphysics—made nonsense of the idea that he was an evolutionary primitive.

Three months after the double funeral at Paradise Farm, Brian Nollinger's point of view received some convincing support from the surgeons who had operated on Adam to enable him to speak. With permission, they released to the press several X-rays of Adam's skull. Taken from different angles, these X-rays created a small sensation. Never before had RuthClaire or Adam permitted anyone to examine him with an eye to precise physical measurements or speculative comparison. These X-rays, along with the plastic surgeons' computer-generated "blueprints" of Adam's head, revealed that he had a cranial capacity of 870 cubic centimeters. This figure exceeded that of most known fossil representatives of *Homo habilis*, but not by a great deal. Even more spectacular was the discovery that in its overall shape and proportions, Adam's skull bore a clear point-by-point resemblance to Skull ER-1470 in the Kenya National Museum in Nairobi. Because 1470 belonged to a creature once identified by Louis Leakey as an *H. habilis* individual, this startling resemblance led many paleoanthropologists to classify Adam, too, as a habiline. What RuthClaire had surmised about her future husband on the first day she saw him, the scientific community had now also officially conceded. Even Alistair Patrick Blair was beginning to come around.

By this time, however, the Montarazes had left the country. A few of their friends in Atlanta, among them the Blaus and the Loyds, knew their general whereabouts, but adamantly refused to divulge the information to either reporters or scientists. RuthClaire and Adam had gone away to *escape* the public's prying, to renew themselves on fresh and exotic shores. Moreover, I privately suspected that they mailed the postcards pinpointing their "current" locations only after having made up their minds to go elsewhere. Once they reached this new place, they lay low. Lying low, I told myself, was a survival strategy at which a Lolitabu habiline dispositionally excelled. If he did not want to be found, he would *not* be found—except by the rarest of accidents.

But the Montarazes apparently wanted to be found. Soon after she had sent us a postcard from Rutherford's Port, RuthClaire wrote us a bona fide letter. It reached us early in April. Here is what it said:

Dear Caroline and Paul,

Once, in a letter, Adam described Paradise Farm as his "unjumping Eden," because although everything else might go blooie for him, Paradise Farm would remain the fixed center of his Coming of Age as a civilized being. It was where he and I met, it was where he outgrew the feral habits of his youth, it was where his son was born. Today, of course, it's where his son lies buried, next to the coffin of his murderer. Well, Paul has sold Paradise Farm, and Adam's Eden has—forgive me, there's no other word for it—*jumped.* We've come "home" to Montaraz, an Eden somewhat more Edenic than Paradise Farm but probably not quite so paradisiacal as the dusty Lolitabu Hills (chronologically speaking). It's like Chinese boxes, isn't it? Edens inside Edens.

I'm writing not only to give you news of our doings but also to ask you a favor. One *big* favor, actually, with at least three little favors nesting inside it like—well, you know. Ready for the *big* favor? It's this: Adam and I want you to drop whatever you're doing in June and come down here to Rutherford's Port (our beach cottage, actually) for at least a month. We've already petitioned for and received the special permits to visit Montaraz that you'll need from the Haitian Ministry of Tourism, and Adam has succeeded in extorting from the publisher of *Popular Anthropology* enough money to cover your travel expenses, round trip. Caroline must simply agree to write an article for that magazine about your visit with us. This shouldn't be too hard because the article will consist almost entirely of an historic taped interview at which she'll function as moderator.

But I'm getting ahead of myself.

The first little favor nesting inside the *big* favor of coming down here requires you to bring Tiny Paul's ashes with you. Because Adam's entire preconscious past belongs to Montaraz, we've decided to make the island our permanent home. We'd like to have Tiny Paul's physical remains close to hand. Sentiment rather than reason talking here, but sentiment has compelling reasons all its own. The distasteful part for you guys— for Paul, anyway—is that you'll have to dig up our baby's burial urn and carry it down here virtually in your arms. No checking it with your airline baggage. No consigning it to steerage or the cargo hold when you board your Cavalcade Caribbean cruiseship out of Miami. It's too valuable for that, of course, and you'll probably come to regard it as a nuisance before you've actually handed it over to us. Forgive us for asking such a thing, but we—or, to be fair to Adam, *I*—have no other choice. Do you understand?

The second little favor inside the *big* one: David Blau tells us that in only a few months Paul has become an able artist's representative. (He wasn't too bad at that while we were married, but he was always more interested in peddling avant-garde marinades and sauces than avant-garde paintings and sculptures.) Adam and I would like Paul to ply his new trade on behalf of a small contingent of local artists whose work you can see when you get here. You'll need to bring photographic equipment with you to capture some of this work, however, and high-speed color films capable of producing quality images in poor, sometimes nearly nonexistent, light. (See the attached list for the recommended brands and quantities.) What Adam hopes will result from this, Paul, is a modest habiline show at Abraxas similar to the Haitian exhibit of fifteen months ago. (Probably, though, we won't want to label the artists habilines.) As you may have already guessed, these artists are Adam's habiline relations. They exist. They live here. Because I've met them, I know they're more than just the diminutive Caribbean equivalent of the Northwest's elusive Bigfoot. Adam wants you and Caroline to meet them, too.

And the third little favor: Caroline's interview/article for *Popular Anthropology*. If you arrive in June, Caroline will be able to moderate an historic meeting between Adam and the Zarakali bigwig A. P. Blair. This is the man who once argued that a photograph of Adam was in fact a photograph of a black man in a shaped latex mask. This past autumn, Blair hosted the PBS series on human evolution called "Beginnings." Right now he's trying to raise money for his digs at Lake Kiboko in Zarakal. Under the aegis of the American Geographic Foundation, he'll spend the late summer and the early fall delivering paid lectures to audiences all over the United States. He's stopping in Montaraz in June before going on to Miami and then Pensacola. Adam and I invited him to come—with the proviso that he withhold any written account of his visit until our own authorized account of the meeting has seen print in *Popular Anthropology*. He agreed. Not without some epistolary grumbling, of course, but he did agree. And it's Caroline whom we want to do this piece.

As you know, Adam and I spent most of last fall on the Greek island of Skíros, working and recuperating. In mid-November, there was an international convocation of paleoanthropologists in Athens. This affair lasted a week, and the rumor of our presence less than a hundred miles away (as the Olympian eagle flies) somehow got back to these men and women. Blair was in attendance from the University of Marakoi. (Richard Leakey was there from Kenya, Donald Johanson from the United States, and so on and so on.) Blair didn't want to commit himself to a wild-goose chase, but, if the rumor were true, he didn't want to miss out on talking to Adam in person, either. So he sent a graduate student from the University of Marakoi, an apprentice paleoanthropologist in his party, to Skíros to check out the scuttlebutt. She was a native Zarakali of the Sambusai tribe, a very efficient young woman, and she tracked us to our little villa as expertly as her forefathers had tracked their enemies across the salt flats of the Lake Kiboko frontier. She wanted us to go back to Athens with her. If that was unacceptable, she wanted us to grant Blair an exclusive audience on Skíros at the conclusion of the big paleo-powwow in Athens.

We didn't want to go to Athens, and Adam wasn't sure he was ready to meet Blair face to face. So we gave the young Zarakali woman a letter outlining the conditions under which we might later grant Blair an interview, and, as soon as she had left, we made our own plans to leave. We didn't actually pull up stakes until December, though, and by January we were in Mexico City. There, feeling guilty about denying Blair's interview request, Adam wrote to the Great Man in care of the Interior Ministry of Zarakal, clarifying the conditions set forth in the first letter and specifying a June meeting here on Montaraz. Blair responded surprisingly quickly. A June meeting in the Caribbean suited his schedule and his travel itinerary almost perfectly. So, at long last, it's going to happen. Adam's going to be able to show the old bastard that he's not wearing a latex mask.

Let us know if you'll be able to come. We'll help you out financially as far as we can, but both Adam and I believe you can *make* some money from this trip. Just exercise your professional skills and try to get some funding in addition to the *Popular Anthropology* travel money. It's tacky to poormouth, but Adam and I are not wealthy. I've made almost nothing since forsaking the porcelain-plate business (a decision I *don't* regret), and, as you may imagine, we've spent a small fortune pretending to be jet-setters and establishing residences here and there in the course of our travels. At last, though, we're home. *H.O.M.E.*

Much love,

Ruth Clare

P.S. Three days ago, I saw Brian Nollinger at the open-air market in Rutherford's Port. You thought he was somewhere in the Dominican Republic, didn't you, Caroline? Well, he's not. Austin-Antilles has apparently relieved him of his duties as a canecutter demographer there. Adam says it's possible he made suggestions for improving the workers' lot that struck company officials as dangerous boat-rocking. On the other hand, maybe he's simply doing the same kind of work for them on their Montaraz coffee plantations. Forgive me, Caroline, but I can't help seeing his presence here as highly suspicious. Oh, yes—he didn't see *me* when I saw *him*, and I was very careful *not* to let him see me. I finished doing my marketing and drove home as quickly as I could.

P.P.S. Please do us these favors. Adam and I have really missed our friends from stateside. We really have.

CAROLINE AND I decided to go. Our honeymoon over the Christmas break had consisted of five days in Savannah and two on Tybee Island, a week of blustery weather that we had managed to enjoy even while dreaming of the voluptuous dazzle of summer. Our trip to Montaraz, then, would be an extension of—an improvement upon—our December honeymoon. We would conscientiously seek to combine business with pleasure. Caroline had not committed to teaching a summer class, and I was free to set my own hours. That we could deduct almost everything we spent as legitimate business expenses had escaped neither of us—RuthClaire and Adam had cleverly arranged our visit to make that possible.

The P.S. to RuthClaire's letter disturbed me. Last summer, Brian had gone to the Dominican Republic for Austin-Antilles Corporation; now he had shown up on Montaraz at a most auspicious time for someone who had once told the world that Adam was a habiline. Coincidence or stealthy premeditation? Had Brian received a tip through the paleoanthropological grapevine that A. P. Blair was traveling to Rutherford's Port for some undisclosed, but promising, reason? Had he received a tip from some other source? I looked at Caroline, remembering her former interest in the man, and my heart misgave me. In my most self-critical moments, I told myself that I had caught her on the rebound.

"When's the last time you heard from your old flame?"

Caroline's eyes cut across me like lasers. "In January. He sent us a card wishing us happiness and long life. You saw it. I'd told him we were getting married, and he sent that card."

"What need was there to tell him anything? To rub it in?"

"Brian meant something to me once," she said, still staring at me hard. "I still consider him a friend. I like to stay in touch with my friends."

"Yeah."

"You've seen every card or letter Brian's written me since he left Atlanta. There've been four, all but the last one mailed before we got married. What's the matter with you?"

"He's in Montaraz, Caroline, and I don't want to see him."

"Well, I didn't have anything to do with his showing up there, and I'm not going to pussyfoot around everyplace we go on that damn island trying to avoid him. If I see him, I'll speak to him. He may not even *be* there when we arrive. He may have been taking a holiday from his work in the Dominican. He may have been trying to satisfy his natural curiosity about Montaraz. Okay?"

"Okay."

"Get off my case, Paul. I'm not guilty of defrauding my husband through the mails. I'm not Brian's pen-pal paramour."

The conversation ended. I had very nearly provoked a serious quarrel, but Caroline had refused to let me. She had kept her anger in check. As a kind of penance for my boorishness, I took her out to dinner at Bugatti's, and we spent nearly the entire meal making plans for our departure.

In mid-May, I drove to Paradise Farm to disinter Tiny Paul's ashes. The Hothlepoya County Sanitarian, Jim Stevens, approved my request to do so; and one of the new owners of my former property escorted me to the burial plot, which, in fulfillment of a contract stipulation authorizing the sale, his cooperative had enclosed with a shoulder-high fence of treated redwood and a barricade of flowering shrubs. I did the actual digging myself, and it took no more than twenty minutes to unearth the miniature casket containing the urn. I removed the urn from the casket without pulling the casket clear of the grave and then carefully refilled the hole with displaced soil and sod. A small pink-marble headstone with a brass plaque remained to mark the site. I let the plaque stay, a memorial as much to Adam's idealism as to the ludicrously brief life of my murdered godson.

In June, Caroline and I flew to Miami.

The following day we set sail aboard the Cavalcade Caribbean cruiseship *Zepaules* for Cap-Haïtien. Our voyage was leisurely and uneventful. We docked in Cap-Haïtien on a mild summer evening, spent the night in a plush hotel, and took a tour boat to Rutherford's Port with a small group of French-speaking Europeans who held themselves aloof from Caroline and me.

On the boat, the only person who took any notice of us, and who smiled at us each time he caught our attention, was a dark-skinned member of Duvalier's *Volontaires de la Sécurité Nationale*. This militia is better known locally, and abroad, as the "Tontons Macoutes," a folkloric appellation implying that its "volunteers" are evil uncles who sometimes bag up unoffending citizens and, without charge or trial, spirit them away to nowhere, never to be heard of again. Our smiling Tonton Macoute wore the rural "uniform" of the species, namely faded blue jeans, a faded denim vest, scuffed military boots, a crushed black beret, and a pair of huge mirror-lens sunglasses. These monstrous lenses led me to suspect that the man was spying on us even when he appeared to be half-facing away. On a shoulder sling, he carried an ancient Springfield rifle whose barrel he had lovingly oiled and whose stock he had either waxed or lacquered. A bulge under his denim vest told of another weapon, probably a revolver, in an armpit holster. He made me nervous, this smiling man. And, to my great dismay, he finally sauntered nonchalantly across the open deck to the rail at which Caroline and I were standing. Rather like a Muslim, he touched his forehead in respectful greeting.

"Americans, yes?"

We admitted that we were.

"On what business do you come?"

I looked at Caroline. How much did we have to tell this bogeyman? Was he simply making polite conversation, or were his questions subtle commands for full self-disclosure? His teeth, when he smiled, reminded me of nicotine-stained cuff links—that big, that yellow.

Caroline played coy. "How do you know we haven't come for pleasure?"

"Rutherford's Port is, uh, *ennuyeux*. Dull, I think you say. Real pleasure-seekers go to Port-au-Prince. Habitation Leclerc, maybe. Those gentlemen—" he nodded at three of the French-speaking travelers—"they are coffee buyers from the mother country. Not playboys, not drug dealers. They come to Montaraz to work. You, too, I bet."

"Does it make a difference?" I said, more hostile than inquisitive.

The Tonton Macoute did not stop smiling. "I am practicing my English, is all. Sorry to trouble you so." He touched his forehead again.

To make up for my rudeness, Caroline introduced us by name and told the man that we had come for both business and pleasure. We were friends of Adam and RuthClaire

Montaraz, the artists. Had he heard of them? (But of course.) Did he know anything about the habiline remnant from which Adam had supposedly sprung?

"Officially, I know nothing. Unofficially, I know that it is hard to find this remnant because Papa Doc, the first Duvalier, well, he—" The security volunteer gave an exaggerated shrug.

"What did he do?" I urged him.

"He encouraged the local *houngans*—voodoo priests, you see—to cast spells against these creatures. He said they were demons. And the priest most powerful on all the island, Odilon Roi, was not only a famous *houngan* but also the local chieftain of the security volunteers. Roi and his followers cast bullets as well as spells at these habilines. This was over twenty years ago. A dozen or more of the little *cigouaves* were shot. My father was a civil volunteer under Roi and he remembers."

"Duvalier, a medical doctor, thought the habilines were demons?"

"For purposes of the *vaudun* persecution, Monsieur Loyd, yes. In reality, he feared any part of the population that had a certain . . . uniqueness. He thought such persons dangerous. They would corrupt others, or they would somehow be corrupted. Castroites and Marxists would maybe turn the *cigouaves* against him. This, you see, made him decide that they had to go."

Caroline said, "What would your current President-for-Life, Baby Doc, do if he heard you telling us these things?"

"Is it your wish to inform on me?" asked the macoute, smiling.

"Of course not. But suppose we went home and had your allegations printed in a newspaper as the story of a talkative civil guard on Montaraz? Wouldn't your loose tongue convict you as a traitor to the late Duvalier's memory?"

"Things are more free under Baby Doc. Besides, I haven't told you my name, have I?" His enormous ivory teeth reflected sunlight off the water. "Do you suppose me the only security volunteer on the island?"

"What about all the habiline hunters who swept through

here last autumn?'' I asked. ''Did you tell any of those
eager people your persecution story?''

''*Mais non, Monsieur.*''

''Why not?''

''I had not even heard it then myself. It was this recent
sweeping-in of foreigners in quest of the *cigouaves*—the
demon habilines—that reminded *mon père* of *la petit terreur*
of twenty years past. He told me the story but cautioned
my discretion. It's foolish to confess to outsiders the crimes
of one's own family. How do Americans say it? Hanging
out the dirty laundry for the hoi polloi to gaze upon?''

''But you're telling *us*,'' Caroline said.

''Because you are nicer people than the pushy ones who
came last year. Also, it's an interesting story. Also, too, I
think nobody anymore will see the *cigouaves* again. So
what harm?''

''You think they've all been wiped out?''

''*Oui, Monsieur*. What irony. A dozen deaths is no very
formidable massacre—think of the thousands upon thousands whom Trujillo killed—but on this island it makes a
type of genocide.'' No longer smiling, he shook his head.
''I had nothing to do with it. The sins of the father is not a
doctrine I care to embrace.''

''Do you think Adam Montaraz is a demon?''

''Oh, no, sir. He's a great man, a great artist.'' He
touched the forward bulge of his beret. ''Call upon me,
please, if I may be of service to you during your sojourn
here.''

''But what's your name?'' Caroline asked him.

He looked over his shoulder to reply: ''Lieutenant
Bacalou, Madame and Monsieur Loyd. Ask for me at our
security headquarters in Rutherford's Port.''

It was only later that we learned that *bacalou* is a Creole
word for an evil spirit, either a demon or a werewolf, that
feeds on human flesh. But our Tonton Macoute was making no attempt to conceal his identity from us; rather, he
was providing us with the fearful *nom de guerre* by which
his comrades and presumably the common people under
his jurisdiction already knew him. We likewise learned
that *cigouaves*, the term he used for the island's elusive

habiline remnant, has its own superstitious connotations. It refers to yet another kind of lycanthropic demon, creatures with wolfish bodies and human heads whose singular method of attack supposedly results in the violent emasculation of their victims. Lovely. We had come to an enchanted isle, a territory possessed by black magic and primitive dread. The police were bogeys, and everyone who opposed them was an upright piece of meat animated by a malignant spirit. You exorcised the demon by killing the body of its host. Never mind that the rifle-toting exorcists, the Tontons Macoutes, were possessed by malicious demons of their own. . . .

RUTHCLAIRE MET us in Rutherford's Port. The city consists of ancient quays, government buildings and churches of a prerevolutionary Spanish architectural style, a series of palm-lined public squares, a military barracks, and, still at sea level, dozens of private residences designed and built around 1900 by such masters of Gingerbread Gothic as Eugène Maximilien and Léon Mathon. These houses feature balconies, cupolas, and arabesque grillwork even more fanciful than the gimcracks distinguishing the former Montaraz house in Atlanta. (I was beginning to see why Adam had purchased that house.) The yellow bricks used for walkways, foundations, and low decorative walls, RuthClaire told us, had arrived in Rutherford's Port as ballast in merchant ships coming for the island's coffee, sisal, and cacao. The most famous house in the city belonged to the grandson of local architect, Horacius Dimanche, who had attended the Paris School of Architecture with Léon Mathon. Later, if we wished, RuthClaire would give us a tour of the Old City.

Above the Old City, climbing the forested flank of the mountain behind it, were two contrasting enclaves. On the western side, condominiums of steel and glass, charming old hotels and restaurants (survivors of a fairly recent effort at urban renewal), and a monolithic terra-cotta business complex. On the eastern side, shantytown. Shacks with corrugated tin roofs, slatted or cardboard walls, and doors consisting of rusted scrap metal or ragged woolen blankets. Sunlight ricocheted among these hovels like a bouncing ball above the lyrics of a wretchedly amelodic song. A sluice of mud ran down the slope of one precarious neighborhood from a broken pump that provided water for half of the hillside's inhabitants. Shantytown's only saving grace, in fact, was the open-air market at the foot of the mountain. It boasted colorful pennants, hundreds of booths with thatched roofs, and prodigious mounds of tropical fruits and vegetables. The bazaar abutted a section of the Old City, through which we rode in RuthClaire's rented jeep on our way up the coast to the secluded beach cottage where she and Adam were staying.

"He didn't come himself," RuthClaire was explaining, "because he creates a lingering sensation wherever he goes."

"What about you?" Caroline said.

"Me? I'm just another American tourist. That's why I came after you. Adam's a local hero, and he's tired of being mobbed."

"Don't they follow you to your house?"

RuthClaire lifted her eyebrows at me. "The people themselves, no. They don't have wheels. When we first got here, the local press asked for interviews, but we respectfully declined. Then Haitian security put out the word that we weren't to be bothered. Militiamen with rifles go up and down the road fronting our beach property, patrolling. Only one or two at a time, on their way back and forth between coastal villages. They're not actually *assigned* to us."

"Tontons Macoutes?"

"That's not the approved term, Paul."

"We met one on the boat over from Cap-Haïtien. He used the term himself. I think he took a certain pride in it."

"They do that, I guess. Instilling terror's one of their collateral duties. They've been good to *us*, though."

Caroline said, "The one we met on the boat told us that the habilines here are extinct, victims of a Duvalier purge in the early sixties."

"He's right about the purge, wrong about extinct."

"How many remain? When will we get to see them?"

RuthClaire laughed. "All in good time." Still laughing, she swung the jeep sharply to the left to avoid hitting an old man wearing a straw hat and a polka-dot neckerchief of red and yellow. Behind the old man stumbled an aged donkey piled high with foraged firewood.

"What about Blair?" I asked.

"He's already here. That's another reason Adam didn't come. He's entertaining the Great Man."

"With or without his latex mask?"

Squinting at the unpaved, gully-riven coastal highway, RuthClaire sniggered appreciatively. She was enjoying herself. We were traveling ten miles per hour over terrain designed to impart permanent kidney damage, and she was having a good time. I was happy for her. She had not even asked about Tiny Paul's ashes, and I was damned if I were going to remind her that we had brought them.

FROM THE air, Montaraz looks like the three-fingered hand of a Disney cartoon character, Goofy or Mickey Mouse or Donald Duck. The hand is tilted in Manzanillo Bay so that the thumb points northeast across a hundred miles of ocean at Grand Turk Island. The middle finger shoots a bird—a Donald Duck?—on a lengthy northwesterly diagonal at Miami Beach. (So far as I know, no one in Miami Beach has ever taken umbrage.) Rutherford's Port nestles in its harbor at the base of the thumb, closer to the Dominican coast than to the Haitian. Our destination, RuthClaire explained, was an arc of beach on the inside edge of the island's forefinger. Had there been a road straight across the interior, our trip would have taken no time at all, but no such road existed. Moreover, the Austin-Antilles Corporation limits traffic on its coffee plantations, and their accessways, to company vehicles. Consequently, our switchbacking journey along the coast took nearly an hour and a half.

The beach cottage was slightly more than a cottage. It was an adobe bungalow of beige stucco nearly three hundred yards from the highway. A ridge of volcanic tuff and a phalanx of coconut palms and prickly-looking beach shrubs concealed it from passersby. Whoever had stuccoed the cottage had adorned it at waist level with a foot-high frieze of sea shells, shark's teeth, sand dollars, and crab pincers. Red clay tiles shingled the roof, and an L-shaped screened-in porch of roomy dimensions clung to the building on two sides, one of them fronting the miniature inlet that local people called Caicos Bay. The sand along the bay sparkled like refined sugar. RuthClaire and Adam had turned the porch overlooking this secluded strip of brightness into a studio. Easels, acrylics, canvases, and uncleaned brushes littered the shady L.

Blair, when we arrived, was sleeping, recuperating from a three-legged flight from Zarakal and a vicious case of jet lag. He had reached Rutherford's Port yesterday afternoon. He was seventy-one years old, and although still vigorous by most physiological yardsticks, he no longer found it possible to move from time zone to time zone without suffering painful temporal discontinuities. His advisors liked to tell him that in flying westward he was "gaining" hours, stockpiling minutes that he could later add to the biologically determined span of his life. But the Great Man reminded them that they invariably depleted this stockpile by flying him home the same way he had come. Why didn't his advisors ever think to route them back to Marakoi over the Pacific Ocean and the Indian subcontinent? Because jet lag hung on to him like an unshakable bout of intestinal flu, he felt that he was a time-traveler whose time was rapidly running out.

Adam told us this story after embracing us and showing us around the cottage. He recited most of it, in fact, while Caroline and I stood with him just outside Blair's open bedroom door, looking in on the paleoanthropologist's inert form and the sun-burnished tonsure of his massive head—like parents looking in on a sick child. Blair snored while Adam talked, walrus-whistle arpeggios that overrode the gentle lapping of the surf in Caicos Bay. No Great Man (I then and there decided) can communicate the full extent of his eminence in jet-lagged snooglings. It was unfair to expect him to. We tiptoed off, and, in RuthClaire's absence, I gave Adam Tiny Paul's burial urn.

"Thank you," he said simply. "Thank you from my heart." He carried the urn into his and RuthClaire's bedroom and set it on an end table by their bed. When he reemerged, he closed the door behind him.

Later, on the porch, Caroline and I had cold rum drinks with our host and hostess. We talked and talked, never getting very close to subjects that might be either emotionally painful or pertinent to our having come so many air and nautical miles to see them. But that was the way we all wanted it on this first day, and we had a good time, anyway.

The next day, Blair was better. He was gallant and gracious and witty. He spoke in the orotund tones of a word-drunk Welsh poet—sort of a cross, said Caroline, between Dylan Thomas and Captain Kangaroo. It was hardly his fault that his every utterance put me in mind of a constipated sea lion.

That afternoon, Caroline got out her notebooks and her recording equipment. The interview that she had agreed to moderate for *Popular Anthropology* took place in the cottage's living room. RuthClaire and I were present, but we refrained from saying anything, and the tape spools turned inside their cassettes with a relentless whirr that trembled in the tropical air.

CAROLINE: It's on, Dr. Blair. Why don't you and Adam talk about whatever you like? I'll stay out of the conversation—except for some followups and maybe some general explanatory comments. Okay?

BLAIR: That's fine. Adam, I've spent better than fifty

years digging up the bones of your ancestors and your collateral relations. It's a surprise, and a profound honor, to meet a representative of your species in the flesh.

ADAM: Thank you.

BLAIR: Once, of course, I doubted. Except for you, I presume, your species is extinct. That *any* of your people have survived to this day is nothing short of miraculous. I would scarcely be less astonished, Adam, if I were to go out and find *Homo habilis* fossils in a strata containing the remains of Neanderthals and early Cro-Magnons. Your intrusion into even *that* strata would have struck me as utterly fantastic. Six months ago, anyway. I would have had to assume that some smart-aleck mischief-maker was perpetrating a hoax. An *inept* hoax. How much more astonishing it is, then, to find myself face to face with a hominid of that otherwise extinct kind—a living, breathing, English-speaking exemplar of Early Pleistocene humanity.

ADAM: *Very* much more, I would guess.

BLAIR *(laughing)*: You'd be right, too. Listen, Adam, I hardly know where to begin. I'm a digger, not a diva of the interviewing trade. I'm far better with a fossil brush than a microphone.

CAROLINE: Your Peabody Award for "Beginnings" notwithstanding?

BLAIR: Never mind that. It was scripted. Adam, let me begin by asking you how you feel about the taxonomic terminology by which the scientific community has designated your species.

ADAM: *Homo habilis?*

BLAIR: Exactly. How do you feel about that nomenclature?

ADAM: About it, to be very candid, I have no feelings at all. Sticks and stones can break my bones, as the

children sing, but names can never touch me. *Hibber*
never touched me, either. It was to shrug off.

BLAIR: Does it strike you as accurate, *Homo habilis?*

ADAM: "Handyman"? Probably not. I am an artist,
but around the house I am no good at all. Miss
RuthClaire can vouch for my great *un*handiness in
household matters. Dripping faucets confound me.

BLAIR: You're a living fossil with your own fair share
of funny bones, aren't you? That's quite a droll observation, but it's not what I'm angling for, Adam. I was
wondering how you'd feel about adopting a somewhat
different nomenclature. *Homo zarakalensis,* to be precise. I ask because it's an unwritten tenet of contemporary civilization that free nations and free peoples
have the right of self-determination when it comes to
the matter of what they wish to be called. Rhodesia
became Zimbabwe, for instance; and in the United
States, fairly recently, most thinking Afro-Americans
determined that they would rather be called blacks
than Negroes. Do you see what I'm suggesting, Adam?
Extinct speciecs can't tell us what they would like to
be called. Living species, provided of course they're
human, *do* have that important option.

CAROLINE: Excuse me, Dr. Blair. Isn't *Homo zarakalensis* a term you coined two years ago for a hominid
skull that one of your Kikembu assistants found in the
Lake Kiboko digs?

BLAIR: Yes, it is. It means "Zarakali Man."

CAROLINE: But there's controversy over that designation, isn't there? Your skull appears similar to those
of the habiline specimens unearthed by the Leakeys at
Koobi Fora in Kenya. Richard Leakey, in fact, claims
they're identical.

BLAIR: That may be. We paleoanthropologists are
aggressively territorial creatures. What I've always
stressed, however, is that my discovery is somewhat

older—perhaps by as much as a half million years—than the Leakey "habilines." In other words, this distinctive hominid probably *originated* in what is today Zarakal and only somewhat later *migrated into* what is today Kenya. For that reason, if for no other, it ought to be called Zarakali Man.

CAROLINE: But *habilis* is altogether neutral in regard to the hominid's place of origin. It suggests the creature's tool-making ability. Is it fair to discard that bit of preexisting descriptive nomenclature for a term that has only your own egotistical chauvinism to recommend it?

BLAIR: *(chuckling benignantly)*: Well, that's what I'm trying to ask Adam. You see, it's his place to decide. Just as American blacks decided they wished to be called blacks, Adam ought to be the sole authority in *this* matter. It directly affects only him. I'm not going to throw a tantrum if he opts to go with *habilis*. He's the one who'll have to answer to Handyman, Handyman, Handyman.

CAROLINE: Dr. Blair, it seems to me—

BLAIR: For someone who was going to let Adam and me converse, young lady, you're becoming a fair threat to monopolize our talk.

CAROLINE: *(forthrightly)*: Forgive me.

BLAIR: Now, then, Adam. Which do you prefer? *Homo habilis*—Handyman, you know. Or *Homo zarakalensis?* Your word, I have a feeling, will be the paleoanthropological community's command.

ADAM: Is not *Homo sapiens sapiens* within my humble purview? I'm not a handy person, and never in my life have I set foot in Zarakal.

BLAIR: *Homo sapiens sapiens?*

ADAM: *Mais oui.* With Miss RuthClaire's tender help, I fathered a human child. And thanks to the surgeons at Emory, I speak even as you do, sir. Also, I have many perplexing spiritual longings and a freshly emergent concept of God. Considered in these lights, am I not a twentieth-century human being whose archaic bone structure is irrelevant to his dignity and worth?

BLAIR: But *many* species are interfertile, Adam. And your ability to speak is an acquired characteristic. A *surgically* acquired characteristic. To assign yourself to a species classification on that account is to fall prey to insidious Lamarckian error. Please, Adam, *think*.

CAROLINE: He's thought, sir. He wants to be called *Homo sapiens sapiens.* You said you wouldn't quibble with him.

ADAM: In truth, I'd prefer to be called Adam. Adam Montaraz.

CAROLINE: That's fine with me. How about you, Dr. Blair? Is that fine with you?

BLAIR: It's perfectly acceptable. But let's get on with this. We've many important things to talk about.

(At this point, the participants took a short break. Caroline checked her recorder. Then the conversation resumed.)

BLAIR: I'm afraid that I've been doing all the talking, Adam. What I'd like to know, of course, is how you were raised, what you remember of your childhood and youth, and whether any of your people, be they called habilines or *Homo sapiens,* still exist on this island. Would you mind addressing those questions?

ADAM: Very happy to. The first two are more difficult to answer than the last one, however. I can only do my best.

BLAIR: No one asks more of you, Adam. Begin with the easiest of the three and then proceed as you like.

ADAM: Miss RuthClaire told me once of the Yahi Indian called Ishi, about whom Theodora Kroeber wrote eloquently. Ishi was the last of his tribe in the state of California. Well, like Ishi, I am the last of my tribe—my species, you would say—on the island of Montaraz. In the entire great world, too, I fear.

(I glanced at RuthClaire. Her letter, of course, directly contradicted Adam's testimony. Ostensibly, after all, I had come to Montaraz to see, evaluate, and perhaps represent the work of an unspecified number of habiline artists. Was Adam deliberately lying to the Great Man, or had RuthClaire lied to us to give us an irresistibly compelling reason to come? Wearing a sheepish grin, she merely shrugged and looked away.)

BLAIR: What happened to your people?

ADAM: Exterminated. Persecuted, hunted, killed. Those who escaped the Duvalier pogrom—a very, very few—were scattered on the devil-may-care winds of politics and commerce. Off the coast of Cuba, five years ago, I saw two of my people die at the hands of a man greatly more animalish than we. One who died was my brother. These deaths, I think, ended all our desperate struggles to prevail in a world such as this. I was then the last one of us all.

BLAIR: Weren't there any women on Montaraz to keep things going? Isn't it possible that some of your far-scattered fellow habilines may still be alive elsewhere?

ADAM: No sightings, no reports. Such a hope seems foolish.

BLAIR *(sighing audibly)*: Ah, well. Yet another proof of contemporary humanity's unparalleled ability to muck up or destroy what clearly ought to be preserved. It makes me ashamed.

ADAM: Don't reproach yourself too harshly, sir. Should I die, after all, before *H. sapiens sapiens* obliterates itself along with this oh-so-lovely planet, why, your kind will have outlasted mine. Only by a little, of

course, and only after a reign much briefer than the
furtive persistence of us habilines—but you must take
your victories, Dr. Blair, where you find them, even
if they are most upsettingly Pyrrhic. Not so?

CAROLINE: You seem to be identifying yourself as a
habiline now, Adam. Do you mean to?

ADAM: I am identifying myself with my people, whom
others have called habilines. Also, of course, I'm a
good *H. sapiens sapiens* myself. Perhaps my people
were likewise, even lacking speech. In my mind,
Miss Caroline, they will always seem human—nobly
human.

BLAIR: I take scant comfort from surviving by a mere
breath an ancestral human species that preexisted us
by at least two million years.

ADAM: Then you are noble, too, sir.

BLAIR: Thank you, Adam. I appreciate your vote of
confidence.

CAROLINE: Adam, Dr. Blair's other questions concerned your childhood and youth, your memories of
habiline society and culture here on Montaraz. Those
strike me as topics of crucial value to any study of
your vanished people. Would you tell us what you
can about those things?

ADAM: You and Dr. Blair must never forget that that
portion of my life corresponds to the portion of ongoing human experience that you call "prehistory." I
have a prehistoric life and an ego-documented life.
I'm speaking to you now out of the latter context.
Recovering the prehistoric elements of my life from
the vantage of my crystallized ego—well, it's hard,
very hard. Distortions arise. Who I am now contaminates what then I was. Contaminates and discolors.

BLAIR: You're completely unable to reconstruct your
early life?

ADAM: Of course not. It goes around in my head like

a dream. It's a hard dream to tell, though, because then I had no language with which to chain and tame it. I had *heard* language spoken, but I had none of my own, and if you had seen me in those days, you would have thought me a feral creature surviving by instinct rather than wit. I had an invisible umbilical cord to my family, and another to the island's soil and vegetation, and another to the snakes and capybaras, and yet another to the sea and air. Everything around us was magical, and I was a kind of joyfully suffering magician. Falling down might hurt. Getting kicked might hurt. Going hungry might hurt. But the *living* of life, the living of even these many cruelties and hurts—oh my, Dr. Blair, that was ever and always magical.

BLAIR: But was the population of habilines from which you sprang a patrilineal or a matrilineal society? Was sexual dimorphism a factor in the assigning of domestic tasks and leadership roles? Did you have any noteworthy rites of passage to mark your movement from one stage of life to another? Did you hunt, scavenge, or forage for your livelihood? That's what my colleagues are going to ask me, Adam. Can't you remember, can't you tell me anything about such basic matters?

ADAM: In the absence of the people themselves, Dr. Blair, such knowledge seems—forgive me—irrelevant. Keenly and profoundly irrelevant.

BLAIR: Hardly, Adam. Knowledge of the world is knowledge of ourselves. What you can tell us of habiline mores, customs, and survival strategies will enable us better to comprehend who and what *we* are.

ADAM: To know the habiline life in any sense truly meaningful, sir, you would have to live it. You would have to stop scrutinizing it from afar and plunge into it with uncritical abandon. That's possible no longer. Gone, gone.

BLAIR: If nothing else, can you tell me *where* you lived?

ADAM: Dominican slaves were freed by Boyer in the eighteen-twenties, but it was not until eighteen-seventy-four, when Peter Martin Rutherford ceded Montaraz to Haiti, that we habilines obtained our liberty from his cacao and coffee plantations. We left en masse and made a secret republic for ourselves on one of the island's little-populated fingers. That is all I can say. For a long time, no one bothered us. Then the twentieth century happened, and everything changed. Gradually, oh so piecemeal, for the worse. I'm speaking now, you understand, from the vantage of my crystallized ego.

BLAIR: Can you take me to the site or sites of that "republic"?

ADAM: No. It is impossible. They're gone, and I've forgotten.

BLAIR: But, Adam, the island isn't that large. Suppose the Haitian government were to authorize travel and archeological research in various areas. Don't you think you'd assist? Don't you think you'd cooperate with me and others in uncovering your people's past?

ADAM: I think not, Dr. Blair. Let the dead rest forever. Let them rest in the remembering of their loving kin.

BLAIR: But isn't it true that you had your son's ashes disinterred and brought here to Montaraz by your friends the Loyds? I don't think I understand the distinction between that and excavating the living sites of your extinct habiline relations.

ADAM *(coldly)*: Apparently not.

BLAIR: Sorry. I meant no offense.

(The participants took another break.)

CAROLINE: All right. I've flipped the tape. Dr. Blair, you can begin again, if you like.

BLAIR: I think this has been a somewhat frustrating exchange for both of us, Adam. Let me apologize for that again. You see, I never expected to have the chance to sit down with a surviving representative of any of the hominid species whose bones I've been digging up and cataloguing these last fifty years. It's not a conversation I ever imagined taking place.

ADAM: Of course not.

BLAIR: You don't knap flint, do you? You don't chase hyenas off the remains of a lion's kill. You don't recall walking upright through the ash storm of an erupting East African volcano. You can't tell me anything about the other hominid species—*Australopithecus robustus, Australopithecus africanus*—with whom your people shared the savannahs. You can't even tell me much about your people's millennia-long trials and tribulations in the hills of present-day Zarakal.

ADAM: Regretfully, I can't. I am a product of Montaraz. So were my parents. So were *their* parents. On this island, we go back nearly seven generations.

BLAIR: Doesn't the allure of Africa niggle at you, Adam? I've seen some of your paintings. Baobabs, volcanoes, grass fires, hunting parties. It's hard for me to believe that the continent of your origin—your earliest origins—doesn't arouse your curiosity. Wouldn't you like to visit? Wouldn't you perhaps like to emigrate?

ADAM: I would like to see a giraffe.

BLAIR: A giraffe?

ADAM: Yes. It would be exciting to see a giraffe doing its dreamy, slow-motion gallop across the great African steppe. Otherwise, sir, I have no ambitions to fulfill on that score. I am home again. Montaraz is home, and it puts me in touch with earlier homes.

BLAIR *(after a lengthy pause)*: A little while ago, Adam, you mentioned that you have—let me see if I can remember your phrasing—"many troubling spiritual longings" and "a freshly emergent concept of God." Would you care to expound a little on those matters?

ADAM: Only a little, only a little.

RUTHCLAIRE *(her one and only interjection)*: Thank God.

ADAM: Before my ego crystallized, here on this island, I was an unconscious animist and also a lip-servicing Catholic. The magic all around me overwhelmed the dogmas of the Roman church. Then, in the late seventies, my ego began to take shape—in response, I am sure, to economic and political realities. At last, not long after the murders off the Cuban coast, it was precipitated from the terrible pressures of exile and refugee-ism. My ego, I mean. I became neurotically self-aware.

BLAIR: Neurotically?

ADAM: Even as you and everyone else alive in your world. To survive today, as "reality" is presently constituted, one must have a competitive neuroticism. So I surrendered to ego development in order to survive. I became an "I."

BLAIR: And your spiritual longings?

ADAM: Much that my new "I" heard in your world was disparaging of my personhood. I was an animal. I had no soul. On the boat from Mariel Bay to Key West, the passengers were not physically cruel to me; the opposite, rather. They patted my back and laughed at my japeries and treated me like a friendly performing dog. The "I" that my once-innocent self had become—well, it realized that in their private estimation, I was . . . soulless. I was excommunicated from real human fellowship because of my unhappy lack of this attribute.

BLAIR: Quite a tortuous chain of reasoning for a brand-new ego, Adam.

ADAM: Yes, but in my brand-newness I was very stupid. I made the mistake of appropriating these misinformed people's concept of the soul. I began to think of it as an item separable from the body. Like, perhaps, a pocket watch. I wanted such a pocket watch. A pocket watch, after all, may very well survive the death of its owner. It can exist without that person. It can continue to keep its time in a drawer. But it isn't coequal with its dead owner, and ultimately it, too, will perish. Nevertheless, I wanted this kind of soul, the sort that nearly everybody else mistakenly believes they possess—if, of course, they are "religious." Having that kind of soul, I thought, would bring my crystallized ego into fellowship with those of the human beings around me.

BLAIR: But you learned better?

ADAM: I learned better than they, Dr. Blair. If you wish to touch your soul, if you wish to handle it, place your fingers on your own body. This was something I had known as a creature without ego here on Montaraz, but in developing an aggressive "I" to make my way in civilization, well, I forgot this knowledge. The soul is not a pocket watch. It is inseparable from the living body. It does not reside in a pocket, it resides systematically throughout the body's systems. A dead body does not possess one. It's dead, in fact, because its soul has been disrupted.

BLAIR: No immortality, then?

ADAM: The fatal disruption of the personality would seem to preclude it, Dr. Blair. But only rigidly crystallized egos despair on this account. A self that understands its interdependency on the living systems around it—family, plants, animals, water, air—knows that the way of healthy living matters more than the egotistical lingering of personality after death. God's grace is on those who know this.

CAROLINE: Not everyone would find that comforting, Adam.

ADAM: Well, it is the neuroticism of the developed ego that prevents them, I fear. It is the unfortunate psychic investment they've made in something called "salvation." They've paid in too much for too long to gracefully withdraw from this investment. Or perhaps they deeply love others who have paid in too much for too long. It's a hard thing. I have much sympathy for all such travelers on the path to spirituality.

BLAIR: Do you think your spiritual journey recapitulates that of humanity as a whole?

ADAM: Only in the long view, and yet I have no great hope that the human species will ever adopt a holistic faith without imposing some kind of lethal rigidity upon it. And maybe, Dr. Blair, the interplay among current faiths, the tensions and slacknesses even yet linking them, is itself a holistic system with certain virtues. I don't know. A nonneurotic human species would be a species nearly unimaginable. You would have to think up a new taxonomic designation, Dr. Blair.

BLAIR: Perhaps not. Maybe the one we have now would finally begin to imply something other than self-congratulation. . . . What about your "freshly emergent concept of God," Adam? You deny the immortality of the soul apart from the problematically immortal body, and yet you retain a belief in a transcendent deity?

ADAM: Yes, I do. Perhaps, though, it is unimportant. I am getting tired of talking. Do you hear how my voice rasps?

BLAIR: Quickly, then, just a hint of your formulation.

ADAM: It sounds like a paradox. Perhaps it is. I hold that God possesses both a fundamental timelessness— that he exists outside the operations of time—and also a complete and necessary temporality, permitting him to direct and change *within* the stream of time. There's a hint, then, of my theology.

BLAIR: But isn't that like saying that a man both has a head and doesn't have a head? Or that a certain person happens to be both a Haitian citizen and not a Haitian citizen? It's self-contradictory.

ADAM: Only because our temporality makes the situation appear to be baldly either-or.

(*Adam's voice had gotten thicker and thicker. He cleared his throat.*)

No more for now, please. I think I would like to take a swim.

CAROLINE: We'll wrap it up with that, then. Thank you, Dr. Blair. Thank you, Adam. It's been a strange but stimulating journey.

AS MATTERS fell out, the interview was never resumed. Blair wanted to question Adam further; indeed, he wanted to mount an impromptu expedition to the island's various peninsulas, to go traipsing about among the pines and wild avocado trees in search of Adam's "secret republic." But late that afternoon, one of his advisors arrived from Rutherford's Port to tell him that the American Geographic Foundation had added to his tour three new lectures in south Florida; tomorrow morning, then, he must fly to Miami from Cap-Haïtien. Storming about the bungalow like a petulant Hollywood executive, Blair cursed his advisor. He even impugned the good name of the director of American Geographic. Finally, though, he subsided, confessing that without this tour a great deal of important work at Lake Kiboko would go undone. After gathering together his suitcases for the trip back to town, he came back into the living room to bid us all goodbye, as downcast and jet-lagged a figure as I could imagine. He was genuinely disheartened to have to go.

Abruptly, his mood changed. He had remembered something. Grinning, he knelt beside one of his leather bags and undid the straps on a bulging side pocket. From this pouch he extracted a magazine.

"Adam, would you and RuthClaire do me the favor of autographing this cover for me? I'm not ordinarily a souvenir collector—fossils are the only souvenirs a man in my line requires—but I'd really like to frame this for my office in the National Museum in Marakoi."

It was the *Newsweek* with the infamous Maria-Katherine Kander photograph of Adam and RuthClaire. Only Blair, of all the people in the room, failed to detect the palpable air of embarrassment that had congealed about us. Even his advisor, a young black man in an expensive western suit, flinched. Adam, although not himself embarrassed or offended, clearly understood that Blair had discomfited his wife and his house guests. He took the magazine from the paleoanthropologist and hastily initialed it with a ballpoint pen. Blair was beaming. He nodded at RuthClaire to encourage Adam to pass the magazine to her for her signature. With some reluctance, Adam did so. She accepted it with her head down and a crimson flush on her forehead and cheeks. I wanted to kick the insensitive Zarakali's shin.

"Nothing to be ashamed of," said Blair cheerfully, buoyant again. "You've got quite a respectable little body there."

"Thank you," RuthClaire murmured. (Blair was a father figure, and you never upbraided Daddy for bad manners or an absence of tact. That would be unmannerly, that would be tactless.) But when she autographed her portrait, she wrote her name in an angry vertical loop that partially obliterated her two-dimensional nakedness. Then she shoved the magazine back into the Great Man's chest. It trembled there at the end of her outstretched arm.

A small cloud of confusion passed over Blair's features.

He took the magazine, looked at it as if it had been vandalized (maybe it had), and, kneeling again, slid it regretfully into the side pouch of his carry-on bag. No one spoke. When he stood again, his expression was abashed and apologetic.

"Body shame's one of the saddest consequences of western civilization," he said. "On the other hand, the commercial exploitation of nudity is a reprehensible thing, too. It's a prurient outgrowth of that same unhealthy body shame."

I was sure that this was an astute analysis of something, but a something sadly peripheral to our joint embarrassment. Blair started to speak again, but stopped himself. He cleared his throat. He rubbed his hands together.

"Sir," said the young Zarakali, "it's time to go."

The Great Man agreed. He shook hands with Adam and me, embraced Caroline, and, when she failed to respond to his attempt to hug her, too, kissed RuthClaire on the forehead. Then all of us but RuthClaire trailed Blair and his aide outside and waved them goodbye. Their enclosed four-wheel-drive vehicle spun through the sand, at last obtaining purchase on the road back to Rutherford's Port. Inside again, we found RuthClaire standing in the middle of the living room with her hands hanging limply at her sides and tears flowing freely down her face. Adam took her in his arms and tenderly held her.

Over the top of Adam's head, RuthClaire said, "Paulie's dead because of that damn photograph, and I thanked the stupid old coot for telling me I've got 'quite a respectable little body.' I *thanked* the son of a bitch!"

THAT EVENING, near twilight, Adam and I took a walk along the secluded beach below the cottage. Caroline and I had argued because although I had wanted to walk with *her*, she had insisted on sitting down with the tapes to begin their transcription and editing. Her holiday would only begin, she had declared, when she had successfully accomplished this work. She could not enjoy herself with it hanging over her head, and I was selfish and unreasonable to pressure her to go for a moonlight skinnydip while the task remained undone. Damn Calvinist, I had thought—for, Alistair Patrick Blair's little lecture about western "body shame" notwithstanding, I wanted nothing quite so much as to hold my unclad flesh against Caroline's in the gently lapping waters of Caicos Bay.

Instead, my companion was Adam Montaraz. He was naked, but I was shuffling along beside him in sandals, loose ebony swim trunks, and a short-sleeved terrycloth jacket. Sea shells crunched beneath my feet, and stars began to glimmer in the high tropical sky.

"You told Blair that you're the last of your kind, but RuthClaire's letter said there were habiline artists here. That's why I came. To look at their work, maybe even to represent it in Atlanta. What the hell's going on, Adam?"

"I lied to Dr. Blair."

"Why?"

"Why do you suppose? To protect the tiny remnant that survives. Five persons, Mister Paul—only five persons."

"But if I go back to Atlanta touting their work as the glorious result of an innate habiline aesthetic impulse, this place'll be overrun again. You'll have blown their cover for good. The art will *prove* they're here, and bingo! another mad influx of bounty hunters."

Adam halted. "Not if you represent their paintings as the work of *deceased* Haitian artists. Say they are dead, the artists. Each item you put up for bid is a discovery from their estates. It is not even necessary to identify the artists as habilines. Haitian art has many aficionados in the United States. You can sell it as Haitian art—nothing more, nothing less."

"It would sell for a lot more if I could reveal the identity of the artists. If I could somehow document their identities."

"But I am not interested in 'mopping up.' "

"What *are* you interested in?"

"Secure futures for these last five people. After them, no more. After me, no more. RuthClaire and I want enough money to look after them here on Montaraz, enough money to see to their remaining needs."

"Your own work isn't selling? Let me represent *that*, Adam. We'd all make money, and you wouldn't even have to mention your last five habiline relations."

Adam explained that although their recent travels had stimulated a good deal of creative activity, it had also denied them sufficient time to bring many of these new works to completion. Further, RuthClaire's latest paintings—the series entitled *Souls* that she had completed in Atlanta—had not yet found an audience. Gallery directors declined to put them on show. If RuthClaire rented space in malls or department stores to counteract the insulting gallery boycott, the public ignored them. Newspaper critics lambasted them as dull, flat, colorless, repetitive, picayune in concept, and generally uninspired, particularly in light of their grandiose overall title. Even more dismaying, one critic who hated what he called "decadent decal work for the AmeriCred porcelain-plate scam" had cited the acrylic paintings *Souls* as evidence of the "steep falling off" of RuthClaire's talent since *Footsteps on the Path to Man*. Indeed, you could almost say that these unpopular and much-belittled paintings had destroyed RuthClaire's marketability. Adam's work continued to sell, but his artist wife had run headlong into an immovable brick wall. That was one of the reasons they had summoned Caroline and me to Montaraz.

"They're good," I said. "It's just that nobody sees."

"For a time, *you* didn't see. And maybe they *aren't* good, Mister Paul. Maybe it's only an accident of light that redeems them from mediocrity."

"To be truthful, my appreciation of them came and went—just like the light. It's not hard for me to understand why she's having trouble selling them."

"Okay. But that's why we require money." He began walking again, his hands clasped in the furry small of his back.

I took a couple of long strides to catch up with him.

"When do I meet these habiline artists, Adam? When do I see their work?"

"Tomorrow."

"Where?"

In the early starlight, he grinned at me. "On the middle finger, Mister Paul. On the bird we shoot at Miami." Whereupon he turned, trotted toward the water, and threw himself out into the surf with a splash whose falling canopy of droplets iridesced like the bladder of a Portuguese man-of-war.

After shedding my jacket and slipping out of my sandals, I followed Adam into the water. Just as I had hoped, it was warm without being strength-sapping. My habiline host was dog-paddling about the inlet, sometimes rolling to his back like a sea otter, sometimes treading water with the lackadaisical finning motion of a manatee. I sidled up to him with an easy breaststroke. He began dog-paddling again, but stayed in my vicinity so that we could talk.

"From what you told Blair in that interview, you've abandoned Christianity for some kind of new-fangled theory of the interrelatedness of biological systems." I blew salt water away from my mouth.

"Nonbiological, too."

"Where did it all come from, Adam?"

"It's Batesonian. For a man named Gregory Bateson." He was circling me.

"Familiar, I guess, but I don't really know him."

"You can't know him. He died the year my ego was beginning to crystallize out of the Edenic anonymity of my youth."

"I meant that I don't know his work. Have you uncritically adopted this Bateson's metaphysics? Jettisoned your time-tested religion for some kind of trendy Californian nonsense with pseudo-scientific underpinnings?"

"There is *nothing* I adopt uncritically, Mister Paul, and if you don't know Bateson's work, you understand absolutely nothing about its underpinnings. They are evolutionary. I like them very much."

"I was worried about RuthClaire."

"Why? I love her."

"I'm sure you do, Adam, but it's hard for me to believe she's going to be crazy about a 'religion' based on the evolutionary interrelatedness of biological—and nonbiological—systems. She's a traditionalist, but you've name-called traditional faiths like hers as egotistical and neurotic."

He treaded water in front of me. "But *I'm* egotistical and neurotic. So was the young man who killed our son. I am trying to discover meaning, Mister Paul. I am trying to cure myself of neurosis. Everyone should wish to cure themselves."

"T.P.'s murder sent you down this path?"

"Of course. You heard the eulogies I spoke. I hurt. RuthClaire hurt. Maybe the family of Craig Puddicombe hurt. My choice was to seek consolation in the orthodox hereafter or to discover my place in the great systemic neurosis that devoured our son and so begin to heal myself from the inside. My gift to him."

"Is it really an either-or situation, Adam?"

"Maybe not. But first things first."

"How does what you believe now, right now, differ from this Bateson's world view?"

"He sees Mind and Megapattern. I see those things, too, but I also continue to postulate God. It's a matter of hopeful, nonneurotic faith."

"Sez you."

This tickled him. "Yes, sez me." He brought the heels of both palms down hard on the water, launching stinging fusillades of spray right into my eyes. I yelled, clutched my face, and then blindly grabbed for him. He had already dived out of reach, however, and was sea-ottering from side to side through the inlet toward the web of its enclosing fingers. Once there, he scrambled up onto the beach. Gasping, I waded ashore a minute or two later to join him on the ever-darkening strand.

"Do you mean you've thrown over all your favorite theologians for Charlie Darwin and Gregory Bateson? Adam, I don't know what to say to you. It's beginning to look as if we're brothers under the skin, after all. Rational pagans, both."

"But I am *not* a pagan."

"No?"

"I don't deny the divinity of RuthClaire's Savior. I don't deny the possibility of historical revelation. Not at all, not at all. It's only that the New Testament revelation came at a time and a place inaccessible to my earliest people. I know of another revelation more topical and timely. For me, anyway. For me."

"What?" He had completely lost me.

"Tomorrow, Mister Paul. Let's go back to the cottage."

So we proceeded up the beach, stopping once for me to retrieve my sandals and jacket; and when we entered the little house, I heard Adam's recorded voice saying, ". . . *no great hope that the human species will ever adopt a holistic faith.* . . ." The rest I blotted out. Caroline was still hard at work, and I was still resentfully horny.

I AWOKE with my lust unslaked. Caroline was not in our bed. I dressed and went looking for her. Neither she nor the Montarazes had waited for me. They had gone down to the bay for an early swim. I could hear their voices—or, at least, RuthClaire's and Caroline's—piping cheerfully on the palmy morning breeze. My resentment increased. Last night, Caroline had refused to stop work to accompany me to the water's edge, but rising an hour or so ahead of me—after retiring an hour or so later than I—was apparently no obstacle to her enjoyment of the beach. I banged into the L-shaped porch overlooking the inlet and made an eyeshield of my hands. Pressing them against the screen, I peered down at the revelers.

Adam, as a concession to the women's southern sensibilities, was wearing a black monokini, while both his wife and mine had outfitted themselves in modest one-piece maillot suits, Caroline's a serene turquoise-and-navy, RuthClaire's a brilliant blood-orange. Arm in arm, they were dancing into, and then awkwardly scampering away from, the lacy charges of the surf. The hilarity of this game had them struggling to stay upright.

"Shit," I murmured.

Something on the porch moved. I nearly jumped out of my sandals. One hand went to my heart, the other groped for a support to which to cling. I found the nearest wooden stud bracing the screen and held on to that.

Looking at me from the far end of the porch was a wizened, gnomelike creature wearing a pastel-blue chemise and a grubby white head scarf. She sat on an upturned box with her gnarled hands hanging between her legs and her bare toes going up and down on the hardwood planking like so many soundless piano keys. I assumed her female only because of her clothing; for a moment, in fact, I had thought this strange person might be Adam in drag, playing a trick on me. But Adam was cavorting with RuthClaire and Caroline beside Caicos Bay, and my visitor seemed to be many years older than the habiline. A habiline herself, she scrutinized me with beady, alien eyes.

"Good morning," I said. "I'm Paul Loyd, a friend of Adam's." I jerked a thumb in the direction of the surf-teasing trio.

Her eyes remained on my face, more watchful than curious.

"Why don't you tell me *your* name?" I urged her.

"Ga gapag," she said.

This expression meant nothing to me, but I was surprised that she had spoken at all. Until his operation at Emory, Adam had been incapable of speech. True, he had never lacked the ability to *vocalize*, but uttering recognizable phonemes had had to wait for surgery. This woman's *"Ga gapag,"* by contrast, represented something vaguely like intelligible human speech. A Creole habiline dialect, maybe; a primitive patois.

"Gaga pag," I imperfectly echoed her. "Is that your name?"

She shook her head.

"You're one of the Rutherford Remnant, aren't you?"

With unmistakable contempt, she everted her bottom lip. The wet pink flesh curled back on her receding chin like a fan. Chimpanzees perform a similar trick when bored or irritated. Then her face went back to normal, and she looked away from me as if I had committed an asinine social blunder.

"Wait here," I said angrily. "Just wait here."

My command to the haughty female gnome was superfluous; she sat stolidly on her upturned crate, "obeying" me only because she had already independently decided to remain where she was. I yanked open the screen door, descended a set of treated wooden stairs, and put my foot on the first island in a miniature archipelago of stepping stones. Then I floundered through a cut between two sand dunes and stumbled down the beach to my wife and our hosts.

Caroline, seeing me, broke free of RuthClaire and Adam. With a gait at once coltlike and touchingly feminine, she came running toward me on tiptoes. "Paul!" she cried, and her smile wiped out every other attractive natural sight on my horizon—diamond-blue water, glittering sand, even a gliding formation of brown pelicans at the mouth of the bay. She put her cool hands on my shoulders and kissed me on the bridge of the nose. I gave her in return only a miserly peck.

"Why the hell didn't you get me up, too?"

"Sleeping, you looked about five years old. How could I possibly wake up a tuckered five-year-old?"

I made an irritated head gesture at the cottage. "There's a rude little *enana negra* up there. One of Adam's kind. A habiline. You left me the rude little biddy to wake up to, didn't you?"

Adam appeared at Caroline's shoulder, RuthClaire behind him. "I did not expect her so early. You were alone in the house when we came down here. Not for anything, Mister Paul, would I have caused you discomfort."

"She scared the bejesus out of me."

"You probably frightened her, too," Caroline said.

"A platoon of marines with a howitzer might frighten her. Me, she found about as terrifying as a terminally ill ladybug."

"That's Erzulie," Adam said. "My grandmother on my father's side."

"Erzulie?"

"Her *vaudun* name. I do not remember how we called her when I was a boy with no ego. Probably, we had no spoken name for her at all."

"*She* speaks. She said, '*Gaga pag.*' Something like that."

"She meant, '*Pa capab.*' That's Creole for '*Pas capable.*' It means 'No can do.' That is just about all the language she has, Mister Paul. She says it very seldom because, outside of speaking, there is *not* a great deal she cannot do. Unlike me, however, she has never developed an ego. And so she avoids identifying what she does not possess with the imperfect label of her *vaudun* name."

"If you can follow that," RuthClaire said, laughing.

"What's she doing here?"

"She is an artist," Adam told me. "Also, even though RuthClaire and I know the way, she wished to act as our guide. Now that you're awake—and now that Erzulie is here—we can eat our breakfasts and go."

We returned to the cottage. Although Caroline kept her hand in mine, I felt subtly betrayed and so declined to answer her friendly squeezes with squeezes of my own. By the time we reached the cottage, then, she was casting me puzzled looks, squinting at me for some sign of affection or thaw. I liked that. It served her right. Who the hell enjoyed being told that he resembled a tuckered five-year-old? Not me. I had had adult games in mind, but Caroline had chosen to sacrifice my hedonistic ambition on the altar of the Protestant work ethic. I was aggrieved.

We had fresh eggs from the market in Rutherford's Port. Although I cooked a reproachfully splendid breakfast, Erzulie, the habiline woman, spurned the platter of fried eggs that I set out. Standing at a counter in the kitchen, she drank her eggs raw from a ceramic cup. For a chaser, she downed a jelly jar of native *clairin*, or crude rum. And when we left the cottage in the rented jeep, Erzulie carried with her in the back seat a small Tupperware container of *rapadou*, a coarse brown sugar that many Haitians rely upon as both a sweetener and a staple food item. Like a mountain woman taking snuff, she would put pinches of this sugar between her gums and her rotted teeth and noisily suck at them as we followed the coastal road around the island's middle finger.

Adam was oddly dressed. Everyone else had put on jeans and rugged shoes, but Adam was wearing the same frock coat and top hat that he had worn to the double funeral at Paradise Farm. Horn-rimmed glasses with no lenses adorned his dark face. (For a time, Adam had worn real glasses to read with, but since his operation at Emory, he had depended on contact lenses to correct his vision, and today he was wearing his contacts beneath the phony horn-rimmed glasses.) Sitting beside RuthClaire in the front seat, he had a walking stick between his legs and an unlit cigar in one hand. He had to hold on to the brim of his top hat to keep it from blowing off. Occasionally, though not often, we would pass a straw-hatted laborer or a child-toting mother, who, startled, would gape at the jeep—but especially at Adam—as if seeing a disquieting revenant from the island's past.

"Why the getup?" I shouted from the back seat. (Erzulie was between Caroline and me, sucking her *rapadou*.)

"Because it has religious significance," Adam said over his shoulder.

"Religious significance?"

"He's dressed like Baron Samedi, a voodoo spirit," RuthClaire said. "Some of the Haitians call this traditional spirit Papa Guedé, but whatever the god's name, he's a ribald authority figure associated with death and cemeteries."

"Oh, good," I said. "What's the point?"

"The point is religious and ceremonial," Adam snapped, as if he had already explained this and I was being willfully obtuse.

"I thought we were on our way to the secret habiline republic, not to just another funeral."

"Listen, Paul," RuthClaire said, "that republic's dying. It's been dying for more than twenty years. You're privileged to be visiting it, but you'll have to remember that visiting it is a lot like attending a magnificent funeral mass. So humor Adam in this, okay?''

"I'm here because you guys asked me to be here. Don't get testy if I can't help wondering aloud what the hell's going on!''

"Paul," Caroline admonished me.

On the dark, fertile slope to our left were the terraces of one of Austin-Antilles Corporation's coffee plantations. The regularly spaced shrubs, most of them more than thirty feet tall, loomed over us like fragrant emerald geysers. Their white flowers stirred in the breeze; so did their bountiful crimson clusters of cherries—in this spot, if nowhere else, ready for harvest. Coffee, coffee everywhere, but not a cup to drink. I realized that for breakfast RuthClaire had brewed a pot of tea while Erzulie had opted for rum. I *needed* a cup of coffee. I needed *something*.

RuthClaire said, "Papa Doc, the first Duvalier, sometimes dressed in top hat, horn rims, and tails. 'I am the revolution and the flag,' he liked to say. Well, he also liked to present himself as a champion of the people's folk religion, *vaudun*, which they continue to practice hand in glove with Roman Catholicism. Duvalier exploited this unorthodox dualism. In the Port-au-Prince newspapers, he declared himself Christ's chosen leader, and he made a habit of appearing on his personal reviewing stand in the guise of Baron Samedi. He wanted his identification with Haiti to be total. He wanted the respect, love, and fear of every Haitian, intellectuals and peasants alike.''

"Certainly their fear," said Adam.

"So now you're dressed as Baron Samedi," I said. "You're emulating Papa Doc, who almost everyone agrees was a paranoid megalomaniac. Pardon me if I see that as a nasty little imposture.''

Adam turned around to look at me. "Baron Samedi—Lord Saturday—was here long before Duvalier. So were we habilines, *les nains noirs* of the original Rutherford estate. I am not copying the paranoid Papa Doc, I am honoring a Haitian religious tradition.''

"Wouldn't superstition be a better word?''

"*Pa conay*," Adam said, Creole for "I don't know." "Do you call something a superstition if it works?"

That shut me up. If throwing spilled salt over your left shoulder neutralizes the bad luck otherwise assured by having spilled it, do you call that preventive act superstitious? At the moment, I had no idea. I looked down at the habiline woman Erzulie. Maybe she knew. She looked up at me from beneath the band of her head scarf and the bony ridge of her brow. A coquettish glimmer pirouetted in her eyes, reflecting the sea on our right. Then her tiny Tupperware container bumped me in the chest, and I saw that she was offering me a pinch of *rapadou*. The lumpy brown stuff repulsed me. I turned my head.

The road began to climb, slicing tentatively inland. Caroline and RuthClaire talked, but Adam, Erzulie, and I held our places like bound hostages with gags in our mouths. After another twenty minutes of traveling, RuthClaire swung the jeep into a foliage-capped side road that was mostly gravel and eroded channels. It ended about a hundred twisty yards from the main road. "Here we are," she said, jamming the vehicle into park, and we all got out, pilgrims on a hidden path to mystery. No one on the main road would ever see us. Indeed, I was trying to figure out how RuthClaire had even spotted the turnoff. Creepers netted the rocky ground, and eerily hairy lianas dangled from the trees—a stand of mahogany, if I were any judge—in profligate loops and slings. The coffee plantations of Austin-Antilles lay far behind us to the south, or far enough behind us to *suggest* our isolation and remoteness. A feeling of claustrophobic uncertainty sped my pulse and opened my sweat glands.

Erzulie, barefoot, plunged into the wall of foliage without any further ado, but Adam called her back. We had to unload and fasten on our backpacks, which contained canned goods, cooking utensils, water bottles, bedding, fresh clothes, and all our recording and photographic equipment. RuthClaire had even brought some art supplies for the habilines. I could hardly blame her; they were so rarely the recipients of Federal Express or United Parcel Service deliveries. Everyone wore a backpack but Erzulie. Adam—

his carry-frame in place, his top hat at a jaunty angle, his walking stick at least a foot taller than he—reminded me less of a voodoo spirit than of a Victorian chimney sweep. Into what sooty recesses of Montaraz did he intend to lead us?

Actually, Erzulie did the leading. By sore-footed necessity rather than choice, I brought up the rear. As a consequence, I could never even *see* the chemise-clad habiline. She was always thirty or forty yards ahead of me. To prevent me from being outdistanced and abandoned, Caroline had to lag well behind RuthClaire and Adam, occasionally signaling for rest stops. I had thought myself in better shape. Discovering the truth about my physical condition was a new source of resentment and chagrin.

I began to think that Caroline and the others had deliberately set out to humiliate me, not only on this fatiguing hike but earlier that morning at the beach cottage. How many jokes had they told about me? How many laughs had they milked from silly speculation about my response to Erzulie's presence on the porch? Was it possible that the three of them—Adam, RuthClaire, and Caroline—constituted a clandestine *ménage à trois?*

"Paul, you're as red as a beet," Caroline said. "Stop right there." She poured some water onto her neckerchief and began to wipe my forehead and temples. For a moment, I let her. I was too tired to resist.

RuthClaire and Adam came back along the unmarked trail to see what was happening. Their faces had outline but no definition. Their features were amorphous blurs against a revolving backdrop of emerald and turquoise. One of them asked me if I wanted to lie down with my head propped against a sleeping bag.

"You'll dump crickets on me," I said. "Crickets and red wigglers and a butter tub full of dirt."

"He's out of it," RuthClaire said. "Let's get him to lie down."

I grabbed the wet neckerchief out of Caroline's hand and flung it at a nearby tree. "Bitch! Two-timing bitch!"

"She's trying to cool you off," RuthClaire expostulated. "You've gotten overheated. It's not your fault. We didn't give you any time to get acclimated. It's too much too soon.''

"I'm Adam and you're Eve," I said. "Who are these other two people? I've never seen them before."

"Lie down, Paul. You're delirious."

"I'm delightful. I'm delicious. I'm delovely."

Caroline, whose name I couldn't then recall, turned away, and a dwarf in a blue dress and a white scarf limped out of the higher woods to peer into my flaring nostrils from below. A cockatoo screamed, or a blood vessel in my temple began to hiss. I waved at the dwarf in the chemise, waved her out of the way, and sat down next to the tree. I was breathing hard, and I was angry. My new wife had disappeared, and my old wife was kneeling in front of me. Beside her crouched a chimney sweep who was trying to unbutton my collar. (Did my chimney need cleaning?) His fingers kept poking me in the throat. I knocked his hand aside. As soon as I did that, however, a lid of some kind slid over the sky, blotting out sound and color alike. During this extended eclipse, my temples went in and out, as if my brain were struggling to breathe in a suffocating darkness. Then a familiar female voice said, *"The bastard's still in love with you."*

Although the voice was familiar, I didn't recognize it. I may not have even heard it. I may have simply imagined it. . . .

I AWOKE sitting in the same spot. The light dappling the forest floor betrayed the fact that my delirium had lasted two or three hours. Noon had come and gone. Erzulie was hunkering at my side with a thermos cap full of orange juice. Seeing her, and no one else, panicked me. My wife, my ex-wife, and my ex-wife's husband had absconded. They had left me alone in an obscure upland glade with a wizened hominid woman whose name, Erzulie, was also

that of the preeminent voodoo goddess of the Haitian
religion. Erzulie Freda, an imaginative yoking of the eternal female and the Virgin Mary. Why was this queer little
person staring at me as if I had somehow upset the balance
between divinity and the material world.

"*Bwah,*" she said. "*Bwah!*"

That was pidgin French, wasn't it? *Bois.* Didn't that
mean "wood"? Well, of course, there was a wood all
around us, trees and shrubbery and vines galore. What
could be more obvious? But when Erzulie said "*Bwah!*"
again, touching the thermos cap to my bottom lip, I realized that she was commanding me to drink, and I slurped
the orange juice greedily, grateful for its cold sweetness and
for the brief reprieve from my panic.

Then the panic came back.

I was lucid, I was refreshed, and I was scared. I pushed
the thermos cap away and levered myself upward against
the tree trunk. I shouted Caroline's name. I shouted it two
or three times. Then I began calling for RuthClaire and
Adam. Erzulie grimaced, turned her back on me, and sat
down on an outcropping of rock, embracing her knees with
her thin, hairy arms.

"I'm here," Caroline said, sliding down a mossy in-
cline next to Erzulie's rock. "Are you all right?" She
embraced me.

"I don't know. I could have died. You guys ran out on
me."

Caroline explained that she had never been more than
forty or fifty feet away, that Erzulie had voluntarily stayed
by my side to moisten my forehead with makeshift
compresses, and that we were now only about ten minutes
away from the habiline village. RuthClaire and Adam had
each been back two or three times to check on me. If any
of them had believed me in real danger, they would have
carried me bodily to the jeep and driven me lickety-split to
the hospital in Rutherford's Port. However, my fever had
departed with the application of the second compress, and
it had seemed to Adam that an hour or two of sleep, even
if delirium-induced and fitful, would probably restore my
physical and emotional equilibrium. My forehead was still

cool, Caroline noted, touching me, and I *looked* a helluva lot better. Adam had been right.

These explanations failed to appease me. Maybe the rest had restored my physical equilibrium, but I was an emotional shipwreck. In two days I had accumulated more grievances against Caroline than in our previous five months of marriage. Our working "holiday" was going to hell in a canvas backpack. I was the object of gross neglect and a truly odious conspiracy of sexual exclusion. Using somewhat blunter language, I told Caroline so.

She stared at me aghast. "You're kidding."

"I know what I know, Caroline. I feel what I feel."

"Paul, you could run this country. You're as paranoid as the first Duvalier." I could see that she was waging a fierce internal battle to keep her composure from falling in ruins. "Maybe we *shouldn't* have left you sitting here. You've had some pretty weird fever dreams, old boy, and even though you're awake again, you're still under their brain-damaging influence."

"Old boy?"

"Look, if I can forgive you for something you inadvertently revealed while you were talking out of your head—if I can be big enough to do *that*, even though it hurts like hell to find out—well, *old boy*, you can have the decency to forget the nonsense you dreamt sitting under this tree!" Both fists clenched at shoulder height, she began to cry.

My stomach flip-flopped. "Something I inadvertently revealed?"

"You're still in love with RuthClaire, you brain-damaged klutz! You called her Eve and yourself Adam. Me, you called a two-timing bitch. Then you said you didn't know who I was. Adam, either. In the insular little paradise of your subconscious, it's just you and RuthClaire, world without end, amen. You think finding out something like that doesn't hurt? My gut's in a minor uproar, my nerves are knotted, and the irony of ironies is that from your paranoid point of view, *I'm* the perfidious two-timer! *Me*, not you!"

"Caroline—"

"Why don't you just shut up? Every time you open your

mouth, you put another foot in it. If you were a centipede, you'd've gagged to death by now."

"That's not bad, kid," I said. A wan chuckle escaped me.

"*I'm* not bad. There's nothing about me that's bad. I'm so goddamn saintly I can go on living with a selfish yahoo who's still in love with a woman who's happily married to somebody else."

Erzulie, whom I had virtually forgotten, made an ugly hacking noise and spit into the leaves beside her flat-based rock. Then she got spryly to her feet and vanished into the uphill barricade of foliage. Caroline wiped her eyes with the sleeve of her blue work shirt.

"I didn't know what I was saying," I began.

"You did when you accused me of neglecting you. And, for God's sake, when you accused me of getting kinky with Adam and RuthClaire."

"I meant when I called myself Adam and RuthClaire Eve. A man's not responsible for *all* the crap in his subconscious, Caroline. I loved RuthClaire for a long time. We lived with each other for ten years. I was still in love with her when we divorced. I'll never utterly eradicate those feelings. I really don't think you'd want me to, either. So long as you realize that here and now, it's all you, Caroline, every bit of it. My jealousy, my unfair resentments—they just go to prove it."

"Hey, sport, that's really comforting. Just *hugely* comforting." But, her sarcasm aside, Caroline *did* appear to be comforted—or, if not comforted, then mollified. She had spent her anger. She had disillusioned me of the belief that I was the victim of a conspiracy.

"Caroline, I'm sorry."

She gave me a grudging smile. She put her arm through mine. "Come on, you jackass," she said. "Let's walk on up to Prix-des-Yeux."

"Prix-des-Yeux?"

"The habiline village. We're almost there. RuthClaire and Adam are waiting for us. The habilines, too, I guess."

Prix-des-Yeux means Eye-Price or Eye-Prize. In the special lingo of *vaudun*, the term connotes a state of mystical clairvoyance obtainable only by practitioners at the highest level of faith. Arm in arm, then, Caroline and I climbed toward that state—even though neither of us believed.

RuthClaire, Adam, and the habilines were not the only ones waiting for us when we arrived ten minutes later. Also on hand in the hidden village a hundred yards from the top of the mountain was Brian Nollinger. Once an anthropologist at Emory and a former beau of Caroline's, this unexpected apparition was sitting on a rosewood log next to the crude peristyle of the village *houngfor*, or voodoo temple. As soon as we had emerged into the ragged clearing encompassing Prix-des-Yeux, Brian stood up, turning his wide-brimmed hat in his hands like a steering wheel. I looked at Caroline. She looked at me. God blast me for a green-eyed fool, the first thought into my mind convicted her of a premeditated infidelity.

"Hello," the interloper said. He was wearing bush shorts, hiking boots, calf-high socks, and a khaki shirt with epaulets and three or four button-down pockets. His hat kept turning in his hands.

Caroline said, "My God, Brian, what are *you* doing here?"

"That's what I was going to ask you about him," I told Caroline. "Please don't try to pretend you didn't know he was here."

"But I didn't—"

"That's insulting, Caroline. You must think I'm an idiot."

RuthClaire, hearing this exchange, came out of the *houngfor* in front of which Brian had been sitting. A voodoo temple generally consists of a thatched enclosure with walls about two thirds of the way to its ceiling; the roof, as on this one, is wimpled with palm fronds. Hang-

ing on cords beneath the ceiling is an eclectic jungle of
sacred objects, including colored bottles, dried gourds, tin
trinkets, and hand-carven mahogany charms. Exiting this
shabby peristyle, RuthClaire walked straight across the
small clearing to Caroline and me.

"She *didn't* know he was here, Paul. He got here about
fifteen minutes ago. He followed us from the cottage."

Tentatively, Brian approached. As if afraid that I might
leap forward to bust him in the chops, he halted about five
feet behind RuthClaire. The wispy Fu Manchu that he had
shaved off before showing up at Abraxas for Adam's first
formal exhibit was back again, but two or three days'
growth of patchy stubble had started to encroach upon its
territory. In another three or four days, his beard would
cover most of his lower jaw, with only the Fu Manchu's
dubious head start to mark it out from the newer sprouts.
His hat, the kind that an African big-game hunter might
wear, continued to whirl—I was reminded of a bus driver
trying to get out of a crowded parking lot.

"That's true," he said. "I have a little French motor
scooter, very quiet and economical. I'd been watching the
Montaraz beach cottage ever since Blair got here. When he
left yesterday, I was afraid maybe Adam had canceled any
plans to come up here again. Why would a restaurant
owner or a vacationing sociologist be interested in visiting
the Rutherford Remnant? But I hung on through the night,
and this morning, *pop!*, a habiline woman appeared at your
cottage and the five of you piled into your jeep and drove
on up here. For once I succeeded in finding the damned
turnoff. The previous three or four times I tried to follow
you, well, you gave me the slip. It's the turnoff that
flummoxed me. I kept puttering right on by it. It's no
more than a tear in the roadside foliage."

"We knew you were on Montaraz," RuthClaire said.
"But we thought you were working on the coffee plantations behind Rutherford's Port for Austin-Antilles."

"I am, Mrs. Montaraz. How do you think I managed to
buy a motor scooter down there at import prices?"

"You're supposed to be in the Dominican Republic,"
Caroline said. "You're supposed to be doing demographic

studies of the canecutters there. To take that splendiferous job, you beat it out of Atlanta without even telling me goodbye.''

Christ, I thought. Caroline's really getting to clean out her psychic cupboards today. . . .

"Caroline, I wrote you about not saying goodbye, and I *did* do demographic work in the Dominican. But I took that job for only two reasons—to get me out of an intolerable situation at Emory, and to position myself close enough to Haiti to be able to do some independent research on the Rutherford habilines. As soon as I could, I finagled a transfer from the Austin-Antilles sugar operation to the coffee ranches here on Montaraz.''

"Doing what?'' Caroline asked. "Installing punch clocks for the peasants?''

"Supervising the construction of concrete drying platforms, Caroline. They've had them since the thirties on Haiti itself, but the workers here on Montaraz have always resisted the washing and drying process. Austin-Antilles was afraid to push them too hard for fear of provoking work stoppages. About three months ago, I implemented an education program with the help of the Pan American Development Foundation. A month ago, we actually got platform construction under way.''

"Platform construction? What's demographic about that, Brian? Where does your anthropological background come in? What's it got to do with helping the laborers themselves?''

"Not much maybe, but it's the job that got me transferred over here. It's valuable work economically, Caroline—it benefits the company. But my ulterior motive all along was to find Adam's people. I've searched this island a dozen times since March, using my work as cover, and when the Montarazes themselves settled here—well, I knew it was only a matter of time. Blair came. And then, icing on the cake, you and—'' He gestured at me.

"Caroline's husband,'' I said.

"Icing on the cake?'' Caroline mocked. "Because you were finally able to get what you wanted, namely, unauthorized access to the habilines.''

"With you and Mr. Loyd along, it wasn't hard to follow you up here, if that's what you mean. Mr. Loyd was so slow I had to sit down every couple of minutes to keep from stepping on his heels. Finally, he cracked up and went down on his fanny for a couple of hours." He put his hat on, tightened its draw string under his chin, and stuffed his hands into the pockets of his bush shorts. "I'm glad you're okay, Mr. Loyd. I hung back a long time, trying to figure out what was going on—but when Caroline came back to you and the two of you started arguing, well, it didn't seem fair to sit there listening to you, so I made a big circle around you and came on up here to Habiline City."

"Prix-des-Yeux," RuthClaire corrected him. "You think following people without their knowledge is less despicable than eavesdropping on them?"

"Ma'am?"

"Why didn't you come to our cottage, knock on the door, and *ask* us to bring you here? Didn't that ever cross your mind?"

"I was pretty sure you didn't want to see me, Mrs. Montaraz. You ducked me in the market one day." He shook his head. "Don't deny it. Don't apologize. Just tell me this—if I'd done that, if I'd come to you and asked you to bring me up here, I mean, would you have done it?"

"Of course not," RuthClaire said.

Brian Nollinger shrugged. Well, then, his shrug implied, I had no other choice. He glanced about to see if anyone were sneaking up behind him to knock him senseless with a monkey-coco club.

I glanced about, too. On either side of the *houngfor* was a squatter's hut of cardboard, plywood, scrap metal, palm thatching, and broken cinderblocks. These were dwellings that might have been transported here from Shantytown in Rutherford's Port—except that whoever made them had refrained from using any tin or glass, and had been careful not to employ any scrap metal on their roofs. I knew why. The habilines had no wish to disclose their village's location to searchers in small aircraft or helicopters. Consequently, Prix-des-Yeux had an earthy drabness and a natural

green canopy that concealed most of its modest area from
aerial snooping.

"Now that you're here," RuthClaire asked the intruder,
"what do you intend to do?"

"Well, study the habilines, of course. What else? With
your permission, I'd like to do anthropological field work
here."

"*With our permission?* You went out of your way to get
around having to acquire it, mister!"

"But now that I'm here—now that I know where the
Rutherford Remnant makes its home—surely you'll let me
follow up. I'm an admirer of Adam's. I'm sympathetic to
his people's desire to live out the remainder of their days
as an autonomous community. Most of my work has been
in primate ethology, it's true, but that's not an entirely
inappropriate background for research like this. I'm strong
on method, I'm a good organizer, and I can do almost
anything I put my mind to, given half a chance. Supervising the construction of coffee-drying platforms for Austin-
Antilles proves that. Moreover, I'm able to—"

"Brian, old boy, you've *got* a job," I interrupted him.
"So how about skipping the self-serving résumé."

"What you lack," RuthClaire angrily told him, "is both
discretion and a basic regard for others' feelings. To you,
these people—" she gestured at the temple and the nearby
shanties, a township barren of visible inhabitants—"well,
they're nothing but *subject matter*. Just as I'm nothing but
an obstacle to research and Adam's nothing but a means to
personal advancement."

"Mrs. Montaraz, that's not fair. Do you remember
when I showed up at the art gallery to apologize? Mr.
Loyd here hustled me off, but I was completely sincere in
my intentions."

"I'm sure that's true," Caroline told RuthClaire.

"Caroline!" I exclaimed.

Brian hurried to add, "Can you blame an anthropologist
for being obsessed with Adam's personal history? The
secret of the origin of the human species may rest with
these persecuted habilines, Mrs. Montaraz."

RuthClaire slipped her hands into the pockets of her

designer jeans and walked several steps away from our
mutual nemesis. "Suppose you do your precious 'field
work' here. Suppose Adam gives you a free hand. What
then?"

"Ma'am?"

"What would you do with the results of your research?"

"Publish them, of course. That's essential."

"To whom?"

"To Brian Nollinger," I said. "He one-ups the entire
paleoanthropological community, not excepting its high
muckety-muck, A. P. Blair."

"And destroys the Rutherford Remnant in the process,"
RuthClaire predicted. "It was something of a miracle they
outlasted the first onslaught of scientific fortune hunters.
Like their ancestors in Zarakal, they had to go underground—literally—to survive that dismaying siege. Montaraz
is a small island, but their cunning and nimbleness, an
inherited ability to lie low for long periods, saved them. A
published account of their culture would be its death knell
and eulogy. That's not melodramatic alarmism, Dr.
Nollinger—that's a realistic assessment of the likely consequences of human curiosity and greed."

"Including yours," I told my wife's ex-beau.

Caroline crossed her arms and shook her head. "Paul,
why don't you shut up? RuthClaire's handling this."

"What if I purposely refused to pinpoint the location of,
uh, this village?" Brian countered. "It's almost impossible to find without prior knowledge. The proof's that even
though thousands of people have suspected the existence
of a habiline hideaway, no one's ever found it."

"Until today," RuthClaire said. "And in this case, the
exception doesn't prove the rule—it sabotages your entire
argument."

"You folks were careless, Mrs. Montaraz. You let that
habiline woman visit your cottage, and then you put her in
the jeep with your two foreign house guests. You took off
as if you were going on a three- or four-day picnic. You
never tried a single dodge to see if anyone was following
you. And once on foot, you let Mr. Loyd and Caroline

jibber-jabber like school kids on a weekend field trip.
Without that kind of carelessness, I wouldn't be here now.

"Well, you don't *have* to be careless," he continued.
"You can do things differently. You can insure the total
anonymity of the site, and you can keep doing it even after
I've published my monograph."

RuthClaire lifted her chin and spoke to the blue Haitian
sky: "Too bad I don't believe in murder. I could put an
end to this whole perplexing mess by putting a bullet in
Dr. Nollinger's brain." She fixed her tormentor with an
exasperated stare. "Do you think anybody would ever find
your body, mister?"

"Probably not," he admitted.

"Your bones, maybe. Two million years from now. But
only by a rare conjunction of skill and luck. But murder's
not in my behavioral armory, damn it. Where's a blood-
thirsty Tonton Macoute when you really need one?"

"Why don't you talk to Adam?" Caroline suggested.
"Brian may be just the person to do an ethnography of the
Rutherford Remnant. I mean, if *anyone's* going to do one.
I can vouch for his character."

"And the Pope could vouch for Colonel Khadafy's," I
said. "Never mind that he'd be an idiot to do it."

Pointedly, the two women ignored me.

WHERE WAS Erzulie? Where were her fellow citizens of
Prix-des-Yeux? For that matter, where was Adam?

RuthClaire led us across the small clearing to the
houngfor. We entered. Inside, we found Adam seated at
the base of the *poteau mitan;* this is the central post of the
roofed part of the temple called the *tonnelle*. Down this
post, RuthClaire explained, the gods of the voodoo pantheon, known both individually and collectively as *loa*,
descend upon the service from their spiritual abode in

"Yagaza," which translates as either "Africa" or the "immaterial world beyond death."

But Adam, still in his Baron Samedi costume, was not alone in the *tonnelle*. Facing him at the foot of the spirit pole sat Erzulie, her legs crossed lotus fashion and her hands clasping his in the same viselike way that the couplings on two railway cars achieve an unbreakable grip. Adam's eyes were shut, and when we advanced deeper into the peristyle, walking cautiously beneath its hanging gourds and trinkets, we saw that Erzulie's were too. The wizened habiline woman and her well-traveled grandson were communing with each other through the agency of trance. What disturbed me even more than their abstraction from the present moment, however, was the fact that providing another Laocoon link between them was the sinuous body of a python nearly twelve feet long. It curled about Adam's torso, made a spavined loop around both his and Erzulie's arms, and, after lazily girdling the woman's waist, rested its flat, evil-looking head atop her grubby scarf.

"My God," Caroline said. "Are they all right?"

"They're fine," RuthClaire assured her. "It's just that we're not going to be able to talk to them for a while."

"But the snake—"

"It's not poisonous, Caroline. There aren't any poisonous snakes in Haiti or its coastal islands."

Brian said, "It's a local variety of python called a *couleuvre*. Islanders revere them. That's because they eat rats. I've been in both Dominican and Haitian homes where they put out food to *attract* the blesséd things. Saucers of milk, fresh eggs, little dishes of flour. You're lucky if you've got a *couleuvre*, Caroline." He tilted his head to look at it. "Pretty, don't you think?"

Even in the shade, the python glinted bronze and garnet. Its eyes sparkled like beryls. No one could reasonably dispute its prettiness, but it stank. The unmistakable odor of serpent drifted through the *tonnelle* like a thin gas. To ward off nausea, I had to cover my mouth and nose and turn aside.

"Cripes!" I exclaimed. "How do they stand it?"

RuthClaire looked at me with some sympathy. "It affected me that way, too, at first. You get used to it. Just as you get acclimated to Montaraz."

"But what are they doing?" Caroline asked.

"You have to look at the three of them as a symbiotic unit of ancient Arada-Dahomey spirits—Papa Guedé, Erzulie, and Damballa. There are plenty of other *loa* in the voodoo pantheon, but on Montaraz, well, that's the Big Three. Damballa's personal symbol is the serpent. He's the god of rain, a guardian of lakes and fountains. Erzulie is Damballa's mistress. Adam says that when they link up like this, they establish a metaphorical conduit between past and present, Africa and the New World, the spiritual and the material. The python's the flow—the electricity, if you like—necessary to convey the gist of their messages."

I was standing just inside the temple's door again. "That doesn't sound like Adam, RuthClaire. It sounds like superstitious gobbledegook."

"The gist of *what* message?" Brian Nollinger demanded. "What kinds of information are they supposed to be communicating?"

RuthClaire said, "The kinds that can't be verbalized."

"That's appropriate," I said. "Erzulie can't talk much, the snake's probably no orator, and Adam's natural eloquence is lost on their likes." Oh, yes. *The kinds that can't be verbalized.*

"Telepathy?"

"I wouldn't call it telepathy, Dr. Nollinger. That has an unsavory paranormal ring. Mostly, though, it's inaccurate."

"How about witchcraft?" I said. "When it comes to savoriness, witchcraft takes the cake. Give me witchcraft over telepathy any day."

"You're making fun," RuthClaire said, "but witchcraft—the term, I mean—implies an element of inexplicable spiritual interplay that telepathy lacks. If you're going to explain what's going on here, that element has to be accounted for. It's religious, Paul, not crassly materialistic."

"I'm beginning to think that with you and Adam everything's 'religious.' "

"Try 'holy.' Or 'sacred.' That's even better."

Avoiding the vaguely cabalistic *vevés* that had been laid out on the floor with cornmeal, flour, and colored sand, Caroline picked her way across the temple and crouched behind the center post to look at Adam and Erzulie. The *couleuvre* flicked its tongue at her. She drew back from the serpent so suddenly that she had to reach a hand behind her to keep from falling on her butt. Recovered, she shifted position and continued staring at the habilines.

Without looking up, she said, "Can't you give us a general idea of what they're not talking about?"

"It's really hard to say," RuthClaire confessed. "Details of Adam's life on Montaraz before ego-crystallization. Possibly some stuff about habiline history both here and in the Lolitabu catacombs. It may even go as far back as the beginning of the species. In fact, Adam says that it does. Erzulie's knitting him back into the unraveling fabric of his people without tearing him out of the life he's made with me. He does this at least once every time we come up here. In a way, I envy him."

"Why?" Caroline asked.

"Because it's making it easier for him to forget what happened to Paulie. I could use that kind of help myself."

"Can't you do this, too?"

"I'm afraid to. And I'm not a habiline."

"Do you have to be a habiline? I would've thought that simply being human was enough. It was enough for you and Adam to marry."

"That's one of the sad things about this," RuthClaire said. "He's human, but I . . . well, I'm not a habiline. It's like time's arrow, I guess—a one-way street. So I'm frightened and envious."

"If you were an anthropologist," Brian began, "you could. . . ."

"I could what?"

"Try to make a professional identification with the habilines. Take part in their ceremonies. Translate the nonverbal images that Adam and this woman are exchanging into an impressionistic history of human origins. You can see what that would mean. You can see why I'm badgering you to let me try it. It might very well revolu-

tionize our entire species' self-concept, our most fundamental notions of who and what we are.''

I said, "You never let up, do you, Brian?"

At which point Adam leaned his head back and released
such a piercing cry that all four of us ducked away from
the noise. Then Adam's eyes sprang open. So did Erzulie's.
The *couleuvre*, Damballa's living avatar on Montaraz,
slipped the knots that it had tied around Erzulie's waist and
Adam's torso and crawled sedately away from the couple.
Caroline had to jump aside to let it pass.

The snake knew exactly where it was going, namely, up
onto a crude wooden dais beyond the *poteau mitan*. On
this dais, the habilines had arranged the three sets of
Arada-Dahomey drums traditionally played during a *vaudun*
ceremony. The python, taking its time, gripped the base of
one of the *asotor* drums and flowed up its commanding
height to the leather drumhead. Here the serpent balanced,
as if on a fulcrum, until it could bridge the chasm between
the drum and one of the posts supporting the *houngfor*'s
outer wall. Still calmly flowing, the great bronze-and-
garnet snake reached the top of the truncated wall, and, as
its weight shifted from the drum to the flimsy rafter of the
peristyle, the entire temple shook. To prevent the *houngfor*
from collapsing on me, I stepped outside. Soon, though,
Damballa had found a resting place on the rafter, and the
temple stopped swaying.

Adam and Erzulie awakened from their trance. They
had ceased to be *loa*—they had become themselves again.
Adam pulled Erzulie to her feet, and the two groggy
habilines turned to face us with a reluctance, or an apathy,
that was palpable. The reality of the present moment, no
matter how strange, could not compete with the colorful
intensity of their possession by the Haitian gods. Adam's
pupils were huge, as if he had been drinking in light with
which to illumine the visions of his trance. He stumbled a
step or two toward RuthClaire before finding both his
balance and his place in our small consensus world.

"Are you all right?" RuthClaire asked, catching him.

He was looking at Brian Nollinger. In an instant, his
pupils had contracted to the size of microdots. Something

inside him, I thought, wanted to squeeze the anthropologist utterly out of his sight.

"I was," he said, his guttural voice scarcely audible. "I was."

THE FIVE of us remained in Prix-des-Yeux for three days. Brian Nollinger was permitted to stay because he had found us and would probably have little trouble finding us again; too, he earnestly reiterated his promise not to divulge the location of the habiline village, if only Adam would consent to his undertaking a respectful ethnographic study of the Rutherford Remnant. Adam gave his consent, but a lack of enthusiasm suggested that he regarded Brian's plea as a subtle form of blackmail. If he had withheld his consent, the anthropologist could have avenged himself by going back to Rutherford's Port and telling what he knew. Then Adam's people would have had no choice but to move. Tearing down their *houngfor* and their huts would have posed no real problem, but, on an island as small as Montaraz, finding an equally well-camouflaged site for a new village would have. So Adam told the blackmailer that he could stay.

The decision irked me. I understood it, but it irked me. That Caroline had offered the Montarazes unsolicited testimonials on Brian's behalf did not sit well with me, either. What stake did she have in his remaining with us? Why did she so highly value his talents—completely untested talents—as an ethnographer? Why did she remember him with such fondness, when he had deserted their earlier relationship without so much as a flippant ta-ta? I tried to discover reasons. He was younger than I. His brief career in the Caribbean, begun out of something like Byronic desperation, gave him an irresistibly romantic air. Or, the least palatable of all my conjectures, Caroline was still in love with him. She had married me on the rebound, albeit

a *long* one, and Brian's abrupt reappearance in her life had
come to her as a godsend.

Self-doubt. Paranoia. An absence of charity. I was the
possessor of all these negative attributes. I kept thinking
about what RuthClaire had jokingly said about killing the
interloper. The surreal tropical setting of Prix-des-Yeux had
deprived me of all adult perspective. I was a teen-ager
again, a teen-ager not terribly shy of his fiftieth birthday,
and the fact that I was living a kind of oblique Lost Race
fiction right out of Bulwer-Lytton and H. Rider Haggard
merely heightened my adolescent self-doubt.

And the Lost Race whose tiny society Brian hoped to
observe, whose art my new wife and I had come all the
way from Atlanta to see, and whose survival the Montarazes
wanted to insure?

Well, on the afternoon of the day of our arrival, we met
these unusual people one at a time over a period of approximately two hours. At Adam's bidding, Erzulie left Prix-
des-Yeux, hiked into the dense shrubbery uphill from the
huts, and returned in twenty or thirty minutes with one of
her habiline compatriots. Then, after mutually awkward
greetings of a pantomimic kind, Erzulie would accompany
her charge back up the mountain to fetch the next. Each
habiline came to us dressed in a togalike garment that
varied not at all in style or color from person to person.
With the appearance of the third habiline, I understood that
Erzulie's relatives were all wearing the same garment. An
ochre stain on its hem gave the game away. Although the
motto "one size fits all" was not strictly true (the smallest
of the four members of the Rutherford Remnant had to
gather up the toga's skirts and carry them across one arm),
they pretended otherwise. I began to understand that in the
absence of visitors they probably wore no clothes at all.
Hence these serial debuts.

Erzulie's head scarf and chemise were dictated solely by
her current status as a go-between, a role that she must
frequently have played with the superstitious islanders grub-
bing out poverty-level livings farther down the mountain.
Older and more worldly-wise than most of her naked
conspecifics, she could pass herself off as a deaf-mute

mambo or *vaudun* priestess. The Haitians might suspect that she was actually a habiline, but to regard her as a witch—rather than a dissimulating weredemon or a quasi-human survivor of Sayyid Sa'īd's slave market—conferred a certain degree of safety on their dealings with her. *Cigouaves* and habilines, after all, you were supposed to report to the Tontons Macoutes, and the fewer contacts with those guys the better. You could trust a four-foot-tall witch a lot further than you could a six-foot-tall policeman with mirror-lens sunglasses and a Springfield rifle.

In any event, Erzulie—both *mambo* and goddess—introduced us to her people.

The first of the four habilines to greet us was a grizzled old man with a broad flap of flesh for a nose and eyes the color of cloudy gin. He was blind. Adam told us that his name was Hector, but, as with all the names that Adam subsequently gave us, I felt sure that he had invented it as a convenience for the rest of us. Although blind, Hector oriented himself to every rock and blossom in the landscape as if he could see. Once, when a tropical butterfly with iridescent moiré patterns and peacock eyes on its wings tumbled past us, Hector moved his head as if to follow its flight. RuthClaire conjectured that an acute sensitivity to air currents and minuscule temperature changes had enabled him to perform this trick.

The remaining three habilines came out in turn. They included a furtive, middle-aged male whose incongruous pot belly pooched out the fabric of the toga; a relatively young female with a deformed pelvic structure that gave her a gimpy walk without really slowing her down; and an adolescent male whose fierce mistrust of us revealed itself in his flashing eyes and the uncontrollable tendency of his upper lip to pull away from his teeth. Adam called these three Toussaint, Dégrasse, and Alberoi. French names, every one. I reflected that in the days before Peter Martin Rutherford deeded Montaraz to President Nissage Saget, most of the habilines had probably had either English or Spanish names—if they had had names at all. It hardly mattered, though. Among themselves, they must have used primeval East African syllables, throaty names with no

modern counterparts; or maybe they had communicated
solely by touch, gesture, facial expression, and eye movements. Because none of the Prix-des-Yeux habilines spoke,
we had no way of knowing.

Toussaint, we learned, was young Alberoi's uncle.
Toussaint's brother—the father of the edgy Alberoi—had
been a member of the same gunrunning crew on which
Adam had worked early in 1980. Adam had witnessed the
murders of Alberoi's father and his own brother by a
Cuban thug (whom Caroline, entirely by coincidence, had
later interviewed in the Atlanta Federal Penitentiary). As
for Dégrasse, she had broken her pelvis in a fall from one
natural stope in the cave system above Prix-des-Yeux to a
chamber far below it. She had been carrying an unborn
child. The child died, and she had almost died herself.
Friends managed to get her to the level on which she and
her husband had made their home in the catacombs, and
here she had eventually recovered. Destroyed along with
her baby, however, was her ability to conceive. As the
only surviving habiline woman of child-bearing age, she
suffered from the knowledge (dim and unfocused perhaps,
but ever-present) that her tenacious species was finally—
after nearly three million absurdly self-abnegating years—
doomed to pass away. Alberoi might well be the last of
them to die, but Dégrasse had been their only viable hope
for continuance.

Gone, that hope. All that was left was for the males to
mate with human women. Ironically, Adam had pioneered
that option with results that had persuaded him and
RuthClaire not to try again. Hector was old and blind.
Toussaint and Alberoi might one day seek willing Haitian
brides, but their fear of the human world—their past experiences with Tontons Macoutes, plantation overseers, fortune hunters, and Marxist revolutionaries—argued against
their doing so. Their people were universal victims. Even
people who wished to protect them often endangered them
by shining upon them the light of sincere concern. Adam,
a habiline himself, had inadvertently done that. So it was
unlikely that the anxious Toussaint or the feral Alberoi

would ever venture down from their village to woo the sloe-eyed daughters of men.

I asked Adam why he had limited our first contact with his people to these stiff, serial meetings. He explained that it was simply to give them a chance to get used to our presence. They were suspicious, and they were shy. Erzulie had had some experience with outsiders, but the other habilines were innocents. They had soft ego structures. They had threaded their lives into the elemental natural beauties and terrors of the island itself, but latter-day humankind absolutely confounded them. Tomorrow, and the following day, we would see more of them. Meanwhile, we must let them think about our first meetings with us. In the darkness of the caves—I finally began to understand that there were caves higher up the mountain— they would begin to weave us into the psychic patterns tying them to Montaraz and their immemorial family past. Or so, at least, he hoped.

That night, we lit candles in the *houngfor* and shared a rude picnic near its center post. We included Brian, who had brought a backpack of his own, and made nervous jokes about the *couleuvre* coming down to join us. After-ward, Brian began asking questions about Blair's visit to the cottage, and Caroline made the mistake of telling him about her tapes of the Great Man's conversation with Adam. Since we had brought our taping equipment with us, Brian insisted on hearing them. RuthClaire and I told Caroline that she would be crazy to let Brian eavesdrop on a privileged interview, especially before it saw print in *Popular Anthropology*, but Adam, having surrendered once, saw no reason to hold firm on this point, either. Besides, he wanted to hear the tapes himself. Up here in Prix-des-Yeux, what other entertainment did we have?

We listened to the tapes. Brian was as intent as I had ever seen him. Like a man praying silently at an altar, he leaned forward in the flickering candlelight. Although he laughed aloud during Blair's attempt to persuade Adam that *Homo zarakalensis* was a better species designation than *Homo habilis*, he was reverent and respectful through the latter two thirds of the interview. Only when Adam

claimed to be the "last of my tribe" did Brian raise his
eyebrows and let his gaze travel around the shadowy circle
of our faces. The concluding section of the tape about the
soul, the ego, and God, he listened to raptly, without
criticism or censure.

"Good stuff, Caroline. But incomplete. You ought to
do another interview like that—with *me* as the third
participant."

"No," said Adam clearly. "No way."

WE SPREAD out our sleeping bags in the *tonnelle*. The
serpent in the rafters made me uneasy, but RuthClaire
swore that it was only interested in small rodents, birds'
eggs, and *vaudun* offerings. No need to fear waking up as
a paralyzed lump in its throat. We slept.

During the night, all the other habilines but Hector
returned from the caves to the village. Alberoi and Erzulie
had one of the Shantytown huts, Dégrasse and Toussaint
the other. All four of them were up and about by the time
we rubbed the sand out of our eyes and pushed our creaky
selves off the ground. The men had donned walking shorts,
and Dégrasse was a vision of yellow and brown in a
floral-print chemise whose pattern reminded me of nursery-
school wallpaper—groups of baby ducks swimming through
stands of graceful reeds. From hidden larders, the habilines
had produced a small black cauldron of red beans and rice
that they were heating over a fire not far from the *houngfor*.
We emerged to the oddly pleasing aroma of this stew.
Alberoi was stirring the pot, Erzulie ladling globs into
chipped porcelain mugs, and Dégrasse passing out cheap
metal spoons to the people walking by to be fed. Seated on
the log by the temple, Toussaint was already greedily
eating.

After breakfast, Brian declared that it was time for the
habilines to hold free elections.

"For what?" RuthClaire asked. "Five people hardly require a president."

"To see what they want to be *called!*" the anthropologist buoyantly replied. "As Alistair Patrick Blair himself pointed out, even the scientific community will be bound by their decision. Let's get them all together so that we can propose alternatives to *Homo habilis*, and to *Homo zarakalensis*, and have them vote. It's rightfully their decision."

"Adam," RuthClaire said, "this is preposterous."

Surprisingly, Adam had entered into the spirit of Brian's early-morning madness. "I know. I like it because it *is* preposterous. I like it because Dr. Nollinger recognizes the egotistical absurdity of his eminent colleague's campaign for *Homo zarakalensis*."

"Does it have to be a Latin term?" I asked.

"Of course not," Brian said. "The habilines themselves are the sole arbiters. It can be *anything* they want."

The habilines themselves were sitting on the rosewood log beside the village *houngfor*. When Hector came into the clearing a moment later, Adam escorted him to a place on the log beside Erzulie. Every member of the Rutherford Remnant was on hand, and Brian, speaking alternately in English and French, explained to them the significance of this morning's election.

"Adam, don't let him continue with this demeaning nonsense," RuthClaire said. "You're betraying your own kind."

"Only if you suppose Erzulie and the others incapable of deciding what they wish to be called. *I* give them more credit."

"So do I," said Brian. He looked at me. "Any suggestions, Mr. Loyd?"

"Well, they're not too much bigger than a singing group. They could call themselves the Ink Spots."

Brian translated this for the habilines. "*Les Taches de l'encre?*"

"Oh, my Lord!" RuthClaire exclaimed. She shook her fists at shoulder level and then stormed off into one of the huts to escape an outbreak of silliness that she saw as low and pernicious.

"That really dates you," Caroline told me. "The Ink Spots, for heaven's sake. I didn't know you were *that* old."

"What about the Jackson Five, then? Is that any better?"

"The frivolity of singing-group names," Adam said, still adroitly deadpan, "is altogether inappropriate."

"Then what about the Dodgers?" I suggested. "The Rutherford Port Dodgers?"

"The Society for Self-Perpetuating Anachronism?" Caroline said.

"*Homo nollingeri?*" Brian said.

"The Survivors?"

"Friends of the Earth?"

"Adam Montaraz and the Voodoo Vagabonds?"

"Old and Young Republicans?"

"Enough!" Adam said. "I have one final proposal, *Les Gens*. I now demand that the choices be put and the vote itself recorded."

Les Gens—the People—won hands down. (Well, to be truthful, hands up.) And there were no charges of election fraud or ballot stuffing.

"It's not particularly original," Brian said after the count. "But at least it has the force of tradition behind it."

"Exactly," Adam said. "Now RuthClaire can write Dr. Blair and inform him of my people's decision." He went into Erzulie's hut to tell her of that decision. A moment later, the sounds of RuthClaire and Adam's argument drifted out to all eight of us in the clearing.

I WAS frightened. Exploring caves, even in the company of a knowledgeable guide, strikes me as the physical equivalent of exploring the teeming darkness of the id. You have no idea what you will find. And there is never any guarantee that once you confront this darkness, you will find the strength to overcome it and reemerge a saner person than you first went in. There is no guarantee that you will reemerge *at all*.

"Come on, Paul," Caroline said. "The People do it all the time. Hector, who's blind, has been doing it for years."

"It might help to be blind."

Still dressed as Baron Samedi, Adam led us away from the *houngfor*, from the village itself. We climbed through a dense obstacle course of bushes and scrub pines to a strip of open terrace. This terrace was probably only thirty or forty feet wide and ended abruptly in an upslope barricade of sablier trees. This tree takes its name from that of a tusked hog found on Haiti—for the tree, too, has tusks, an array of evil spines on its trunk and lower branches. RuthClaire explained that you seldom find the sablier so plentiful and closely spaced at the higher elevations, but that this imposing stand was the result of deliberate plantings undertaken by the habilines to conceal and guard the cave mouths farther up the mountain. Until such hedges were outlawed as threats to the public safety, in fact, property-owning Haitians had often used sablier trees to fence their homes and gardens. Innocent passers-by, as well as would-be thieves, had sometimes suffered puncture wounds, lacerations, lost eyes, and even death upon unexpectedly running into a phalanx of sablier spines.

"Doesn't a barricade like that call attention to itself?" Caroline asked, gesturing at the prickly wall.

"Only from the air," RuthClaire said. "And the only people on Montaraz with helicopters and light aircraft are Austin-Antilles employees. They don't overfly Pointe d'Inagua very often because they've already got most of the good coffee-growing land tied up, anyway. It's a little weird, a sablier hedge this high, but it's not so strange as to invite inspection trips. It just keeps tourists and local curiosity-seekers at bay."

Hector was with us. He stared unseeingly at the wall, a look of fond contentment on his runneled face. He was walking unassisted, without even a stick to help him feel his way, and his sure-footed strides amazed and humbled

me. How, though, was he going to negotiate this murderous barricade? How, for that matter, were *we* going to be
able to?

Adam seemed to have read my mind. "For Hector and
the others, venturing into the sablier trees is very like Br'er
Rabbit from Mr. Harris's stories being thrown into the
briar patch. Come."

Adam and the old man set off across the terrace, climbing boldly toward the sabliers. Brian, RuthClaire, Caroline, and I followed, glancing around ourselves as if an
army of Tontons Macoutes might appear at any moment to
gun us down.

Hector led us through the barricade. His clairvoyance—
his uncanny second sight—allowed him to duck sideways
into an opening of spiny boughs that immediately chan-
neled us into yet another corridor requiring a sideways
twist to enter. Each time Hector sensed, or remembered,
the next arm of spikes ready to stab him, his head bobbed
expertly to avoid it. And so we tiptoed along behind him,
bobbing and feinting as we saw the person in front of us
do, trusting that each of our dodges was a replica of one
already expertly performed by Hector. I felt like an upright
slug trying to prevent my own vivisection in a forest of
jumbled razor blades.

At last we got through. The top of the pine- and
hardwood-studded mountain still loomed over us, but off
to our right we could see a wedge of glittering blue from
Inagua Bay, and a peaceful triangular sail on the water,
and the red-tile roof of a solitary villa next to the sea. The
clarity of these images—after our claustrophobic hike from
the coastal road to Prix-des-Yeux and from Prix-des-Yeux
to this narrow overlook—stunned me.

"See if you can find an entrance to the caves," Adam
challenged us.

We stumbled along a dark-soiled cut between the sabliers
and the lichen-coated rock formations above us. Hector and
Adam stood at the opposite end of this cut waiting for us
to pass their test. I began to weary of it.

Turning around, I said, "How long are we supposed to
look?"

Adam was alone on the spot where he had been standing. Hector had disappeared. Had he fallen through a metaphoric trap door into the maw of the mountain? I scrambled down the cut to Adam to see if I could solve the mystery.

Beside the habiline were three or four blasted-looking bushes. They had grown together so that it was hard to tell their number. One of them stuck out and downward from the wall of the gravel-littered cut. Even though the slope of the mountain and the curve of the gully protected this bush from the wind, its inner branches were languidly waving, like sea anemones in a gentle current. I stuck my arm into the bush. The air striking my flesh was cool—refrigerated-feeling, in fact. This was undoubtedly Hector's point of entry into the underworld.

"Here," I said. "Right here."

"Go on, then," Adam encouraged me.

I had to wade into the tangled bushes, stoop to get my head beneath the bush growing out of the wall, and sit down to keep from scratching my face on its branches. As soon as I had sat, my legs were dangling invisibly beneath me and my upper body was enmeshed in brambles like a fly in the pod of a carnivorous plant. RuthClaire, Caroline, and Brian approached. I could see their faces through the interlocking twigs of my prison.

"Drop," Adam encouraged me. "Drop on down."

"I'm not sure I want to be first."

"You won't be," RuthClaire said. "Hector's already down there."

"Wait!" Caroline barked. She knelt and shoved a Nikon into my hands. "Hang on to that, Paul. It's expensive."

"I know that. Who the hell do you think bought it?"

But I gripped the camera more tightly and edged forward until my rump had nothing under it to support it. Like Alice, I fell. As in my worst nightmares, I fell into obsidian blackness. Then my feet hit rock and went out from under me, and I was sitting again, less comfortably than before. My coccyx had been jarred, and I could see nothing at all. A hand touched my forehead and then discreetly withdrew.

''Hector? Hector, is that you?''

A hand grabbed my shirt and push-pulled me off my tail to a hunched standing position. It was indeed Hector. He was blind—but, down here, so much less blind than I, or anyone else, that his clairvoyance made him king. I was afraid to straighten up for fear of bumping my head.

''That's not the way you're supposed to do it,'' RuthClaire called from above. ''You're supposed to *slide* down.'' Her words echoed through the catacombs.

Caroline shouted, ''Paul, are you all right?''

''I think I've loosened the bolt that holds my ass on, kid. Otherwise I guess I'm okay.'' It gratified me to note that my ex-wife had scolded me, while Caroline had inquired after my health. Maybe at some fundamental level of its dubious operation, the world was running smoothly, after all.

Then Brian Nollinger cried, ''Hang on, Mr. Loyd, we're coming down!''

Adam came first, then RuthClaire, Caroline, and Brian. They slid down a natural ramp two feet over from where I had been sitting, and this bodyworn slide deposited them next to Hector and me without fracturing either their feet or their tailbones.

''I am very sorry you hurt your butt,'' Adam said, touching my arm. ''On this walk-through, then, we will avoid the most treacherous galleries, the little coves and crawlways that speleologists call horrors. No wriggle rooms, or rock bridges, or *chatières*, Mister Paul.''

''*Chatières?*''

''Cat holes,'' RuthClaire told me. ''You can guess what those are.''

''*En avant*,'' Adam said. He shone his battery lamp straight into the depths of the tunnel. Its beam illuminated the glassy black walls of the cavern and a high rugged arch beyond which ran a wall that shone as if basted with coal oil. We began to walk toward the wall.

In its center, maybe fifty feet away, writhed a statue— its writhing was a trick of the light, the oily dampness, and the sinuous lines of the sculpture itself—of a hominid creature very like a habiline. It was carven from a hunk of

dark, banded rock. Its contorted face had smooth hollows
for eyes but an angry mouth and a flat nose with flared
wings and nostrils. Simultaneously, its face seemed to be
that of both a protohuman and a rabid canine. Its hands
were fists, and its arms were raised either to embrace or
assault whoever approached it. It boasted an erection as
big and shiny as a Coca-Cola bottle, and testicles as
distended and uneven as parallel drippings of candle wax.
An agony of love, hunger, and rage emanated from the
figure, which RuthClaire told us was supposed to represent
Homo habilis primus.

The primeval habiline. The father of his species.

"Who did it?" Caroline asked. "Hector?"

Adam said, "No, not Hector. Even he can't remember
who shaped it, or how our ancestors set it here. For as
long as any of us can recall, it has stood at the base of this
wall, at the mouth of this gallery—a memorial and a numen."

"A numen?" Caroline said. She handed me a flash
attachment. I plugged it into the Nikon and took a series of
photographs of the statue.

"A presiding spirit," Brian told Caroline. "The creative
energy of the caves and of the habilines."

"Abraxas," RuthClaire said cryptically.

I looked at her in the wavering light of Adam's lamp.
"What?"

"Not the art gallery," she said. "In Christian Gnosti-
cism, Abraxas was the god of both day and night. Well,
the long, bitter day of Adam's people is nearly over.
Down here, it's already given way to night."

"We must move on," Adam said. "To stay too long is
to tire the eyes so that they begin to play tricks. You will
see statues where none exist, wall paintings where none
have been painted. Huge figures at a distance will seem to
you tiny figures in a nearby niche. Tiny statues near to
hand will seem colossi viewed from across a chamber of
humbling bigness. Please, then, let's move on."

We obeyed, and what Adam predicted would happen,
happened. The longer we stayed underground the less
reliable our perceptions of what he was showing us. Today
I have a photographic record of our trip through the Montaraz

catacombs, but these photographs cannot communicate the impact of beholding such powerful art in its hallucinatory natural setting. Even my panoramas of the largest subterranean vaults are incapable of evoking the *feel*—the claustrophobic awe—of actually standing in those places and drinking in the glory of what the habilines had done. Once it is sundered from the context of the caves, the art loses meaning as well as immediacy. Like the Upper Paleolithic artists who painted the deep galleries of Lascaux in France and Altamira in Spain, Adam's people had decorated their grottoes, corridors, and rotundas for complicated religiohistorical purposes—rites of initiation and socialization— that would fail of fulfillment anywhere else. You had to *be* there for the art to have its context, and the art had to have this context for its beholders to internalize the sacredness and force of what they were seeing. That the caves eventually deceive the eye and disorient the body only adds to their importance in shaping the experience of the initiates.

What, then, whether "correctly" or "incorrectly," did we see?

With Adam as guide, and with Brian and RuthClaire as subordinate torchbearers (they had flashlights), we saw all that we could see without crawling, rappelling, or sprouting wings and flying. Here on Montaraz, a school of habiline Michelangelos had rendered the entire history of their species in red, black, yellow, and glowing-white symbols. This chronicle began with a parade of East African animals migrating in discrete herds along the wall leading away from the primeval habiline; it concluded with a procession of gunrunning boats, cruiseships, and propellerdriven pot planes along the way leading back to this anguished figure.

In between, deeper into the mountain, these same artists and their descendants had accomplished awesome murals synopsizing their people's years on the savannah, their uneasy early relationships with *Homo erectus* and *Homo sapiens*, their furtive exile in the foothills of Lolitabu, the terrible dwindling of their numbers during this protracted time, the capture of their surviving remnant by Kikembu warriors, their humiliation and sale in the slave market of

Zanzibar, their painful sea voyage from the Island of Cloves to the Isle of Coffee and Cacao, their years of anonymous labor on the plantations of the Rutherfords, and their near-extermination by the Tontons Macoutes of Papa Doc Duvalier in the early 1960s.

These sprawling, almost phosphorescent murals took our breath away. Moreover, in front of each mural stood a rock carving that subtly glossed the mural's principal theme. Among these statues were a droll granite hippopotamus, a dying australopithecine, a family of cave bats hanging upside down, and so on. I thought that Brian was going to squeeze his eyeballs out of his sockets examining these works. Adam was continually having to remind him to keep his hands off the statuary and the paintings, particularly the murals, for too much touching would probably alter or deface them. Although the habilines' pigments had good durability and color fastness, and although their artists had applied these pigments only to the most absorbent rock faces, the preservation of this subterranean wonder still depended on the respectful manners of its visitors.

"You can't continue to keep this secret!" Brian exclaimed, his words bouncing off a stagger of receding walls.

"We have to," RuthClaire said. "To save it."

"But Mr. Loyd's taking pictures of everything. Do you really believe that after they're published, another plague of professional schemers won't swoop down on Montaraz?"

Adam said, "But these pictures, you see, he won't be publishing."

"Why am I taking them, then?"

"As a record," Adam told me. "In case anything happens to destroy this magnificence—vandals, war, volcanic eruption."

Caroline asked what photographs, of what art, I *would* be allowed to publish or to carry around to gallery owners in my agent's portfolio. Adam replied that he was not asking me to represent the deceased habiline cave artists, but instead Erzulie, Hector, Toussaint, Dégrasse, and Alberoi. It was their work that I had come to photograph for business purposes, not the paintings and statuary now

surrounding and thoroughly overawing us. I would also be
given the chance to take some of their work back to
Atlanta with us. Granted, I was presently taking celluloid
inventory of these refrigerated basilica naves, but that was
only a sidelight—albeit an important one—of Caroline's
and my voyage to Montaraz. We had come to help the
living rather than the dead. The dead were beyond our
help, if not our memory and our gratitude.

"Where are Erzulie and the others' paintings?" Caroline asked.

"In Prix-des-Yeux," Adam said. "Mister Paul could
have photographed them this morning, I suppose, but we
became very involved, then, in our free election for a
species name. It's best to visit the caves early in the day so
that nightfall has no chance of catching one below ground.
When we get back, you can see the paintings in Erzulie's
hut."

"They couldn't possibly compare to these," Brian said,
making a sweeping gesture with one arm.

"Why should they?" RuthClaire said. "They're altogether
different."

"Not altogether," Adam corrected her. "Hector and
Erzulie did some of the cave paintings—farther on—of the
Duvalier persecution. Bogeymen with wicked rifles, our
young ones thrown from cliffs, and so on."

"I can understand their doing so," Brian said. "Hector
and Erzulie were alive during that very bad time. But *this*
stuff—" he pointed at a graceful two-dimensional scene of
a habiline hunting party chasing a pack of jackals off a
kill—"well, none of the Rutherford Remnant could have
possibly experienced it. None of your cave painters ever
lived in Africa. Even more obvious is the fact that none of
them lived there *two million years ago*."

"Very true," Adam acknowledged.

"So how did they do these paintings? How did they
render the *entire* history of their people in this unbelievably
glorious way?"

"*Vaudun*," RuthClaire said.

"I beg your pardon."

"Voodoo and revelation," RuthClaire told Brian. "Local *houngans* and *mambos* began putting *Les Gens* in touch with their species' collective unconscious all the way back in the eighteen-seventies. Adam figures that the earliest of these paintings date from then. Later, of course, some of the habilines became priests and priestesses themselves. Erzulie's a current example. In a less thoroughgoing way, so's my Adam. He always dresses like Papa Guedé—Baron Samedi, if you prefer—when he comes up here. That's to insure a sympathetic continuity between the dead habilines of Africa and those here on Montaraz who spiritually rediscovered them through voodoo.''

"That's what Adam was doing last night," I said. "What Adam and Erzulie were doing, I mean. With the snake.''

"Exactly," RuthClaire said. "Getting in touch with their habiline past. And a trip through these caves can do the same thing in a way that brings all the participants in the rite closer together. The first of the cave painters probably began their work believing that it would help their people survive. It would educate and unify them. It would give them a sense of the sacred. Unfortunately, the twentieth century has been pretty efficient at destroying the sacred. And how could any of the cave painters have known that a man named Papa Doc was going to be their Stalin, their Hitler, their Pol Pot? They'd never heard of any of *those* butchers.''

"Voodoo and revelation," Brian said. "You mentioned both those things. What did you mean by revelation?''

Adam's lamp lit him from beneath, giving him the look of a disembodied floating head. "That God revealed himself to early *Homo habilis* as he later revealed himself to the Hebrews. Even as we approach extinction, we know that we were favored by the earliest manifestation of God to a hominid species yet on record—even if it is on record only with us. We know that we have our own Christ.''

"Your own Christ?''

"Not a prehistoric Jesus of Nazareth," Adam told Brian. "But God in a form of flesh that any habiline—mute, illiterate, and naked—would see as holy. Our own Christ.''

Somehow, our sensoriums overloaded with data, we

groped our way to the surface and then back down the
mountain to Prix-des-Yeux. Hector remained behind in the
absolute darkness of the caves. He, after all, was their
curator.

IN THE village, Adam took Caroline and me into the hut
that Alberoi was sharing with Erzulie. The hut's interior
was larger than its haphazard outer walls and askew car-
pentering had led me to think possible. Alberoi himself
was on his knees toward the rear of the shanty, beneath a
hole in the roof through which fell a dusty column of
sunlight. Was he sick? I thought for a moment that a
stomach cramp had taken him, that he had assumed this
hangdog posture to vomit—but then I realized that he was
hovering over a small sheet of canvas tacked to a piece of
plywood lying flat on the floor. With the edge of a rusted
spoon, he was applying paint to the canvas. The artist in
his studio. Indeed, the hole in the roof was serving as a
skylight. A rain-warped hatch cover rested on one end of
this opening, just waiting for the hut's occupant to grab its
handle and slide it firmly into place. In the event of rain,
that act would provide a bit of protection. Mostly, though,
it would plunge the hut's interior into leaky gloom.

Speaking hesitant but surprisingly well-accented French,
Adam told Alberoi that we had come to see his and the
others' paintings. The habiline backed off his canvas and
squatted in a corner with his spine to the wall and his eyes
cutting back and forth between RuthClaire and me. He still
had his spoon. The pigment on it was a crimson acrylic,
making it appear that he had been sneaking tastes from a
forbidden bowl of strawberry Jell-O. A naughty boy caught
red-handed. We stepped around the clutter in the room—
including a large crate resting on a foundation of bricks, a
strip of oilcloth covering it—to see what Alberoi had been

painting. Fortunately, he was fairly far along in the work, and I could tell a good deal about his talent.

He *had* talent. The painting was a colorful market scene in the "naive" style that had dominated David Blau's Haitian exhibit at Abraxas. Accessible, representational art. Its human figures had an affinity with the human-habiline figures on the walls of Hector's caves, but its setting was modern. I recognized the market as the market in Rutherford's Port. Vegetable stalls, milling people in bright clothes, a pair of buses with baskets tied to their roofs, a group of native musicians soliciting money from tourists. What drew my eye faster than any of these conventional elements, however, was the grinning, dawdling giraffe in the midst of the crowd, none of whose members regarded the African animal's presence as a cause for either alarm or celebration. The giraffe belonged to the scene as surely as did the buses or the women balancing market items on their heads.

Adam was so delighted that he laughed out loud, one of the few times I had ever heard him do that. "Very good, Alberoi. *Excellent*."

"A giraffe?" Caroline said.

"He knows my secret," Adam said, as if that explained anything. "Do you think you could sell a painting like this, Mister Paul?"

"Sure. Without too much trouble, either."

"Come, then. Come see the others." He led me to the crate that was up on bricks—like a teen-ager's engineless jalopy, I thought—and when we were out of his way, Alberoi crept back to his painting, laid the spoon aside, and took up a fine-tipped brush from a tray of acrylics on the floor. With this brush, he began stippling in the mountain shrubbery behind the market. His concentration was intense. Adam, Caroline, and I might as well have been in Miami Beach.

Adam lifted the oilcloth covering the crate, which thin plywood dividers sectioned into at least a dozen compartments. Its cover off, the crate looked like a clumsy sort of filing cabinet. Each compartment held canvases, some of them rolled, some of them stretched taut on narrow frames.

We began pulling the paintings out of the crate and examining them. Almost all of them were in the bright naive style of the market scene that Alberoi was finishing. Several were portraits—or self-portraits—of the people of Prixdes-Yeux, the best being those of Erzulie and Dégrasse, as if the artists preferred doing the female countenance to the male. Three or four of the paintings, in stark contrast to the majority, radiated a gray or muddy-blue pessimism rather than a gaudy Caribbean joy, but *their* subjects were Tontons Macoutes or demons from the local voodoo lore. Flipping past these, I saw several moderately "realistic" renderings of such *loa* as Damballa, Petro Simbi, and Ogou Achade, who is famous for being able to drink a great deal without becoming drunk. Unlike the demons, the *loa* were presented positively—in citrus-fruit colors and broad but enigmatic smiles. Most of what I saw, I liked.

"Am I supposed to photograph these?" I asked Adam.

"Only if you want to. You can take some of them with you, if you like. Take a few, and champion them about, and sell them for modest prices. Keep your commission and send the rest to RuthClaire and me. We can ship others to you, if you believe your markets will bear such an influx."

"I'll take ten or twelve," I said. "It's probably best to see what kind of interest they're going to generate before taking the lot."

"You don't want *all* of them?" Caroline asked me. "You'll be able to sell every habiline painting, or toenail clipping, entrusted to you."

"But he's not going to let me identify them as habiline artifacts."

Caroline looked at Adam. "No? That's self-defeating."

"I am not trying to mop up, Miss Caroline, only to preserve what's preservable and to pay for the privilege as we go."

I had noticed an unusual, although perhaps not surprising, fact about all the paintings in the crate. "Adam, none of these is signed. Not one. What names do you want to give the artists? I'll need names for gallery owners and department-store buyers."

"Not *names*, Mister Paul. *One* name."

I glanced at Alberoi. "He didn't do all of these, did he? I thought you said that Erzulie painted, too. And all the others, for that matter."

"Erzulie does. Likewise the others. But only one name is required for all the paintings, don't you think? Look at them closely."

I did as Adam asked. Caroline helped me compare. The canvases, no matter their subjects, did in fact appear to be the work of a single hand. Brush strokes, color choices, draftsmanship, compositional techniques, overlay patterns— all these telltale criteria suggested but one artist. Even the bleak portraits of the Tontons Macoutes and the Arada-Dahomey demons differed from the other paintings only in the area of color choice, and it was hard to think of many artists who did not sometimes deliberately vary their palettes to encompass the full spectrum of human feelings. (RuthClaire had stayed with murky pastels for the *Souls* series, of course, but that series composed only a small fraction of her total output.) So, yes, it would make some sense, and tremendously simplify my marketing approach, to offer these paintings to prospective buyers as the work of a solitary talented naïf.

"How did they manage this? It's uncanny, Adam."

"There is nothing to manage. It happens. In this creative endeavor, at least, the feelings of one are the feelings of the others. Also, the talents. Because art requires leisure, they take turns at painting. They work turn by turn, by months. This is Alberoi's month. Next, Dégrasse's again. And so on. While the artist does art, the others tend their cassava patches, or forage for firewood, or barter at night with trustworthy islanders for food items and such. It works very well. No one becomes disgruntled."

Caroline said, "The canvases. The paints. Where do they get them?"

"Of late, RuthClaire and I have supplied them, but before we came, Erzulie would go to Rutherford's Port for them. She took small carven figures of rosewood or mahogany to trade in the art shop next to *Le Centre d'Art* near the International Hotel. It was her idea to begin this. She saw primitive paintings like these—not so good, really—selling to tourists in the bazaars. This crate holds almost three years' work. Not quite, though, because Erzulie has sold some of these paintings already. To guess who may have them is impossible.''

''Used-car dealers from Ohio and Arizona,'' Caroline said. ''Not knowing what they have, they hang them in their dens right next to these enormous paintings of bull-fighters on black velvet.''

''Maybe,'' Adam said. ''I don't know.''

I asked him what name he favored for our solitary naïf. We had to have a name. Would it be wrong to use his? Adam rejected this notion out of hand. He was not ashamed to put his signature on these canvases, but no one who knew his own paintings would believe for a moment that he had done these, too. The styles diverged too widely. He worked with the advantage, and the disadvantage, of a crystallized ego, whereas Alberoi and the others painted from the soft core of their unspoken common experience, from a collective unconscious too rubbery for any ''I'' ever to get a firm grip on it.

''What, then?''

''Fauvet,'' Adam said. ''Call this unknown artist Fauvet.''

''From *fauve?* That's a school of painters, Adam, not a single artist. And it means 'wild animal.' ''

He smiled broadly. ''Yes, I know.''

WE COULD have selected a dozen paintings, rolled them up, fitted them into our backpacks, and bid farewell to Prix-des-Yeux, but Adam insisted that we must not leave Montaraz without taking part in a *vaudun* ceremony. A ''rational pagan'' like me, he declared, ought to subject himself to at least one powerful mystical experience in his life, and he and Erzulie were just the people to see me safely through it. The other habilines would form a chorus, a kind of upland rara band, to play the drums and chant the necessary chants. By great good luck, tomorrow was Saturday, and the voodoo service would begin a split second after nightfall. In the day-long interval, of course, I must try to conclude my photographic inventory of the caves—while Caroline and RuthClaire drove into Rutherford's Port for the items essential to the service. None of these arrangements appealed to me, but the others voted in a block against me (two cheers for democracy), and so it was decided.

"There's danger?" I asked. "Adam and Erzulie have to see me *safely* through the ceremony?"

RuthClaire said, "You'll be all right, Paul. It's only dangerous if you provoke the *loa*. Keep an open—preferably, a blank—mind."

Caroline laughed. "He ought to be able to manage *that*." She was teasing, not being malicious, but the remark prompted RuthClaire's laughter, too. The resurgent chumminess of the two women, united again in playful ridicule, stung. That Brian Nollinger was also present did nothing to pluck out the barb.

"Why the hell do they have to go to Rutherford's Port?" I asked.

"To do this right," Adam said. "We require a baptismal gown large enough to fit you, Mister Paul. Also some rum, some *orgeat*, some Florida water, more cornmeal and oil, and two chickens."

"Chickens?"

"Don't ask," RuthClaire said, and she and Caroline began laughing again, their arms around each other like long-lost-but-lately-found sisters.

"Do we . . . do *we* have to get the chickens, too?" Caroline managed through this sputtering.

"I'll drive them," Brian volunteered. "They can do the trinket shopping. I'll buy the chickens."

"Live chickens," Adam cautioned him.

"They don't need you to chauffeur them, Herr Professor," I said.

"I *like* to buy chickens," RuthClaire interjected. "Even live ones. It's hauling them home in a jeep that rapidly loses its glamor."

Brian tried to explain himself: "I've got to check in with my employers. They give me a fairly free rein with this PADF project, but not so free that I can let them think I've skipped the island."

Adam's eyes widened, narrowed again. The anthropologist noticed. I think both men were remembering that nearly two years ago Nollinger had betrayed Adam to an agent of the Immigration and Naturalization Service. What was to prevent him from calling in the Tontons Macoutes in the hope of some kind of reward, either money or preferential treatment?

"I won't tell anyone what I've seen here," he said hurriedly. "You have my word."

A cynical snort escaped me.

"What would be the point?" he went on. "I'd destroy my chance to do important field work here. I'd put myself in competition with dozens—maybe hundreds—of other would-be ethnographers. Do you really believe I'd do that?"

"He wouldn't," Caroline said, speaking up for him. "Brian's not stupid. He knows what he's got in Prix-des-Yeux."

"And I want to see the *vaudun* ceremony tomorrow night. I'll buy the damn chickens. I'll truss them so they won't flap. I can't promise they won't cackle, but that's chickens for you."

"You could always crumble sleeping tablets into their feed," I said. "Do that methodically enough and maybe you'll get research funding from the National Institutes of Health. You could call your paper 'On the Tendency of Barnyard Fowls to Fall Asleep When Administered Mickeys.'"

This time Caroline and RuthClaire laughed with me, rather than at me, and I had the pleasure of seeing Good Old Brian's look of annoyance. But, hat in hand, he continued to argue that he would be foolish to reveal what he knew and that RuthClaire and Caroline would be better

off with him along than tooling down the coastal road
unaccompanied. He would help them load their purchases—
he would help them haggle for every item on their list. He
was an expert at open-air bargaining, a skill he had picked
up in the Dominican Republic.

"We'll keep an eye on him," RuthClaire told Adam.
"He'll report to his bosses at the Austin-Antilles office,
and that's it. No side trips. No private telephone calls.
Nothing like that."

"Okay by me," Brian said.

He had won. He gave me a look, eyebrow raised, of
ironic triumph.

Because RuthClaire and Caroline wanted showers and a
good night's rest before going into Rutherford's Port, they
hiked down the mountain that same afternoon and spent
the night in the beach cottage on Caicos Bay. Brian Nollinger
drove them. He made a pallet for himself on the porch,
and, the next morning, he wrestled the rented jeep along
the coastal road into the city so that the women could do
their *vaudun* shopping. This summary of events, of course,
I report second-hand, trusting that it does not deviate too
much from what actually happened. I slept very little that
night, though.

AT SUNRISE, the coolest part of the day, Dégrasse brought
me breakfast—mild Haitian coffee with *rapadou* and a
spoonful of powdered milk, a stew of plantains, and a
piece of odd-looking but tasty fish. The stew and the
coffee were hot, but the fish seemed to have been forked
out of a lukewarm brine. Although groggy from lack of
sleep, I ate ravenously. In the lee of the *houngfor*, Toussaint
and Dégrasse ate with me, neither of them paying me the
slightest heed. Then Adam appeared, wearing walking
shorts and a pair of Adidas sneakers. He handed me the
camera equipment and led me uphill through the fortifica-

tion of sablier trees to Hector's secret entrance to the caves.

We spent all day exploring them. I took so many pictures that my forefinger began to throb. Hector led us through the main rotunda and the most accessible galleries, but Adam, more nimble, took me into places that I had not already visited: *chatières*, rock chimneys, lofty crawlways. I saw ritual statuary, painted symbols, and weird faces cut out of the abrupt dead ends of labyrinthine tunnels. On at least six occasions, each time through a different corridor of stone, we surfaced to rest our eyes and let our minds clear. Then we would plunge back into the darkness, to grunt and wriggle our ways to deeper grottoes and more disorienting bouts of vertigo. It was a day-long dream, this activity.

A nightmare at tropical noon.

BY THE time Brian Nollinger and the two women returned, I was long since exhausted. Stars were beginning to wink through the twilight sky over Prix-des-Yeux, and all I wanted to do was sleep. Adam declined to let me. So I was standing bruised and bone-weary beside the *houngfor* when the marketing party came into camp with their duffles and baskets and trussed chickens, laughing ruefully through their own weariness, happy to have completed their journey.

Toussaint and Dégrasse fed the marketgoers, and Adam urged them to finish eating so that in his capacity as priest—in his self-appointed role as Lord Saturday—he could initiate the service that would allow Caroline and me to experience the full mystery and power of the *vaudun* gods. Only then, after all, would we be able to go back to Atlanta with a real appreciation of the spiritual forces that had sustained *Les Gens* in their Caribbean exile.

It was completely dark when Caroline, Brian, and I

entered the sacred peristyle of the habilines. In his top hat and tails, Adam led us inside. RuthClaire was waiting for us in the palm-thatched *tonnelle* with Erzulie, Toussaint, Dégrasse, and Alberoi. Even Hector was present, although he sat cross-legged in one corner next to a series of stylized cornmeal designs that Alberoi had laid out during the day. The three younger habilines occupied the low platform on which the *vaudun* drums rested, while Ruth-Claire and Erzulie walked about sprinkling water on the ground from flip-top metal pitchers like the creamers you might see in a roadside café in the states. An odd improvisatory touch.

Only Brian, Caroline, and I were going to be "couched" tonight, "put down on the floor" as potential communicants with the Yagaza gods. This service was for us; expressly for us. We wore white baptismal gowns similar to the cambric robe in which the habilines had first introduced themselves. RuthClaire and Caroline had bought our garments in Rutherford's Port, and they were spotless when we donned them, as immaculate as new wedding gowns. Candles in small globelike pots were burning at various places around the temple, and again I was reminded of the tacky accoutrements of a cheap stateside restaurant. Brian kept saying that he wished only to observe, not to participate, but Adam quite forcibly rejoined that no one who came to Prix-des-Yeux could do so as an observer, that participation in its life and rituals was a requisite for staying.

Erzulie lit two tall red tapers in cast-iron holders at either end of the drum platform. Then she centered herself in front of the platform and nodded at Adam. Behind her, Toussaint began to tap out a light beat on the tallest of the drums; he was seated on a rickety stool that permitted him to lean forward over their taut skins. Alberoi picked up this beat on the set known as *mama*, largest of the ceremonial drums, and Dégrasse began to counterpoint these rhythms on the drums called *boula*, smallest of the three kinds. Although the beat from these instruments was hypnotically insistent, the drummers played with a curious delicacy, as if fearful of waking the birds that had already

gone to roost. The faintness of the rhythms, even inside
the *houngfor*, mocked their purpose, which was to induce
a trance state in us communicants. And then I realized
that, to keep from revealing their presence and their whereabouts to any hostile strangers on the mountain, the habilines
must always conduct their *vaudun* service so.

"Lie down next to the *poteau mitan*," Adam commanded us. "Arrange yourselves like so many nesting
spoons."

Spoons don't nest, I thought. Spoonbills maybe, but not
spoons.

Brian Nollinger and my wife were not so literal in their
thinking; they went down to their knees by the center post
and then assumed clumsy fetal curls beside it, facing it.
The anthropologist was first, with Caroline cupping her
body into his and touching her chin to his shoulder blade. I
lay down behind her in the same intimate posture, vaguely
grateful that Brian had not tried to come between us in this
matter. I pressed my groin into Caroline's buttocks. Our
robes were no longer immaculate, our first contact with the
ground had soiled them.

Hector and the habiline drummers began to chant—faintly,
in a guttural singsong that either counterpointed or precisely echoed the rhythms of the Arada-Dahomey drums.
The sound was reminiscent of Adam's singing before he
had learned to speak, but at once rougher and more ritual-
ized. Caroline shuddered, and I shuddered with her. My
position on the floor kept me from seeing much, but the
ceiling of the *tonnelle* and the upper portions of the wall
were visible to me, and down one of the posts of the
peristyle came gliding the *couleuvre* that had linked Adam
and Erzulie on our first evening in camp. I wanted to get
up. A paralysis of either fear or fatigue had gripped me,
though, and all I could do was watch. The guttural chanting of the habiline choir veered into spooky falsetto registers.

Like a spry gnome, Erzulie began to dance. I could feel
her bare feet slapping the floor not far from the center
post. The python continued to flow down its own post
behind the drum platform, its bronze and garnet body
shimmering in the candlelight. A chicken began to cluck.

Two chickens. Erzulie's hand came into my line of vision,
swinging a chicken by its bound legs. Adam, who appeared above us near the *poteau mitan*, took this flapping
fowl from the little woman and promptly bit off its head.
He spat the head onto the floor, and also a mouthful of
feathers, and gouts of blood leapt from the decapitated
chicken's neck, fountaining around us in a gaudy, queasy-
making rain. Our white cambric gowns were spattered by
it, and the stench of the hot blood filled our nostrils along
with the fainter scent of flowing serpent.

"O great *loa*," Adam chanted, "your horses await your
mounting. Your horses invite you to ride." He had dropped
the headless chicken; it was beating the ground near the
center post with impotent, reflexive wing flaps. "*O loa,
come!*"

The second chicken, which Erzulie suddenly thrust aloft,
was cackling hysterically now. It, too, could smell blood;
it, too, could sense that a similar fate lay in store for it.
And, in fact, Erzulie beheaded the creature as quickly and
surely as Adam had executed the other. Blood parachuted
away from her like the pyrotechnic streamers of a crimson
Roman candle.

I shut my eyes. I covered my mouth and nose with my
palm. Caroline was as tense against me as a vibrating
metal pole. When I pushed my groin against her again—to
reassure us both—I was acutely conscious that my cock
was a shriveled nub. What, exactly, was mystical about
this ceremony? So far, it was nothing but an abomination
and a horror, and I wanted out.

Drumbeats, chanting, dancing.

Opening my eyes and peering down the length of Caroline's body, I saw that the *couleuvre* had reached the
ground. Only an arm's length from Caroline's feet, it was
loosely coiled at the base of the wall. My eyes strained to
see what it was doing. Having unhinged its lower jaw, it
was methodically swallowing—with terrible, wavelike
gulps—one of the headless chickens that, a moment past,
had been lying next to the center post. Feathers and all, I
thought. That damn serpent is gagging down its dinner,
feathers and all. I shut my eyes again.

Drumbeats, chanting, dancing. It seemed to me that Adam was dancing barefoot with the barefoot Erzulie. The drummers on the platform—or, at least, Dégrasse and Alberoi—were moving behind their instruments like impatient revelers in a stalled conga line. Even Hector had got to his feet. He was bouncing up and down behind us, stutter-stepping between the *vevés* that Alberoi had designed. I could *feel* him moving. I could feel *everyone* moving. The drumbeats, the chanting, and the dancing had begun to pulse in my temples like angry blood. Brian groaned, and Caroline's head came back so quickly that she split my bottom lip.

"O Legba," Adam cried, no longer dancing, "let the *loa* descend into this temple, permit them to mount their horses. We call for Agarou, god of ancestors, and Aïda Ovedo, virgin wife of Damballa, and likewise for Damballa himself, whose serpent we have propitiated. Let these three descend, and let them ride their horses, and let their horses run beneath them like thoroughbreds!"

Someone yanked my head back. Erzulie, I think. Over my split lip, she poured some *orgeat*, a syrupy drink with a strong tang of almonds. This, Adam said, was another offering to Damballa and his wife, consumed by us prostrate horses so that the *loa* could enjoy it once they had mounted us and brought us to our feet. If nothing else, the taste of the *orgeat* briefly routed the sickening odors of *couleuvre* and slaughtered chicken. Then I could smell rum. One of the habiline drummers was splashing it about, renewing the baptism of the already baptized ceremonial drums, being prodigal with the native *clairin* simply because *Les Gens* had it to be prodigal with.

"Come, Agarou! Mount your horse!"

The center post shook. Brian reached out to grip it, maybe to steady it. The electricity coursing through the *poteau mitan* galvanized him, imparted its energy to Caroline, and battered my own body like a thousand miniature tidal waves laboring to erode my identity. One moment, then, I was Paul Loyd, and the next I was nothing but obedient meat for the *loa* possessing me. In short, I was a horse.

AGAROU, THE *vaudun* god of ancestors, leapt down the lightning rod of the *poteau mitan* to convulse the robed body of the human being gripping its base. From this person, the god passed into Caroline Hanna, who kicked out spasmodically, and on through her briefly seized person into the terrified consciousness of her husband. Agarou *mounted* Loyd. Racked by the god's overmastering spiritual horsemanship, Loyd began to thrash, as a mustang ridden by a determined cowboy will buck for its helpless pride's sake, foreknowing itself tamed. In just that way, Loyd thrashed. He threw himself away from Caroline. He writhed about so violently on the hard-packed floor that his gown erased or smeared portions of the *vevés* drawn there.

Where stars had been earlier, storm clouds massed in dark bands above the mountain. Still putting up a token fight for his own body, Loyd could hear thunder cannonading across the sky as if from the ramparts of the Citadelle Laferrière, south of Cap-Haïtien on Haiti itself. And with each new roll of thunder, the mounted man convulsed.

Even as they continued to drum or dance, the habilines were watching Loyd. Hector, the blind one, had moved into a corner to escape being knocked down by the erratic flailings of his arms and legs. Erzulie, however, had taken his predicament as a challenge to her skill as a dancer; above him, she was leaping from foot to foot, guessing with uncanny instinct where to place her feet without stepping on him. Adam, meanwhile, had renewed his plea for Aïda Ovedo and her husband Damballa to come down the center post into the temple.

The thunder above the mountain boomed even louder, and the submerged kernel of Paul Loyd's consciousness realized that the noise of the storm would completely drown out that of the *vaudun* service. He could no longer hope for rescue by sympathetic islanders. Agarou had him.

"Up, Agarou!" Adam encouraged the *loa*. "Ride your horse to revelation! Show your horse the god who showed himself to our ancestors!"

Loyd could feel himself surrendering to the inevitable. His movements became less violent. He bridged his *loa*-possessed body so that his heels and the back of his head were holding him off the ground. His eyes searched the trinket-hung enclosure for sympathy. Where was RuthClaire? At last, he found her. She was in the corner opposite Hector's, regarding him with a grimace of appalled compassion. How must he look to her? It was all he could do to hold his eyeballs still so that they could focus her image. Maybe she had never seen a possession exactly like this one. She was frightened as well as appalled.

"Adam!" she said, trying to be heard over the drumming and the thunder. "Adam, stop it! I think it's killing him!"

Killing me, thought Loyd dispassionately. This is killing me.

The habiline in top hat and tails turned to his wife. "Oh, no, Miss RuthClaire, it is bringing him to life. It is bringing him, I think, to a knowledge that, otherwise, he could not so vividly acquire."

Loyd placed his forearms on the floor parallel to his arched body. Pushing with them, he sprang up off the ground like a limbo dancer who has just crept beneath the lowest level of the bar. Upright, his body swayed in the candlelit geometries of the temple. He could see Caroline and the anthropologist lying beside the center post, entranced but not yet possessed, their blood-spattered baptismal gowns giving them the appearance of murder victims. An interesting, but not an especially disturbing, sight. They weren't dead, after all, and once Aïda Ovedo and Damballa mounted them, he would have company in his spiritual slavery.

"*Aaaawwgh*," he said. Spit ran down his lip and chin.

In his Baron Samedi costume, Adam did an ironic bow. "Welcome, Agarou. Welcome, Agarou. Welcome, Agarou."

Agarou did a scissoring dance step.

"After such an entrance," Adam said, "you must have great hunger." He swept a headless chicken off the floor, dug the nails of both hands into its breast, and broke it open with a wicked popping motion. From this bloody rent, he pulled those pieces of the entrails that Loyd had never used in his culinary operations at the West Bank. Adam handed these items to Agarou, who, to Loyd's helpless consternation, began to eat them. They were warm and slippery, hard to chew, but Agarou got them down almost as easily as the *couleuvre* had engorged the entire unplucked body of the other chicken.

RuthClaire (Loyd noticed, stealing a look through the *vaudun* god's eyes) had left the *houngfor*. Why? he wondered. Once, not so long ago, she had tolerated the barbaric eating habits of her habiline husband.

Rain began to sheet down. It rattled the palm-frond thatching of the *tonnelle*. It blew in through the openings at the top of the peristyle's walls. It dripped from the eaves and from seams in the underside of the roof. No longer inhibited by the need to play softly, the drummers began to pound their instruments with abandon. The noise inside and outside the swaying building crescendoed and crescendoed again. In Loyd's benumbed body, Agarou turned his face upward and opened his blood-stained mouth to the life-giving waters of which his fellow *loa* Damballa was the presiding deity. He had led his horse to water, and he had made him drink.

Loyd was drowning not only in this sudden deluge, but also in the ancient personality of the *loa* riding him. Rain veiled his eyes. It broke through the roof of the *tonnelle* and extinguished the candles in their plastic pots. The pots hissed their dismay. Or maybe it was the python hissing, swimming toward him in the blinding downpour like a great ruby and golden eel. In fact, of all the former inhabitants of the structure dissolving in this summer rain, the serpent was the only one that Loyd could see. He knelt—Agarou made him kneel—to embrace the creature, which lifted its head from the floor and kissed him on the lips with a double flicker of its tongue. Whereupon the rain ceased, and the dripping echoes of its cessation were heard, and Agarou found himself alone on the flank of his Caribbean Olympus.

"Giddyup, horse," the *loa* said.

Facing uphill, Loyd began to walk. (*Agarou* began to walk.) He felt himself to be two consciousnesses at once, and he had the further conviction that as he strode away from Prix-des-Yeux (which had dissolved in the rain along with the *vaudun* temple) he was climbing not one but two mountains. First, of course, was the mountain on the tip of Pointe d'Inagua here in Manzanillo Bay, but superimposed spiritually on that landscape were the lineaments of Mount Tharaka in the present-day African nation of Zarakal.

Each time Loyd stopped and looked back down the mountain, he saw—by the sheen of intermittent lightning flashes—first the ebony ripples of the Atlantic Ocean and then the vast antelope-dotted expanse of the Zarakali plains. They alternated, these contrasting features, and with them Loyd's twentieth-century present and East Africa's Pleistocene past likewise alternated—so that, ridden by Agarou, he was two different consciousnesses at two different places at two different times. How could such a thing be? Well, the *vaudun* service had done its work. The drumming, the chanting, the dancing. And then, of course, the python had kissed him, both to acknowledge Agarou's power over him and to link his fitfully self-aware consciousness to distant places and earlier times.

Loyd-*loa* continued his hike uphill. The fragrant scent of coffee blossoms hovered over everything, wonderfully fresh after the rain. Where was Agarou going? It occurred to Loyd that if the *loa* riding him tried to take him very far, he—his body—would probably collapse. (You can't ride a dead horse.) He had worn himself out crawling through the habiline caves, and a forced diet of chicken innards was not likely to counteract his body's fatigue. Then Loyd heard himself laugh. It was Agarou laughing through him: the god had found his ignorance of the mechanism of possession amusing. His body would do whatever Agarou demanded of it for as long as Agarou spurred and controlled it. (You *can* ride a dead horse—at

least until its last vestiges of mind have d....
insentient randomness.) Loyd resigned himself to a ....
hike, and an even longer captivity.

At last the horse came to a palisade of mastodon skulls,
sabre-tooth tiger tusks, and chalicothere skeletons twenty
or thirty feet high. These bones were locked together like
pieces of an enormous ivory puzzle, alternately grim and
dazzling in the lightning-riven night. Loyd-*loa* approached
them, intent on discovering a solution. He gripped a pair
of weather-polished tusks and swung himself between them
into the labyrinthine heart of the puzzle. Inside the barrier,
he ducked and climbed and contorted his body to find
passage through the bones. A spur on a set of wildebeest
horns stabbed him in the side, and he cried aloud. Let me
out of here, Loyd thought, and his plea was for escape
from both Agarou and this maze of treacherous ivory.

More coherently, Loyd thought, I'm in the picket of
sablier trees, not a pile of interlocking tusks and antlers.

And he was. The image of a bone-surrounded Mount
Tharaka had disguised from him the reality of the Haitian
mountain. It was Agarou who preferred the surrealism of
the ancient African past, and because of Agarou's ascen-
dancy, Loyd had not been able to see the sablier hedge.
Well, they were through it now, scrambling uphill in the
open toward the shrub-lined cut where the entrance to the
caves was concealed. Agarou-on-Loyd halted in a three-
point stance and in a gust of ozone-heavy wind looked
down the mountain at Inagua Bay. Sea and savannah did
their dizzying switch, a sail boat briefly metamorphosing
into an albino elephant and a flight of bats into a flock of
prehistoric flamingos.

Then reality came back.

How am I going to see down there? Loyd protested.

His hand raised a flashlight to face level (an instrument
he could not recall the god picking up), but when he
thumbed its button, no beam shot forth. The silly thing
was useless.

This won't do, Loyd told the god of ancestors.

Agarou replied, Do gods need eyes to see in your
material darkness? We possess the second sight of divinity.

betrayed into long

377

...e no more. And Agarou laughed at
...k of faith of his human horse, and
...he bush through which Hector habitually
...es, and slid him down a body-worn slide into
...ss and the breathy cool of the buried past.

...see! Loyd cried to his *vaudun* rider.

Open your eyes, mon! Open your eyes!

Not realizing that they had been closed, Loyd opened
his eyes. He could see. What he saw, however, came to
him as if by ultraviolet illumination. The cave walls glinted
silver and purple-red, as if each rock fracture disclosed a
sweating seam of either liquid mercury or grape jelly.
Also, in order to make out the size and shape of the
objects around him, Loyd had to look at them peripherally.
A straight-on gaze dissolved into formless mist whatever
he was trying to view. As a result, to penetrate the secrets
of the ultraviolet gloom, he was constantly doing quick or
slow double-takes, lifting or lowering his eyes, ducking
and feinting. He felt like a soul in hell.

Yagaza, Agarou corrected him. Africa. The afterlife.

At which point he understood that Agarou had permitted
his own consciousness to resume control of his body. He
was still possessed—the *loa* had not dismounted, had instead merely dropped the reins—but now his own peculiar
Loyd-ness was free to direct his steps either here or there
in these weird caves. Agarou had retreated to a spectator's
position behind his eyes. (Undoubtedly, it was Agarou
who was *allowing* him to see.) Therefore, it was Loyd's
will rather than the *loa*'s that counted, now. My will be
done, Loyd thought. My kingdom's come, and it's hell
rather than heaven. . . .

Shadows in the ultraviolet told him that he was not
alone. He was surrounded by habiline wraiths, a hunting
party of naked males from the Early Pleistocene. He was
walking in their midst in his glowing cambric baptismal
gown, a sunlit saint in a pit of resurrected time. He told
himself to stop, to turn back and climb out of the gloom
the same way he had entered—but the habilines all about
him carried him forward against his will. *My* will, he

thought. I can't do my will. I'm doing *theirs*. And although he marched along with them in apparent freedom, a head and a half taller than the tallest of the ghostly hominids, he had no real choice but to follow their lead and to wish that he were less gaudily dressed and a good deal smaller. And when the habilines began to run, they pulled him along—he tottered above them like an effigy on a shoulder-borne float in a religious procession.

They were in the caves, and yet they were also in a dry arroyo on the African veldt. The paintings that Loyd had already photographed spun by on the arroyo's walls like fissures and fault lines, intrusions and alluvial deposits. The habilines were on the track of a potential kill. They were carrying bone clubs and primitive stone knives. One of the two-legged shadows in front of Loyd threw its club, which disappeared end over end into the darkness—to strike something that vented an echoing yelp of pain. In the wake of this yelp, more clubs were flung. If Loyd could trust the piteous sounds that then ensued, many of these tosses also hit their target. Excitement built among the hominids. Loyd was pulled along even faster than before.

A gravity well, he thought. A singularity. I'm being sucked into bottomless night with a horde of protohuman spirits. . . .

These agile ghosts scampered away from him, toward their kill, releasing him confused and breathless to the dark. Now, if he wanted, he could turn around and grope his way back to the exit. No. No, he couldn't. Curiosity about what the habilines had wounded here in this pocket of space-time had him in its grip. He had to see—if seeing it really was—their mysterious victim for himself. And so, self-conscious in his blood-spattered robe, biting his split lip, he walked toward the place that the habilines appeared to have gone. Gradually, the odd red light visible all about him overlapped into this hidden place, and he pushed his way through the befuddled hunters to look down on their prey.

It was a monstrous hyena, a prehistoric specimen. Or else it was a large quasi-human creature with the head of a

hyena. In the bad light, Loyd had trouble deciding. Whatever it was, the weirdness of its anatomy had halted the
habilines in their tracks. It was sitting against a chromium
outcropping of rock like a man trying to recover from a
long run. Hyena or hominid? The head gave one message,
the body another. Chest, arms, pelvis, and legs suggested
a vaguely deformed primate, but the ears, snout, and teeth
said hyena . . . or dog . . . or jackal. The eyes had a
pleading human twinkle that further confused things. The
habilines knew that no wounded hyena in their experience
had ever assumed this manlike posture, and they were
chary of the beast.

Once, Loyd suddenly understood, something like this
had actually happened. With Agarou's blessing, I'm wit-
nessing what a real band of habiline hunters witnessed in
Africa over two million years ago. For them, this is an
archetypal event. It defined them as human—before the
advent of speech—in a spiritual or metaphysical sense.
And they know it. . . .

Exhausted and bleeding, the hyena-hominid pulled itself
to its feet. It towered over the hunters. If only by a little, it
was taller than Loyd, too. Although by every objective
sign the creature appeared to be at the mercy of the
habilines, they made no attempt to deal it a death blow.
The creature commanded their awe. Humbling them by its
majestic height and its indifference to its own great suffering, it completely disarmed them. Loyd was frightened.
He felt like running, but the habilines, anticipating revelation, held their ground. This eerie stand-off continued.

Finally, the hyena-hominid bowed its doglike head. This
gesture of resignation or reverence or bodily surrender
turned into something else, an act both grotesque and
moving. The creature, stretching out its arms and gripping
the rock face behind it for support, kept bending forward
until its snout was nuzzling its left breast. The vertebrae on
its neck and spine strained against its taut hide. With a jerk
of its head, the creature tore the flesh of its own pectoral
muscle. Then it straightened, removed one hand from the
wall, and cupped from this narrow wound its own vividly
beating heart, which it held out to the wonderstruck habiline

wraiths as an offering of love and validation. All who partook of it would know that the Mind implicit in Nature had consciously affirmed their lives—through the agency of this hyena-headed messenger. Their salvation lay in this knowledge and in their ability to live harmoniously with one another in a necessarily imperfect world.

Come, the hyena-hominid challenged its pursuers, still holding out its heart. Come and partake of my life's blood.

The largest of the habilines, the alpha male of their spectral hunting party, went forward to accept the offering. Dwarfed by the dog-headed messenger, he tasted of the heart. Having tasted, he carried the heart to each expectant member of the band, and they, too, cupped the beating organ to their mouths and bit into it and took into themselves a living piece of their miraculous prey. Loyd could only watch. None of the habilines brought the heart to him—clearly, they regarded him as alien to their world, too alien to benefit from this rite—and he was grateful to them for ignoring his presence. When the heart was altogether eaten, the gloom of the catacombs absorbed the hominids into itself, and Loyd found that he was alone with the creature that had sacrificed its heart to feed a small remnant of feisty but unprepossessing human forebears.

Agarou, the *vaudun* god of ancestors, had mediated this confrontation in the immaterial realm of Yagaza, but now it was Loyd who had to face the hyena hominid and to demand of it some explanation for its behavior. His fear came back. What authority did he have to question such a being? What answers—if any—could he expect from it? The silver-crimson light of the caves coalesced around the two of them like a contracting womb. . . .

LOYD: Who are you?

(*The hyena-hominid only laughs. Its demeaning animalish laughter echoes in the half-light like a huge coil unwinding.*)

LOYD (*apprehensively insistent*): I said, Who are you?

I AM: Names fail. If you like, call me Yagaza, or

Lord, or Logos, or even *Anima Mundi*. None of these titles suits absolutely, but if you have to have a name, pick something that doesn't belittle me.

LOYD: God?

I AM: In this context, Yagaza might be more appropriate. After all, I'm Adam's God—Adam Montaraz's, that is. But, ultimately, I'm yours, too.

LOYD: I thought Yagaza meant Africa—either Africa or the afterlife.

I AM: In the *vaudun* scheme of things, it does. Because you're here through the good offices of Agarou, perhaps we should honor him by adopting *vaudun* terminology. Without that body of ritual, we wouldn't be talking like this.

LOYD: I can't call you Yagaza. I'm not a voodooist. I'm a victim of possession, but I'm not a voodooist. And you—you call yourself Adam's God, but all I can see, squinting and cocking my head, is a heartless chimera, part man-ape and part African scavenger.

(*The hyena-headed being reaches up and places both palms against the sides of its face. It lifts this face away like a mask, revealing the horror of a human countenance that has been three quarters obliterated by .38-caliber ammunition. Loyd is reminded of Craig Puddicombe in the parking lot behind Abraxas; he cannot understand why God would choose to appear to him in the mutilated guise of a dead murderer. He tries to turn aside, but he cannot make his possessed body obey even the simplest internal command.*)

LOYD: Please. Don't make me look at you like this. It's crueler than you know.

I AM (*restoring the hyena mask*): That I doubt. It's just that I have no desire to slip my share of responsibility in matters that you must regard as terrible manifestations of evil. I don't explicitly order them, but I can't arbitrarily countermand them without sabotaging creation itself.

LOYD: But you *can* inject yourself into the affairs of your temporal creation, can't you? You did that with your hyena-hominid revelation to Adam's Pleistocene ancestors. You've just let me witness a reenactment of that "disclosure event."

I AM: What I've permitted you to see is an *allegory* of that event intelligible to your contemporary human understanding. Had I given you a reenactment of the event as it actually occurred, you would have utterly misinterpreted it. More than likely, you would have missed its sacred aspect completely.

LOYD: But you *were* there, weren't you? You made yourself manifest in the otherwise mundane history of the planet. You appeared to a small band of habilines whom most of us today would dismiss as protohumans.

I AM: I did.

LOYD: Why?

I AM: You've already anticipated me here. To demonstrate my love for them. To affirm them. To validate their struggles to survive and evolve.

LOYD: Can your appearance to them possibly have had any measurable effect? At first, you terrified them. Momentarily, you made them forget their terror by appeasing their hunger. That's all, surely.

I AM: The Rutherford Remnant—Adam, Erzulie, Hector, Toussaint, Dégrasse, and Alberoi—demonstrates that it *did* have a lasting effect. They continue to celebrate my earliest quasi-human incarnation by observing Voodoo Saturday Night. In fact, *you're* celebrating that pivotal event with them. Possessed by Agarou, god of ancestors, you're a *vaudun* devotee in spite of yourself, Mister Paul.

LOYD: But what if there were no Rutherford Remnant? What if the species known as *Homo habilis* had died out approximately when most paleoanthropologists once supposed, namely, two million years ago?

I AM: Does a falling tree land with a thud if there's no one there to register the thud? Yes. The thud exists as a receivable potentiality in the sound waves generated by the tree's impact with the ground. Because I was received by creatures now dead hardly suffices to demonstrate that I wasn't received at all. I appeared to them, and they knew themselves blessed—validated, if you prefer—by my holy concern.

LOYD (*shaking his head*): Impossible.

I AM: It wounds your vanity to think that *Homo sapiens* was not the first hominid species to experience a sacred disclosure event?

LOYD: You wrong me, Yagaza. Frankly, I'm by no means certain that *Homo sapiens* has ever experienced its *own* such event. Frankly, I doubt it. Frankly, I've *always* doubted it.

I AM (*laughing in a melancholy-merry hyena voice*): Then what about this, Mister Paul? What's happening to you now?

LOYD: I'm possessed. I'm dreaming. I'm talking to some sardonic corner of my own consciousness, not to—God forgive me—God.

I AM: But God has a corner of your consciousness, doesn't he? If God created you, why, then, he has a lien on all the physico-spiritual systems making up your identity. You're one of my most valuable means of comprehending myself—along with all the other self-aware entities, terrestrial or otherwise, of an ever-questing creation. You ought to take advantage of your dreaming—your *possession*—to assist me in this self-reflexive quest.

LOYD: You called yourself Adam's God. Why? Because you appeared in hyena-hominid form to his ancestors?

I AM: In part, certainly. But also because in searching for an element of the sacred to append to his Batesonian philosophy of evolutionary holism, which lacks such a dimension, he decided to repostulate God. I'm the God That Is, but I'm also the God that Adam humbly repostulated. Your species' hunger for the sacred, going back even to Pleistocene times, doesn't arise in the *absence* of satisfying spiritual meat, but in response to its availability in the miraculous slaughterhouse of creation. I AM that meat. I AM the architect of the sacred abattoir. Those who refuse to ignore their hunger will eventually find me.

LOYD: Adam told Alistair Patrick Blair that you have both a timeless aspect and a necessary temporality that involves you in the time-bound doings of the material world. Is that true? It sounds paradoxical, probably even impossible.

I AM: Like a man who simultaneously *has* a head and *doesn't have* a head?

LOYD: Exactly. That was Blair's precise objection.

I AM: Well, my temporal aspect hardly requires lengthy justification, does it? In that aspect, or one manifestation of it, I am talking to you now. And in one manifestation of that aspect, I possess both a hyena's head and the mutilated face of the man who killed your godson. And, if you must know, no head at all.

LOYD: All right. Fine. If you're conversing with me, then you obviously depend on the flow of time to achieve such communication. But how can you simultaneously—ah, but that's the wrong word, isn't it—how can you also have the quality of timelessness that places you either outside or above the ongoing mayhem and muck of the physical universe?

I AM: Because you're a captive of time yourself,

Mister Paul, this is going to be hard to explain. Timelessness is not an attribute you're particularly well-equipped to understand.

LOYD: Oh, I see. You're gearing up for a cop-out.

I AM: Not at all. If you can accept Heisenberg's uncertainty principle in its specific application to quantum theory, confessing that one may know either where a subatomic particle is or how it happens to be moving, but not both attributes at once, why can't you adopt a similar uncertainty principle to a concept as grand and ineffable as that of God? Or, to employ another analogy, if light can be either a particle or a wave depending on the perspective and the intentions of the observer, why can't God be a temporal being within the context of creation and a timeless entity in his orientation above, or outside, the universe of matter and mutability? The supposition that he must be one or the other is a reflection of human limitation, which arises not only from the finite capacity of human understanding but also from your existential immersion in time itself.

LOYD: This isn't fair. A man who's spent most of his adult life concocting recipes for cheesecake and pasta dishes shouldn't have to argue theology with God.

I AM: Who better than you, Mister Paul? A person who has fed publicans and sinners, sociologists and habilines, knows something of what it means to satisfy hunger—as well as to fail in that task.

LOYD: Okay, okay. You've mentioned subatomic particles—our ability to know either their location or their motion, but not both. And you've mentioned that light can be either a particle or a wave depending on what the observer is trying to find out. But these analogies break down in this situation because atoms and light are temporal phenomena themselves. They don't have any atemporal attributes at all.

I AM: Congratulations on underscoring the obvious.

Can you think of *any* phenomena that aren't finally time-bound or time-determined?

LOYD *(chagrined)*: I'm afraid I can't.

I AM: Then maybe you can see the difficulty of what I'm trying to explain. If you *could* think of any examples, I'd try to work them into illustrative metaphors for the coincident timelessness and temporality of God. But since you can't, I'm stuck with phenomena that operate within the dimension of time. As a result, everything I tell you is an approximation of something largely inexpressible.

LOYD: Go on. I'll try to follow.

I AM: Only in my timeless aspect—my supratemporal identity—am I utterly without blemish. There, I AM perfect and fulfilled and all-knowing and, yes, changeless. What I know never alters because it encompasses—until the "end" of "time"—the totality of changes past, present, and future in the physical universe. At my deliberate impetus, time began—space-time began—on the boundary between timelessness and temporality. And one day, in figurative temporal terms, I will put period to time by allowing it to run the course that I have already omnisciently calibrated and clocked. Whereupon I will necessarily subsume my temporal avatars and once again simply BE, perhaps from Everlasting to Everlasting. I can't be more specific than this because my own immersion in the flow of universal time clouds my clairvoyance. Trapped here with you, Mister Paul, I see through a glass darkly—but with a vision, in comparison to your own, pristine and pellucid.

LOYD: Why would a perfect, fulfilled, all-knowing, and changeless deity even bother to inflate the balloon of the physical cosmos? Isn't that a capricious act? An unnecessary waste of energy?

I AM: I like your metaphor. It has a festive spontaneity totally in accord with the motives of God in my timeless aspect. These motives are complex, innate, and immutable, but they center on the impulse to celebrate my self-awareness with living consciousnesses outside myself. This impulse requires a physical creation—the Big Bang that gave birth to space-time and eventually all the galactic populations.

LOYD: How can you describe a God with impulses as "fulfilled"?

I AM: In temporal terms, I can't. But temporal terms are all we have here. It might be more accurate to say that even in my timeless aspect I possess the positive attribute of generosity. In the absence of beneficiaries, however, no one but I could possibly document my possession of this trait. Therefore, I inflated the balloon of the cosmos to affirm the otherwise pointless fact of my generosity. I didn't *need* to do so, I *wanted* to do so. Even this falls short of the reality, Mister Paul, but, here and now, I can scarcely do better.

LOYD: Never mind. What about suffering and death and injustice? How do you square the murder of an innocent child with your hypothetical generosity as the God Beyond Time?

I AM: I don't. I don't even try. Every secondary creation of any complexity is flawed. Perfections of various wonderful kinds may occur within it, of course, but the encompassing whole—well, its imperfections are equally numerous. In fact, some of the perfections depend upon them. The just recognize justice by unhappy exposure to its opposite. The wise distill their—

LOYD (*waving his hand in the gelatinous light*): I've heard all this before. It's a recipe for carrion-comfort, dog-god.

I AM: What you have to remember is that no matter how terrible the world sometimes seems, no matter how cruel or pointless, the Mind that nudged its various ecosystems toward the evolution of self-aware consciousness did so out of an inexpressible generosity.

LOYD: A ponderous vanity, you mean.

I AM: And the timeless Mind whose temporal avatars intrude upon creation to shape and direct it in their puny ways—well, that Mind releases them like antibodies into the besieged body of the world. There they help the sentient creatures of faith and good will neutralize the poisons of entropy and accident. I came for that reason. So did Buddha, and Jesus of Nazareth, and Gandhi, and perhaps even the latter-day habiline whom you know as Adam Montaraz. In any case, Mister Paul, Adam came to extend the family of humankind. He came to demonstrate—via his struggle for personal revelation—the interconnectedness of creation.

LOYD (*flailing at the womb of visible darkness containing him*): Well, I *curse* you in your impotent timeless aspect! The holy physicians you send us are quacks! Better for us never to have been than to suffer so grievously from the imperfections built into your misbegotten creation!

I AM: Not at all. Not at all.

(*Yagaza, the dog-god, catches Loyd's hands and pins them to his sides. The snout of the upright creature hovers only inches from the possessed man's face. Loyd can smell the odor of carrion on its breath, the unmistakable stench of the decaying human features— Craig Puddicombe's—behind its hyena mask. He grips the wound in the creature's chest with one hand and averts his face.*)

LOYD (*mockingly*): Not at all. Not at all. How does knowing that God possesses both a temporal and a timeless aspect improve our lot, Yagaza? What difference—*what goddamn difference*—does it make?

I AM: By repostulating me as the Alpha and Omega, the supreme primal-and-ultimate holistic concept, you can believe in me again. You can rediscover in me the ground of your own existence.

LOYD *(struggling in Yagaza's powerful hands)*: What the hell for?

I AM: To realize again that you were spawned by a multidimensional, paratemporal Benevolence and that even your most pointless-appearing torments *mean*, Mister Paul. They resonate forever in the all-encompassing Mind of God.

LOYD *(weeping bitterly)*: Hooray for our resonating torments. Hooray, hooray. What a comfort, what a comfort. . . .

THE POSSESSED man slumped from Yagaza's immaterial embrace. Meanwhile, Agarou, god of ancestors, was climbing out of the deep psychic grotto into which he had earlier purposely withdrawn. He was climbing out of it to remount the body of Paul Loyd. His intention was to ride his human horse back into the rainy compass of Prix-des-Yeux and its *houngfor*. Regaining control was not hard. Because Loyd had so little fight left in him, Agarou easily routed the man's defenses, occupied his overloaded mind, and looked out through his eyes. He found that Loyd was sitting at the feet of the agonized statue of *Homo habilis primus*. One of Loyd's hands tenaciously clutched the statue's stone phallus, apparently to keep him from toppling all the way over.

Let go of me, Loyd told Agarou. I'm sick and tired of the selfish double dealings of gods.

The one who must release you is coming now, Agarou said. Patience.

Loyd peered through the *loa*'s eyes—*his* eyes, if only he could get them back—at the flashlight beams crisscrossing in the entrance shaft to the upland cave system. A small party of people was approaching him. He could see them limned in nappy silhouette behind, or off to the sides of, the bobbing flashlight beams. These were figures of blood and substance, not habiline ghosts, and the closer they came, the more palpable and realistic grew the light accompanying them. The darkness in the catacombs began to relinquish its ultraviolet character to the dim grittiness of the visible spectrum. That meant that Agarou's hold on him was weakening.

Caroline knelt beside him. Adam knelt beside him. Their clothes were drenched, their faces beaded with tropical rain. Behind them, looking down on him, stood two sinister-looking men whom Loyd could not place and whose postures bespoke an alert and belligerent impatience. They were carrying weapons—rifles or submachine guns. Even the *loa* possessing him recoiled from the shadowy image of these figures, and Loyd found himself struggling to focus on Caroline and her habiline protector. Caroline looked like a drowned angel; Adam, a refugee from the bombed-out set of a 1930s Hollywood musical starring Fred Astaire. (It was the top hat and tails that did it.)

"Come forth, Mister Paul," urged Adam in his hoarsest whisper. "Come forth from your possession by Agarou, god of ancestors."

I SAT up straighter. Embarrassed, I let go of the smooth lustrous prick of the statue behind me. I blinked against the flashlight beams of the armed men regarding me with equal measures of curiosity and contempt.

"What the hell's going on?"

Caroline kissed my forehead. She nodded in the direction of the nearer of the beret-wearing security men. "You remember Lieutenant Bacalou, Paul? We met him on the boat coming over from Cap-Haïtien."

''Hello again,'' Lieutenant Bacalou said, saluting me with a curt nod. His face was only partially visible, but I imagined that he had just flashed me a quick, superior smile.

Groggy, I tried to stand. Caroline and Adam did all they could to help me. With their support, I made it, but momentarily teetered like an inflatable punch-me toy trying to regain its equilibrium. Five minutes ago, after all, I had been talking to God—scoring points against him in an emotional metaphysical debate that had utterly wrung me out. To find this grim pair of Tontons Macoutes in his place, holding my wife and my friend at gun point, seemed a bleak variation of a nightmare that had already taken place in Beulah Fork. E. L. Teavers and the Klan, Lieutenant Bacalou and another of Baby Doc's rifle-toting bogeymen. They were mirror images. Or maybe this cave was the darkroom in which the negatives of the unsmiling macoutes would reveal themselves as pernicious double exposures. No matter where we went, we could not escape the merciless pursuit of zealots.

''All right,'' I managed. ''Tell me something about this.''

Caroline explained that Lieutenant Bacalou and his men had burst into the *houngfor* shortly after I, as Agarou's human mount, had left it. The rain and my sudden leavetaking had forced their hand—they had had to show themselves before assessing the entire situation to the lieutenant's satisfaction. By accident, then, the macoutes had disrupted the *vaudun* ceremony at exactly the right moment to foil the efforts of the rain god Damballa and his bride Aïda Ovedo to possess Brian and Caroline. (I was almost glad to hear this. The idea of Caroline's being the anthropologist's consort, even in the twilight world of *loa* possession, was repugnant to me.) The men under Bacalou's command had entered the peristyle so unexpectedly that RuthClaire had screamed and the habilines had panicked. Toussaint was dead. He had attacked the first man into the *tonnelle*—not Bacalou, but an agent from the Pointe d'Inagua security post—and the man had riddled him at close range with his submachine gun. In the resultant confusion, Alberoi and Dégrasse had broken through the wall behind the drum platform and escaped into the night.

"Erzulie? Hector?"

"They're okay," Caroline assured me. "Under guard in a dry corner. Brian and RuthClaire are with them down there, likewise under guard."

I looked at Bacalou. "Did you bring a whole army up here with you?"

"Not even a platoon," he said with easy irony. "At first, Monsieur Loyd, it was only Philomé and I who followed the two women and the Austin-Antilles man up here from Rutherford's Port." He swung his flashlight in an arc that briefly illuminated his stocky partner's face. "Monsieur Loyd, Philomé Bobo."

"*Enchanté*," said Bobo. But if there was anything he did *not* sound, it was charmed.

"On the edge of the *cigouave* encampment," Bacalou continued, "I sent Philomé back down the mountain to Pointe d'Inagua for reinforcements. Who could say looking at their shabby habitations how many demons might dwell there? Soon enough, thank goodness, Philomé returned with Charlemagne and Jean-Gerard—almost in time to see you leaving the *houngfor* with a *loa* on your back. It was needed, monsieur, to call enough assistance to be fully prepared."

"You'd make a good Boy Scout," I said.

Bacalou ignored the compliment. "We still have no idea, of course, how many *cigouaves* must live up here. There could be dozens, couldn't there? This *caverne*—it's very big."

"Not counting myself only five of my people remained in all the world," Adam said. "You murdered Toussaint. Now there are only four."

"*Peut-être*," the lieutenant replied. "Maybe." He nodded at his partner. "And what Philomé did was not murder, Monsieur Montaraz. It was a very quick, thoughtful defense of the self."

Further discussion revealed that while holding the remaining occupants of the *houngfor* at gun point, Lieutenant Bacalou and his men had decided that I must be brought back for questioning. Adam and Caroline had volunteered to lead the macoutes to me, Adam because he knew where I was and Caroline because she feared for my safety in my possessed state. Negotiating the uplands had not been easy in the dark and the rain, nor had their torturous journey through the palisade of dripping sablier trees, but at last they had reached the cave entrance and here they were. Their torn and sodden clothes testified to the pains to which they had gone to find me. Now, Caroline said, we could all be under arrest together.

"What are we under arrest for?" I demanded. "What have we done?"

Lieutenant Bacalou considered. "You have aided and abetted the *cigouaves*, who, during the previous regime, did many treasons against the government of Papa Doc. The order to rid the island of them has never been officially put away. We could kill those two old ones down there, and you their cunning accomplices, and any other demons we might find in this impressive hole, and do it, you see, with the blessings of Baby Doc and also, maybe, the present U.S. administration."

"I doubt that," Caroline said. "If RuthClaire and Adam disappeared, you'd have world public opinion, a dozen American Congressmen, and Amnesty International breathing down your necks to know why."

"Probably," Lieutenant Bacalou conceded. "It makes me tremble."

"And there's no sense killing Hector and Erzulie, or Alberoi and Dégrasse, either. They're the very last of the Rutherford Remnant, and when they die, Lieutenant Bacalou, their species will be extinct. They're trying to hang on here, not overthrow the corrupt tub of butter who pays you to terrorize the citizenry."

This sally offended the lieutenant. "We are *not* terrorists, Madame Loyd. We're policemen. We keep the peace."

"A goal that murdering Toussaint has greatly furthered," Caroline angrily retorted. "Do you have any proof that he or any of his kinspeople have tried to bring about the collapse of the Duvalier government?"

"How could I?" Bacalou shouted, gesturing with his

flashlight. "Until this evening, I had no proof that he and the other *cigouaves* continued even to *exist*."

Adam interjected, "Please think for a moment about what you have just said."

"Proof of the latter is proof of the former!" Bacalou declared. Somewhat less emphatically, he added, "At least in the eyes of my superiors." He shone his flashlight to the left of the statue, picking out portions of the murals glistening on the cold rocks and undulating across their seams and crevices. "In any case, the acme of their criminality—theirs *and* yours, my friends—is that you have all conspired to keep a big secret of this mighty national treasure. You have worked together to steal from the Haitian people one of the true marvels of their cultural heritage. And *that* is clearly criminal. *That* cries out for your arrest and punishment."

"Bullshit," I said. "This is one of the true marvels of *habiline* endurance and creativity. It belongs to Adam's people, not to Baby Doc or the hordes of fat-cat foreigners who'll come pouring in here to see the place if its secret is betrayed. Is that what you want, lieutenant? Pizza Huts and neon signs and helicopter overflights—right here on Pointe d'Inagua?"

"*Mais non*," Lieutenant Bacalou said. He was very unhappy. His partner had shot Toussaint; he and the other macoutes had summarily arrested us for crimes that the lieutenant was having trouble defining; and now the poor man was beginning to regard these magnificently decorated catacombs as a potential threat to the beauty of this peninsula, the only finger on the island not already overlaid with Austin-Antilles coffee plantations and bean-washing facilities. Was it more patriotic to betray the secret of the caves to Baby Doc or to keep it from the government for the sake of the disadvantaged local people and the indigenous wildlife? An influx of new tourists would bolster Haiti's staggering economy, but it would also make new headaches for the security personnel charged with protecting the foreigners. Worse, leftist spies and agents provocateurs would try to use the influx as cover for their own nefarious activities. The ramifications of his dilemma weighed heavily on Bacalou.

"What are you going to do?" Adam asked him.

"For a man in this kind of work," he lamented, "I have too much education. I am not ruthless enough."

"Philomé is," Caroline said, and I was glad that the other macoute had no English. "Maybe you should let him do a 'very quick-thoughtful defense of the self' against all three of us." She smiled at the stocky *volontaire* to show him that his name had not been taken in vain. (Even though it had.)

"Let me see more of this," Bacalou said, ignoring Caroline's barb. Abruptly he marched into the rotunda at the end of the righthand corridor. The rest of us followed. Both Philomé and the lieutenant splashed their flashlight beams on the ceilings and walls of this vast chamber, and Adam used his battery lamp to supplement their feeble lights. For a long time, no one spoke. The macoutes were wonderstruck. Caroline slipped her arm around my waist and supported me because she had noticed that I was falling prey to dizziness, the peculiar sensory lag of one recently released from possession.

I shut my eyes. Agarou was there in the darkness, and the hyena-headed godling of the habilines, and a vast, expanding interior light that I recognized immediately as the signature of the Mind Beyond Time that had brain-stormed all three of these apparitions. What had I to do with Beulah Fork or Atlanta or the frigid caves of Montaraz? In Caroline's loving grasp, I was bound for a temporal union with the source of all being. There, freed from my time-bound prejudices, I would meet and embrace the dead—from spiritually inclined australopithecines to materialistic Bolsheviks. Agamemnon. Cleopatra. Francis of Assisi. Queen Elizabeth. Montezuma. Feodor Dostoevski. Jesse Owens. My parents. Elvis Lamar Teavers. Tiny Paul. Nancy Teavers. Craig Puddicombe. Toussaint. They'd all be there, frozen in the timeless medium of God's all-encompassing, unifying, and compassionate Thought. . . .

Adam was talking to Lieutenant Bacalou. He was explaining that this exquisite habiline cave art required a champion. Why not Lieutenant Bacalou himself? Surely, he could convince Philomé Bobo to forget what he had seen here. Or, if not forget, *pretend* to forget. As for the pair of Tontons Macoutes still in Prix-des-Yeux, the lieutenant need not even tell them that he and Philomé had seen these caves. Of course not. Instead, they had found me aimlessly wandering the mountainside or perhaps huddled in a rock shelter several hundred yards below the summit. To announce the presence of the caves would be to unleash on this lovely peninsula the inevitable apocalypse of development, exploitation, advertisement, and ruin. What good would that do anyone?

"None," Lieutenant Bacalou said. "But it is my duty to do so. It need not happen the way you say."

"But it will," Adam pursued. "You and I, we both know that." He spotlighted another incandescent historical mural, another lovely sculpture. The hallucinatory rapture of protracted cave-crawling had begun to overtake us all, even the miserable lieutenant. He was beside himself with awe and indecision.

"What must I do?" he wondered aloud.

Adam intuited that a bribe might work. A bribe would present Bacalou with a material rationale for (a) shirking the stringent dictates of duty and (b) surrendering to the call of his own natural decency. A bribe would preserve the tortured man's self-respect. Succinctly, then, Adam explained that Caroline and I were going to take a number of habiline paintings back to the states and market them as the work of a mythical Haitian naïf by the name of Françoise Fauvet. Bacalou could pretend to be Fauvet. For this imposture, he would receive a commission on every painting sold. If the work of "Fauvet" proved especially popular, Adam would see to it that Bacalou toured North America with an exhibition of "his" paintings. Further, to keep Philomé Bobo from revealing this ruse to the authorities, Adam would finance Bobo's complicity in it by outfitting him as Bacalou's amanuensis and valet. Otherwise, of course, the lieutenant might have to kill the man or frame him as a clandestine Castroite bent on the establishment of a Marxist regime in Haiti.

"But Philomé *hates* Castro," his superior told us.

"Then persuade him to be your valet," Adam said. "You can both resign from the *Volontaires de la Sécurité Nationale*. I will use my influence to help you do so. Your lives as an artist and his traveling secretary will enrich you beyond telling—in a spiritual, as well as a monetary, sense." Adam added that they would both be able to take great private satisfaction from the knowledge that they had delayed, if not forever prevented, the commercial despoliation of the caves.

After pondering a moment, Bacalou said, "I don't like the name Françoise Fauvet. It has, I think, the ring of phoniness."

"What do you prefer?" Adam said.

"Why not my own? My real name, I mean, not my *nom de guerre*."

"And what is that?"

"Marcel Sam," the lieutenant said. "I have not used it since I was a boy, but it's a real name, not an invention, and quite pretty too, *n'est-ce pas?*" He looked at Caroline. "An *artiste* should have a pretty name."

"Very well," Adam said. "Marcel Sam it is."

But Marcel Sam's short-lived happiness in this solution began to evaporate. He struck his forehead with an open palm. "Philomé is married. He has seven children. It's not going to be easy for him to resign and become a traveling valet."

"Then kill him," I said impatiently, half meaning it. "Frame him as a Castroite."

Adam shook his head. "Nothing so desperate as that is necessary. We will think of something, Monsieur Sam. We will think of something."

And, in fact, we did. We went back down to Prix-des-Yeux with the erstwhile Lieutenant Bacalou in our pocket and his gullible partner persuaded that what he had just seen was a subterranean annex to the Duvalier family's complicated secret banking and warehousing system, whose existence on Montaraz he dare not bruit about. He could talk of it only at certain peril to his wife and seven children. For the time being, at least, Bobo, too, was in our pocket, a dupe of a story too plausible to dismiss as fantasy.

THE UNPLEASANT banal truth is that every story of individual consciousness—except, perhaps, God's—concludes with a death. Toussaint was dead. What had I really known about the little man? Almost nothing. Of the five surviving habilines who had tried to make a community-in-hiding on Pointe d'Inagua, Toussaint had probably made the least impression on me. Hector, Erzule, Dégrasse, and Alberoi all had physical handicaps or personality quirks that quickened them in both my affection and my memory. By contrast, Toussaint was a cipher, a pot-bellied, middle-aged little man with no conspicuous talents and no ingratiating idiosyncrasies. (He could paint, Adam assured me, but June was not his month to do so.) Back in Prix-des-Yeux, then, it surprised me to find that RuthClaire had wrapped Toussaint's bullet-riddled body in clean linen and squatted down beside him in the *tonnelle* to stroke his cold brow and to cry a little over him. To me of scarcely more consequence than someone's pet dog, to RuthClaire this dead habiline had been a person of . . . well, sacred worth. His private story was over, but it continued in the impact, whether forceful or modest, that he had made on others.

A banal truth. A banal consolation.

Like enemies observing a holiday cease-fire, the Tontons Macoutes and our own little party cooperated in giving Toussaint an impromptu funeral and burial. Mud and mire impeded our labors, but at last we got him into the ground in such a way that an evil *houngan* or *bocor* would not be able to resurrect him as a zombie. Alberoi and Dégrasse, who, earlier, had fled, did not return to help us—but I had the feeling that from some hidden vantage they were watching and carefully evaluating our methods.

Lieutenant Bacalou assured his fellow *volontaires*—
Philomé, Charlemagne, and Jean-Gérard—that there were
no charges under which to hold Toussaint's companions.
He assured Adam that for our promise not to report the
unfortunate shooting of the habiline (who, in any case, had
no certifiable status on the island), he would make no
mention in his mandatory summary of tonight's events of
the discovery of Prix-des-Yeux. Officially, then, the incident had never happened. We were all dependent on one
another to keep the lid on this tragic collision of purposes
and personalities.

Lieutenant Bacalou led his men back down the mountain
ahead of us. Alone again, our own party puttered back and
forth between the *houngfor* and the huts trying to tidy up
after the rain. We were going back to the Caicos Bay
beach cottage—all of us but Hector and Erzulie—and I
gave myself the task of gathering together the paintings of
"Françoise Fauvet," to be known henceforth as Marcel
Sam. I rolled each canvas as tightly and as carefully as I
could, removing from their frames those that were stretched
taut and tacked down. I was inserting these paintings into
my backpack, almost like a sleepy boy getting ready for
his morning paper route, when Brian Nollinger came into
the shanty and wordlessly began to help me. My stomach
did a queasy flip-flop.

After a while, he said, "Mr. Loyd?"

"Yeah?"

"What are you going to do with all your photographs?
Of the caves and so forth."

I wanted to reply, What the hell's it to you?—but
instead said, "File them away until the last of *Les Gens*
has died." I looked him squarely in the eye. "I *don't*
intend to publish them."

"Alberoi's younger than you, Mr. Loyd. He could outlive you. He could outlive you by a great many years."

"I hope he does."

In the muggy damp of the hut, poor Brian looked down.
The rolled painting in his hands was trembling.

"You're afraid he might outlive you, too, aren't you?"

I said. "Well, that's a possibility I've got my fingers crossed for."

"I was going to do an ethnography of this wretched place. I wasn't going to reveal its location, I was just going to try to record the lifestyle of these remaining habilines under truly oppressive conditions. A rigorous scientific study of a lost race of only five individuals. It would have been good, Mr. Loyd. It would have been an unparalleled—an unduplicatable—piece of work."

"Buck up. You've still got your coffee-drying platforms to build."

"Those stupid Tontons Macoutes ruined everything. They came barging in, they shot Toussaint, and now, to preserve the fiction that Toussaint never existed, we're all having to abandon Prix-des-Yeux. Doesn't that offend you?"

"Not half so much as the death of Toussaint." (A noble sentiment. Had I not seen RuthClaire crying over him, though, I might never have thought to utter it.)

"They ought to be exposed, Mr. Loyd. They ought to be made to pay for their arrogance and cruelty."

"Yeah, well, exposing the macoutes means exposing the habilines. That's what you really want, isn't it? Once the world knows that the Rutherford Remnant is real, you can blithely publish your I-was-there-when-they-victimized-Toussaint memoirs without a twinge of conscience."

Brian sighed. "You're really going to put those photographs away in a drawer somewhere?"

"What's wrong with that? Did you want them to illustrate your paper? Text by Brian Nolo Contendere, pictures by Judas Loyd?" I chuckled. "Of course, you could leave my name out of it altogether. There's precedent, isn't there? You once took credit in the Atlanta papers for a photo of mine."

"I was trying to do you a favor. I was trying to keep your name out of a controversy that might've—"

"Do me another favor and shut up."

He shut up. The damp canvas backpack held as many rolled paintings as I could stuff into it. To get those still remaining in the homemade filing cabinet, we would have to make a second trip. I hoisted the pack, squared it across my shoulders, and bounced it a couple of times to make sure I could carry it.

"Do you remember when RuthClaire told you that murder wasn't in her behavioral armory, Brian Old Boy?"

"Yes, but—"

"Shut up. Well, it may be in mine. It's my bewildered conviction that if you try to make capital of what you've seen here by publishing anything at all, down to and including a squib in *Reader's Digest*, I'll actually go to great pains to seek you out and do you malicious bodily harm. I might even kill you. You're the only person in the whole of God's creation I feel that way about, *Brian*, but the reality—the down-and-dirty grunginess—of that feeling just can't be gainsaid or whitewashed. Believe me, *Brian*, I'd do it."

"That's bullshit," he said, but the furtive bleakness of his eyes told me that I had really frightened him.

"I'm talking about the states, of course. Down here in Montaraz, well, it's Lieutenant Bacalou you'll have to be wary of. If you make any noises about the habilines while you're still a guest of Baby Doc, expect a late-night knock at the door. Expect the key in your motor scooter's ignition to turn over a bomb. Expect your very next shower to greatly gratify the ghost of Alfred Hitchcock."

"You're all talk, Loyd."

"That's possible. I may be. I'm talking tough just to work myself up to actually carrying out the talk. But Bacalou, well, this Lieutenant Bacalou you can't write off so easily. He knows who you are, and he's bayoneted babies for breakfast. He's a butcher, a trained assassin. Just because you think *I* might hesitate to cut your liver out, don't sell Bacalou short. That'd be a terrible, terrible error."

"Don't you give a damn for the light that Adam's people can shed on the history of our species?"

"I'm much more concerned that we let Adam's people—*Les Gens*, thank you—live out their own little histories in peace. I'm much more concerned that those caves up there remain a habiline secret until there ain't no more habilines to keep it." I looked him square in the eye again. "What about you, Dr. Nollinger?"

He took off his wire-rimmed glasses and rubbed their lenses on one of the front pockets of his bush shorts. "Okay."

"Okay what?"

"Okay, okay, okay!" he sang in annoyance. "I'll lock everything I know in a vault in the very back of my brain and let it molder there until the Montarazes relent and let me bring it out again. Not you, Mr. Loyd, the Montarazes. You're hardly even a walk-on in this—hardly even a walk-on." He put his glasses back on. Distractedly, he pulled an original Fauvet/Sam from the crate, rolled it, and began tapping it lightly but obsessively on the cabinet's edge. A voodooist coaxing Arada-Dahomey rhythms from some arhythmic recess of his soul. I grabbed his wrist to make him stop.

"There's one thing about you I'll never understand," I said.

His expression was neutral. I could explain myself or not explain myself—it made no difference to him.

"I'll never understand what Caroline saw in you."

"That's because you're of the wrong generation," he said indifferently. "And because you really don't understand people, anyway."

I let go of his wrist and stalked out of the hut. My legs felt as flimsy as licorice braids. My backpack contained more than a major portion of the habilines' output in acrylics; it contained the weight of everything that had happened that day. I needed help getting down the mountain, but I needed no help falling asleep on the feather bed in the guest room of Adam and RuthClaire's cottage on Caicos Bay. The white noise of the surf ebbed and flowed through my sleep like the hydrogen hiss interconnecting the myriad stars. . . .

THE FOLLOWING evening, Adam and I were sitting on the L-shaped porch of his cottage, darkness slowly thickening around us. Down on the beach, visible as lithe silhouettes, RuthClaire and Caroline were building a bonfire. They were going to bake yams deep in the accumulating coals and barbecue several varieties of fish on a smutty grill that RuthClaire had found in the storage shed. Adam and I were supposed to be preparing exotic tropical drinks, but the women—who had *chosen* bonfire-building over tending bar—were still gathering driftwood and poking experimentally at the feeble flames licking up through the scrap lumber that we had helped them drag down there earlier. It was going to be a while before we ate. No matter. In the anticipation lay much of our pleasure.

Adam said, "Alberoi and Dégrasse joined Hector and Erzulie in the caves today. They're all well—the last of *Les Gens*, the last of my people."

I said nothing. Prix-des-Yeux was going to have to be abandoned and torn down. Maybe we had dealt effectively enough with Bacalou and his partner Bobo, in delaying the disclosure of the caves' existence—but, with their own eyes, the other two macoutes had seen the habilines, too, and chances were good that they would tattle. Rumors would spread, and Pointe d'Inagua would suddenly become a very popular vacation site, a mecca for rock hounds and hikers and amateur naturalists.

Shifting in his rattan chair, Adam said, "Agarou carried you to revelation? You saw God?"

"I saw *something*, Adam. The prehistoric creature who gave your ancestors a divine validation of their survival struggles. It didn't look particularly holy, Adam. It was a kind of monster, in fact."

"All gods, Mister Paul, are monsters in human eyes. That is to say nothing very terrible against it."

"It looked something like a hyena or a dog. Its head did, anyway."

Adam smiled. "I know. With a hominid body, yes? Well, what you saw was the avatar of God most meaningful to every prehistoric specimen of the human family—by some reckonings, the Master of the Hunt. It lived in the collective unconscious of *Homo habilis, Homo erectus, Homo neaderthalensis,* and early *Homo sapiens.* It lives in many so-called primitive peoples even today. It ties, you see, the human to the divine and the divine to the animal—so that they are all interconnected not merely by Mind, but also by a unifying perception of the Sacred."

"I saw the Sacred?"

"Yes. A projection of the God Beyond Time into the evolutionary aesthetic of his creation. You saw *meaning,* Mister Paul, and you spoke in your possession to a messenger from its source."

"Not Buddha or Jesus but the Master of the Hunt?"

Adam—I could barely see him in the indigo twilight—lifted both hands in an unsettling draw-your-own-conclusions gesture.

I leaned toward him in my rocker. "Why didn't bells go off, Adam? Why didn't the sky open up and light pour through? Why didn't I feel like I could float eight feet off the floor of the cave? I mean, if that was a religious revelation, Adam, I prefer falling in love. With falling in love you get fireworks and light-headedness and invisible champagne bubbles. With that business in the caves all I got was horror-movie special effects and a theological lecture. And a lingering headache. How can I put any credence in a revelation like that?"

"Did you learn anything that you did not know before?"

"I was *told* some things I didn't know before. Why?"

"Because if you didn't know them before, or hadn't been told them before, well, then, you would be foolish to conclude that what you experienced was nothing but your own subconscious talking to you. Something outside yourself was putting in its two cents of worth."

"I don't feel any different than I did, well, two days ago. I'm the same materialistic rational pagan."

"Who has been ridden by the *vaudun loa* of our African ancestors. Who has broken through one of God's masks to talk to him face to face."

I shivered. "Only in a manner of speaking."

"It will all come gradually, Mister Paul. Your bells will sound like they're ringing at the bottom of the sea. Your fireworks will unfold in great slow-motion umbrellas. You'll float only at the most modest, and so nearly imperceptible, heights. But it will come, and each instance of its happening will have its own design, and the many individual designs will compose an all-embracing pattern, and that pattern will have its ground in the Mind and Megapattern of God."

"You sound like one of those crackpot Indian gurus, Adam."

"Then I'll shut up. Right now. Better to think about eating—" he gestured at the beach—"than get lost in the metaphysics of another."

We sat in silence watching our wives pull coals into a circle of stones upon which they would soon place the greasy grill rack. Paul and Caroline, Adam and Ruthie Cee. Just another pair of sophisticated fun couples partying in a secluded cove on Montaraz. The bonfire ten feet away from their makeshift barbecue pit was leaping upward like the funeral pyre of a Roman emperor. Caroline's and RuthClaire's bare shoulders gleamed in its roaring blaze as if made of bronze. I watched them tong strips of filleted fish out of a metal cooler onto the grill rack. I watched them take turns basting each strip with the sauce that I had made. I watched them for a long time.

Finally, RuthClaire stood up and shouted, "It's nearly time to eat!"

Adam and I carried two pitchers of iced daiquiris down to the beach, and, sitting on the sand at a safe remove from the bonfire, we ate and drank—somewhat solemnly, considering the late hour and the formidable size of our appetites and thirsts. Tomorrow, Caroline and I would be flying back to Miami from Cap-Haïtien. That knowledge may have contributed to our solemnity, but, of course, a lot of it had to do with Toussaint's death, the upheaval at

Prix-des-Yeux, and the uncertainty of our own several futures. I found myself thinking forlorn thoughts about Livia George, Paradise Farm, and the West Bank. To keep from getting maudlin, I limited myself to three small lime daiquiris in a ceramic coffee mug. In fact, I did everything in threes—three strips of fish, three baked yams, and three avowals of either eternal love (that one for Caroline) or eternal friendship (one for RuthClaire, one for Adam) for my companions on the beach.

The bonfire started to die.

RuthClaire murmured, ''We've got to build it up again,'' pulled herself up to her feet, and trudged up the sand toward the cottage. Halfway there, she turned around and beckoned to us with an uncoordinated looping wave. ''C'mon, you guise! He'p me get some stuffer th'fire!'' Adam, Caroline, and I struggled up and followed her on her drunken anabasis.

Over the next hour or so, we hauled from their various storage niches inside the cottage all of the paintings in RuthClaire's series *Souls*. Then we tossed each canvas, whether loose or affixed to a stretching frame, right into the greedily crackling pyre. They burned very well. In fact, in the fire they had the kind of stunning luminous beauty that they had had for me on only one previous occasion—a memorable occasion in the upstairs studio at Paradise Farm. Very soon, though, they scrolled and spit and blackened and turned to oozy char. It amazed me that we were abetting RuthClaire in this enterprise—Adam as eagerly as anyone else—and yet I purposely asked no questions until we had flung the last painting in.

''You destroyed them because they weren't popular, is that it?''

RuthClaire straightened, as best she could, and said, ''It was either them or my porcelain plates. Porcelain won't burn.'' She started to laugh. She laughed so hard that she had to grab Caroline for support, and, once again, the two of them shared a sisterly hilarity that had a rationale impenetrable to male intellects. Adam and I had no choice but to wait them out. Finally, still leaning on each other, they regained a sort of uprightness.

''The concept was all wrong,'' RuthClaire said, swaying a little. ''In spite of what the hot-shot critics said, I did 'em okay. I mean, I *executed* 'em okay. But a soul's not a soul's not a soul.''

''Who said that?'' Caroline asked.

''Gertrude Steinem,'' RuthClaire said, and they both started giggling again. Then RuthClaire waved her hand and said, ''What I mean is, the pastels were to show the insubstantiality, the immateriality, of souls—but souls are living bodies, and so my stupid concept is all wrong. My stupid paintings never lived except when the light hit 'em just right, and they looked better burning than they ever did in the morgue of my studio gallery. I had to get rid of 'em, I have to start over, thash—*that's*—all there is to it.''

''Adam liked them,'' I said.

RuthClaire broke free of Caroline, tottered over to Adam, and put her arm through his. ''Adam's my husband, Paul.''

He grinned, and the bonfire illuminated his teeth as if they were a bracelet of ancient ivory charms.

Still later, more in control of herself, RuthClaire fetched the burial urn containing Tiny Paul's ashes down to the beach and asked me to open it. I was T.P.'s godfather, after all, and the honor of scattering his ashes on the waters of Caicos Bay was rightly mine. If it *weren't* rightly mine—by the standards of Emily Post or proper cremation etiquette—well, she and Adam had decided to countermand those standards with an appeal to simple sentiment. I took the urn to my chest with one arm and tried to unstopper it. Nothing I could do would budge the form-fitting lid, and I began to fear that I would break either it or the urn itself trying to get it loose.

''My hero,'' Caroline said. She took the urn from me, set it down on the sand, squatted next to it, fiddled with it for forty seconds, and abruptly began to unscrew the fire-baked clay stopper. Then she stood and placed the urn back into my arms. I accepted it, smelling sea and ash and particulate spirit.

''Go on,'' RuthClaire said.

So with the urn in my arms the way small children

sometimes carry a rubber boot into the water to give them both ballast and a fragile sense of security, I carried Tiny Paul into the shallows of Caicos Bay. Like his father, he was home. Without looking back at the people who had sent me, I sowed the murdered child's ashes on the murmuring inlet. Those that stuck to my palm I washed away in the gentle lapping of the evening tide. They weren't inconsequential, I told myself, and they weren't lost. They were afloat in the consciousness of God. And I tried like crazy to believe it.

THE BEST IN SCIENCE FICTION